praise for

ghostflowers

"Atmospheric, suspenseful, passionate, entertaining, and fun! In ***Ghostflowers***, Rus Wornom puts a vampire of myth and legend onto the back of a motorcycle, and sets him loose in the Virginia countryside in the 1970s. Put an Allman Brothers album on your turntable, and enjoy the ride." —Jamie Malanowski, author of *Commander Will Cushing* and *The Coup*

"As immersive and lyrical as it is brutal and bloody, ***Ghostflowers*** is an unputdownable examination of love, fear, and desperation—a thrill-ride launched from page one that never lets up." —Mandy McHugh, author of *Chloe Cates Is Missing*

"Romantic, mysterious, dark and beautiful, a journey to the alien and familiar, a 1970's small town world of bikers and diners. Thoroughly entertaining!" —Colleen Doran, Eisner Award, Bram Stoker Award winner, Neil Gaiman's *Snow, Glass, Apples* and Neil Gaiman's *Chivalry*, Creator of *A Distant Soil*

"Moody, atmospheric and thrilling. ***Ghostflowers*** is one hell of a ride. Rus Wornom has crafted a unique vampire tale that hits you like a burst of sunlight after leaving a dark room." —Darin De Paul, actor, *Shazam!*, *Justice Society: World War II*, *Apex Legends*, *Overwatch*, and *Final Fantasy XV*

"***Ghostflowers*** gripped me from the first page to the last. It's a glorious blend of horror and romance, a story as shocking as it is beautiful and firmly rooted in the southern gothic tradition." —Michael Howarth, author of *A Still and Awful Red*

"…Brilliant… I read more than half in one sitting. Dinner was late that night. … ***Ghostflowers*** is steeped in the heat of passion and a melting-pot summer. A black Gothic rose of a novel, its petals drip with blood of the deepest red. It's a love story with deadly consequences as its many layers peel back to reveal the strange truth of the man who came to Stonebridge. There is ecstasy, pain, blood and much more in this story steeped in atmosphere and the vampire mythos. It is a horror-love story—that bites. …I loved it." —Catherine Cavendish, author of *The Garden of Bewitchment* and *In Darkness, Shadows Breathe*

"Like a classic rock song that comes on the radio, ***Ghostflowers*** will get stuck in your head and make you want to read this on repeat! A dark blast!" —Steve Stred, Splatterpunk-nominated author of *Sacrament* and *Mastodon*

ghostflowers

RUS WORNOM

ISBN: 978-1-68510-037-7 (sc)
ISBN: 978-1-68510-038-4 (ebook)
Library of Congress Control Number: 2022934161

First printing edition: July 8, 2022
Printed by JournalStone Publishing in the United States of America.
Edited by Sean Leonard
Proofreading and Interior Layout: Scarlett R. Algee
Cover Design: Don Noble | Cover Concept and Layout: Rus Wornom
Cover Images: Enrique Meseguer (front) and Epic Images (back) from Pixabay

JournalStone Publishing
3205 Sassafras Trail
Carbondale, Illinois 62901

JournalStone books may be ordered through booksellers or by contacting:
JournalStone | www.journalstone.com

For Maria

For all her love, her infinite support,
and for her terrible, awful, wonderful idea.
8 i9f3 697

verismo

midnight rider

thursday, july 1, 1971

It had to be the heat.

It slammed her as she stepped out of the diner, enveloping her. She smelled the green trees towering across the street, black silhouettes in the gloaming, and the moisture in the air tickled her bare arms with infinitesimal dewdrops.

It had to be the heat that did it.

And then—she couldn't breathe. Her vision blurred, grew fuzzy around the edges. She swayed backward, and it felt as though the bottom dropped out of her soul, and every muscle went as limp as a dish rag. Her knees weakened, let go—

And—

And—

the heat—

No. It wasn't the heat.

It wasn't the heat at all.

It was his eyes.

1

THE BIKER WAS a night-black blur, leaping for the waitress as her knees buckled and the star-speckled blacktop raced toward her.

At the door, the sheriff bellowed something incomprehensible. Rob yelled, "Hey!"

The waitress moaned as the biker gathered her into his arms. He hurtled past the sheriff and kicked open the glass door. He blinked in the diner's white fluorescent glare.

Tina Tyler spun, serving tray on one arm. A gravy-spotted spoon clanged to the tile floor.

"This woman has fainted," the biker said. "Is there someplace—"

Conversations dropped into silence. An older couple stared at him from a booth. Deputy Duke turned at the counter, chewing a bite of his cheeseburger. He saw the biker's long, dark hair and his worn jeans, and whispered, "The sheriff's gonna shit."

"Yeah. Yeah, over here." Tina pointed toward the swinging doors leading to the kitchen.

The bells on the glass door jangled. Sheriff Hicks strode back into the diner, his hand on the butt of his revolver. His jowls glowed pink. "Now, look here—"

The cook burst through the swinging doors. Ruthette's eyes were wide with worry, yet her low voice was as strong as steel. "Don't you drop her, boy, or I'll kick your butt all the way to Richmond."

The rider cradled Summer's head. He smiled. "No need for butt-kicking, ma'am. I've got her."

Sweat trickled down Ruthette's dark skin. She slung a dish towel over her shoulder and shoved open Ralph's office door. "You damn well better."

The room smelled like old grease. Ralph Jenkins spun around at his desk. On a small black and white, a blind detective was shouting for help. "The hell?"

Ruthette swept a stack of *Playboys* off of Ralph's napping sofa. "You put her over here." She saw Summer's boyfriend in the doorway, craning to get a look past the sheriff. "Robby, you go and get me a nice, cold dish towel, you hear?"

Rob West raced toward the wash sink. The rider placed Summer onto the sofa. Ruthette slipped a red and orange crocheted pillow under Summer's head. The rider looked down on her. Her hair spilled over the pillow in a blonde waterfall.

Tina Tyler peered behind the sheriff. "She okay?"

Ruthette felt Summer's forehead.

The rider said, "She fainted."

"Yeah, well, I'll be the judge of that," the sheriff said.

Tina glanced at the sheriff, then at the rider, then back at the sheriff. "Yeah. Okay, I've got the front. No worries."

Rob slipped past the sheriff and handed Ruthette a cool, damp towel. She folded it and draped it across Summer's forehead.

Summer's lips moved, and Ruthette leaned toward her.

Hicks stepped forward. "Did she say something?"

Ruthette said, "Michelle?"

Hicks grunted and watched the biker. He motioned for Duke. "Take our friend into the kitchen. Get his ID. And search him."

Ralph Jenkins spun in his chair and said, "Somebody want to tell me what the hell is going on?"

Duke grabbed the rider's elbow and read the name patch. "Come on, Mr. Trager."

Trager let himself be led into the big kitchen. It smelled like bacon and french fries.

"You better hope she's okay," Duke said.

Trager looked back towards the office door. Under the screech of tires from the television, he heard the beating of her heart, her steady breathing. "She'll be fine. Glad I caught her before she hit the ground. Besides"—he glanced at Duke's badge—"I didn't do anything wrong."

Duke nodded. "I didn't say you did. Sheriff might be of a different mind though." He held out his hand. "I'm gonna need some ID."

2

"WE NEED TO call the doctor?" the sheriff said.

Ruthette shook her head. "Looks like she just fainted. Heat, I s'pose. Ralph, we got any smelling salts?"

Ralph ran his hand through his sparse grey hair. "Maybe in the medicine cabinet?"

"Shit, there ain't nothin' in there exceptin' a bottle of mercurochrome and some Paregoric from the 1940s. Robby!" she shouted.

Rob had been hanging around in the background, fidgeting. "She breathing?"

"Well, of course she's breathing. Now, go get that first aid kit under the cash register. Might be something in there we can use."

"You got it, Ruthette. Be right back." He turned around and, just then, Summer moaned aloud. Rob stopped in the doorway. "Is she—"

Summer's eyes popped open, and focused on the cook. "Ruthette," Summer said.

"I'm here, girl."

"Ruthette," Summer said, "why am I in Ralph's stinky office?"

Ruthette smiled. The staff all knew that Ralph's office collected the amalgamated aromas of burgers, fries, the Friday fish, and the stench of Ralph's tennis shoes—worn without socks—which, together, multiplied the odors exponentially. "Sweetheart, you passed out."

"I was outside."

Ruthette nodded.

"The guy on the motorcycle?"

"He carried you in."

"He *what*?"

Sheriff Hicks stepped closer. "Summer, did he hurt you?"

Summer frowned and stared up at Hicks. "Hurt me? Who?"

"The hippie. On that motorbike."

Summer looked away; then it came back to her in a rush of images: the bike, the rider, the heat that had risen inside her—

"No. No, he never touched me. I was— I fell. The heat—No, he caught me."

Hicks frowned.

Summer started to sit up. "My customers. Ruthette, my tickets—"

"Tina's got it for now. You stay here and rest. You want me to call your mama?"

Summer's eyes widened. "No. Hell no."

Ruthette smiled. "That's what I figured." She turned toward Rob. "Robby, you go and get Summer a big glass of ice water, okay?"

Rob rushed into the kitchen, and Summer lay back on the sofa. "I'm all right, really."

"Maybe we should get you home soon."

"God, not that," Summer said. "Suddenly this office isn't so smelly anymore."

"Hey. My office don't stink. I clean," Ralph said.

"Sure you do," Ruthette said. "Last year."

Ralph stood up and took the high road. "Well. I better go man the grill."

Ruthette whispered, "Yeah, you better."

Summer smiled.

The sheriff cleared his throat. "Ruthette, you keep a watch on her. I'm going to have a talk with Mr. Motorcycle."

Ruthette's gaze flicked to the doorway. Back in the kitchen, the biker leaned against a steel cooking table, his arms crossed.

She shivered, suddenly feeling cold, chilled to the bone. The biker turned his face toward her. Something small, a tiny little voice, shouted at her for attention. Then an icy shadow fell over her.

His eyes. It was his eyes.er

The hairs on her forearms were standing up straight.

And she knew.

Something just ain't right here.

3

DUKE HELD OUT the biker's IDs like a pair of playing cards. Hicks took them and snapped them against his palm. He read the California driver's license, issued a few months ago in April, then concentrated on the light green military ID. "Trager, James Phillip."

"That's *Colonel* Trager," the biker said.

Hicks glanced up at him, but asked Duke, "You search him?"

Duke held out a six-inch hunting knife. "On his belt."

Hicks took the blade, flipped it in the air, and caught it by the handle. His eyes never left the biker's.

"Don't look like no colonel to me."

"What's a colonel look like?" the biker said.

The sheriff pulled a crumpled pack of unfiltered Pall Malls from his shirt pocket and lit one. "Like a soldier," he said, exhaling blue smoke. "A hero. Respectable. Clean. Not like some dirty hippie." He stepped up and glowered in the biker's face. "What the hell you doing in my town, boy?"

"Do I need you to approve my passport or something? You want to see my papers?"

"I asked you a question."

The biker's gaze didn't flinch. "I shipped back from 'Nam a couple of months ago. Retired. Riding across the country. I've never really been through the South before. Thought I'd see your natural stone bridge. Maybe write a book about my ride. Sure didn't expect all this Southern hospitality."

The sheriff *hmphed.* "A book."

"Yeah. It's one of those things you read."

Hicks watched him. He listened to him too. His voice, his accent. Sounded weird. Not American enough. And a retired lieutenant colonel at only twenty-eight? His gaze moved to the name stenciled on his jacket.

TRAGER.

His hair is too long. He's a biker freak. He's too damn young to be a real colonel, much less a retired one. And he sounds like a goddamned foreigner.

"Sheriff!" It was Ruthette, shouting from Ralph's office. "It's Summer."

Hicks exhaled and threw his cigarette to the floor. He ground it out with his steel toe. "Stay here."

The biker almost laughed. "I wouldn't dream of going anywhere else."

The sheriff entered the office. Summer was sitting up against the couch's armrest, sipping a Coke through a paper straw. Ruthette said, "She's doing all right."

Hicks looked at Summer.

"I'm fine," she said. "Really."

“Obstinate as hell,” Ruthette said.

Hicks glanced at the black and white TV and snapped it off. “Sure you don’t want me to call Doc Bragg?”

Summer shook her head. “No. Not a chance.”

“It was just the heat,” Ruthette said. But her round face was creased with worry.

“Summer,” Hicks said, “are you sure the biker didn’t do anything to you?”

She placed the Coke on an end table. “I’m fine. He didn’t do a thing.” She stood up, then wobbled on her feet. Ruthette pushed off the sofa to help her, but Summer waved her away. “No. I’m okay. I’m ready.”

She looked the sheriff in the eye. “I need to talk to the—” She didn’t know what to call him. The stranger? The biker?

—the night man?

“I need to talk to him.”

Hicks looked at her with distaste. “What the hell you want to talk to that punk for?”

Rob cleared his throat. “Summer, I’m with the sheriff on this. If he—”

She stepped past the sheriff and looked at both Rob and Hicks from the doorway. “I would have been flat on the ground if he hadn’t caught me. I need to thank him, at the very least.”

Hicks started to object, but Ruthette was up, and she put her hand on his chest. “Come on, now. You boys need to go back and finish your dinner. It’s all got to be ice cold by now. Let’s go. I’ll heat everything up.”

Hicks stared at her. His right eye twitched.

The stranger stood at the back screen door, looking out into the dark trees beyond the loading dock. Deputy Duke saw Summer and smiled. “Feeling better?”

She nodded, eyes on the biker. “Duke, give us a few, will you?”

He glanced across the room. Ruthette was pushing Hicks toward the front room. “I don’t know, Summer,” Duke said.

She smiled at him. “Come on, Duke. It’ll be okay. You’ll be right over there.” She nodded to Hicks and Ruthette. “This guy’s not going anywhere. I promise.”

Then the stranger turned toward them. His eyes, his face, seemed unusually shadowed. He was focused on Duke. She looked closer, and all she could see was darkness where his eyes were supposed to be.

Duke looked at her, then the biker, then looked away, as if confused.

“Okay,” he said slowly. “Okay. Yeah. My burger is cooling. Right. Okay.”

Duke followed the sheriff and Ruthette into the dining room. Summer watched them go, then turned toward the biker.

He took a step toward her, into the light.

She almost gasped.

He was stunning.

His night-dark hair framed his head with the mane of a black lion. He moved his tall, lanky frame toward her, like a panther, and the slow smile that spread across his face lit his wide, black eyes with a glint of humor, a hint of secrets.

She could focus only on his eyes—so wide, so dark. They clutched her in a dark embrace. They were liquid, black water, depthless, and she was floating, helpless, trapped in his gaze.

I know you.

I've seen you.

She blinked. She had never seen—she read the name on his jacket—this TRAGER before in her life.

"Trager. Army," she said.

He nodded.

"You been to Vietnam?"

He nodded.

She crossed her arms. "Do you ever speak?"

He nodded.

"Okay. So who are you?"

He opened his mouth to answer, then realized he had no idea what to say. He could smell her—perfume, with hints of lavender and vanilla; the aroma of cooking grease in her hair; and underneath it all—

—roses.

His mind, his being, was suddenly adrift, floating in the dream that was her.

He didn't know how to answer. There was a lifetime of things he wanted to say—and not one of them would she understand.

"James. Trager."

"James," she said, testing how the name felt on her tongue.

"Yeah, well." He stepped closer. Even with the smells of the kitchen and the old grease, she smelled the outdoors on him—a freshness, a wildness that spoke to the part of her heart that was yet untamed.

"I'm Summer," she said. "You cause this much trouble everywhere you go?"

He shrugged. "Whenever the sun goes down. My buddies in 'Nam called me the Midnight Rider."

She grinned. "Then you're only half as good as me. I cause trouble all the time."

He laughed softly, watching her, the fear tickling his spine like a nagging itch.

Is this her?

"Somehow," he said, "I believe that."

"Listen. Thanks for, like, saving me."

"I was afraid my bike had scared you, or—" He trailed off, not knowing exactly what the hell he was saying at all.

She flicked her eyes toward the dining room. "I think you scared the old people out there, maybe. I—I kind of like the bike."

They stared at each other awkwardly.

"Anyway," they both said simultaneously. She laughed. He smiled.

"Anyway," she said, "thanks for being there."

"Glad I was. Glad I'm—"

"Me too." *Now, why did she say that?*

In the corner of her eye, she saw the kitchen doors swing open and the sheriff's bulk filled the doorway. He walked toward them, staring straight at Trager, bouncing the biker's knife in his palm.

"'Scuse us, Summer. I've got business with Colonel Sanders, here. Duke'll give you a ride home."

"No, I'm sticking around for a while."

"Now, you listen—"

"No," she said, facing him. "Did you hear me? I have work to do. I can get a ride later from Rob or Tina. Besides, I haven't done anything—and neither has James."

Hicks turned to Trager. "If you know what's good for you, you'll hop back on that kiddy bike and ride it out the same way you came in."

"This town ain't big enough for the both of us? Is that it?"

"Listen, *Colonel.* Me—I'm the law in this town. And we don't take kindly to your kind of trouble around here."

"My kind—"

"In other words, we ain't puttin' up with any of your goddamn hippie crap, you got that? Biker boy?"

The rider smiled. "Some of us in 'Nam had a saying. 'You didn't see me, I wasn't here, and I'm not here now.' That about right?"

"You're getting the picture."

The rider glanced over at Summer and said, "I'm glad you're well."

"I am now. Thanks."

He stared at the sheriff a moment, then looked back at Summer. He winked.

He shoved open the back screen door, and it slammed shut behind him. The sheriff followed the biker out and hung back at the edge of the diner, watching Trager climb onto his motorcycle. Summer came up a few steps away from him.

The night roared with the growl of the bike's powerful heart. Summer watched the bike turn in the parking lot and leap onto the road. The taillight disappeared around a bend, hidden by a thick curtain of trees, and she wondered why the night felt so empty now.

Hicks exhaled smoke into the night. "Don't you come back here, boy. Don't you even—"

Summer went back into the kitchen. She felt a smile growing across her face, reflecting something she felt in her heart, opening like a midnight rose.

Then Rob came in through the swinging doors. "Babe, are you all right? I really don't want you to work any more tonight, okay?"

She shook her head. "No, I'm all right. I just want to finish up tonight and—"

"What happened out there?" Rob said. He tried to be casual, but there was a note in his voice that told her he really meant, *Who was that guy, and do I have anything to worry about?*

"I guess it was just the heat. I could have broken something if that guy hadn't been there."

He tried to look into her eyes. Then Tina came up and put a hand on her shoulder. "Summer, I can hold down the fort. Go home. Get some rest."

At the grill, Ruthette took a spatula out of Ralph's hand and pushed him away. "Listen to her, girl. We can handle it, even with Ralph here, messin' things up."

Summer shook her head. "I'm okay. Just a little while longer, that's all, just to help out."

"Stubborn," Ruthette said.

Tina grinned. "Stupid too."

Summer smiled. "You got that right."

"So what really happened out there?" Tina said.

Summer stared toward the road, into the shadows where the biker had gone.

"Hell if I know," she said.

—but his eyes—

4

earlier

HIGH ABOVE THE blacktop parking lot, DIXIE DINETTE flickered in letters of bright red and blue. The X bore flashing white stars in the design of the Confederate flag, and the sign was topped by an elongated shooting star whose yellow light sputtered erratically.

The Dixie Dinette occupied a low-slung building of brick and wood at the intersection of Route 1 and Route 38. In the heat, without a breeze, the aroma of burgers and hot grease hung in the moist air like a fog. Around the dinette, crickets chirruped in the grass, and beyond, in the dark trees, sang an overture of locusts.

All in all, it was just another hot summer night at the Dixie Dinette.

The clock above the jukebox read 9:45. The first movie at the Shenandoah Drive-In, The Green Berets, was just about halfway over, and Summer Moore and Tina Tyler were dealing with the influx of tourists and teenagers who had nowhere else to go during summer vacation. The dinette was busier than usual—it always was around July Fourth—and it was so humid inside and out that Tina's thick, frizzy hair was already threatening to fluff up into a brown wedge. With both drive-in theaters open and tourists sticking around to take snapshots of the Bridge and Carter Caverns, Ralph had decided to stay open till midnight.

Summer didn't mind. She needed the extra cash, and she wanted away from her ma. She wanted a vacation, a break. She wanted out.

She stared at the county sheriff sitting at the counter.

She wanted out.

Sheriff Hicks had pulled up in his cruiser around 6:30, and parked himself at his usual stool near the dessert case, next to Deputy Duke. His sheriff's uniform, crisply starched, was a nether shade somewhere between a dull brown and an olive green. An enamel flag pin adorned his collar, his one breach of regulation. His duty was to his flag, his country, and his town. His town. And if wearing the American flag was against regulations, then by God, you could call him a criminal and lock him behind bars, but that flag would stay right where it was, right above his all-American heart.

Summer had done her best to ignore him for more than three hours. He had complained to Duke—and to anyone else who'd listen—about leftists and politics, about those traitors Jack Anderson and goddamn Ellsberg, and all the damn hippies, and he'd been bossing her and Tina around as if he owned the place.

Hicks glanced up from the afternoon paper out of Richmond and lit his fourth Pall Mall. "Girly girl," he said. He jabbed a pudgy finger repeatedly into his coffee cup.

Summer stared at his finger, then took the coffee pot off the burner. She poured it all the way to the rim.

He laughed once. "Paper says you damn kids got the vote now. You all won't even know what to do with it."

She looked him in the eye. "Sure I do. I'd make John Lennon president. And then I'd put the Chicago Eight on the Supreme Court."

Beside the sheriff, Duke almost spit out his coffee.

The bell rang in the kitchen window. "Order up!"

Summer turned away, grinning.

Behind her, Hicks said, "That girl is a goddamn commie." He lifted his mug, and hot coffee spilled onto his fingers. "Shit!"

Ruthette Haskins slid a cheeseburger platter with a mountain of fries across the window. Ruthette's dark brown skin gleamed with perspiration, and Summer got a whiff of the sweet pomade glistening in her hair. "There's your boyfriend's dinner now. A little pink, like he likes it." Ruthette paused. "You know he shouldn't eat it like that."

"He won't listen."

"I know. Don't you come crawlin' to me when he gets sick."

Summer turned and placed the platter in front of Rob West at the counter. She leaned in close and said, "I will pay you to get me the hell out of here. Cash money."

He smiled and shook salt and pepper over his burger. "Your mother?"

"Evil, as usual. I think she's taking lessons from Satan." She unwrapped a stick of Juicy Fruit and folded it into her mouth. "By the way, I didn't get that job."

He looked up. "What? Crap. How come?"

She shrugged, then rested her elbows on the counter. Her long, sandy blonde hair tickled the back of Rob's hand. The jukebox at the end of the dinette played something about being with the one you love. She flicked her eyes toward the end of the counter. "He's been awful tonight."

"Yeah, I heard." He took a bite of his hamburger. "John Lennon's from England, you know."

"Yes, I do know where the Beatles come from, doofus."

"So, Lennon's a foreigner. Legally, he can't be president."

She stared at him, half-smiling, then tapped the tip of his nose. "You are a nerd. And he can be president because I say so."

He smiled and chewed his burger. Then someone at the counter called her name, and he watched as Summer poured coffee for Pearl Seabury, the clerk over at the courthouse. Summer was full-bosomed and already tanned brown from laying out in her garden since May. Her straight, sandy blonde hair spilled to a teardrop point below her shoulder blades, and with her ice-blue eyes, she was just too gorgeous for a regular guy like him—and he knew it. They had been going steady for three years, since senior year at Stonebridge High, "The Home of the Undefeated Confederates!!!" In August he would start his junior year at Virginia Tech; Summer had decided to forgo college again this year, and Rob was beginning to think she'd never achieve anything better than her high school diploma. Damn shame. She was too smart to let life pass her by.

The sheriff suddenly cleared his throat. It came from deep inside him, a wet, raggedy sound that echoed through the diner. The old couple at the window looked up.

Ruthette leaned in to see who had made that godawful sound. "Did a giraffe just die in here?" she muttered.

Summer came back over to Rob. "God."

"Be proud," Rob said. "We are in the presence of the prototypical redneck lawman."

"Prototypical. Good one. College word." She glanced at the sheriff. "How about pig?"

"Don't say that too loud."

"Pig," she repeated, glaring at Hicks. "Piggy piggy piggy."

"Summer, shh," Rob whispered. You didn't say pig anywhere near a cop in the South unless you were ready to get your knuckles busted and spend a night in jail.

She snorted, hog-like.

"Summer—"

"Well, he is a pig," she said, just loud enough for Rob to hear. "He's everything I despise about this town." She stared out the window and saw her own reflection in the glass above the old couple in a window booth, Kate and John Juniper. "Welcome to Hee Haw." A pair of headlights shone through the windows as a car bounced into the driveway. The dark car aimed straight for a space below the Junipers' window.

"You know, that new movie, **Klute**, is coming out."

"**Klute**? You still haven't taken me to **Summer of '42**."

"All right then. Only the finest for you."

"Hm. The drive-in—and a cooler of Rolling Rock?"

"Well. Of something."

"Romance lives." She kissed him on the cheek. "And you are the Prince Charming of Hooterville."

The Junipers turned to look at the headlights bearing down on the diner. The car tore straight for them. The high beams flicked on.

The car screeched into the space by the Junipers. John flinched away from the window. A brunette riding shotgun in a gleaming convertible flicked out a cigarette in a glowing arc that scattered on the black pavement. She grinned at them and hopped out of the passenger side, her breasts bouncing beneath her deliberately tight t-shirt. Ronnie Sheffield. Kenny Cousins sat behind the wheel.

"Look at that," Summer said. "He got it."

Kate Juniper took a bite of her fried chicken. "Damn fool kids."

The brass bell clanged on the door and Ronnie strutted in, her face beaming. "Summer," she said, "Kenny got the Mustang. Do you believe that? He got it."

"It's beautiful, Ron," Summer said. "He's been talking about it for, like, how long now?"

"God, like, forever," Ronnie said, flicking back her hair. Rob went outside. The lights in the parking light gleamed off the polished, dark green hood. Kenny pulled his bulk out of his new car. Ronnie went to the door, then turned to Summer. "You coming?"

Three Dog Night played from the jukebox, singing about nights out in the country. A single headlight, bright, sliced through the darkness outside. It bounced in the driveway, and a motorcycle rolled into the parking lot. Its engine was the muted purr of a thunderbeast.

Summer called out, "Be right there."

The bell jangled as Ronnie stepped into the moist night. Then she heard the low growl of the bike.

Moonlight rippled like water off the shiny black motorcycle. The rider shut off the motor, and it ticked soft in the still night.

The rider was a rugged dream. An animal. Feral. A rebel. The army shirt and his faded jeans, black boots, and his mane of jet-black hair branded him an outsider, a hippie, to

Stonebridge's geriatric establishment. Ronnie's heart skipped a beat. Something in her shifted, something secret, something nasty.

Ronnie whispered, "Too cool," just low enough so Kenny wouldn't hear.

Kenny looked at the biker and squared his shoulders. He lit a Marlboro and stared him down. Three knuckles had band-aids wrapped around them, spotted with blood. He had been in a fight yesterday. Ray Ray Pollard had finally and willingly ponied up the two hundred dollars he'd owed him. Now, the Mustang was his—and so was Ronnie. He'd make damn sure this biker knew it.

Deputy Duke turned to see who had ridden up, and he looked long and hard enough at the rider to know that trouble had just driven in. Well, well. Take your shoes off and sit a spell. He glanced at the sheriff. Hicks was silent, folding the paper, staring straight ahead. There was a reason Hicks always took this stool. From here, he had a vantage point where he could see through all the windows. Duke looked closer. The sheriff was staring into the polished glass of the dessert case, watching the biker.

"Huh," Hicks grunted. The biker's reflection was dark. Indistinct. Like smoke. "Huh."

Summer called out, "I'll be right back, Ruthette." The cook looked up, then saw the rider through the window. She flicked her eyes toward the lawmen at the counter.

"Don't need no trouble here tonight, Sheriff," she whispered. "Don't you start nothing here tonight."

The rider was peeling off his gloves when Summer stepped outside. The combination of heat and moisture slammed her, and sweat beaded down her sides, but she was grateful even for a few brief minutes outside in the fresh air, away from the grease, under the stars. She looked the Mustang over, gleaming in the lights from the diner's flashing neon sign high on the edge of the road.

"You did it," Summer said. "You actually did it."

She'd bought her '69 Camaro last year for three hundred dollars, used. Kenny's car was sweet—the perfect shade of forest green—but hers was black and tough, a muscle car with a crimson interior and red detailing. Rob called it the Batmobile.

"It's gorgeous, Kenny," she said. "It's perfect. It's you."

Her words hung in the still, moist air. No one said anything. She looked up.

It was the guy on the motorcycle.

Firm features, a thick mustache, black hair flowing over his shoulders. His jawbones, his chin, seemed chiseled, all hard angles. The only softness she could see was in his eyes—eyes filled with sadness, yet glinting cold, with flint or steel. He was a night dream, a raider; and as he stared at her, she felt his gaze bore into her, flooding her. His dark, wide eyes reflected the red flashing neon; and the heat of the summer night, mixed with a strange chill, passed through her simultaneously: two opposing currents weaving through her blood, rushing like a virus. They enveloped her with the warm night.

She felt his heat, his icefire, pounding through her blood, and a bead of sweat trickled down her spine.

The rider swung his leg off the cycle and stepped onto the pavement. Then his eyes met hers.

It hit her with the sudden snap of a steel cord, or a whip.

His eyes—

Inside the diner, Sheriff Hicks put down his coffee. He turned to watch the rider. The sheriff took a tiny white pill from his shirt pocket and washed it down with coffee. "All right," he said to no one but himself. "It's time."

The rider reached out for Summer's hand. One of his gloves dropped to the asphalt, and his fingertips—ice cold, yet burning like a dying sun—brushed her skin. She shivered, and her senses exploded with the aroma of roses; a sea of moonlight and sweat, and roses.

His eyes—

—a dream. It has to be a dream.

His voice seemed distant, eons and centuries away, yet she felt his words—

—his essence—

—echo throughout her body.

And he said, "Is it you?"

Summer blinked.

—Is it you?—

Then he faced her, and his eyes were black, midnight black, blazing like twin black suns, the light around them flickering around the rim of his soul. She couldn't turn away. She couldn't breathe. She saw a woman's face, a brief glimpse, as if shrouded in mist—

The bell jangled as Sheriff Hicks shoved open the glass door. He said something, something empty and important and sheriff-like. "What's going on here?" or, "Hey, you, stop right there!" or something official and pointless; but no one heard him. His words were muffled; they hung empty in the air, for all Summer could hear, all she could see, in the tunnel of darkness that swallowed her senses, was the rider, and the depth of his dark eyes—eyes she had known forever—and his shallow intake of air, his pulsating need ringing through her soul.

Is it you—

And she whispered on the warm night breeze, through the long emptiness, between lifetimes—a whisper that echoed down the songlines, into darkness.

"Yes."

Yes.

Oh, yes—

Then the earth spun. Her knees buckled. Someone called her name.

—and in the shadows, she saw his eyes—

5

HE RIDES THE long night, a dreamline, an infinite echo, from lifetime to lifetime. The night stretches ahead, and behind him come the shadows, trailing like hungry remoras.

Behind him.

Forever behind him.

The low chorus of the summer locusts was muted by the growl of the Electra Glide as he roared back up Route 81, toward the mountains, away from the Dixie Dinette. Chances were there'd be a service station on the main road. He'd top off the tank and decide what he was going to do, now that he was finally here.

The hot wind buffeted the rider's face, streaming his long hair behind him in a black wake. The heavy, olive shirt he had been issued in Di An billowed with the breeze. On his left shoulder, a division patch bore a red numeral 1 inside a squared-off shield of green, the insignia of the First Infantry Division. The strip of tape over his left pocket read U. S. ARMY. The strip over the right read TRAGER. His right collar bore a simple silver eagle.

His ears throbbed from the engine's roar. Yet the rider heard the crickets, the locusts in the trees, the breeze whistling through the soft, black hairs on his arms. A bald eagle swooped over the road and dove into the trees. He smelled sweet dew forming in the hot, humid air.

The long night was alive.

He had ridden the night through the British countryside; past the ruins of marble columns in the hills outside of Rome; through kilometers of verdant brush surrounding Johannesburg; following interstates and freeways; down old country roads where dogs howled as he passed. Running, always running, ahead of the shadows.

The cone from the headlight illuminated the road only seventy feet or so ahead, but his eyes easily picked out a green exit sign a quarter of a mile away. He read it by starlight: **STONEBRIDGE**.

He leaned into the exit and the road blurred beneath the tires. The curve straightened into a two-lane road that led down into the valley. A mile farther in, two rows of hills spread out and formed a vague crescent, meeting again as mountains five or six miles farther in the hazy distance.

He pulled onto the grassy shoulder and shut off the engine. The abrupt silence was broken only by the soft *tap-tap* of the hot engine as it began to cool. Then he made out the sound of crickets moving in the grass on each side of the road, and the flutter of wings deep in the trees. Yet there was silence in the earth, and a heavy silence in the shadows between the trees. The land felt strange here; old, yet unfinished, as though it were waiting.

At the edge of the headlight's reach stood a painted metal sign, shaped like an open book:

WELCOME TO
STONEBRIDGE
"Home of the Eighth Natural Wonder of the World"
The Gem of Crescent Valley
CARVED BY THE AWESOME MAJESTY OF MOTHER EARTH AND THE TIMELESS GRANDEUR OF ETERNITY

Affixed to the sign was a vinyl sticker of the American flag, partly covered by a bumper sticker proudly bearing the Confederate flag. Bullet holes cratered the sign.

He looked up at the velvet sky. The stars that night would have seemed unusually bright to us, for the sky above Stonebridge was clear and there were no streetlights for several miles. But to him, the canopy above was ablaze with suns most can only see through telescopes or in astronomy books. He followed the track of the Milky Way, and smiled at the smoky shape of a nebula, just a pinprick of light, hanging over the black tree line.

The nights had been this clear in the north, and that vista was the only thing he missed from his journey through Canada. After his plane had landed at LAX, he had ridden his bike through California for almost two months until the white knights had gotten wind of him in San Francisco. Then he had ridden up into Oregon, then Washington, trying to throw them off, sensing them always somewhere on the road behind.

He couldn't judge them. He had been hiding in Southeast Asia for five years, and the things he had seen—the things he had done, in the tunnels, in the trees—he would wish upon no one. He had walked the jungles and the humid killing fields, had smelled the blood and the napalm and the sweet stench of death, and he had seen the results for himself. He had been part of it.

He had even liked it.

When he returned across the New York border, he could no longer sense his pursuers. He had lost them again—only for a short while, he was sure—and once more he had kept his promise to Angeline. The Hawkbournes would not come to harm by his hand. He had sworn it to her as she lay still and silent in his arms, her eyes burning into his, her crimson blood spreading down her crinoline dress.

That was a lifetime ago, and a promise he would never break.

So he raced the endless night, a shadow chased by shadows.

He bent down and placed his palm in the grass, feeling the earth beneath it. Feeling its memory. Feeling it *breathe*.

A light flared against the trees. He looked up, expecting to see the bright tail of a meteorite as it streaked through the atmosphere. Instead, the light on the trees grew brighter, more artificial.

His first instinct was to hide, to seek cover from incoming fire. Then headlights appeared around the curve and flashed on a tourist billboard.

VISIT CARTER CAVERNS!

The headlights angled toward him. They would be focused on him in seconds.

The shadows along the edge of the trees grew darker, longer, as the headlights approached. The concentrated blackness of the woods stretched out, kissed the tip of his boots, then slipped up his leg, smooth like black ooze, swallowing him with shadow.

A dark green '69 Mustang convertible bore down upon him—the kids from the Dixie Dinette. The headlights cut through the night, slicing through the shadows between the trees. The passengers in the car would never notice a too-thick patch of darkness along the side of the road, a solid sliver of midnight that light could not penetrate.

Music beat from the Mustang's radio, some pop song he recognized from Armed Forces radio back in 'Nam. The rider smelled a whiff of cigarette smoke, of beer; the odor of hot engine oil; a young woman's perfume, the scent of summer sweat.

Then the Mustang tore past him, never slowing as it headed toward the country. "—you got me running, and hiding, all over town—" faded down the road, and the young woman's laughter shimmered on the air like rain.

The taillights disappeared behind a bend in the road. Starlight sparkled in the rider's black eyes as the shadows around him slipped away in silence. A cricket finally chirruped, then the insects in the trees resumed their nighttime song.

He stared back the way he had come.

There, in the valley. He'd find the comfort of friendship, at least for a short while, and perhaps even find a respite from the loneliness, the feverish hungers, that he had lived through in unpronounceable jungles halfway across the world.

He placed his hand on his shirt pocket, and touched the outline of the letter he had received in Saigon.

—and a promise to keep.

He had ridden this black night many times before, into valleys, into darkness. The engine growled to life. Rocks spit out from the back tire, and the Electra Glide leaped away from town.

He followed the odor of the car's hot engine. The road curved and the trees began to thin out, and he saw the Mustang's taillights a quarter of a mile ahead as it flew past a gas station.

A bell clanged twice as the rider drove over the station's black rubber hose. He shut off the engine and stared at the faded green dinosaur painted on the cinder block wall. The new logo, a big red diamond, shone through a plastic and neon sign at the edge of the road. It was nothing, he thought, compared to the simple artistry—and the deeper connection—of the original Sinclair dinosaur.

He had first seen the cartoon dinosaur at the World's Fair in Chicago, the first time he had experienced the vibrancy of Chicago's night life, and a wonderful time in a South Side night club listening to Big Bill Broonzy and his band.

A head popped up inside the office—a skinny, tousle-haired boy, maybe fifteen, curly blond hair. He waved and smiled, exposing a big goofy grin.

The boy loped outside. He wore a pale blue t-shirt with an ironed-on picture of the Woodstock logo. He stared at the bike, and then at the biker.

"How about a fill up?" the rider said.

The boy blinked behind thick glasses. "You sure, mister? Gas just went up a coupla cents."

The rider glanced at the sign. **REGULAR 33¢**.

"I'm independently wealthy," he said, unscrewing the gas cap. "Go to town."

The boy adjusted a metal lever on the pump, and a bell clanged inside. He filled the bike's tank and replaced the nozzle on the pump. "Gallon and a half. 51¢, mister."

The biker handed him a dollar from his pocket. "Keep it."

The boy broke out in a big, wide, buck-toothed smile, and the rider kickstarted the bike. It woke with a roar of metal. "Cool!" the boy said.

Cool.

It hit him then. Out in the open.

He was too high profile for this sleepy little town. Too different. Too cool.

He needed cover. "Hey." The kid looked up, eyes wide. "This place got a hotel?"

"Oh, sure, mister. A couple of them. There's a new fancy one out by the natural bridge, but there's a motel right up the road." He pointed north.

Away from the diner. Away from—

Without a word, the boy ran off toward the office. He rummaged around behind the counter, then came back. He held out a map. "Here ya go, mister. It's free." He snatched it back and unfolded it, then pointed his finger on the red line that was Route 81. He memorized the main roads and their pattern, the location of the diner, the stone bridge—

—and St. John's Cemetery.

The rider took the map, folded it, and said, "Thanks. I can use—" And then the boy held out a small, stuffed dinosaur—green, fuzzy, wearing a tiny t-shirt that read SINCLAIR.

"Free with every fill up. I guess a gallon counts, don't it?" He shuffled his feet. "Besides, we got four boxes we gotta unload."

The rider took the dinosaur and watched the fluorescent lights gleam off its round, blackbead eyes.

"I'm in first-year ROTC at Stonebridge High." He pronounced it *Rot-See.*

The rider nodded. "Okay."

"You seen any action? 'Nam, I mean."

Did he mean the heat of the flame throwers? The intermingled smells of sweat and urine in the fetid tunnels? The aroma of charred flesh?

"Yeah. Five years. I saw a little."

"Man!" The boy beamed like a kid with his first BB gun. "Hey, you kill anybody?"

He stared at the boy and said, "Yeah."

"What—"

"It's not pretty," he said. But he had wanted to be truthful. He had wanted to say, *It's not good. It's not civilized. It's not human.*

"Wow."

"Yeah. Wow."

"Must be great to, like, get out of here and, like, see the world, huh?"

The rider sighed. Frogs chorused from the lowlands behind the service station. The trees hung motionless along the road, and stillness ruled the night.

He looked up at the night sky. "What's your name?"

"Steve. I'm Steve."

"I wish you could shut off all your lights for just a minute or two."

Steve looked back at the office lights, then turned to the rider. "Uh—"

"Tonight, when you shut down for the night, Steve, look up before you go home. The sky is darker here in Stonebridge. There aren't the streetlights that cities have, or flashing signs, or marquees. In New York, L. A.—hell, Saigon, even—you can't see the stars at all. Too much light. Too much gets in the way."

Steve watched him, but finally glanced up at the sky.

"Keep looking up. Enjoy the night for what it is. What it can be. Sometimes, life is written in the stars. There's magic up there, if you can see it. Sometimes, it's down here too."

And in his mind's eye, he saw an oval face, framed in sandy blonde hair; an upturned nose, pouting lips, and piercing blue eyes.

He straddled the bike, kicked it, and spat gravel behind the tires. In his mirror, he saw Steve, standing away from the sheet metal canopy, staring up at the tapestry of stars.

6

THE MOTEL WAS a long, one-story building, a central A-frame roofed with bright green shingles, and two wings of clapboard siding. The tall sign along the road was lit by floodlights on each side of a giant, tri-cornered hat. *Patriot Motor Inn* was painted in an antique script. A red neon **VACANCY** sign sputtered below the colonial hat.

The rider parked in front of the office door and went inside. The desk clerk sat tilted back in an office chair, snoring against the background noise of a flickering black and white television. He was in his fifties, and he wore thick, black-rimmed glasses and a stained, short-sleeve white shirt. His pudgy stomach rose and fell with each wet snore. A plastic nameplate lay angled on the counter.

TUCKER COE
ASSISTANT MANAGER ON DUTY

The rider rapped his knuckles on the countertop. The man snorted awake.

"You must be Tucker," the rider said.

Tucker pursed his lips in concentration and focused his wet, bulbous eyes at the rider. Long hair, late twenties. A hippie? He glanced out the window and spied the motorcycle.

Yep. Hippie.

The sheriff was gonna crappity-crap.

"How much for a room?"

Tucker blinked his pink eyes.

"The sign says vacancies. I only need one."

"One?"

"One room."

Tucker's eyes suddenly widened. "Oh. Okay. A room." *Crap, crap, crappity crap.*

Tucker said, "$10.50," deliberately quoting the highest rate. He slid across a registration form. "Two double beds. But you might could find a cheaper place out by the old bridge, if you—"

"I knew a Tucker in 'Nam. Saved a platoon from the VC with a couple of grenades." He placed twenty-one dollars on the counter. "One night in advance."

Tucker reached for the cash, then paused, his hand in mid-air. Tucker's fear emanated from him in waves. "Look, mister—"

"Trager. *Jim.*"

"Yeah, okay," Tucker said, trembling.

The rider let himself focus on the man; let his perception reach out and *touch* him.

The sheriff.

His fear was physical. And it went back a long time, back to high school.

Stonebridge High, where Hicks had been the schoolyard bully, the big dog that pissed on the little pups.

Tucker had always been the runt.

The rider felt his fear, absorbed it. The room slowly faded around the desk clerk, growing darker. The television was an incomprehensible murmur in the background, the picture an out of focus static that no longer registered to Tucker's watery eyes. There was only this stranger, Mr. James Trager—colonel, the jacket says—and his silhouette was a black hole, a singularity darker than night.

—Tucker.

Tucker blinked. The voice had come from everywhere.

—Tucker. There's nothing to be scared of. You're certainly not scared of me, are you?

Tucker nodded once, slowly.

—The sheriff is a clown, isn't he?

The clerk almost smiled.

—If the sheriff asks—if anyone asks—you have no reason to keep watch on me. No reason at all.

Tucker's lips parted slightly, moved soundlessly.

—I am the perfect guest. You don't want anyone to bother me. Understand?

A thin line of drool dripped from the corner of Tucker's mouth.

—You like me. I'm a great guy. Funny. I even told you a few jokes.

Tucker blinked, swaying slightly in the chair. The line of drool dripped onto his chest.

The rider slid the cash across the counter and cleared his throat. Tucker blinked. He looked up at the rider, then down at the counter. The form had been filled out. The rider placed another twenty on top of the first. "Let me ask you for a favor, Tucker. My bike is kind of loud. Can you give me one of the rooms on the end? That way we can keep it quiet and peaceful for everybody else."

"Oh, oh sure!" Tucker almost leaped out of the chair. He opened a shallow lock box on the wall and took down the last key on the bottom. "Room 34. All clean and ready to go!" He handed over the key, then picked up the cash. "And thanks, mister—I mean, *Colonel.* Thanks for everything you did over there in that godforsaken jungle."

The rider nodded, afraid Tucker would next salute him.

"God bless America," the rider said.

"Yes, SIR!" And Tucker saluted.

The rider parked his bike a few spaces over from a two-tone '66 Caprice filled with cardboard boxes and piles of laundry. He untied his duffel bag from the seat and looked out across the parking lot, toward the forests and the wooded mountains sloping up against the sky. This town was too small, too close knit. He had to get the lay of the land, but the bike was too loud, too high profile for a Mayberry like this.

He unlocked the door and slung the bag into a chair by the window. He left the lights off, seeing only by a slit of moonlight shining through a gap between the window's thick curtains. The carpet was an ugly green shag that needed vacuuming. The beds were made with identical lime green and pale blue patterned comforters. The sink was in the center of a simple Formica counter, and four glasses covered with crinkled paper tops were on a cork tray with an empty ice bucket. The white ceramic bathtub was cracked in a couple of places, and the toilet underneath a small window—*Excellent*, he thought—was bound with a white paper wrapper.

SANITIZED FOR YOUR PROTECTION

He placed the stuffed dinosaur atop the television between the V of the rabbit ears. There was a red, painted coin box on the bed's headboard:

MAGIC FINGERS

25¢ FOR A RESTFUL VIBRATING MASSAGE!

"God bless America," he murmured.

He lay across the bed closest to the window and stared at the rough, stucco ceiling, stained with the brown blood of a dead bug near the corner, and tried not to think about her.

He hadn't expected this. He had long ago given up believing it would happen again. But why here? He never would have come to Stonebridge if he hadn't received the letter. After all this time—*What? Fifty-nine years?*—why was it happening here? Why now?

He shut his eyes, wishing away the vision of her face, her soft, round curves, her aroma, the light behind her eyes.

"No," he said. "It cannot be her."

He was on his feet without knowing it, pulling off his pants.

The night called.

He had to run.

Naked, a sliver of moonlight slicing across his back, he messed up the sheets and punched an indentation into a pillow. He turned on the air conditioner beneath the window. He snapped on the TV and turned the volume low, then filed a water glass halfway and placed it on the nightstand. He ripped the wrapper off the toilet seat and balled it into a trash can under the sink. If anyone came looking in the morning, it would appear as if he had spent the night.

He opened the window over the toilet, and he smelled the wildness of the Virginia hills; the rich loam of the earth, the sharp scents of flowers growing wild and free. Except for the low murmur of locusts in the pines, it was silent outside. And in the darkness, a silent shadow slipped through the window, fleeting down the wall. It slid over a gravel drive leading behind the motel, then merged with the shadows between the trees. It rose in the darkness, a night-thing, feral, and loped between the elms and pines, growling low in its throat like a beast loose in the night.

7

SHE LOVED THE sound of locusts on hot summer nights.

Thunder was an annoyance; but the sound of rain, the incessant patter on the roof, disturbed her in a way she never understood, and always put her on edge.

Locusts, though, singing, alive and invisible, their song cascading high in a symphony through the trees, then crashing like a wave to shore—that was magic.

The Hollies harmonized slow on the radio as Summer relaxed beside Rob in his blue '67 Falcon. The headlights cast weak, yellow beams that bounced across the blacktop, and she gazed through the open window as the trees rolled by, loving the way the warm breeze through the window vent caressed her skin.

She had surrendered to Ruthette forty-five minutes after the biker had left. She had over-poured coffee into two cups just minutes after Duke and the sheriff had driven off. Then a couple of her tickets had come back—she had done the math and taxes all wrong, and one table complained they never got the peach pie they had ordered.

She took care of things for them, and then she hid in the kitchen. She scooped up a handful of cubes from the ice machine and held them against the back of her neck. She smiled at Ruthette, the cook, bustling at the flat grill.

"Long night," Ruthette said.

Summer closed her eyes, felt the cool trickle of the ice as it melted down her spine. "Long damn night," she said. "Do me a favor, will you? Drop some broken glass or Clorox in the sheriff's dinner."

Ruthette smiled. "Heh."

Summer turned up the radio. The Turtles seemed happy, singing together; but her music wasn't working. She shut her eyes and leaned back against a refrigerator. She kept an old Magnavox clock radio in the kitchen, tuned to the top 40 AM station from Hampton, or WNOR, the cool FM rock station out of Norfolk. Whenever Stonebridge and its blue hairs pressed in on her, or when redneck truckers leered at her figure just a little too long to be comfortable, she would disappear in the back for ten or fifteen minutes, and let the songs wash over her. She'd float into the beat, feel the lyrics vibrate inside her like her heartbeat. When "Bridge Over Troubled Water" played on the radio, the sadness it evoked would wash over her in waves. And when the Stones' "Paint It Black" came on, her heart would beat with an almost forbidden rhythm that pounded with soul. Songs took her away and made her feel alive.

Ruthette glanced over and saw the sweat stains spotting her pink waitress outfit. She shook her head. "Girl, you need to—"

"No," Summer said. "Don't you even start. I'm too tired to hear it."

Ruthette went to a metal cabinet and pulled out a brown moccasin purse.

She took down the tip jar from the shelf above the grill. "Seventeen dollars," Ruthette said, stuffing the bills into the purse. She slipped the purse over Summer's shoulder.

Summer tried to smile. Oh well. At least she had made enough tips to buy a few new paperbacks and the latest Stones album.

"Go." Ruthette pointed toward the door. "Get your boyfriend and go."

Rob watched her hug Summer through the grill window. He hopped off the stool and held open the glass door, and then Summer shuffled out of the kitchen and waved goodbye to Tina.

Outside, the night heat washed over her. She stopped and inhaled, tasting the humidity and the thick richness of the woods deep in her throat, and she felt the night take hold of her.

Rob said something, she didn't know what, and she dimly heard him open the door for her. But something stirred deep inside her, waking, squirming like a soul-beast first sensing its surroundings, testing the bars of its flesh cage—hungering, restless.

Rob had disappeared. There was only the night—the night, and the rider's dark, deep eyes.

"Hey."

Summer looked up. "Huh?" She had zoned out. She was already in the car. Rob had closed her door and had the key in the ignition. He started the engine. The radio lit up, and Mama told someone not to come. "Summer, are you okay?"

She gave him a thin smile. "Tired. Maybe fainting has affected me more than I thought."

He put his hand atop hers. "Why don't we forget about going to the movies tomorrow night? We don't even have to go to the party on Saturday. I just want you to be okay."

"I know," she said, looking out at the night.

"Maybe it'll do us both some good to get away together." He turned the radio down a notch. "A friend at Tech has a cottage on the beach at Nag's Head."

"A one-night stand at the beach?" She tried to smile.

"At least two," he said.

"Rob, I don't know. I just don't know."

"So come back to Tech with me. Stay with me in September."

"Rob—"

"You don't have to go to college. We'll find you a job in Blacksburg. We'll get an apartment. I'll read to you at night. Gothics. Tolkien."

She rolled her eyes. "Oh no. No singing dwarves."

It wasn't the first time he had brought up living together.

"Rob, not again. You know I can't move in with you. Mama would kill me."

"Screw your mother."

"—or she'd never speak to me again."

"There's a big loss."

"We've gone over this."

"I know. Look, I know. But—"

But.

Always *But.*

How could she tell him without hurting him that she just wasn't ready to move out and shack up with her high school boyfriend? That something about it just wasn't right, no matter what *Cosmo* said, no matter what couples were doing in the big cities. Rob was a wonderful guy—he and Summer had been best friends since kindergarten—but in his faded t-shirt and glasses, he was too cut and dried, too clean. Too Stonebridge.

"I'm just not ready," she said, looking out into the darkness within the trees. "I just feel like— One of these days, I'll be ready."

"For what?"

She glanced at Rob, then looked away quickly. Too quickly. She felt her cheeks grow warm and hoped that Rob wouldn't notice, because she was scared. Scared that she suddenly didn't care about the drive-in, always the damn Friday night drive-in; scared that the Fourth of July party in the woods was only two days away, but it could be months away for all she cared. And she was scared because something behind her eyes, in her heart, deep inside where yearnings wait, she felt something growing.

Something was happening, and she felt so stupid, so weak, as though she didn't know a single damn thing.

But that just wasn't true.

No matter what Ruthette or the sheriff believed, it had not been the heat that had knocked her out.

She had always felt just fine in the steam and the heat of the diner's kitchen. Tonight had been no different. When she had stepped outside to look over Kenny's new set of wheels, out in the darkness and the open air, the warmth had embraced her. She had always reveled in everything that was summer—the heat, the sun, the aroma of suntan lotion, the feel of wet sand between her toes.

She knew perfectly well what had started it all.

It was him, wasn't it?

The Midnight Rider.

She squeezed her eyes shut, trying to force the deep night of his eyes from her mind. But they were so dark, so endless—and the touch of his hands, so strong, so hot.

No. She could not feel this. Not here with Rob, not now.

"Shit," she whispered.

Rob looked her way. "Summer? You okay?"

She nodded, and when she opened her eyes, she was surprised by her tears. "Just a little headache. I'll be fine tomorrow. I think I just need to get to bed."

"Should you try to stay awake some? I mean, you did fall."

"Rob, I only fainted—" Her voice trailed off. Her mouth hung open, and her eyes went blank, focused inward, on an image that sprang unbidden to her mind.

Summer?

Rob's voice was only an echo, a whisper in an endless cavern. She stood beneath a wide, gnarled tree. It towered over her, spreading its dark green canopy across her field of vision. It was an ancient and vast tree, an oak, wide and green; the oldest tree in the world. Stars blazed between its branches, and its roots burrowed deep into her being.

She blinked.

Driving.

Rob.

Through the windshield, the headlights illuminated a neighborhood street sign.

"Here," she said. "Turn here."

"What?" Rob stopped at the intersection of Augusta and Main. "But that's downtown. Nothing's open this late."

"Turn." She pointed toward the brick and concrete blocks that were downtown Stonebridge.

He stared at her, then spun the wheel.

Main Street after sundown was a ghost town. Once past the empty hulk of the old Langley Theatre, Summer remembered seeing her first movie there, *Lady and the Tramp*, when she was only four, the tiny specialty shops like Patty's Peanut Place and all the town offices were dark and empty, closed since 4:30 or five, except for Howard's Hot Dogs, a glorified beer joint where half the old guys in AA at the First Stonebridge Baptist spent their paychecks after meetings. A sign over the door read **NO HIPPIES ALLOWED**.

Twin spotlights illuminated the American flag, hanging listless high above the post office. Rob stopped at the intersection of Prince Street, and they sat in the silence of the town, listening as the Stones wailed softly through the radio about a honky tonk.

Rob broke the spell. "Why'd you want to come this way?"

She shook her head, slowly, and gazed across the intersection.

St. John's Episcopal, a two-century-old brick and marble cruciform, was awash in yellow floodlights, illuminating the stained-glass windows crafted in 1813. But she didn't see the church where she had been baptized, the cemetery where she had played among the Civil War tombstones and cracked marble slabs.

It was the wide, overhanging silhouette of the churchyard's ancient oak that she focused on. Its gnarled, verdant limbs rubbed against the church's shingles and spread out over Main Street, almost to the opposite sidewalk. She did not notice that the locusts around the car had grown silent.

The pounding of her heart was a violent, hard rock drumbeat. Why had she wanted to come here? This was *stupid.* What the hell had she been expecting?

"Holy—" Rob pointed through the windshield. "What the hell is that?"

A dark thing bounded out of the dense blackness beneath the twisted oak, trailing shadows behind it like mists. It moved catlike into the street with silent footsteps that pounded inside her, the beat of a wild and forbidden heart.

The thing stood almost five feet tall at the shoulders. Its eyes shone like scarlet and gold, twin hearts of redfire burning deep within. The buried floodlights on the church dimmed, flickering erratically, like blue sparks erupting from the earth.

It nudged the bumper with its great, black snout. Then it looked up, into the windshield, its eyes narrowing into angry, feral slits of fire. It was an animal, a monster; the concentrated essence of night, of a passion she felt in her soul.

This *thing* was impossible. This was a shadow thing, a creature straight out of a dream, a dream of heat and sweat.

Its ears flattened atop its broad black skull, and it slammed its giant head straight into the grille. The car rocked backward with a crunch of metal. The chrome crossbar in the grille popped like a spring, and the tip of the hood crumpled like tin foil. They heard the tinkle of glass as a headlight shattered and sprayed across the road.

"Holy *shit*!" Rob shouted. "My *car*!" Rob punched his fist on the horn. "God, Summer! The window! Roll up your window!" He jammed his right hand on the horn and fumbled for the window knob with his left. Summer stared motionless through the windshield, breathless. The thing was huge. Mighty.

Beautiful.

It leaped up onto the hood. Its massive paws crumpled the hot metal. Its black, shaggy head seemed as large as a buffalo's, and its fur rippled, almost like tendrils, or smoke, or *something*.

"Oh, Jesus! Summer! Summer, the window! Now!" Rob's fist beat down on the horn. One hand accidentally hit a knob on the dashboard, and the wipers suddenly flicked back and forth, *sliiip tick sliiip tick*—

The thing followed their movement with its black eyes, left, right, left.

Then, it suddenly snapped forward and crunched a wiper between its shark-like teeth. It tossed back its head in fury, and threw the blade into the gutter. The thing bared its ragged teeth, exposing its long yellow canines, sharp like the fangs of a sabretooth, and bellowed its challenge.

Summer caught herself panting in short, intense breaths. She watched this thing, this *monster*, enrapt. There was great power in this thing, this night beast—and savage beauty.

Rob was babbling. "What the hell? What— Is it a wolf? My God, it can't be."

The thing's eyes locked with Summer's. Slowly, its ears lifted away from its head. Its black eyes widened, somehow became *softer*. The thing whimpered once, shook its massive head, then leaped off the hood. It bounded into the black depths of the cemetery. From within the deep shadows, it howled—long and high, a scream of rawness, of endless pain. It was more than the howl of a wild beast. It was a wail, a cry of infinite loneliness.

She knew when it was gone—she *felt* it, deep inside—just as something inside her had told her to be here, right here, right now.

She heard the locusts spring back to life outside in the trees, and the radio was playing that goddamn stupid "Chickaboom, Chickaboom," and she didn't like it one damn bit.

"Summer, that was a wolf! That had to be a wolf, didn't it? Look what it did to my hood! Holy shit! Can wolves even *do* that?"

"We don't have wolves here," Summer said, softly. "Canada, maybe. The Rockies. But not here."

Rob gazed through the windshield. "Not a wolf? *Had* to be a wolf! I thought for sure it was a wolf. A bear! It was bigger than a wolf! It had to be a bear! It was too big for a wolf anyway, wasn't it? *Had* to be a bear!"

Summer said nothing.

It wasn't a bear, and it wasn't the Big Bad Wolf.

Rob hadn't seen. She had. She had seen the night curl around its limbs in wisps of shadow as it had stepped into the street from the darkness of the graveyard.

It was pure ferocity. A wild thing. A shadow beast, prowling the night.

And it was loose.

Something inside her relaxed.

Free.

"We gotta call the sheriff! Tell him we've got a wild bear in town!"

She turned to him, calmly, her eyes half closed. "Rob, you need to get me home. I fainted, remember?"

He blinked at her. Then his mouth fell open. "Oh, God, Summer! I'm—Yeah, yeah, you're right. Let's get you home. Jeez, Summ, I'm so sorry!"

She forced a smile. "It's okay. You can call the sheriff from your place."

Rob nodded and stepped on the gas.

She looked out the window.

Rob could call the sheriff all he wanted.

Somehow she knew—she was *sure*—that beast would never be caught.

8

"CHRIST. MY DAD is gonna kill me."

They stood in the road in front of Summer's house on Croatoan Avenue. A lone streetlight cast a cone of pale light over the Falcon. Rob's hand seemed stuck to his forehead, his eyes wide with disbelief.

Jagged chrome fragments stuck out from the grille. The front bumper and hood were crinkled accordion-like into uneven V-shapes. The hood was cratered by the thing's heavy paws, swirls scratched into the paint by its long claws. The driver's side headlight was only a bent cup of shiny chrome, some bare, wrangled wires, and a few shards of glass.

"Christ," he said. "Oh, Christ."

Summer took his hand. "Rob, it's going to be all right. Listen to me. Your insurance will take care of it. It was an accident, right?"

"Insurance. Yeah, I forgot about that."

"So, you get home, you go tell your dad everything that happened, and you call the insurance company tonight. Okay? Right after you call the sheriff's department."

"Sheriff?"

"To report the—"

"Right, the bear. It had to be a bear, didn't it?"

Summer smiled for him. *It was no bear.* "Of course it was a bear. What else could it have been?"

Rob stared at the twisted grille.

"Show it to your father. Call the sheriff. That'll make it all legal. Call the insurance company."

Rob nodded. "Okay. Okay."

She leaned over and kissed him. "Rob, I'm sorry, but I have to get to bed. I still don't feel right, and—"

"No, no, I'm sorry. You're the one who fainted. And I'm just whining about my car."

"Thanks for being sweet." She kissed him again, then he pulled her close and kissed her deeply.

She started up the sidewalk, then turned and smiled. "I'll see you tomorrow."

Rob pulled off, and Summer watched him fade away down the dark street.

The house was two stories, whitewashed, with green shutters and a dark green roof. A wide, L-shaped porch wrapped around the front and left sides, fringed with her mother's ugly damn azaleas. Holly bushes stood sentinel at the corners.

Croatoan Avenue had been the most prestigious lane in Stonebridge in

1919, when the house had been built. In summer the trees along the green medians spread their limbs across the avenue in a long tunnel of foliage, their leafy fingers intertwined with the trees lining the town's most luxurious lawns. But towns grow old, and neighborhoods fall in and out of favor, and things that were once considered fashionable eventually become old-fashioned or second-rate.

Summer's home, and the other homes on the verdant lane, were now a testament to a rich, Southern heritage: archaic architecture built on streets named after the South's conquered and forgotten peoples. Algonquin. Powhatan. Kecoughtan. Croatoan.

Lost.

The screen door creaked as Summer stepped inside, and her mother's acrid cigarette smoke washed over her. The television's glow flickered blue along the orderly arrangements of commemorative plates along the mantel, the Hummels in the china cabinet, the Chinese Foo dogs and Asian trinkets on the floor and on tables, and her mother's ancient family antiques—a heritage of memories Summer thought were prehistoric and ugly.

Louise Moore sat at her usual nightly perch on the sofa, chain-smoking and watching Dean Martin on TV. She wore her short, silver-blonde hair in a style left over from the '40s, and she looked up over her thick glasses. "How come you're home so early?" She brushed ashes off her shiny, Chinese blouse. "You didn't get fired, did you?"

Summer shook her head and walked into the kitchen. Over her shoulder, she said, "Why do you always think the worst?" She opened the refrigerator—the ice box, her mother called it—and popped open a Coke with the bottle opener over the sink. She took a deep swig, then held the cold bottle to her forehead. "I left early. I wasn't feeling well."

Louise *hmphed* in the living room. "You were out late with that Rob again. Carousing all over town. Trifling."

Trifling. Summer never, ever had fun. She just *trifled.*

She leaned against the arch leading into the living room. "Mom, Jesus, can't you just for once—"

"Don't you take the name of the Lord in vain! I don't know where you get this stuff. You didn't get that from my side of the family, that's for sure."

Summer stared at the grainy image of Dino singing atop a piano. Her mother smoked furiously. "Look," Summer said, softly. "I was sick. I kind of fainted."

"*Fainted?*" Louise spun to face her.

"God, Mom, I didn't die or anything. I just didn't feel good. I was sick, okay?"

Louise sucked her Winston. "Well, you go out too much, if you ask me."

Summer muttered under her breath, "I *didn't* ask." She wanted to argue, she wanted to tell off her mother, but even more she wanted to climb straight into bed. "Look, it wasn't because I had too good a time. I wish. Maybe you should try it sometime."

Her mother's mouth dropped open. "Maybe your mouth is what got you in trouble with that job."

She had gotten a phone call this morning from Words-N-Tunes, a small chain of book and record stores that came out of Roanoke. She had interviewed last week with the owner, a graying forty-something man named Wallis, for a job—anything to make more bread than the diner gave her—and maybe she'd be able to score some new novels and albums with the employee discount. Wallis had brushed a hand against her left breast and made a not-so-subtle pass at her, and she politely turned him down after mentioning how nice his wedding ring shone in the light.

The bastard called this morning and told her she didn't get the job.

Her mother blamed her, first thing off. Summer couldn't tell Louise that Wallis had propositioned her; Ma would march down to the store and threaten him with court action. Summer didn't want to cause a scene—besides, she'd spread the word later, and none of her friends would ever buy anything there—so she told Louise that she didn't know why she didn't get the job, and Ma, of course, said she had obviously done something wrong. It was the way Summer dressed, or her damn know-it-all attitude, or she wasn't serious enough about her future.

Trifling.

Summer said, "I'm going to bed." She started up the stairs, passing framed black and white photos of dead relatives she had never met. "Same damn pictures," she said, loud enough for her mother to hear. "Same old shit."

Louise smoked. On the TV, an invisible audience guffawed on a laugh track recorded decades earlier. Dean Martin had never been funnier.

9

CIGAR SMOKE FROM a house fifty yards behind him. The smell of car exhaust from the blue Falcon parked at the curb. The scent of flowers hanging thick and sweet in the night air.

He watched them kiss, then she turned away. The boy drove off down the street and turned at the corner. And he smelled her perfume in the air, the smell of her sweat, the soft shampoo in her hair.

She went inside and closed the door. He heard the deadbolt lock. His nostrils were suddenly filled with the perfume of the roses behind the porch, and he knew, he *felt*, that somehow roses were a part of her secret soul. It was as though he had found a mythical place where he finally belonged.

Voices, hers and an older woman's, came from inside the house. He crouched back into the shadows beside the tall hedge. In a few moments, there was silence, then the hollow sound of faint footsteps twisting up to the second floor. A light snapped on in the upstairs windows. There was a metallic *clunk*—an air conditioner coming on.

Music, then, a stereo. Beyond that, nothing, nothing but the sound of his own breathing, and the scratchy voice of a blues singer wailing about the summertime. Music to shut down the day. Music made to help forget it all.

In a moment, he was gone, a shadow, bounding on all fours across the lawns, over hedges, back into the darkness from which he was spawned.

10

SUMMER FLICKED ON the overhead light, then locked the bedroom door. She plopped her purse onto the dresser, then cranked the window air conditioner to HI.

She had picked up the stereo system—turntable, eight-track, AM/FM radio, and twin speakers—with S&H green stamps she had saved during her junior year, working part-time down at the Be-Lo Market. She had christened it by dropping the stylus on Track 1 of *The White Album,* and she had relaxed in her bean bag, next to a stack of unread paperbacks from the five and dime, and had been swept away.

Music and prose; guitars and stories. Her heart would always beat to the euphony of make-believe and reality and magic.

A flick of the **ON** switch; a toggle from **8-TRACK** to **STEREO**. She glanced at the title of the album on the turntable, then moved the stylus to the top of the third track, her favorite, and she fell across her bed, sheets still rumpled from last night, and closed her eyes and waited for the A/C to turn icy cold as Janis wailed about the days of living easy.

Her room, at least, was home. She had taped posters above two of her paperback book shelves: two fingers making the peace sign, painted red, white, and blue, and the movie poster for *Love Story* that Rob had given her last year. A glow in the dark Barnabas Collins poster watched over her from a spot next to her vanity, and a door-length purple and orange poster from a surfing movie was taped to the back of her door. She loved to sit in her gold velour bean bag chair—velour, Captain Kirk gold, Rob had once proclaimed—under the window that overlooked her garden and watch her portable TV or listen to the stereo with her headphones on, and just look at her belongings and feel welcome.

"Shit," she whispered.

That had become her favorite word. It was the way she felt about everything lately, the way the whole world seemed to her—the way life worked.

Shit.

She let Janis fade out, then went down the hall. A small window air conditioner had been chugging in the bathroom all day, and the bath rugs under her feet felt soft and cool. Maybe in some future decade her old lady would spring for central air, but Summer wasn't holding her breath.

She splashed cold water on her face, just to feel the chill. Then she took down a jar of Noxzema from the medicine cabinet and wiped the makeup off her face.

Shit. She seemed pale in the mirror, despite the tan she had been working on since March, sneaking an hour every now and then in the garden under the sun. She knew her color was a reaction from fainting. *It had to be, right?* But she loved having a tan. She loved the heat, the feel of the sun baking her skin.

She had gone to Virginia Beach for a three-day weekend last year with Tina and Ronnie, and she longed to smell the ocean breeze and the scents of cocoa butter and suntan lotion again. She'd tasted oysters for the first time on that trip, and had steamed shrimp with cocktail sauce. And they had let three guys pick them up—*Rob could never find out about that!*—and buy them beers. They sat around in the dunes and drank and made out. Ronnie, at one point, had her bikini top off, and she disappeared over the dunes with whatever his name was.

And the headache the next morning—

She smiled.

She went back to her cool bedroom and let her pink polyester dress fall to her feet. She hated these damn outfits. Tina called them "diner duds": pink, sky blue, pale yellow, cherry red, and puke green, all with starched, white collars and white hems.

One more day. One more day of grease and burgers and cleaning toilets, and cheap-ass five-cent tips from truckers.

Then, there'd be Friday night, and then the party Saturday; some dancing, some drinking, and then nothing to do on Sunday. Just time to sleep in and relax, and do absolutely, blissfully, nothing.

His eyes.

Damn it, his eyes.

She sat at her vanity and stared at her reflection, her too-pale cheeks, her tired—

His eyes. And suddenly it was his face she saw, the biker, standing in the parking lot, watching her, his eyes dark and smoky; his fingers, his touch, electric.

Darkness and light. His eyes, and fainting, falling—her mind, spinning; the drive home, a blur. And the beast. Its eyes—

His eyes.

She had seen his eyes before.

Could it really be? That long ago?

She put another Janis Joplin album on the turntable, and the room filled with the soulful anguish of "Little Girl Blue." She crossed to her closet and stood on tiptoes, moved aside a red and white plastic megaphone from good ol' Stonebridge High, and pulled down a cardboard box.

She had used colored markers to draw flowers and clouds and hearts across the cardboard sides. Inside were all the diaries she had kept since second grade. She had started them when she was stuck at home with the mumps for a week. There was nothing to watch on afternoon TV except for her mother's stories, and she had read most of her Nancy Drews at least twice. But Daddy had come home with a couple of blank diaries and some colored pencils, just to keep her busy.

So she started drawing pictures of her best friends, and describing them, and how she felt about them, and about school, and life; and suddenly she was keeping a diary.

She opened the oldest diary. She hadn't looked at them in years. Too much

Leslie Gore and Fabian; too many rainbows and ponies and hearts.

Kid stuff.

The diaries from second and third grades were bound with dark, leatherette covers creased from little girl fingers. She had drawn throughout with crayons, pencils, and ballpoints.

She skimmed over an entry about a book she had read, *Cinderella; or, The Little Glass Slipper*, and read another about a fight in the cafeteria, and how Kenny Cousins was a big bully for beating up on Mikey Stubbs at recess. There were sketches of her best friends, Tina and Ronnie, both with big eyes, thick eyelashes, and bright red lips.

She wrote that poem when she was eleven—that stupid Easter poem for Sunday school, that her mother then sent to her elementary school newspaper. God, that was embarrassing—mimeographed, purple, typewritten bullshit. That was when she still sang in St. John's junior choir, way back when she still believed.

She reached in and plucked out her fourth-grade diary, and looked at all the sketches she had made of her friends and teachers, of whomever, and their eyes.

—dark

—filled with ink—

Fifth grade started with "Mrs. Mason is such an old hag!" Mrs. Mason taught math and science for fifth and sixth grades, and demanded them all to exceed her expectations and to excel at the level of Curie and Edison.

After a series of Ds on her report cards, Summer learned that math was not her finest subject and dreaded bringing home her grades.

A few entries later, Summer recounted how Mrs. Shields, furious beyond speech and to the point of spitting, punished her for taking artistic license with the first page of a two-page report on the American Colonies. Instead of writing her name in the upper right corner of the first page, she wrote her first name on the left, her last name on the right, and in between she drew thirteen stars that represented the original Colonies. To Mrs. Shields, such creativity was not the patriotic gesture Summer had intended, but was instead an unpardonable sin, and she paid penance in the principal's holy office. When Ma showed up that afternoon, she swore that Summer would always and forever and from now on write her name, class, and date in the upper right-hand corner just like everyone else, following the rules, coloring inside the lines, and bowing to the dictates of church, state, school, and authority.

She lobbed the diary back into the box.

Sixth grade. The diary was bound in padded vinyl, bearing a photo of a field of colorful flowers waving in the sunshine. She and her mother had been in Richmond for the annual Christmas parade, and Summer had found the diary at G. C. Murphy's.

> *Rob says he followed the stupid instructions* TO THE LETTER! *for an earth science experiment. They said to use a shoebox lid, fill it up with dirt, and then put water all over it. Then, of course, Mrs. Mason* SCREAMED *at him in front of*

the WHOLE CLASS for being so quote unquote IGNORANT as to follow the instructions! The shoebox lid fell apart from all the water, and mud went EVERYWHERE!

She felt sorry for Rob. First, Mrs. Mason never should have yelled at him like that, and second, she never should have totally embarrassed him in front of the whole class. Each classroom had a door leading to the outside, and Mason had sent him outside with his dirt in a bag to get rid of it. Then she had locked the door behind him, in forty-degree weather in December, and wouldn't let him in until the bell rang between classes.

She learned something that day: following instructions was for losers. Blind obedience to teachers, to Mom, to authority—any authority—without question, would screw you over every time.

She woke up in sixth grade. One day she was writing Sunday school poetry about the glory of God, and the next she was sizing up the people sitting around her in church. Mr. Blair, married for thirty years, who, according to her mother, flirted with anyone in a skirt; Yvonne Parker, a housewife who got liquored up every day during "The Edge of Night"; Steve Stone's big brother, who did time for stabbing someone in a beer joint out on Stonewall Road. It came to her that church was a club for hypocrites, acting holier than thou and passing their judgment on everyone else.

That, her eleven-year-old mind started piecing together, was what church really was all about: security in numbers. Believe this, preach that, pretend to follow the rules, then keep on breaking them under the protective umbrella of the All-Forgiving Cross.

Poems and songs, written and forgotten in her dim, distant high school past:

"Away from Home"
"Polaroid Soul"
"Black Tears"
"Hot Burning Rubber"
"Daddy's Gone"
"Paperback Colors"
"Sneakin' in the Roses"

She smiled. She wrote that one after laying out one summer in her garden, getting tan and trying a cigarette she'd sneaked out of her mother's purse.

"The Faerie Queen Sees Ghosts"
"Is She Cool"
"Empty Eyes"
"Front Row at the Spook Show"
"Trippin' in Home Ec"
"I Won't Forget"

Then she turned a few more pages.

May 17, 1963. Her twelfth birthday.

Two wide, black eyes stared at her from across the years.

She didn't realize she was holding her breath.

They took up both pages, drawn in ballpoint ink and Flair pens; a twelve-year-old's study in lines and shadows that somehow she hadn't even remembered.

Until tonight.

May 17, 1963

Dreams woke me up again. Not a nightmare, because I wasn't scared, not at all. But the eyes staring at me were WEIRD. Just looking at me. Really weird! It felt like they knew me, but how could that happen?

Even weirder: I thought I had seen THEM before!!

I don't know how I know this, but the eyes had been watching me! It was nighttime. In my dream, I mean. I was at school, coming out of 4th grade classroom. Why I was at school at night, I have no idea. Or why the 4th grade?? Dumb. So I stepped through the doorway and into the hall, and SUDDENLY there wasn't a floor anymore! I was standing in grass, covered with brown leaves, and there were trees all over instead of lockers. There was a dirt path and I went down it a little ways into the woods. Then the path turned into flower petals. Some were white and red and yellow, and it smelled real nice, like Mrs. Watkins' flower shop. Like I could live there forever! And then the trees weren't really trees, they were big bushes of thorns all really tight, like growing together in knots. And in the middle of them all these two giant black eyes were looking at me. Sometimes they were glowing red in the dark and sometimes it was all clear, like in moonlight, and I could hear it breathing hard and see its eyes and it blinked at me, and I could see black hair. It was like it was panting like it was hot when it was looking at me. And suddenly I was getting hot and feeling like I was going to throw up and fall. I grabbed a tree so I would stay up, but a big thorn went through my hand and it felt like it was burning and I was bleeding and there was a big hole in my hand and I could see the eyes through the hole and I knew it was hungry and it wanted ME!!!

And that's when I woke up and these are the eyes the best I can draw them, because I can't draw and you know that.

She stared at the eyes in marker and pen, but all she saw were the beast's eyes outside the windshield; twin black stars looking back at her, looking into her.

Hungry.

Below the eyes, she had written a poem. A *song.*

Listen to My Heart
Lyrics by
Summer Moore

Listen.
The night knows tales
told not through words
but through love
and blood
and eternity.
Listen
on soft, autumn nights, when the last scorched breath of summer fades
with the glare of the cold moon,
and you can hear
the song of the night
murmur
through the brittle trees.
Listen
as the cold wind kisses your cheeks
listen to the silence
hugging the hills like fog
listen to the call
of the lonely night
singing in your soul.
Listen
to the darkness
and you will hear its tales.
Listen
to the night
and you will hear its cries.
Listen
to the echoes of sweet, distant voices
unknown
and lost.
Listen
to the beating of two hearts
joined through eternity;
two lovers
trapped in twilit worlds
of shadow and light
dancing between life and death
between sun and stars.
Listen
to a song of summer and sunset.
a crimson nocturne.
a hymn to the endless night.
Listen—

She stared at the drawing, and she whispered aloud, so softly that she didn't even know she was talking to herself.

"You're the one."

She snapped her head up and looked around. She had zoned out again.

How long this time?

Tired, she realized.

She'd had enough for one day.

She dropped the diary on her desk, then rummaged through her albums and put on an obscure LP she had picked up at Woolworth's, by someone none of her friends had heard of, Fred Neil. She turned the volume low and peeled off her bra and panties. The music washed over her in soft, gentle waves, a reflection of the sunlight on the ocean, and the summer breezes that rolled through the song. She ran her hand round her breasts and looked at herself in the mirror—but as her eyes closed, the mirror disappeared, and she saw only eyes.

Its eyes.

His eyes.

11

ITS MIGHTY PAWS padded the soft, grassy earth, owning midnight. Its smoke-black limbs leapt over fences and fallen trees with a grace and strength no wolf could match. The run stirred its blood, and it exhilarated in rabbit and owl and mouse, in blood, in the scents of the night.

There were still a few hours left before dawn, time that belonged to him.

A red brick fence, overgrown with ivy, surrounded the quiet solitude behind St. John's Church. The beast cleared the fence by two feet, bounding between the worn marble markers, scenting its surroundings. It moved silently between grey pockmarked tombstones, beneath the needle-like statue of a soldier bearing a rifle and a squat, diagonal cap. The tall, polished marble gleamed in the moonlight.

IN LOVING MEMORY OF OUR CONFEDERATE DEAD

In the distance, it spotted a line of mausoleums arranged at the far edge of the property. Only a long brick wall separated the cemetery from the woods.

It slunk toward the tombs silhouetted against the trees. They were the final homes for the lineage of Stonebridge's landed gentry. GOODE, the oldest. LIGHTFOOT. HOBBS. One had hand-carved cherubim supporting its marble roof. The chiseled name above the door read SQUIRE. The black iron doors were solid, locked.

The crypt on the right had GARDNER chiseled into the marble above the iron doors. A tall willow at a corner of the brick wall dangled its whip-like strands over the marble roof. Two tall holly bushes grew wild and unkempt between the mausoleum and the brick perimeter. The beast stepped up to the black gates and sniffed—only rust and dead leaves. It pushed on one of the barred gates with its heavy paw, and the door creaked inward.

Brittle leaves lay strewn across the floor. Three raised marble crypts obscured the far wall. The beast huffed in satisfaction. It took a deep sniff of the night air, shook out its black shaggy head, and leapt over the wall, into the trees. It raced through town, between houses where dogs moaned at the silent strangeness they sensed outside their homes.

On a quiet street far on the other side of town, the beast raised its head and scented the air. Across the road, a faded '59 Chevy truck was parked on a cracked, cement driveway. From the ranch home it scented paints and varnishes; it heard the sounds of only one person, sleeping quietly in a room at the back of the house—the scent of someone he once knew a long time ago.

Tomorrow, the beast decided. Someone else had captured its attention.

The beast ran between the shadows, merging with the darkness between house and bush and ditch. Near the center of town, crouched low in the shadows behind her house, he sniffed the air. Moonlight fell upon his naked skin, shining across his pale shoulder.

First, the letter. Now, the girl.

There are no coincidences.

He had been trying to ignore it. But he knew her. He knew her eyes. He knew her scent.

Her *being.*

He could deny it no longer.

He had been called here.

It was starting again.

12

ROSES.

She smelled roses.

Her eyes blinked open. The stereo light was still on, but the album was over and the stylus had moved back onto its stand.

She felt chilly, almost shivering.

Naked. On the bean bag.

Summer pulled on her old white terrycloth robe. The blue of dawn glowed just beyond the horizon.

She had been dreaming. Panting. Feeling dirt beneath her feet. She dimly remembered cries—no, *howls*—echoing through the trees.

Running. Something dark growled beside her. A wolf?

No.

Then the trees were gone, and a huge dark shape leaped into the center of her garden, trampling her bushes beneath its misty, black paws.

Roses.

She went to the side window and peered down, between the drapes. The back light was on; a yellow bulb above the porch intended to ward off the hooligans and bums her mother was sure lusted after her precious Hummel figurines.

Near the back of the house, her rose garden lay wild and alive in soft moonlight. No darkness here; no immense paw prints, no—

From the corner of her eye, she thought she saw something. She had a concrete bench in the center of the roses, and she craned her neck, trying to make it out through the leafy branches.

"What the hell?"

Her digital clock glowed 5:09 a.m. She tied the robe and slowly opened her door. Ma's door was ajar, and she heard her mother snort once in her sleep.

She took soft steps down the staircase, then slipped through the kitchen. She unlocked the back door and undid the chain, opened it gently, then flicked off the metal hook on the old screen door.

The cement steps felt warm against the soles of her bare feet. In the east, the blue of the night was blossoming with an orange glow, just beginning to illuminate the whites and yellows and reds of her garden.

And green.

She picked it up, gently, tentatively, off the concrete bench.

Someone had been in her garden. And they had left her a stuffed green dinosaur, holding one of her white roses in its arms.

She stared at it, into its round, black eyes. She felt her heart pounding. Midnight had followed her home.

pastorale

the night they drove old dixie down

friday, july 2, 1971

1

HERMAN'S HERMITS WOKE Summer at 6:30 sharp, and she slapped her clock radio, muttering, "Screw Henry the Eighth."

Sunlight filtered through the slit between her drapes, and she buried her face into her pillow. She had hardly slept in the hour or so since she sneaked outside. Rob wouldn't have left the dinosaur without at least hinting about leaving her a surprise—and when would he have left it, anyway? No, he was at home, she was sure, having nightmares about car crashes and bears.

And she had heard noises. Animals. Or *something*. Hell, maybe it had been a dream.

—growling—

She sat up. The dinosaur sat on the pillow next to her, staring at nothing. She had not imagined that, at least. It had to have been Rob. She didn't have any secret admirers, that was for sure. Stonebridge was way too small to keep secrets.

She shuffled into the bathroom and took a long, hot shower, washing off yesterday's grease. Then she dried her hair with one of the new blow dryers that had just come out. She had bought it at Kresge's, and her mother had snapped at her when she'd brought it home. "One of your extravagances again. Just like your damn hippie records."

Screw her. Tonight she'd start her weekend off by relaxing at the drive-in with Rob and some beers and some scary movies, and she was going to make damn sure to forget that her fainting spell had ever happened.

She snapped on the radio, and a song came on she had never heard, a favorite of the DJ. She didn't know who Albert King was, but this song rocked. Her foot beat in time with the music as she brushed her hair at the vanity. It was old-fashioned blues, but the man played it with a rock and roll guitar, like something by the Stones. "Born Under a Bad Sign" was now her new favorite song.

She stepped into her uniform, this time the pale yellow with white trim, and put on her makeup. Nothing too stylish or sexy; just enough to draw attention to her best features. The more she smiled and the better she looked, the better the tips. She needed as much extra cash as she could get for new sneakers, new books and albums, and to afford her own place sometime before the 21st Century.

She turned her air conditioner to LO and went downstairs. She smelled coffee and toast, and got a whiff of her mother's second Winston 100 of the day. Her mother was at her usual kitchen spot behind the dinette table, sipping coffee and working the morning crossword. Smoke from her cigarette curled up from an overflowing ashtray.

Louise Moore looked up over the top of her horn-rimmed, Woolworth's reading glasses to watch her daughter open the refrigerator and take out a cold bottle of Tab. Summer popped it open with the bottle opener affixed under the kitchen counter.

"That ain't all you're going to have for breakfast, is it?" Louise said.

The fresh soda bit cold over the back of Summer's tongue. She loved the first drops of an icy cold drink after a long, hot night. "I'll grab something at the dinette, Mama."

Louise puckered her lips and inhaled smoke. "A Coke ain't no decent breakfast."

"Jeez, Mama. I'll eat at work. You know I have a Tab every morning."

Louise tapped her Winston against the rim of the ashtray. "You've got to start taking better care of yourself."

Summer took another swig and closed her eyes. *Not again.*

"You're too young to be sleeping late all the time like you do."

"Mama, I work. I get up early and I go to work. I have a job."

"You sleep till eleven or twelve when you ain't working, 'cause you're always staying out late with that boyfriend of yours, doing who knows what. Trifling."

Summer stuck the open bottle in the door of the refrigerator. "Mama, we've been going steady for like three years."

Louise inhaled and let the smoke trickle out as she talked. "You fainted last night because you ain't eating right. No breakfast in the morning."

"Mama, I eat at the diner."

"And you ain't never home, eating proper meals. You're always out gallivanting."

"Gallivanting?" *Where did she come up with shit like "gallivanting"?*

"Gallivanting all around town with that boy. Dressed the way you do. You're acting common."

"Common? Mama, come on."

"You are working too much at that dinette, and Ralph ain't paying you what you're worth, I know that. And you're seeing that boy too much, instead of staying home and helping me around the house like a decent young woman!"

"Jesus Christ!" Summer shouted. "Don't you ever stop? This is the same shit from last night!"

"NAH NAH NAH NAH!" Louise covered her ears with her hands. "The name of our Lord! NAH NAH NAH NAH! You just pray and listen to what I—"

"The hell I will." Summer's eyes flared. "This shit of yours never ends. I'm almost twenty-one, and you want me to follow you around and do what you say like I'm ten again. When are you going to stop?"

Louise jabbed a finger toward her. "As long as you're living in my house—"

"Yeah? I won't be living here much longer, if I can help it."

"What does that mean, buddy-ro?"

"Buddy-ro?" Summer impulsively snapped Louise's cigarettes off the table and lit one with her mother's brass lighter. Louise's mouth fell open in silent shock. Secretly, Summer was just as shocked. She had never done anything like this before.

She tossed the lighter and the pack of Winstons onto the table and blew smoke toward her mother. "Did you ever hear from Dad before he died, Ma? No? Wonder why? *That's* what I mean. It means you chased Daddy away with all your constant nagging, all your bullshit. And now you're doing it to me."

"Your language! You are no daughter of mine."

"Jesus fucking Christ." Summer stormed out of the kitchen and stuck out her middle finger.

"I know what that means!"

Summer walked straight through the dark dining room, through the living room, past the empty spaces on the walls where once had hung pictures of Mom and Summer and Dad, but Dad didn't exist in this house anymore. He hadn't for a long time.

She yanked open the door, then slammed it behind her. She took a drag off the Winston, exhaled, then threw it to the ground in disgust.

"God, Winstons are *rank!*"

She climbed into her shiny black Camaro and started it up. The radio popped on, and the singer was spelling. "—say M, say E, say R, say I, C—" She backed out of the driveway, threw the Camaro into DRIVE, then sat and just stared through the side window at her mother's house. The white paint. The fading green shutters. The empty metal chairs on the porch. The ugly azaleas.

And she decided right there.

"Done," she said softly. "I'm done."

2

THE RUMBLE OF the Fury's engine broke the still morning as Hicks turned onto Three Stump Road.

The narrow road wound between the low hills on the outskirts of the county, shaded here and there with copses of old oaks and maples, and sometimes fringed with plots of tall corn or green rows of lettuce or cabbage. The houses here were old and low, mostly ranchers built in the forties and fifties, their mowed lawns and sturdy cement wells barely scratching the blanket of uncivilized land.

He drove past the Winters place, where Jasmine Winters, the widow, had her back to him as she planted wildflowers in the row garden that wrapped around her porch. Fine by him. He had never liked the Winterses all that much, especially their boy, Randy. A troublemaker, if he'd ever seen one. Randy would have a few beers and start fights, just for the hell of it.

Not that Stonebridge had ever had a shortage of good old redneck brawlers. There was always a Saturday night bar fight out at the Feedlot off the Boulevard, and lately that damn Cousins boy had been keen on starting things with some of his old high school buddies.

Hicks made a U-turn at the intersection of Three Stump and Bumpass Roads, and pulled up in front of a brick and wood ranch home. The driveway was grey concrete, and a dented '59 Chevy pickup was parked close to the house. He cut off the Dodge Monaco and sat, listening to the engine hiss and tick. It was quiet out here. Peaceful.

He said, "Shit," and finally opened the door.

It had been Iris Salmon's damn fool idea to come out here. Earlier in the office, he'd made Iris put in requests for information on Trager. National Crime Information Center. Social Security. General Service Admin. U. S. Marshal up in McLean. Credit bureaus. IRS.

Iris laughed and said, "Why don't we throw Interpol and Scotland Yard in there too?"

So he did. And then Iris suggested talking to someone local. Trager was Army. "Maybe you should talk to old Ben Castle. He was a general or something in Ko-rea, wasn't he?"

He trudged up the driveway. Small, trimmed boxwoods led the way up the sidewalk to the front stoop.

He pressed the doorbell, heard it chime softly inside the house.

He shifted on his feet. He looked across the street at the Tatum house. A German shepherd barked at him, its forepaws on the top of the backyard's chain link fence.

He pushed the doorbell again, then opened the screen door and rapped his thick knuckles on the front door.

Finally, Hicks heard footsteps inside. Someone *thunked* back the deadbolt, and the door opened.

He wore a paisley silk robe that hung open to the waist, exposing a white undershirt. His hair was peppery, long, and tied into a ponytail with a green rubber band. His day-old stubble was almost silver, and his eyes were bleary and red. He looked at Hicks, then glanced at the cop car at the curb. "Buddy? Is everything all right?"

"Morning, Ben. I hope I didn't wake you up." Shit. Almost 10:00 and this lazy S.O.B. wasn't even awake.

Ben Castle said, "Up until three, finishing a painting. Just making coffee." He waited for Hicks to say something. "You want some?"

Hicks shrugged silently. Ben stepped aside and let him in. Hicks didn't offer to shake hands.

Ben pointed him toward the kitchen. The shades were still drawn, and the living room was twilit and cool. What used to be the dining room was lined with floor-to-ceiling bookcases on each wall. Hicks removed his camp hat and sat at Ben's kitchen table. Its polished walnut top gleamed in the morning light. He smelled the coffee, black and strong, and under it all he smelled the deep, rich aromas of oils and paints.

Hicks wanted to get this conversation over with, pronto, Tonto; so he said, "Ben, I was hoping I could pick your brain. If you've got a few minutes, that is."

Ben blinked at him. "Me?" He took a coffee mug from the drainer by the sink and poured Hicks a cup. The sheriff nodded thanks and sipped it, and it was his turn to look surprised.

"You like it?" Ben said.

Hicks nodded. "Yeah, it's—" He didn't know what to say. It was the richest, most flavorful coffee he had ever tasted. "Yeah."

Ben smiled and sat across from him, moving aside a stack of small, spiral bound notebooks. "Kona, from Hawaii. An old Army buddy retired to Honolulu a few years back, and he sends me some every year at Christmas."

"Damn good," Hicks said. He glanced at the notebooks by Castle's arm. The covers were imprinted with orange and brown chessboards.

"Correspondence chess," Ben said. "Keeps me busy. I've got games going on with, maybe, thirty people across the world." He opened the top notebook. Each page was a die-cut chessboard, and each paper playing piece fit into a slit cut into each space. "So, my friend in Montana sends me a postcard that says, maybe, Q to H8. So I take the Queen and move it to space H8. Then I make my move, write it down on a postcard, and send it off to Montana."

"Don't it take forever to finish a game?"

"Yeah, well, I guess I've got time," Ben said, looking away. "Hell, one game, I've been playing for almost two years."

Hicks nodded. War hero. Artist. Chess player. And a goddamn ponytail.

Nancy boy.

"So, what can I do for you?" Ben said. "It's got to be important for you to come out here and see me."

Hicks cleared his throat and sipped his coffee. He was not about to admit he needed Castle's help. His damn hair was almost as long as that hippie's at the diner.

"Iris, my secretary, had an idea this morning, and I thought it might be best if I followed up on it."

"Shoot."

"See, this biker bum rode into town last night. Stopped at the diner. Not entirely sure how it all came about, but it ended up with Summer Moore passing out."

Ben sat back in his chair. "Is she all right?"

Hicks nodded. "Biker caught her before she ever touched the ground. Carried her in."

"Good for him."

"Says he's a vet. Vietnam. Long hair, hippie type. Army jacket. Patch on the shoulder. The number one, in red."

"The Big Red One," Ben said. "Front line Infantry. It was my division, way back a million years or so."

"Where were you?"

"France. 1917 and '18. Eighteen years old and stupid as hell."

Hicks looked at him, almost in approval. "Guess that makes you seventy-two. I thought you were only in your sixties."

"My mother's genes. So, did this biker hurt Summer?"

Hicks shook his head. "Not as far as we can tell. Just, well, I had the impression he scared her some. She passed out, no matter what. She's okay."

"What about the biker?"

"Says his name's James Trager, colonel, retired."

"Trager?"

"Yep. Sound familiar?"

"No. A retired biker colonel?"

"There's something screwy about him. About thirty years old. A little young to be a colonel, if you ask me. But that's why Iris said to come out this way."

Ben scratched his chin. "Hell, I had a couple of friends who made colonel at twenty-four, twenty-five. Field promotions. Rare, but not unusual."

"Hm." This was going nowhere. "This guy is a certified hippie. Chinese-like mustache, long hair. Talks funny, like maybe he's a foreigner. Anything strike a chord?"

"No idea," Ben said. "I've been retired since '58, Buddy. Last action I saw was in Korea. That ain't why you're here, is it? You think I've got something to do with him?"

Hicks finished his coffee and set the mug down gently. "Nope. Nope, not at all. Just hoping you could tell me something about him by way of association, I guess."

"The Big Red One."

"Yep. Who this hippie might be. What he might be like. Anything." Hicks stood up. "Looks like I'm striking out."

Ben stood and walked Hicks back through the living room. "I wish I could tell you something you wanted to hear. I know a bunch of soldiers got killed four years ago over there. Know some who were in on the Tet Offensive in '68. I think they got shipped back home last year. Kansas."

Hicks looked him in the eyes. "I thought you were retired."

"Yep. But I get the *Stars and Stripes* regularly, and I'm in touch with a lot of my old Army friends. Still do a little consulting for the brass in D.C." He opened the front door. Hicks put on his hat. "Honestly," Ben said, "if this man is wearing the 1, I sincerely doubt he's as shifty as you think he is. And I wouldn't bet against him, no matter how long his hair is." Ben smiled.

Long hair. Just like Trager's. And Castle, with that damn ponytail. Hell, Lonnie had grown out his hair like a girl's when he had up and left, right after Richmond. As far as Sheriff Amberson "Everyone's Buddy" Hicks was concerned, he didn't have a son anymore, ever since Lonnie had protested in Richmond, even spitting on the flag on the Capitol steps. He was hiding out in Canada like a goddamn coward; hiding out from the long arm of Uncle Sam for the last two years.

"Well. Thanks for the coffee. Kona. I'll remember it." He went out onto the stoop. Ben stood in the doorway. Hicks said, "If you can think of anything that could tell me more about this war hero, I'd appreciate it."

"You bet," Ben said. "Say hi to Iris for me."

Hicks turned, and shot him with his finger and thumb. "Sure thing."

Ben closed the door. He listened behind the door until he heard the cop car start up and rumble down the street.

He went into the kitchen, poured himself more coffee, and dropped a slice of bread into the toaster. He leaned against the counter and waited, sipping Kona, thinking about France and the Big Red One all those years ago. Three wars, three tours, two continents, and always the Big Red One.

He ate the toast as he walked into the back bedroom that he had converted into his studio. Two ceiling fixtures cast fluorescent light over the paint-spattered walls. Large canvases were stacked back to front along two walls. A wooden easel took up the center of the room. Ben already had a big blank canvas angled on it, ready for the first brushstrokes of oil and pigment.

His most recent piece, the one he finished at 3 a.m., leaned at the front of one stack: a nightscape of the natural stone bridge, impossibly lit from within by a brilliant smattering of stars that blazed in the darkness inside the arch. This was intended to be the first of a series of landscapes meant to evoke the wonder buried inside the land, juxtaposed with the lure and the mystery of the stars.

At least, that's what he thought now. When he started, he hadn't known what it all meant—or if it meant anything at all. He just thought there was something in the image, something important, hidden there, and he liked it.

Ben swallowed the last bite of toast, washed it down with a gulp of coffee, and set the mug on top of his paint cart. Crossing over to a stack of paintings, he leaned them all toward him, and pulled out the last one. He placed it over the blank canvas on the easel. Stepping back, he appraised it—a dark, charred landscape, lit by small fires and a background explosion, firelight reflected along olive-green helmets, and in errant swirls of smoke and gas.

The soldier in the foreground was leaping over a bloodied body, half buried in a bomb crater. The body wore the torn and muddied uniform of a German rifleman. The American soldier in mid-leap wore a metal helmet that looked like a dented, upside down bowl with a wide, flat brim. He had a black mustache and short black hair, and his eyes burned with a vengeful energy. Over his shoulder, he carried the body of a wounded soldier, seemingly effortlessly.

Ben stared at the portrait, which he had titled "Soulfire" in red paint on the back of the canvas. He stared at the soldier's face, at the emptiness in his dark eyes.

"Finally," he whispered. "Finally."

3

THE DIXIE DINETTE was still packed at 1:30 p.m. with a few locals, but mostly with overheated tourists seeking an hour or so of air-conditioned bliss while on their way to take snapshots of their kids beneath the ancient arch, and posing beside stalagmites in the adjacent Carter Caverns.

Tina Tyler unloaded an armful of dirty dishes into the plastic tub under the front counter. Her dress was damp with sweat under her arms, and her hair had frizzed out like a tangle of steel wool.

"I hate summer," she said.

Summer, pouring coffee behind her, nudged her with an elbow. "I never liked you much either."

Tina snorted in laughter, and Summer could see the exhaustion in her eyes. "I didn't mean you," Tina said, giggling. "Just—"

Summer smiled. "July Fourth weekend is always rough. Just a few more hours."

"Yeah, of tourist torture. I swear they brought all this humidity with them. Just look at my hair." She turned around and whispered, "And they're *stupid.* One of them actually asked me what year George Washington built the natural bridge."

"Oh my God. They really said that?"

"Can you believe it? It's like a 'Be Stupid' switch turns on as soon as they load their ugly kids into the station wagon."

Summer put two coffee mugs and a glass of iced tea on a tray. "At least the tips are decent. I did have a trucker try to pinch my ass."

Tina looked Summer over. "You look as tired as I feel."

Summer put a slice of apple pie next to the cups. "Didn't get a lot of sleep. Plus, my mother is—Hell, she's just insane."

"All mothers are crazy. She still giving you a hard time?"

"When doesn't she?" She turned, lifting the tray, and started toward a booth at the windows.

Tina watched her go. Behind the smiles and the banter as Summer delivered drinks to a booth, Tina saw something else simmering behind Summer's eyes. It was just a shadow, a glimpse. But something new was there.

Ruthette, working up a sweat and running on sheer exhaustion at the flat top, had been watching Summer all day. She looked up at the clock. About three more hours, and Summer could get on back home and relax—although, knowing her, she'd go to the drive-in with Rob, doing anything but relaxing like she should.

Ruthette remembered how she and Arthur had been young thirty years ago, sneaking beers after work when they were only sixteen, and how nothing could stop them when they put their minds to it.

She sighed. Youth, as the man said, was wasted on the young.

Summer slapped a ticket on the steel counter. "Order in." She glanced around. Tina, she knew, was beat, and Ruthette was struggling to keep up, breathing hard, even limping some as she moved between the grill and the walk-in.

Ruthette was not only the nicest and most down-to-earth woman Summer knew, but she made the best home cooking Summer had ever eaten. Ruthette would yell at Ralph whenever she was in a mood, and demand raises and better hours; and Ralph would usually give her what she wanted. She was the best short order cook in the valley.

Ruthette saw her watching. "What?"

Summer smiled softly. "I don't know how you do it."

"Neither do I, child. That ol' paycheck keeps calling me back." She slid a BLT across the counter, along with a club sandwich, an open-faced turkey and gravy, and a double burger with a mountain of hand-cut fries. "Table six up."

Summer started lining the plates up her arm.

"So, how you doin'?"

"Okay, I guess. Nothing a good night's sleep won't cure."

"You're going to work yourself to death, like last night."

"Now you sound like my mama. And look who's talking." She balanced the plates and started toward the booths. "Got to save up. Can't live at home the rest of my life."

Ruthette watched her walk away. Summer's eyes had seemed more than tired. Dark, somehow.

Yeah, I know, she thought.

I know something ain't right.

Summer took the plates to table six, and a young boy clapped at her balancing act. She smiled and refilled their iced tea. Last night, and today's rush, had finally gotten to her. Lunch wasn't even over yet, and she was ready to race home and crank the A/C and huddle in bed for days.

There was just too much to cope with. Her dreams last night, and the dreams she'd had years before—so similar, feeling so real, so *tactile*. The dinosaur in the garden—*weird!* And that thing, that beast, in the road, looking into her eyes.

His eyes.

She shook her head. No. Those were just crazy thoughts.

Sunlight off the chrome fender of a car. She looked through the wide windows. The deputy's cruiser pulled into the parking lot, and Rob's busted-up Falcon turned in right behind him. She watched as Rob climbed out of the Falcon and said hi to Duke.

Oh shit.

Why was Rob here? She had been hoping he would just call her about the movies tonight.

What the hell was wrong with her? She couldn't get the rider's black, burning eyes out of her mind.

She hurried behind the counter. She didn't want to face either Rob or Duke. Why did she suddenly feel like she had done something wrong?

She didn't see Tina watching her from across the dining room.

Outside, Duke and Rob shook hands and spoke briefly. Then Rob laughed at something Duke said, and they walked in together.

Duke was thirty-four, felt twenty-four, but thought he'd be eighteen forever. The long summer nights weren't so long ago when he was listening to the Platters and Bill Haley in the back of his father's Thunderbird, a six pack on the floor and his girl snuggled beside him. He thought those days could never end.

Then college didn't work out, and his girl broke up with him, and he took a temporary job with the sheriff that somehow became permanent, and there were times he wondered if he was already too stuck to move on.

He smiled as he came toward her. He even took off his hat. "Hey, Summer." He nodded at Blanche Mitchell, sitting alone at the counter close to Summer. "I just stopped by to check up on you. See how you're feeling, you know?"

He was smiling too much, and his fingers fidgeted with the brim of his hat.

"Duke, I'm fine. Feeling great."

"Okay, okay, good."

"Thanks for asking though."

"Oh, hey, yeah, no problem. Listen, though." He stepped closer to her. "Has that dude been by?"

She blinked. "Dude?"

"The dude. You know, the biker."

Her heart took a leap.

"Has he been around here today? Bothering you or anything?"

"I thought he left town."

"Not exactly," Duke said. "Tucker up at the Patriot says he spent the night. Hasn't checked out yet."

It popped unbidden in her mind.

Good.

She shook her head. "I haven't seen him. But he didn't—"

Her cheeks grew hot. Where does Deputy Dog here get the right—

Oh. It wasn't Duke who was asking. It was him. Hicks.

Her eyes flared. "Duke, listen. You tell Hicks from the Sticks that that biker dude is the reason why I'm okay. He caught me before I hurt my head or something. Okay?"

Duke heard it in her voice. He'd said something wrong. "Look, what I meant was—"

Shit. She'd had her fill of Sheriff Buddy Hicks. She had detested him since a debate at Stonewall Jackson Junior High in '65—and he probably hated her too. While no one could ever consider Summer a radical—she had been a cheerleader, for God's sake—even when young, she was smart enough to recognize injustice and hatred, and fierce enough to call it out. During a debate between Hicks and the school principal about school integration, she finally had enough of the sheriff's smug superiority and stood up in the bleachers, telling him off in front of the whole school.

"You tell that fat ass boss of yours to go fuck himself, from me."

Duke burst out laughing. "Jeez, Summer. Hicks would have a coronary."

"Then *definitely* tell him. I'd pay good money to see that."

"Man," he said, smiling, "you are one tough chick. I'll tell him you're okay, and that you send your best wishes."

"Yeah," she said. "I guess that's about right, if you ignore the coronary part."

Duke turned for the door. Rob had taken a stool and was drinking iced tea. He fished in his pocket and placed a quarter and a nickel on the countertop—twenty cents for the tea, and a tip for Tina.

Summer picked up his glass and slipped a paper napkin under it. "I didn't expect to see you until tonight."

"I had to go to the library, so I thought I'd stop in and say hi."

"You're checking up on me too."

"Who else checked up on you?"

"Duke. The sheriff, I mean. They wanted to know if I was better." She didn't mention the biker, and the new possibility he might come back to see her—or how that made her feel inside.

"Well?"

"Well, what?"

"Are you okay?"

"Rob, I'm fine."

"Okay." He finished the tea and centered his glass on the damp napkin. "The movies start at 8:30. Why don't I come over at 6:30? We can grab something to eat. My treat."

She grinned. "Lobster and prime rib? I'm ready."

"Burgers or pizza. You choose, my glorious queen."

"I do like Shakey's. Let me think about it. And let's make it sevenish. I might take a nap when I get home."

"Good idea. I don't want you fainting on me again." He leaned over and kissed her.

Tina saw them from the kitchen and said through the order window, "Hey! Get a room!"

Rob squeezed Summer's hand. "Call me if you need anything."

Summer watched him walk away. Her smile faded. *What am I doing?* She didn't know why she had agreed to go to the movies tonight. She was so tired, all she wanted was to go home and sleep forever.

She made herself busy, taking a customer's plate and refilling a glass of water.

But in her mind, all she saw were eyes.

Dark, lonely eyes.

Tina glanced up from wiping down a booth and saw the look on Summer's face.

A man at the counter held up a finger to get Summer's attention. He had a greasy, dyed comb-over and wore a two-piece suit straight off the rack at J. M. Fields. He pointed to the dessert case. "How 'bout a slice of pecan pie?"

There was a white paper doily where a pie should have been. "We've got a fresh one in the back," she said. "Just a sec."

She walked through the swinging doors and opened the walk-in refrigerator. Every summer, Ruthette baked thirteen pies a day: pecan, apple, cherry, blueberry, and one peach pie. She wrapped them in foil, then dated them with a torn strip of masking tape on top. She took a pecan pie and turned to go. Tina stood in the refrigerator doorway.

"What?" Summer said.

"Give," Tina said.

"Give?"

"Give. Talk to me."

"What?"

"You know what. Rob. I saw that look you gave him. There's been something wrong with you all day. Now, give."

Summer stared at the foil around the pie and read today's date in Ruthette's handwriting. 7/2/71.

"Summer, come on. Spill it."

Summer whispered, "Pecan pie." A tear rolled down her cheek.

Tina's eyes softened. "Oh, honey." She placed her hand on Summer's forearm. "Come on. It's cold in here." She led Summer out and closed the door.

Summer looked into her face. "I don't know, Tee. I just don't know anymore."

"It's gonna be okay."

Summer's eyes welled with tears. "I—I've been wondering about him lately. A lot. I still love him, Tee. I know that. I mean, he's always been there for me. We've grown up together. But I think—I mean, I don't know, but—hell, *you* know." She wiped her eyes. "I feel like part of me is missing, or gone all wrong, and—and— *Shit*, Tina, I've never felt so, so stupid, so helpless, before."

Tina grasped Summer's arm. "Sweetheart, let me tell you something. Back in high school, all the girls looked up to you. Including me. And you know I don't look up to anyone."

Summer sniffled. "Now I know you're lying."

"I'm serious. Going out for cheerleading? Dating the quarterback when you were just a junior?"

"The senior girls hated me."

"They were jealous. You were too pretty. Stiff competition for MMC and the other sorority girls."

Summer had always worried about her looks.

"But you were never snooty about it," Tina said. "You were always one of us. Even the sororities came around. And you were pretty damn fearless. Remember the time Daryl Knicke was teasing that slow kid in the hall? And you punched him in the teeth?"

Summer laughed. She hadn't thought about that in a long time. "Yeah. I don't play well with bullies."

"I still can't figure out why you put up with Kenny all the time."

"What can I do? He's Ronnie's stupid boyfriend. If he weren't—"

Tina smiled. "Look. Everybody knew you were one of the cool ones. And smart too. You didn't hang out with any sororities or the cliques, but you were still popular."

"Oh, come on."

"—and you were still a loner too. You almost always had a guy on your arm, but you always sat in the back of class with us bad kids. Dreaming and reading. Never completely by yourself, but always in your own little world. I think you feel bad because, in your heart, you've already made a decision. You just haven't figured that out yet."

Summer's eyes widened.

Ruthette turned away from the flat-top. "Come on, ladies. Customers are waiting. Tables eight and two."

Tina pushed open the swinging doors. "Take that guy his pie. Be gentle with Rob. But you're not gonna be happy until you do what you have to do."

Tina disappeared through the doors.

Reading and dreaming.

Yeah, that was her, all right. Summer placed the pie on a shiny steel counter and unwrapped it. She took a wide knife, sliced into the pie, then sized the pie to make each slice uniform. Each pie, eight slices.

But she thought of Rob, at how mad she was, at herself, at her own stupidity, and she said aloud, "Who am I kidding?"

She angled the knife and made the slice bigger.

It's part of my genes.

I was born to rebel.

She was in fifth grade, eating a PB&J in the school cafeteria, when she had her first period, way earlier than her friends. She felt something warm trickling between her thighs, stood up, and saw blood soaking through her culottes. She was never once scared about the blood; merely curious, cocking her head, wondering where it was coming from and why. Other students were staring. She laughed. "Cool," she said.

At thirteen, she had been so pissed at her mother that she borrowed her old lady's '61 Chrysler. State troopers finally pulled her over halfway to Richmond. Top speed: 93 miles per hour.

She had her junior high school friends over for a party when she was fourteen, while her mother was staying with a sick cousin over in Waynesboro. She broke into her dad's old liquor cabinet and got drunk for the first time. Two hours later, she found herself high in a tree in the backyard, puking all over the patio furniture.

She didn't swear off drinking after that, but she swore she'd never have scotch again.

Along with nine other girls, she skipped a high school pep rally for a bra burning—*Go Confederates!*—and was rewarded with a three-day suspension. In reality, Laura Walsh was the only other girl who burned her bra; the others just wanted to leave school and go smoke outside. Summer wrote pro-feminist, pro-birth control, pro-Chicago Seven, and anti-Nixon editorials for the high school newspaper, *The Battle Flag*, and was summoned to the principal's office each time.

No one really understood, especially not her mother. She always wanted Summer to fit in, to be pretty, to conform, to go to cotillion, to be a mirror image of what Louise thought she was. A doll. *Her* doll.

Not a chance.

Summer had known since she was a child—since *forever*—that she didn't belong. Not in this town of small minds and big prejudices.

Rob had been the only bright spot in this backwater burg. He was educated, gentle, and compassionate—everything all the other boys weren't. Maybe she had made a mistake during her senior year when she finally decided college wasn't for her. Maybe she should have gone to Tech with Rob, and maybe learned how to make something of herself.

But college—

—normalcy—

That wasn't for her.

There was something out there waiting for her, or maybe she was waiting for it.

And last night—

She tried to visualize Rob's face, his smile. But all she could see was the Midnight Rider. James.

No.

That wasn't his name.

It's— *Michael.*

Where did that come from?

His wide, black eyes—somehow they reflected more of her own soul than she had ever understood.

Her heart was pounding, hollow, dull. She was starting to think that, maybe, she had been right all along. Maybe she had found what she had been waiting for all this time. Or maybe it had found her.

She put the slice of pie on a plate and started for the swinging doors. "I love summer," she said.

4

THE SUN HUNG low over the mountains. Heat shimmered over the country roads in pools of illusion, and the shadows between the trees grew longer, hungrier.

Hicks noticed none of this. He sat back in his old leather and wood office chair, reading reports that had come in on Trager.

Iris had left at exactly 5 p.m., as usual, and Duke was the only deputy in the office, finishing up today's reports on two speeders in town. There was a fender bender out in Mosby, and a possible bear sighting that Animal Control could neither confirm nor deny—since there was no physical evidence that Smokey, Yogi, or even Boo Boo had paid downtown Stonebridge a visit.

Hicks tossed the papers onto his desk. No criminal record. No outstanding debts. Not a single parking ticket.

"Horseshit," he said.

He opened the bottom desk drawer and pulled out a bottle of Gilbey's Spey Royal Scotch. Beside it, he placed a shot glass from the Golden Nugget Casino in Las Vegas. He had never been to Vegas—Hicks had never been past the Virginia border—but he had spied the shot glass on Virgil Acker's night table after Virgil had shot his common-law wife in the forehead back in '62, and decided, what the hell, Virgil ain't gonna use it in the pen. So he slipped it into his pocket when no one was looking.

He poured himself a shot, took a pain pill out of his shirt pocket, then slugged them back.

There was something fishy about those reports. They didn't contain much of anything, and to his way of thinking, it was a little too little. Reports like these always had dirt in them somewhere, but not this hippie's.

Old man Castle hadn't helped at all, exactly what he had expected from that old goober. He had always thought there was something off about Castle. Hicks hadn't liked that peckerwood since he came back from Korea, a goddamn war hero.

Hicks' brother, Cecil, had come back in a box.

He put the shot glass away, and poured three fingers of scotch into his coffee mug. Duke had given him the mug on his last birthday. It read **HEAD BALL-BUSTER AND ASS-KICKER** in big red block letters.

Castle and his damn ponytail. His house stinking of fancy paints and books, like some kind of candy-ass city boy. Joe College. Fucking Rembrandt.

He raised the mug to his lips. The whisky went down like sand paper.

He pushed out of the chair and went over to the telex machine tucked behind Iris' desk. He stared at it, waiting. The Army hadn't responded. Neither had Interpol.

Waiting.

He went back to his office and poured himself another shot.

Something was there. That so-called colonel was hiding something—or hiding from someone—and Hicks was not about to let some lousy biker get away with a single thing in his town.

Not one goddamn thing.

5

HIS EYES SNAPPED open, and he stared into the darkness of the still, silent mausoleum, listening to the sounds of life beyond the marble walls. Locusts clacked in the trees. Something slithered through the tall grasses: a snake, he was sure—a small one. A couple of cars honked at each other as they passed on a road a mile and a half away. One was a VW bug; the other an eight-cylinder 440 with a rusted-out muffler.

Twilight.

He sat up, naked, on the cool stone floor, and stretched, enjoying the tension in his muscles. He moved like mercury made flesh, and dressed quickly in yesterday's clothes. Then he was outside in the blue dusk, walking the motorcycle from the gap behind the mausoleum, the tires whispering through tall grasses that the caretakers had ignored for months.

A block away, the rider hopped onto the bike and kicked it to life. This land was too open, too public. If he were going to stick around, he'd need a better place to hole up. The motel was just for show, for the sheriff's benefit; and this, the cemetery, just wouldn't do.

He parked in front of his room at the Patriot, and unlocked the door. Cheap, over-sweet perfume, and the scent of a woman. A maid had been in, to clean the room perhaps six hours earlier.

He peeled off his clothes and showered. After the miles he had ridden yesterday, he needed to get the road and the dust out of his hair, off his skin.

After showering and making the room look lived in, it was time to roll.

The map from the service station hadn't been difficult to memorize. In seconds, his bike was roaring beyond the town boundaries, and he was in the hilly, rural section of Stonebridge County. He pulled up at a neighborhood crossroads and stared at the street sign.

"Really?" he said, grinning.

He parked in front of a long, one-story house. He followed the boxwoods to the front door and rang the doorbell. He felt him, warm, inside the house; heard the *thump* of his heart, slower now than in the years before, yet still strong—the heart of an emperor lion. He also felt the old man across the street.

Glancing over his shoulder, he spotted an old man in denim overalls. The old codger sat on a wooden swing on the long porch of his house, watching him. Then he spat tobacco into a brass spittoon near the edge of the porch.

The rider turned away.

A voice said from the other side of the door, "Do you really need an invitation?"

The rider smiled. "Nope. But seeing as how you're my oldest and best friend, opening the door for me would be nice."

The deadbolt slid back, and Ben Castle stood there, staring at him. "Well, good goddamn."

"Good goddamn, yourself."

Ben stared at him for a long while, and then they embraced and clapped each other on the backs, and the years and the great distances between today and their boyhoods in the line of fire melted away. "Come on in," Ben said. "Get in here."

They looked each other over: Ben, old and craggy, the years lined across his face in a contour map of his life; the rider, with his much longer hair, deeper, sadder eyes, but impossibly the same, just as Ben remembered from the burned battlefields of northeastern France.

"So," the rider said. "Three Stump Road? And Bump Ass Road?"

Ben's weathered face broke out in a shining smile. "They pronounce it Bump-us. Yeah, we're in the cradle of civilization out here. Boardwalk and Park Place. And the town and the county have the same name, in case these rubes forget where they live." He put his hand on the rider's shoulder. "Damn good to see you, Michel. Been too long."

"Haven't heard that name for a long time."

Castle looked him over. "You haven't changed. Not a goddamn bit."

"And you look like a New York hippie."

"I'm a Southern-fried Bohemian. You've grown your hair out too. You should think about a ponytail."

"The Height-Ashbury look works for you."

"Sit down. I'll get us some drinks. You do still drink, don't you?"

Michel said, "Bump ass."

Ben switched on table lamps throughout the living room. The house was clean and orderly, obviously well-kept. There weren't any family photos, though, on any of the tables or walls. Instead there were huge abstract paintings, five or six feet wide: bright colors in spatters and swirls.

"So," Ben said from across the room, "you're the hippie the sheriff is all hot about."

"I guess word gets around." Michel sniffed the air. There were so many odors intermingling. "Linseed oil?" His gaze went from one painting to another. "These are yours?" He stared at a large canvas hung above the sofa. Splotches of colors, merging, contrasting, like waves breaking over each other, broken by smaller, lighter splotches high at the top. "How long have you been painting?"

"Since I retired after Korea. I play."

"Play, hell. These are good."

"I've sold a couple. Been in some shows, in D.C. and New York."

"Stop being so modest. You're really good."

Ben shrugged.

The walls in the den were floor-to-ceiling built-in bookcases, crammed with books packed tight against each other: a wide mix of novels and anthologies, art and photography, history, biographies, even poetry—the library of a Renaissance man, Michel thought. Books were stacked on top of end tables and across a sideboard against the back wall. Unframed paintings hung from shelves. Others on the floor leaned against the bookshelves. All were arranged so that guests who sat on Ben's vintage Art Deco loveseat were treated to an abstract display, while those who sat in the overstuffed reading chairs positioned opposite had a view of Ben's landscapes.

Ben poured them each a tumbler of bourbon. He handed a glass to Michel, who was concentrating on a framed black and white photo. Ben saw where he was looking. "My retirement ceremony in '58."

Michel faced him. "Four stars. I didn't know."

Ben shrugged and sat in one of the reading chairs. "Almost forty years in the service. They had to give me something to show for it, right?"

"I always knew you had a fire inside you." Michel sipped the bourbon, then looked up, surprised. "This is quite excellent."

Ben held up his glass. "It's next to impossible to find this in the ABC stores here. I have to drive to Kentucky a couple of times a year and stock up. Maybe take some paintings to a gallery in Louisville to pay for the trip."

Michel glanced around. Many of the books were from the early half of the century, and he recognized Ben's taste in fiction: a shelf of Zane Grey Westerns, four shelves of Edgar Rice Burroughs hardbacks, shelves of yellowed pulp magazines, volumes of Shakespeare, and so many art books. The den was really a well-tended, private library, and it reminded him of his own library.

He took the letter from his shirt pocket, unfolded it, and placed it on the small, polished walnut table between the two chairs. The reddish-brown letters on the white paper seemed to glow. "Why don't you tell me what this is all about."

Ben looked over the table and met Michel's gaze. "You tell me."

"Exactly how am I supposed to do that?"

Ben concentrated on the letter and took a sip of bourbon. "Only two words and a period. No signature, no return address. And yet, here you are."

They watched each other silently. Michel plucked the note off the table and folded it back into his pocket. "Guess I got the message."

"I guess you did."

Ben slugged back the bourbon. He poured another. "After World War Two, I was promoted to a four-star desk and an office with a window. And that's when I started to get sick of olive-green walls. I jumped at the chance to operate in Korea. Afterward, they set me up at the Pentagon, and I got sick of it all over again—sick at heart with the machine. War after war, just keeping the arms manufacturers and the war machine in the killing business.

"I retired. Moved back home to Stonebridge. Took up painting. Stayed away from the bullshit. But I stayed active in the Reserves.

"Every now and then, the bigwigs bring me in to consult on a task force or some kind of committee. So, late in '69, they asked me to up and ship out for Vietnam on a joint task force, Army, Navy, and the SVA. It'd only take a month, and the pay was good, so I said okay.

"So I'm in Saigon, late '69, and I'm at a restaurant with a bunch of the other officers on the task force. It was a late night. Had one too many glasses of *ruou.* And I paid for it the next morning.

"But, that night, I thought I was seeing things. Across the street, walking with a known Saigon gangster, was somebody I knew. His hair was a lot longer, but it was the exact same face, the same eyes, of a man I knew in World War One.

"And he hadn't aged a day."

Michel took a swallow of bourbon. "So, you're saying you went halfway across the world and found me by accident?"

Ben shook his head. "Not entirely. The task force was investigating some serious involvement of American GIs in the black market throughout Indochina. One name kept popping up—a minor player, but one who had connections to the big boys in Saigon. Some of us were in that particular restaurant because we had learned that our suspect, one Colonel James Trager, was to meet a connection at the roadside bar across the street, in the boonies, about a klick from the Rex Hotel. We weren't going to make any arrests. We just wanted to ID the suspect and see how he operated."

Michel finished his bourbon and held up the glass.

"Glad you like it," Ben said, taking the glass. "You used to be a Wild Turkey man."

"You taught me well."

"Indeed I did." Ben smiled and poured. "You Frenchies had absolutely no appreciation for American fineries." He handed Michel the glass, then set the bottle between them on the table, where the letter had been.

They sipped their bourbon, then stared at each other over their glasses, both so serious. Suddenly they both broke out laughing, and Ben said, "God*damn*, it's good to see you."

"It's good to see you too, my friend." Michel squeezed Ben's forearm. "How long has it been?"

"God. '29, it was. Washington. Forty-two years ago." He looked into his bourbon. "But I thought you had died. Heard about it in 1940. I had to drive to the library in Richmond to read your obituary in the New York Times."

Michel shrugged. "I'd quote Twain, but, under the circumstances—It's convenient knowing people who can plant stories for you." He looked up. "So. 54 years."

"Thereabouts. St. Mihiel. How could I forget?"

Michel stared at his drink, at the light playing along the bottom of the glass. "I recognized the scent. That's how I knew where to find you."

It took Ben a few seconds. "Oh. The letter."

"You have a distinctive scent. Everyone does. I first scented it—you—on the battlefield in 1917, and it's ingrained in my mind. As soon as I opened the letter, I knew it was from you."

"You never forget anything, do you?"

"I don't forget my friends."

Ben nodded. "Good."

"Good?"

"Yeah. Because friends like you and I—I don't forget, either. Not since you saved my ass in France."

"Please. Enough."

"I've been looking after you too."

Michel raised an eyebrow.

Ben raised his glass to his lips and looked at nothing. He tossed back his drink in one swallow, then poured himself another.

"My team was stationed in Saigon for just over a month. I made sure to stay near our operation at the Rex at all times. I couldn't risk you seeing me.

"We pulled together a file against you almost an inch thick. James Phillip Trager. Always in the background. Working through contacts and middle men. At the same time, I started a shadow investigation. On you, when I knew you. On Michel D'Arnot, age 28 in 1918. And on why you hadn't aged a day since I last saw you in D.C. in 1929.

"All this was off the books. I started with France and what you'd told me about yourself. Born in Montmarte in 1890. So, what happened between then and Saigon? I just knew intuitively that James Trager wasn't the son or grandson of my friend. So I looked into Trager's records. Nice, clean, straightforward. I knew it was all a dodge. No such person as Trager.

"So I followed a hunch. If it really was you, why were you in France in World War One, and Saigon in this bastard war?

"What if, I asked myself, you were following wars? Why would you do that? And where were you in between?"

"Where, indeed," Michel said.

"I found you in Korea. Major Spencer Bradford. Far away from where I was stationed. I found you in Hungary in '58. Spain in '37. Italy in '20. You were Charles Montaigne during World War II, on the front lines.

"You were following whatever wars broke out. But why? And the records all indicated that you volunteered for the worst missions—and always at night.

"It took a year, and a bunch of favors from friends in the service, plus a lot of legwork from a couple of private eyes in France and England and the U.S., believe it or not—"

"Oh, I believe it," Michel said. "You have always been tenacious."

"—but when I put all the reports and rumors and false identities together, I had a skeletal biography of Michel D'Arnot, born not in 1890, but in 1846.

"And there were always unproved rumors. Whispers, things I didn't want to believe. But as I kept investigating, it all made some kind of stupid, impossible sense. During wars, in between wars, in every city where you were rumored to be, bodies were found. All unsolved murders, mostly people involved in illegal, let's say, murderous, activities. Vienna. Berlin. Chicago. Rome. Budapest. Sydney. Hong Kong. Always big cities. Always, bodies drained entirely of blood.

"And I *knew* you. I was your best friend. And I knew all of this was goddamned impossible.

"And here you are—a 130-year-old man."

"125."

Ben smiled. "Give or take. And still looking twenty-seven, twenty-eight. Hell, for all I know, you could be getting *younger* as we speak."

Michel said, "Like you said, this really is impossible, don't you think?"

"Sure is," Ben said.

"Hell of a crazy story."

Ben nodded. "Well, my investigators were good. They knew their stuff. Their boss, however, was one crazy retired Army S.O.B."

Michel smiled. "A good man though."

Ben shrugged. "You kept using your real name for too long. That's partially how we tracked you down."

"I used it in the Great War. Thought I was safe for a while afterward too. You missed my activities beforehand though. Spanish-American War. A few others."

Ben looked surprised. "I considered looking that far back, but, honestly, I had all the material I needed."

"Well," Michel said. "May I have another drink before you try to stake me?"

Ben laughed. "Hell, boy, you owe me. I'm the one who got the task force off your back." He poured Michel another glass. "We had you for smuggling. Marijuana, Thai sticks, stolen Army supplies from morphine to Jeeps and generators. We had you for everything from theft to grand larceny."

Michel grinned. "A guy's got to make a living."

"But." Ben held up his finger. "But, I was not about to let them have you. You saved my ass once. And this time, I saved yours. While they were looking at you every which way but Sunday, I had my people work up files on much bigger fish. I threw them a whole damn countrywide infrastructure of heroin smugglers and paid assassins, along with personnel who had gone native and were targeting our troops just for kicks. I gave them every name my people could find in Southeast Asia, and I finally convinced them that you were small potatoes. Just a bit player.

"We completely changed focus. I got them to go after everybody but you. Then I buried your file. I got the task force promoted, and then I got us all home."

Michel was lost in thought. "I knew somebody was on my tail. I could feel it. Then I got wind of it from a couple of informants in the ARVN. But I didn't know it was you. Hell, you're the reason I bugged out of Vietnam."

"Guess you thought it was the Hawkbourne clan again, didn't you?"

Michel's glass was halfway to his lips when he froze.

"And then you got my letter," Ben said. "And now you're here, because you once got a whiff of my blood in St. Mihiel."

Michel's black eyes stared at Ben. "The Hawkbournes."

"Yes," Ben said. "I kept coming across the name, but I don't know much about them at all. The name was occasionally linked to yours, but I couldn't figure out why at first. Then I figured out that mine was not the only shadow investigation sneaking around. And they weren't looking for smugglers or black marketeers, either. They were looking only for you."

Michel stood and looked out the den window. Ben's backyard was even and well-tended. Thick woods bordered the far boundary, and for an instant he wanted to leap into the night and run free through the cover of trees.

"I learned, very early on, to follow wars." Michel spoke softly, almost too low to hear. Ben craned forward in his chair. "One could hide in a war, amid the battles, alongside the dying. War is where blood is. One doesn't have to prey or hide when the dying are all around. And when a leg is missing or there's a hole in a soldier's chest the size of a grapefruit, no one asks questions about the loss of blood.

"Besides, no one sane—not even the Hawkbournes, and they're as rabid as they come—would follow me onto a battlefield. Into the tunnels. They have chased me for almost a hundred years—and they will not stop until my body lay at their feet, falling to dust before their eyes."

"What the hell did you do to piss them off?"

Michel laughed. "Long story. Bottom line: they decided that they had to kill one of their own family members. To eradicate the world of our menace. And I wouldn't let them. I protected her."

He sat and sipped his bourbon. He noticed the orange and brown notebooks on a side table across the library.

"By the way," he said. "Knight to F3."

"Excuse me?"

Michel pointed at the correspondence chess logs. "Knight to F3."

Ben's brow furrowed. Michel smiled. "My next move. I've been playing with you for sixteen years. I'm your chess partner in Seattle."

Ben started laughing so hard a tear appeared in his eye. "No wonder it always took so long for Seattle to respond. You were all over the world, all that time. A mail drop?"

Michel nodded. Ben just kept on laughing. "Holy, holy shit. I went halfway across the world and found you," Ben said, "and we've been in touch all this time."

Michel watched him laugh, and felt the bond between them grow warm, tight. He had missed this old man, more than he had ever realized.

Finally, when Ben's laughter subsided and they both had refreshed their drinks, Michel said, "Okay, Ben. Tell me why I'm here."

Ben took a drink. "Aw, hell." He paused and looked Michel in the eye. "Well, I guess, to save me."

"Save you?"

Ben nodded once, firmly, decisively. "Give me your gift, Michel. Make me like you."

6

THE CALL CAME in twenty minutes after the sun went down. Deputy Duke Crawford was on duty that night, and he called the Dixie Dinette as soon as he hung up with Silas Leggett.

He could hear the sheriff's heavy footfalls as he approached the wall phone behind the counter.

"Sheriff, it's Duke. Just got a call I thought you'd want to check up on. Old man Leggett. Out on Three Stump Road."

A warning flag popped up behind Hicks' eyes. It was a big red warning flag, waving back and forth.

Duke said, "He's complaining about some loud motorcycles or some drag racers out here. Wants somebody to put the fear of God into the hooligans."

"Hooligans," Hicks said.

"You know Silas."

"Yeah. I'll take care of it from here."

Hicks hung up and flipped through the phone book. He dialed the number, listening to the dial as it ratcheted right, then left, in some kind of electronic syncopation.

"It's a goddamn eye-legal biker gang, Sheriff!" Old man Leggett was worked up. "Disturbin' the peace! Sheriff, this cain't be allowed! This used ta be a nice place ta live! Now it's filled up with druggies and scummy bikers out here on their damn moter-cycles! Now, what the hell're you gonna do about these dayum hooligans?"

Hooligans.

Hicks cruised out to Three Stump Road and drove past the black Electra Glide parked at the curb in front of Ben Castle's place—right where he had parked the squad car just this very morning.

"Um hm," he grunted.

The road angled up and curved to the left. He slowed, made a two-point turn, and parked on the inside of the curve, facing Castle's house. He could keep watch on the bike from here, and the biker would never see him.

Hicks looked at his watch. Almost nine.

He felt it stirring, deep in his gut.

Hot.

Seething.

He slammed his hand on the steering wheel.

That old fucker had flat-out lied to him.

Castle knew the biker.

"Liar," Hicks muttered, lighting a Pall Mall. "God damned bastard liar."

7

SUMMER TURNED HER stereo up, loud enough so that Don Brewer's driving drumbeat made her vanity mirror vibrate. She closed her eyes and nodded her head to the hammering beat.

When the drums of "Inside Looking Out" stopped abruptly, in the silence she pulled the 8-track from the tape deck and switched the stereo over to AM. Sly sang about mice elf on WGH. Some songs thrilled her, some hurt her. She cherished the short little stories that that came through the radio. This little song made her want to dance and laugh, like she was part of a secret club with its own secret language.

She had driven straight home from her shift at the dinette. After a quick shower and a Breck shampoo, she had slipped into bra and panties and started to get ready for her date with Rob.

Her Real Girl eye shadow and mascara stood on top of a small tower of paperbacks next to the mirror—her *TO READ* stack. *Valley of the Dolls* was on top, followed by *The Love Machine, Love Story, Hallowe'en Party, The Sensuous Woman* (she had turned the book around so her mother couldn't read the title), *The Andromeda Strain*, and a recommendation from Rob that he had hyped up way too much, *The Fellowship of the Ring*, which she knew she'd probably never read. A hardback leaned against the stack, a new library book that looked scary as hell: *The Exorcist.*

She brushed on her usual shade of pale blue eye shadow, then lightly applied mascara to her long blonde lashes. She loved to look good. It thrilled her when the new issue of *Cosmo* came out, and she had the extra cash to try out new shades of makeup and perfumes.

Tonight, though, she didn't really care. She was going through the motions.

It's only Rob.

She shimmied into a pair of cutoff jean shorts, then she tugged on a tight white t-shirt with blue trim around the neck and sleeves, silk-screened with a red and yellow Superman shield that swelled around the curve of her breasts.

She thought about wearing earrings, or spraying on a little perfume, then decided against it. Rob might consider it an invitation, and she just didn't feel like that complication tonight.

She put on her high-heeled cork sandals, strung with leather thongs and tiny, pastel shells. The radio blasted Johnny Winter, growling, "Rock and Roll, Hoochie Koo," over the twang of his blues guitar. On impulse, she sprayed Blue Jeans under her neck. She could handle Rob.

Louise heard her coming down the stairs and shuffled out of the living room. Summer heard a TV newscaster: something about 6,100 soldiers leaving Vietnam, and she thought, *Will this war never end?*

"You're going out again? Louise said.

Summer opened the refrigerator and took out a bottle of Tab she had left open when she came home. "Date with Rob." The Tab ran sweet and cold over her tongue.

"How come I'm hearing about you hanging around with some motorcycle gang?"

"What?" Summer whipped her head around. "A gang?"

"I heard tell you're dating some Hell's biker."

Summer rolled her eyes. "Ma, when I fainted last night, it was a guy on a motorcycle who caught me. I told you this." She sipped the Tab. "I'm not seeing anyone but Rob."

"Well. I can't have no daughter of mine going out with a common hoodlum."

"Ma, I didn't get to choose who would catch me. Rob is still my boyfriend."

"I suppose he still hasn't asked you to marry him."

Summer glared at her. Then the doorbell rang. "That's Rob."

She opened the front door, and Rob stepped into the foyer. "Hey. You ready?"

"Born ready," Summer said low. "Let's skate before—"

Then Louise stepped around the corner. She smiled at Rob, but there was no warmth in it. "Now, there's Mr. Robby."

"Mrs. Moore."

"I guess you kids are going out."

"Going to the drive-in, Mom," Summer said.

"The picture show?" Louise said, staring at Summer. "Dressed like that?"

"Like—" Summer's face turned bright red. "Mom, it's not *cotillion.* It's just the drive-in."

Rob said, "I think she looks very nice."

"I can see through your blouse."

"Ma, it's a t-shirt. And you can't—"

"You look like a New York streetwalker."

Rob's eyes went wide. Summer's face turned white. She lifted her jaw in defiance. "You should know, Ma. Wasn't your corner at 42nd and Broadway?"

"You always have something smart to say. You're worse than Peck's Bad Boy."

Summer shoved Rob out the door and slammed it in her mother's face. The wooden screen door banged shut, and Summer speed-walked to Rob's car.

She slid into the passenger seat. Rob took the wheel and stared at nothing through the windshield. "Jeez, Summer. I'm sorry about that back there."

She shook her head. "She's just a mean old bitch."

"I always believed you when you told me how she acted, but, *wow.*"

"Yeah."

"And what exactly is a pex bad boy? What is a pex?"

She looked over at him. "She's said that all my life, whenever I got into any kind of trouble. I have no damn idea what she means by that. And I no longer give a shit."

Rob reached behind her seat and took off the lid of a white Styrofoam cooler. "Schlitz for me. For you, I got your current favorite." She heard the sound of ice cubes shifting like glass, and Rob handed her a round, glass bottle dripping with water. "Mateus Rosé."

She smiled, twisted out the cork, and took a long swig. "I wish it were Jack."

He started the car and looked over at her house. "Yeah, you deserve some Jack, all right."

"Tomorrow," she said. She kissed him, and he tasted the cheap wine on her breath. "This is nice. Thanks. And I'm really sorry about my mom."

"So, what about dinner? You in the mood for the Crab Shack?"

"When did you get rich?" She tipped the bottle and swirled the wine around her tongue. "I'll be happy with a BBQ and some onion rings."

He smiled. "Okay then. Sounds like it's a double drive-in kind of night."

He headed for the west end of Stonebridge, where Wythe Boulevard was the town's main business route. They passed the Mountain Shopping Center with J. M. Fields at one end and Kresge's at the other, sandwiching People's Drugs and Thom McAn in between with the new Safeway right in the center. A quarter mile up the boulevard, the tall electric sign for Rockbridge Shopping Center shone bright with neon and painted plastic, where a Miller & Rhoads had just opened last year from out of Richmond, along with a Food Fair at the opposite end, and Kinney Shoes and the A&N store on either side.

Rob turned in to the Atomic Drive-In, Home of the Atom Burger—*"An EXPLOSION of TASTE!"*—and parked in one of the diagonal parking spaces. The carhops were mostly fresh-faced girls still attending Stonebridge High. They were identically dressed in red short-sleeve blouses and tight white hot-pants. Change makers hung from their belts. Bridget, going into her senior year at Stonebridge High, took their order with a big grin and smacks of chewing gum. She noticed the cooler in the back seat. "Hey, save one for me," she said, winking at Rob.

Rock and roll came from almost every car radio, carrying WGH or stations out of Richmond or Roanoke, and a few were tuned to WCST, the AM country and Western station on the outskirts of town. As the sun set behind the mountains, the light from the Atomic sign flashed white and red across Summer's oval face as she smiled at something goofy Rob said, or as she sang along with the radio, and Rob thought there was no woman anywhere as beautiful as she.

Bridget brought their dinner on a metal mesh tray, coated in protective red vinyl. Rob rolled up the window a couple of inches and she hung it on the glass. "$2.71," she said.

Rob pulled out his wallet and handed her four dollars. Her hand went to the change maker on her belt, but Rob held up his hand and in it was one of his beers. "All yours," he said.

She broke out in a huge smile, looked around to make sure no one was looking, and slipped the can into her apron. "You guys are so cool!"

They ate their burger and barbecue and onion rings and pulled pop-tops off the beers under the dash and sneaked sips of Schlitz while the radio played Chicago and Sugarloaf and Wilson Pickett and the Four Tops. When they were done, they balled the foil and paper wrappers and plopped them on the tray. Rob flashed his brights and started the car. Bridget saw the headlights and came up to the window. "Thanks, guys! You made my night!" Rob smelled the beer on her breath. She took the tray, and as he backed out of the parking spot, she turned and made sure he noticed she was waving to him.

Only a quarter mile away, the Shenandoah Drive-In Theatre was positioned at the intersection with Old Mountain Road. The capital letters in SHENANDOAH blinked in unison, except for the DOAH, which had been dark for the last two weeks. Burgie Mallory probably wouldn't fix the lights until profits were in from the July 4th weekend.

They pulled into line behind a wood-paneled station wagon. The features were listed in black block letters against the fluorescent, white marquee:

4 BIG HITS!!!

SCARS OF DRACULAR
HORROR OF FRANKENSTEIN
GINGER
plus 4TH BIG HIT!

SHOW STARTS 8:30 DUSK

Summer laughed, then suppressed it to merely giggles when they finally made it up to the ticket booth and paid Margie Mallory their one-dollar admission. They drove underneath the awning and into the back of the large, triangular parking lot, surrounded by a nine-foot-high privacy fence.

Rob looked at her from the corner of his eye. "Just what is so damn funny?"

Summer started laughing again. "Dracular." She cracked up again, covering her mouth, afraid she'd spit out her Mateus.

"Dracular." Rob snickered, then started laughing aloud. "Man, somebody's got to buy this town a dictionary."

They parked a couple rows behind and to the right of the white, cinder block projection building. The projector was housed in a blockhouse on top; the concession stand and the rest rooms were on the ground floor. Behind the building was a small playground for kids, with hobby horses and a seesaw and a swing set with rusted chains. Rob reached through the window and brought in a metal speaker with an L-shaped plate on the back. He hung it on his window and turned the volume knob. No sound yet.

"What time is it?" Summer said.

He looked at his watch. "Ten minutes to go."

"Half past the monkey's ass," she said, and he laughed.

They kept the radio on and they talked and they drank while the Beach Boys played in the background. Summer smelled car exhaust and popcorn on the breeze. She recognized maybe half the cars that were already here. Kenny was parked two rows up in his new Mustang, ragtop up for privacy, she guessed, since she could barely see Ronnie's blurry silhouette next to him, his arm around her.

Rob pointed. "Kenny's gonna get some tonight. Did you see how Ronnie was all excited last night? That convertible gets her hot."

Summer laughed. Rob touched her thigh. *Yeah. Kenny's not the only guy who wants something tonight.* She yanked the cork out of the Mateus and raised the bottle to her lips.

A burst of static came through the metal speaker, and then the same song that was playing on the radio. "Hey, stereo," Rob said. He cut off the car. The sky was streaked deep blue and purple, with only a rosy glow burning behind the black mountains.

Then a cartoon came on advertising the concession stand: animated candy bars and hot dogs, singing and dancing, extolling the joys of hot, buttered popcorn and grease burgers.

The first preview flickered on the giant screen. Summer said, "Let's get this show on the road."

It was a family portrait: father, mother, and infant, swaddled in a blanket.

And they were apes.

"Cool!" Rob said. "The new *Apes* movie."

Apes in a space ship? She looked at him askance. "New? You mean there are more like this?"

"You know. *Planet of the Apes.*"

"Oh. Yeah."

"And *Beneath the Planet of the Apes.*"

"Never heard of it."

"Mutant humans living in the ruins of New York. The Forbidden Zone."

"Forbidden Zone."

"Yeah. Then Charlton Heston blows up the Earth."

She thought about that. "Okay, so then, if Earth is blown up, how do the apes get to Earth to make this movie?"

Rob shrugged. "Hm. Maybe the same time warp that sent the astronauts to the future in the first movie."

"Time warp," she said.

"Time warp."

"Time-traveling apes."

"Yep."

"You are a nerd," she said.

"Yep," he said.

She chugged her wine.

There was a loud scratch from the speaker, and then there was some guy with a cheesy mustache interviewing Woody Allen about his new movie, *Bananas.*

They watched some clips, some slapstick, some funny lines. But Woody Allen did nothing for Summer.

"Looks dumb," she said.

"Looks hilarious," he said.

"Yeah, but you like apes in a spaceship," she said.

"I do. I do like that," he said.

"Apes and Bananas," she said.

The next preview started. Art Garfunkel was kissing someone. Rob said, "Who is he kissing?"

"Paul Simon," she said.

Then Jack Nicholson shouted, and Ann Margret looked sexy and pouty.

"I don't mind the carnal knowledge," Rob said, "but it looks like relationship stuff and arguments. I'll let you see that one with the girls."

"They might be all arguing and pissy, but the music in the background is 'In the Mood.'"

"Ah," Rob said. "We call that irony."

"Another college word."

"Quite so."

Something devious flashed in her eyes. "You are acting so superfluous and obsequious that I shall no longer converse with you regarding time-traveling simians and Art Garfarkel."

He laughed so hard he spit beer over the steering wheel. "Garfarkel!" Then she was laughing with him, and the preview faded away. Mysterious music swelled from the speaker.

"About time!" Summer said.

The music echoed across the trellised parking lot. The movie opened with shots of a ubiquitous Gothic castle, enveloped in the shadows of the night. Inside, a stone slab had been draped with a crimson-lined black cape. A huge, ugly bat on nearly invisible wires flapped above the slab and oozed blood from its fanged mouth.

"This is one of the English ones you like, isn't it?" Summer said.

Rob nodded, enrapt. "Oh, yeah. Hammer movies are the best. Bats, blood, babes, and breasts!"

You wish. The dripping blood reacted with the ashes or dust on the cape, bubbling. A skeleton started to form, and as the music swelled, a human form took shape, clad in black, elegant, tall, and—

"Dracular," she started to say. Then Christopher Lee slowly opened his eyes, and the joke died on her lips.

A shiver started at the small of her back and tickled cold up her spine. She focused on Lee, on his black-red eyes. She could smell the blood that pulsed cold through his veins. He was grey and his eyes were dead, yet he walked, reborn, from the dust of death.

Rob was saying something—*Lee is like, like, the BEST Dracula ever, isn't he? Better than Lugosi*—but Summer barely heard him. She was shivering, and holy *shit*, she was tingling, she felt the heat building in her loins, and the blood.

A villager bore the drained corpse of a young woman out of the woods, into a clearing. Summer stared at the bloody wounds in her throat, at her pale, voluptuous breasts.

Then there were angry villagers, and a burning castle—all the classic horror movie clichés. Typical crap. So why was she so hot? Why was she breathing so heavily? Why was she *loving* this? This wasn't like *Dark Shadows* at all, and that was her favorite show. No soap opera melodramatics, no werewolves. Just—

Oh. Maybe that was exactly why she loved *Dark Shadows*. Maybe *that's* why this movie made her squirm inside.

The darkness. It was a darkness she could feel, a shadowy, crimson embrace that wrapped around her, a cloak of mystery and blood.

The breeze kicked up. She felt warmth on her cheek, smelled the green aroma of the tall trees bordering the fence. She got a whiff of cigarette smoke from a nearby car, and the acrid aroma from a joint. Rob spoke every now and then, but she was swigging wine and feeling good and wondering if fangs would sting when they bit into flesh, or if they'd feel like iron spikes driven into your neck; or would it be like the pain and pleasure thing guys talk about when they get a tattoo.

Laughter.

She looked up. The church on the screen was strewn with bloody corpses, hanging over pews, dripping crimson on the sanctified floors. "Cool!" somebody said nearby, and she realized it was Rob.

She drank more wine and held the bottle up to the light from the screen. Over half gone.

She grinned.

More wine.

The screen flickered. A cape swirled. Women screamed. Rob leaned in and kissed her. Their tongues met, and she tasted his beer, his cold tongue.

She pulled away and watched the shadows and blood float across the screen.

The speaker thundered. Lightning struck the immortal Count, and he burst into flame. His fiery corpse fell off a parapet and dropped down into the castle's rocky gorge.

The credits rolled. She stared at the screen.

More.

Lights winked on above the doors to the snack bar.

Rob said something.

"What?" Summer said.

"Got to go to the bathroom," he said. "Beer."

"Okay," she said.

He climbed out of the Falcon and closed the door. She rubbed her face, felt her cheeks tingle, felt the breeze on her arms.

Yes, oh damn, yes. I am pleasantly buzzed.

The speaker spat static, and a deep, bass voice sang, "—ada-da-vida, honey—" She saw a shadow coming closer, toward her, and she made out Tina

Tyler, in a checkered shirt and blue shorts. She was smoking, and her eyes looked glassy. She saw Summer and a huge smile crossed her face. "Hot time," Tina sang. "Summer in the city."

Summer said, "How drunk are you?"

"Not too," Tina said. "I figured I'd see you here tonight."

"Where else would I be?" She held out her hand, fingers splayed. "Let me steal one of those from you."

Tina grinned and took a pack of Salems from her purse. She shook one out and Summer took it between her long fingers. Tina handed her a book of matches. "Since when did you start smoking?"

Summer lit the cigarette and inhaled. The menthol tingled her tongue, the back of her throat, and the warm smoke went right to her head. She handed Tina the matches and nodded toward Kenny Cousins' car. "During the movie, I just happened to notice Ronnie's head disappear into Kenny's lap."

Tina laughed. "Maybe that's why her breath always smells like dick. So, what happened to Rob's car?"

"Hit an animal taking me home last night."

"Not a dog!"

Summer shook her head. She knew how much Tina loved her three pooches at home. "It kind of looked like a bear."

"That's crazy. Tell them bears to stay off the road next time." Tina reached into her purse. "Hey, you've got to try this." She pulled out a tall bottle half filled with a yellowish fluid.

"What is it?" The bottle was cold and beaded with moisture.

"Boone's Farm."

"Whatever." She took a long swig. It was a tad too sweet, but it felt good. "Not bad. Better than Rob's Schlitz."

Iron Butterfly faded out. The movie screen lit up, and scratchy folk music floated from the speakers across the lot. People in cars began to laugh and cheer. Summer and Tina looked at the screen.

"Here we go," Tina said, eyes shining.

The Shenandoah Drive-In had been showing the same preview every night for almost two years. At first, Burgie had run it for a few weeks just to stretch the concession time and make a little more food money. Damned if it didn't work, so he decided to keep running it, night after night. *Easy Rider* was a joke at first, something the audience had to sit through and endure. Then, after a while, some of the teenagers came to expect it every week, even complaining whenever Burgie forgot to run it.

The cars erupted in a chorus of voices and laughter, shouting the dialogue. Tina yelled one line, and Summer answered her at the top of her voice; and they were just another part of it all, their ragged voices raised to the skies as Nicholson and the audience cried out, "What you represent to them is freedom!" Then "Born to be Wild" rang from the speakers, a tribal hymn of howls and need, part of the living night.

Then the preview was over, and the audience cheered. A hamburger commercial came on the screen, and then a cartoon ringmaster announced ***INTERMISSION TIME!*** A cartoon clock started a ten-minute countdown until the start of the next movie. Bags of popcorn juggled; candy bars balanced on a tightrope; ice cream cups marched in time. Tina passed the Boone's Farm, and Rob walked up with a bag of popcorn and said, "Looks like I missed the fun." He looked sideways at Summer with a cigarette in her hand and said hi to Tina. She blew him a drunken kiss and went back to the car where her boyfriend, Denny, was hanging out the window and yelling for her.

Rob got behind the wheel, munched some popcorn, and watched Summer. Stray hairs stuck up from the top of his head. Right now he looked more like a boy than a man.

"What?" Summer said. "What?"

"Since when did you start smoking?"

And Summer's laughter rang out, into the clouds, into the hot night.

8

SUMMER TURNED AT the low rumble of thunder. Through the windshield, the night sky wasn't cloudy at all. Then she heard the rumble again, and she knew.

A motorcycle.

Rob turned towards the entrance and saw a single headlight roll through. "Uh oh."

"Uh oh, what?" Summer craned her neck to see, and the headlight winked out. She felt her heart beating faster. The bike growled low and parked far in the back, against the rear fence. *Was it—?*

"Trouble," Rob said. "That biker guy. I thought he'd left town."

"You mean run out of town," Summer said. "Hicks tried last night. Somebody didn't get the message."

She sat back and pretended to concentrate on the movie. A big bald guy dominated the screen, wearing a bulky metal collar and no shirt. *Damn, that boy has some muscles on him.* He sported a broad, rippled chest, even with the cheesy makeup and the flat, shiny head.

A spurt of warmth flooded her, deep inside. She took a long swallow of wine. Red. Dark red. She wished there were a mirror on her side of the car, damn it. It looked dark, really dark, back there, billowing, growing. She felt it, cold, a shadow stretching out, reaching towards her.

Horror of Frankenstein became a blur. She saw none of it.

What she *felt* was all she could think about. It wasn't the darkness she felt, closing in, enveloping her. It was him.

He was a concentration, a singularity, of shadow; a vortex of heat, smoldering, pulling into him all the dark passions of the night.

Summer bit her lip and looked down at her shirt. Drops of sweat were soaking underneath her breasts, staining the stupid Superman logo.

Shit, she thought. *And I had to wear this.*

9

MICHEL LEFT BEN'S house and stood alone on the stoop, staring out at nothing.

"Damn."

He hopped onto the bike and wrapped his fingers around the handles. He looked up at the black, starry sky, and felt the emptiness aching inside him, an endless spiral. He felt—

"Damn."

It burned deep in his belly, spreading through his body, throbbing. The emptiness. It sang through his veins: the night, hot and alive, swirling around him as though he were its obsidian epicenter.

It had been too long. The need was upon him.

He kicked the bike to life and rode toward the light.

And the smell.

The smell.

When Ben had finished and silence hung between them, he had stared at his friend, certain that Ben Castle could not possibly conceive of the long loneliness that would stretch out before him.

"I don't think you know what you're asking."

"Look, Michel. Look around you. No family. No photos. It's all empty."

"Ben."

"All I have is my art. I'm seventy-two, and I have no one else in my life. I never have."

He revved the engine. Heading for the light.

"I'm tired of living life all by myself. A girlfriend here, a lay there. I've never found the right one. And I am tired. I want something different. Something better."

"Ben. What's that got to do with me?"

"It's time. It's over. I'm over."

He had been riding on instinct. Light. Smell. Now he paid attention. Smelled it all, wafting on a warm breeze from somewhere up ahead. Cigarette smoke. Grease. Beer. Exhaust. Sweet wine. Weed.

The smell.

He should have recognized it. It had been all over the house, hiding beneath the oils and paints, in the walls.

"Ben, you've never been the type of man to give up and roll over. I know you. You're a soldier. A fighter. You always have been."

"Christ. Michel, Christ. Okay, it's cancer. I have cancer, okay? The doctors say it's in my groin. My dick. My goddamn dick. Can you believe that? I don't want to not be a man anymore. And the damn thing is spreading."

Michel looked down at his hands. The smell. How could he not have detected it?

"They don't even know what it is. They've never seen this before. Must be pretty nasty,

huh?" Ben slugged back his bourbon, went to pour himself another, then thought better of it and sat back in the chair. "They give me another eight months. Look, I know me. I know what I can take. I give myself a year. Thing is, no one knows, not for sure."

"Ben."

"Damn it, Michel. I'm alone. I want—I need—*a second chance. I've chased enough women away with my life out in the field. I've screwed up royally, and I've come up empty ever since. I need a chance. One more chance. To find the one. The one for me."*

Lights glowed up ahead. The main drag in Stonebridge.

"Michel, it's been a long damn time since we've seen each other. And you. Here you are, the same as you've always been. You."

Ben sat back in his chair and held his empty glass in his hands.

"Tell me. Michel, tell me. Did you ever have someone? Someone you knew meant everything to you. The one woman you couldn't live without. The One?"

He rode on instinct, following the ley lines of the night. Following the scent of sweat, and of blood. Following the *feed.*

"Yes. Yes, Ben."

"And?"

"And what?"

"Well, where is she?"

"She died. She died in my arms, decades ago."

"Michel, I'm sorry.

"I thought she—the one—was gone from me forever. Now, now that I'm here, I'm not so sure. Maybe there is such a thing."

"As what?"

"As a second chance."

He turned into the drive beneath the huge, flashing letters, smiling at the marquee.

"Then you understand. Michel, this could be my second chance. I need your gift."

"Gift? It's anything but."

"It's a blessing. Help me. Help me find her. The one for me. Please. Michel, make me like you."

A monster filled the screen—a half-naked, misshapen hulk wearing a wide, metal collar.

He cut the headlight and parked in the back. He felt their eyes on him, the open curiosity, their small-town apprehension.

He opened himself to the night. The hot, soft breeze ruffled the hairs up his arms. He felt the loneliness inherent with the long, empty night, and the multitude of tiny, blazing lives that burned in the darkness, watching the bloody melodramatics on the screen.

A man, asleep in his car three rows up, was dreaming.

A woman, angry, grinded her teeth.

An owl, in a tree behind the screen, was preening between its feathers with its beak.

The moon gleamed on a chrome fender.

The intermingled aromas, sweet, of beer and smoke, saliva and sex.

A young woman—*There!*—exuding need, panting softly with restrained lust

—*tasting the perfume of her soul*—

The darkness around him thickened. He dismounted the cycle and walked along the dark fence. He moved between the cars, stepping from shadow to shadow. Close to the front, he turned toward the snack bar, then crossed in front of the car where the young woman and her boyfriend were drinking.

He shook out his long hair and reached out, sensing. She was watching him. He felt her heart thumping, felt her heat rising. *Come and get me.* And he walked on. Her gaze was still on him as he turned at the snack bar and stepped into the shadowy playground behind the building.

He grinned in the shadows.

—*Come play.*

And he pulled the darkness toward him, reeling her in.

10

HE WAS TWO rows up, heading towards the snack bar, and Summer froze, staring at his tall silhouette against the monster's sweating, hairless chest up on the screen.

She forced herself to watch the movie. The rider disappeared into the shadows behind the bathrooms. He had parked way in back, she knew. Why hadn't he gone straight to the bathrooms instead of crossing up five rows, and cutting across the lot?

Damn. She wanted to turn around and look for him, but then Rob would ask, *"What are you looking at?"*

She lifted the wine bottle. The light from the screen filtered green through the glass. Three quarters gone.

She finished the cheap wine in a single, long gulp, and said, "There's another dead soldier." She glanced toward the cooler in the back, then got up on her knees in the front seat. Opening the cooler, she looked, instead, out the side window. She dug her hand into the ice so he could hear it. "Want a cold one?" It was dark behind the snack bar. Too dark.

"Sure."

She popped a top and tossed it through the window onto the gravel. The can hissed open, and she handed it to Rob.

"Thanks." He looked at her rear end, round and firm in those shorts as she stretched over the seat. "Nice view."

She turned back to the cooler and reached inside. *Where is he?* A car drove through the entrance, and in the moment before the driver cut the headlights, she glimpsed the rider's silhouette in the playground, sitting on one of the swings.

She flopped around and popped her beer. Ice water dripped onto her breasts, spotting the tight cotton shirt. She felt the cold edge of the can against her bottom lip, and was about to take her first sip when she saw someone walking in front of the car, toward the snack bar, and then turning toward the playground.

Shit.

It was her friend.

Ronnie Sheffield.

11

RONNIE KNEW IT was him as the bike rumbled into the drive-in; snarling, a wildcat at the end of its leash.

He walked in front of the Mustang, toward the snack bar, without a care, like he owned the fucking world. Her nipples poked at the fabric of her tight halter.

"Look. That biker dude from last night," Kenny said. "I'd pay to kick his ass. Can't believe he's sticking around. Sheriff's got a hard-on for him like crazy."

Ronnie watched him walk by. "Where'd you hear that?" She poured the rest of her cheap rum into a can of RC Cola, sloshed it around, and stuck a paper straw into the can. Her red lips engulfed the tip.

Kenny scratched his scalp through his short, brown hair. A cigarette hung wedged against his ear.

"Saw Duke at the gas station. Said they'd heard he was up at the motel."

"What a dive."

He leered at her. "You wasn't complainin' a couple of weeks ago."

Ronnie swallowed her rum and cola. The biker stepped into the shadows of the playground. Her insides had grown warm. No, she was tingling. She felt the heat, the moisture, building between her legs.

She looked at Kenny. He was a dog in bed. Clumsy, panting, pawing. His only saving graces were that he treated her the way she liked it—rough—and he always managed a rock-hard, nine-inch erection.

"That place smells like ass," she said. She sucked her straw and finished the rum with a hollow *slorrp*. There was an open cooler in the back seat. She reached behind her and fished through the ice. "We're out," she said, thinking.

"The hell we are." Kenny reached back and stuck his hand in the cooler, feeling nothing but the chill of the ice and water. "Shit."

"I told you to get us a case."

"Shit."

Ronnie gestured with her sharp jaw. "Ain't that Richie Rich and Jill up there? In his GTX?"

"Yeah," Kenny said. "Least, I think it's Jill. You know Richie."

Yeah, she did know Richie. Too well. And Richie's brother too. And thank God Kenny hadn't found out, or there'd be hell to pay, and another couple of rednecks would find themselves at the wide end of Kenny's baseball bat.

She put her red fingertips on his forearm. "So, why don't you go bum some beers off him? He always has beers."

Kenny smiled. "He should. He steals it out of his dad's garage. His dad has cases of it."

"Get enough for both of us? A six-pack. I've got to go pee."

"Okay." He stuck a cigarette in the corner of his mouth and reached for the door handle.

"Hey." She spoke quietly, sharing a secret. "He's still dealing, right?"

Kenny shrugged. She knew the answer. That's why they called him Richie Rich.

"See if you can get some grass. For later."

He smiled. Her parents had driven to North Carolina for the night, and the house was all theirs, all night.

He opened the door and said over his shoulder, "Back in a few."

Ronnie watched him walk up the rows between cars. Then she lowered her visor and touched up her makeup in the mirror. She painted on fresh lipstick and straightened her halter.

Ready.

Kenny knocked on Richie's window. The glass went down and she saw Richie's elbow on the edge. Kenny cupped his hand around his cigarette and lit it. They spoke, and then Jill hopped out of the other side and held the door open for him.

Kenny slipped into the back seat. Jill closed the door.

Deal.

Ronnie stepped out of the Mustang, slipped behind the car, and moved toward the playground.

With each step in her thong sandals, she felt the loose gravel underfoot. She lost track of the images floating on the screen, forgot there was even a movie. She felt easier, more herself—sexier with each step. There were only the shadows, and the warm embrace of the darkness, smelling of earth and copper; and the gnawing emptiness in her soul; and his muscles, and his eyes, wide and black and everything, everything in the world, watching her. Wanting her.

She breathed harder. She felt herself getting hotter. Wetter.

The playground was outlined with iron chains, painted white, and the openings on each side were bordered with short stacks of chalky, white-washed tires. Inside, the darkness seemed thick, like smoke. Then she heard the creak of a swing, going back and forth in the thick silence, and she finally glimpsed the outline of his shoulders, his long hair, and she stepped onto the playground where the shadows were hot, and her footsteps were muffled in the soft grass, and the sounds from that stupid monster movie were almost nonexistent.

She sees him, seated on a child's swing, rocking, his massive hands wrapped around the chains, and she says Hi, *and he says* Hi, *and she says, I was there last night at the dinette, and he says, Yeah? and she says, Yeah. Nice bike. Maybe I'd like a ride sometime. And he says, Yeah, I saw you, too, and now she's twirling a lock of her reddish-brown hair in her fingers, and she says, Yeah? and he says, You were all I could see last night. I saw you as soon as I drove up, and she says, Really? and he says, Yeah, really, and she laughs and steps closer, and says, I love your hair, really love your hair.*

In reality, Ronnie is unable to speak a word just now, at all, and the words she thinks she is saying are nothing more than low, breathy sounds in her throat, like screams in a muddled dream; and he tugs at her, the night enshrouds her, and the shadows touch her skin with hot, light caresses, and she says, she thinks she says, You like me, don't you? and he says, Mama, I adore you, I want you, and she says, I want you too; and his eyes speak to her, deep in her innermost secret places, telling her tales of bodies slick with sweat, of fingers kneading flesh, of tongues and teeth; and his teeth glint in the moonlight, and his hands are on her, his rough fingers pulling her; and she dances for him, rubbing her ass against his chest; and he rises from the swing, and he whispers his need and his endless passion, and she's shivering, feeling the heat, the tension, squirming in her belly, and she says, Touch me there, and his fingers slip down her belly, under the line of her shorts, between her hot skin and the thin elastic of her soft, thin panties; and they find her, tease her, and his teeth touch the skin of her neck, grazing it, and his voice is a low snarl, the moan of something wild, and he hears the hiss of her blood as it courses, pounds, just beneath the flimsy sheath of pink flesh, and he moves against her slick, pulsing body, and she feels him inside his jeans, feels it, and it moves, thick, coiled like a serpent, and she moans, Yes, yes, and the breeze shifts, and he smells wine, cheap wine, and perfume, and—

He jerked his head up.

He smelled *her.* A whiff of her, in the air.

He felt anew her touch upon his arm as she died in his arms. Her kisses, like the touch of butterfly wings. The scent of her as they made love in the English countryside.

No. Not her.

And now there was Ronnie. And the drive-in.

No. Not Angeline.

Her.

Summer.

And she was walking this way.

12

THE FRANKENSTEIN MOVIE had become an incomprehensible haze of disjointed images, of monsters and boobs and chains, and Rob wasn't even a thought in Summer's mind.

She was riding a good buzz, there was a fresh, ice cold beer in her hand, and the night was hot and pleasant and sweet, and the rider was here.

Trager.

And she knew, *No. Trager isn't right.*

Suddenly all she could think about was his eyes, and how they had looked at her, drawn her in; and the strength in his arms as he cradled her effortlessly.

She had no right.

Ronnie disappeared into the shadowed playground, strutting toward the rider, *her* rider, and she felt it bubbling inside her like acid, hissing, boiling.

Ronnie. You bitch.

The condensation on the beer can dripped over her fingers.

She had to do something. She had seen how Ronnie had looked at the rider last night.

Hungry.

She had to do something. Anything. And now.

“I've got to go,” Summer said.

Rob stared at the screen. “Go where?”

She rolled her eyes. “I've got to *go*.”

“Oh. Got ya.”

She reached for her purse, then stretched her long legs out of the car. At the last minute, she took her beer. She smiled. *Almost full.*

She walked around the back of the car and started toward the rest rooms. Then she made a sudden turn and crossed the row of cars behind the Falcon. Buzzed on Schlitz and tits, he would never spot her.

A few cars down, she turned and weaved between cars, toward the screen. She spied the canvas roof of Kenny's ragtop.

She came up behind it slowly. Kenny was gone. The windows were open, and no one was parked in the space to its right.

She glanced around to see if anyone was watching, and suddenly, she didn't care. She laughed out loud, just once.

She took a long, cold swallow of beer, walked casually beside Kenny's new Mustang, and poured the rest of the beer in the passenger seat.

She headed for the rest rooms.

Her heart was racing, and she was pointedly *not* looking toward the playground. A woman's scream echoed from the scratchy speakers around her. It was dark back there; too dark to see anything.

Darker than it should be.

What did she expect to do back there? Pretend to find them by accident? Ask Ronnie where Kenny was tonight? Confront them like a jealous girlfriend? She didn't even know the guy. How could she say or do anything at all that would make any sense?

She turned into the women's room, into the flutter of fluorescent light and the stench of ammonia, and locked herself in a stall.

Idiot.

What the hell had she hoped to accomplish? To show him how stupid she was?

I am such an idiot.

She had no business going after a guy like that—somebody she didn't even know, who probably wouldn't be around tomorrow.

A bum.

A *biker.*

Maybe her mother was right.

Maybe she *was* a tramp.

She washed her hands and absently glanced at her reflection in the cracked mirror above the sink. The grimy glass was missing a jagged corner at the bottom, revealing bare particle board and a glob of old, yellowed glue. She seemed pale and lost in the synthetic light, washed out, and she had no idea what she was doing here.

So, so stupid.

She touched up her makeup and lipstick, and appraised herself.

"Good enough," she said to her reflection. Good enough for Rob. Good enough for Stonebridge.

And then she said to herself, "Shit."

13

HIDDEN BEHIND THE cinder block building, Ronnie swayed against him in the dark, blocking his view of Summer as she walked toward them.

But Michel felt *her.*

With each light step, her scent filled his senses. Her presence, her being, overwhelmed him, flooding him with the scents and tastes of perfume and honey and Bordeaux.

He forced his mouth away from the smooth line of Ronnie's neck. Her skin was hot and slick. She hummed to herself, listing, swaying to some dance, some lust song only she could hear as it thrummed through her soul. He stroked her throat with his fingers, once, then pulled himself from her, willing his heart to slow its yearning drumbeat, willing his hunger to dissipate, his need to subside.

He took a step away from her. He could not do this now.

Release the prey.

Ronnie slowly stopped rocking as her internal music faded. She stood there, confused. He *pushed.*

—You went to the rest room. He sniffed her. *—The rum and Cokes went right through you. Go back to your boyfriend. You were never with me.*

She tried to think this through. She had gone to the bathroom; she knew that. But why was her heart racing? And why did she feel so horny?

She staggered. Why was she out here by the bathroom? She needed to get back to Kenny.

She stepped out of the shadows and stumbled toward the Mustang.

Michel willed himself to relax; made his heart slow, grow calm. He reached out, seeking—and touched her, sensed her: Summer, awash in the cold light, lonely and alone.

And so, so alive.

14

"SCREW THIS," SUMMER said.

Her reflection stared back, a dark crack in the glass angling diagonally under her breasts. Her makeup was perfect. Her hair was perfect.

"And screw you too," her reflection said.

If the rider wanted Ronnie, then, hell, that was his and Kenny's problem, and they could fight it out.

Let them. If he's all that hot for a little redneck like Ronnie, then he's definitely not the man for her.

She spun out of the rest room and passed the wide, open doorway to the concession stand. She halted impulsively, then turned around.

Why the hell not?

Black smoke curled up in tendrils from a steel kettle, and the smell of burnt popcorn filled the snack bar. Burgie Mallory, stomach spilling over his stained apron, saw the smoke and rushed to clean it out before it ruined the fresh popcorn below it. The next intermission was just minutes away.

Summer fished around in her purse and came out with a quarter, and she dropped it into the cigarette machine. She grasped the metal knob beneath the stack of Salems and pulled.

The rod came out halfway, and then, with a metallic *thunk*, refused to move any farther.

She tugged again, harder, leaning in with both hands. The knob moved only half an inch. "Shit."

Then an arm snaked around from behind her, and a large hand clasped the knob. "Allow me."

With a slight tug, the knob came out all the way. It *chunked* back into place, and a pack of Salems plopped into the bottom bin, followed by a pack of matches.

The rider placed them in her hand. His thick fingers touched her warm skin, and she looked up into his long face, his bottomless eyes.

"Thanks," she said.

"So, how's Supergirl feeling tonight?"

The corners of her mouth turned up in a relaxed smile. She felt completely at ease. And she didn't know why. She should be furious at him about Ronnie.

"Great. Tonight. I guess I just needed a good night's sleep."

"Good."

"Thanks for being there for me. And, look, I'm really sorry about Sheriff Hicks. I don't know why he always has to be such a—"

"An asshole?"

"Yeah." She laughed. "You keep turning up where you're least expected."

"Yeah. I was going stir crazy at the motel, I guess. Thought maybe a movie..."

She looked him straight in the eyes. "That isn't the first time you've lied to me."

"Excuse me?"

She used a fingernail to peel back the cellophane around the cigarettes. "You're not who you say you are." She looked at him. "I've seen you before."

He could not speak. The world around them had grown silent, invisible, and at the apex of his vision, his senses, there was only her.

She lit a cigarette and inhaled, watching him. She didn't know if she should tell him. She didn't know how to explain it, or what to say that wouldn't make her sound crazy. But something was screaming that its time had come.

"This is going to sound nuts. But, I've been seeing you, I think. In my dreams. For a long time. Like, forever. Your face, especially your eyes, staring at me."

He watched her, speechless.

"And Trager," she said, "is not your name."

"Would you like to see my ID?"

"Oh, please," Summer said, almost whispering, as if it were a confession, or the sharing of a deadly secret. "I'm not talking about a driver's license. No. I know, somehow, that this, *Trager*, is not you. Not really. *Trager* is bullshit." She paused, letting this come to her intuitively, looking into his wide, confused eyes. "Michael," she said. Then she shook her head. "No. Not Michael." She looked away for a moment, seeking something inwardly. "I know you. I've dreamed you. How?"

He had no idea what to say, and he held out his palms, almost pleading. "I don't—"

"Michel. Your name is Michel. Isn't it?"

Why? Why is this happening? Why here? Why now?

He said, "Michelle is a girl's name."

"Yeah. But not this time."

She smoked and looked into his face, thinking, then turned toward the exit.

A cold, hollow point blossomed deep in his heart. He felt its chill pulse slice through his veins, and realized what he had been denying—*fighting*—since the two of them had met.

There was no doubt. Not now.

Nichole.

Genevieve.

Angeline.

Summer.

She is the one.

She stepped outside, onto the gravel and dry, packed earth, then stopped. It *was* him, wasn't it? She spun around to face him. "By the way, his name is Delbert."

Michel shook his head, slowly, as though in a daze. "Who? Who is—"

"Delbert." She exhaled smoke and flared her eyes. "Delbert, the dinosaur." She turned and walked away, into the heat, into the dark night.

He stared after her in silent awe.

She swung her hips as she walked back to the car, taking each step almost as though she were dancing to a slow, sinuous song that only she could hear.

Hooked, she thought. *Now I've got to reel him in.*

15

HE REACHED OUT to stop her. His instincts urged him to run, to get her.

To *take* her.

But he held himself back. She walked away with light, playful steps that made her hips and rear sway from side to side, elegant and sensuous. He recognized that walk. It was instinctual and entirely feminine, and he wondered if all women were born with the ability to captivate a man with only their hips.

Gravel crunched under his boots as he walked back to the bike. He straddled the seat and stared at the screen, yet saw nothing.

It had been almost a week, since that cute hitchhiker on Route 66 outside of Carthage. She had tasted of patchouli and pot.

It's time. Past time. And this place, this temple of light, was way too hot for him now. The prey is still here. He could smell her from across the parking lot.

And there was Summer.

He started the bike. He circled around the right-hand curve of the drive-in, then crossed the row in front of Kenny's Mustang. Somebody yelled at him for drowning out the movie, and he throttled the engine and spat forward.

He heard a shout from behind him, but he paid no attention. The need was alive. It was a beast, gnawing at his insides, and he could not be here, this close to her, if it were to become uncontrollable.

It had happened before.

He might not be able to protect her.

To stop it. To stop himself.

He roared out of the theater and drove, following the neon, the red taillights, the light.

And the life.

16

RONNIE WALKED DRUNKENLY across the parking lot. She tripped on a rise of earth, then stumbled into a speaker pole. "Goddamn it!" One of Ronnie's sandals had torn off. She hopped back to retrieve it, slipped her foot into it, then said, "Shit!" A pointy chunk of gravel jabbed into the arch of her foot. She limped back to the Mustang.

Kenny wasn't there.

"God*damn* it!"

She pulled off the sandal and shook out the pebble, then marched toward Richie Rich's GTX.

The windows were up. In the light reflected from the giant screen, she saw that the car was filled with smoke. She rapped on the window. A girl inside said, "Shit!" She heard whispering, frantic. "Put it away!" Then, "Who is it?"

She knocked on the glass again. "It's Ronnie! C'mon, Kenny, let's go!"

She heard his voice from the backseat, muffled through the glass. "Shit, man, it's just Ron. Let her in."

Richie rolled down the window. He flicked back his long, greasy brown hair and looked her up and down. "Lookin' fine, gorgeous."

A hit of acrid smoke went straight up Ronnie's nose. She leaned in the window. Kenny was sitting back, relaxed, in the rear seat. He passed a joint over to Jill, sweaty and bleary-eyed. She had on tight shorts and a tie-dyed t-shirt knotted above her belly button.

"Come on, Kenny. Now."

He laughed again. "Get inside. What's the hurry?"

"Yeah, Ron. What's the hurry?" Jill took a deep hit. "C'mon."

"Kenny, finish up and let's go." She reached in and took the proffered joint from Jill. She inhaled in short bursts, then exhaled slowly in Richie's face. He opened his mouth and sucked in the smoke. "Shotgun," he said slowly.

"Come on, Kenny," Ronnie said. "Like, tonight."

"Baby," he started, "you need to cool your jets."

"Goddamn it. Now."

She spun away, stopped to light up a Marlboro, and paced back and forth behind the car until Kenny climbed out, whispering something to the others. They laughed.

"Whatever," Ronnie muttered. She turned for the Mustang, and Kenny had to run to catch up.

"Ron, what the hell is wrong with you? Slow down, will you?"

They got to the car and slid into the seats. And Ronnie squealed, "What the *hell?*"

"What?" Kenny shouted. "Shut the damn door! What the fuck is wrong with you?"

She slammed the door. "Goddamn it, Kenny! You spilled beer all over my seat!" She sat up and showed him a dark splotch across her butt.

"Holy shit! My new car!"

"Your car? What about my ass?"

"I didn't spill a goddamn thing!"

Ronnie popped open the glove compartment and pulled out some napkins Kenny had pocketed from Burger Chef. "You're so drunk you don't even know you did it!"

"The hell! I wasn't even here! I was up in Richie's car getting high!"

Someone nearby shouted, "Will you two shut the fuck up?"

She tried to soak up the beer in the seat, and got most of it, but the seat—and her shorts—were soaked.

Then the night roared with thunder. The biker rode past. Someone nearby yelled at him, and he revved the engine. A white piece of gravel flew up from his back tire and smacked into the windshield. The crack sounded like a gunshot. Kenny shouted, "Goddamn it! My new car!" And then the shadow shape of the biker roared through the exit.

Kenny's broad face lost its usually flushed color. The crack was a starburst, curing down toward the dash. He gritted his teeth and stared at the exit. First, Ronnie spills beer in his new car and blames it on him. Then, this biker hits his new car with a rock. "That son of a bitch," he said. "That fucking son of a bitch. I'm gonna kill him."

"Big talk, Kenny. He just tore out of here."

He started the car, rolled down the window, and threw out the metal speaker. It clanged against the steel pole. Kenny yanked the Mustang into gear and spun out of the space, sending gravel and dirt in a cloud, and sped around the perimeter toward the red EXIT sign.

Ronnie licked her lips. She didn't know why—her feelings seemed like a memory from a dim dream—but she was still excited. Wet. She stared past the crack in the windshield.

Goddamn biker is gonna get his ass kicked.

17

THE NIGHT EXPLODED behind their car, and it felt to her that the ground vibrated with the rumble of Michel's bike. Summer turned and followed the roar as he drove around the edge of the theater, and in the pale glow from the streetlights outside, she watched Michel's silhouette roll through the gate, and then she was staring at the empty place where he had disappeared.

She glanced over at Rob. He hadn't noticed a thing. He was quagmired in a beer-induced, Gothic haze, dreaming dreams of red velvet draperies, of candlelit castles, and big-boobed victims.

"Goddamn it! My new car!"

Two rows ahead, taillights flashed like flares, and Kenny's Mustang spun out of its parking space in a cloud of white grit. Somebody yelled at him. *Pissed off again*, Summer realized. His temper had always been awful. He had shown it enough growing up: fights at school; nights getting high and cruising for blacks to beat up with that horrible club that he kept behind the driver's seat. He was just an angry little redneck, just like his father.

Rob was absorbed in the movie, and the fleshy English chick up on the screen. He heard only the buzz of invisible mosquitoes swarming in his head, and saw only that chick's big ol' tits.

He sneaked a look over at Summer. He watched her run her long fingers from her hairline straight back through her soft hair. Her lips parted absently. Even as buzzed as he was, he could feel her next to him, her heat rippling away from her, erupting like molten flares cresting from the sun.

He slipped his hand onto her bare thigh. Raised an eyebrow. Grinned.

Mr. Smooth.

And, she thought, *here it comes.*

He moved his hand softly up her forearm, and let his fingers brush the swell of her breast. He leaned in to pull her to him, and he breathed the stench of warm beer over her face.

She took his hand and placed it in his lap. "You are sloshed," she said, "not to mention very stinky."

"Stinky." He reached out for her hand. She pulled away and glared at him.

"Not now, Rob. I'm not in the mood."

He shook his head as though to clear it, his eyes confused. "I—I don't get it. I thought you—"

"Rob," she started. But that was as far as she got.

She cared for him, she knew. She loved him. She loved the man he was. True and good.

Nice.

All her friends had come to believe they were the perfect match, and that marriage would come right after Rob graduated from Virginia Tech in two years.

But she knew now—tonight—that she just didn't love him the way he loved her. She had thought it was love, once upon a time; real love, true love. *Romance*, like in the movies, like Jennifer and Oliver; like *Love, American Style*.

But that was make-believe. It was too high school, like going steady and wearing his class ring on a chain.

"How come you're being such a tease?"

Summer's mouth fell open.

"What are you so surprised about? Come on, don't we always—"

"Take me home."

"Summer, come on."

"Now, Rob. I'm not— Just take me home."

He slammed his palm against the steering wheel. "Shit on a stick!"

Her eyes went wide. *Shit on a what?*

He started the car and jerked the gearshift into DRIVE and stomped on the gas pedal. The Falcon leapt forward, rear wheels bouncing on the gravel hump.

Then there was a loud *clangg* from behind the driver's seat.

Rob slammed on the brakes. Cheers and laughter rang out from the cars around them.

The speaker hung askew in the window, its ripped cord dangling against the side of the car.

"Well," Rob said. "Shit on a stick."

Summer looked at him. He looked at her. And suddenly she was laughing. "Shit on a stick? *Shit* on a *stick*?"

Rob put the car into gear and drove away at a crawl. He reached out and pulled in the cable through the window. "I meant to do that," he said.

She could not stop laughing. And then Rob was laughing. She looked over. The speaker still hung in the window. She snorted out loud, and Rob started laughing again.

"Snortin' Norton," he said.

She wiped tears off her cheeks. "You just couldn't be happy with a busted front end, could you?" She laughed again. "Oh my God, I'm calling you Crash from now on. Crash!" And she started laughing again.

They passed underneath the exit and turned onto Wythe, and they were laughing and smiling as he pulled up in front of her house, the frost between them melted by the heat lightning of friendship.

He put the car into PARK, then took her hand and kissed it. "I was out of line back there."

"It's all right."

"No, I'm sorry."

"Rob, we both had a few too many. It's all right, okay?"

The fact was, she didn't really care. Things were different now, since she'd spoken to Michel. Maybe things had been different for a while, but it had taken a stranger with eyes that blazed like black suns in the soul of the night to make her admit it to herself.

"Well?" he said.

She looked at him, blank. "Well what?"

"The party tomorrow night. Grab some dinner first?"

She stared silently. The beer bash in the woods, at the old Sugden place. Fourth of July.

"Yeah," she said, quickly. "Sounds like fun. Call me tomorrow." She bent over, and they kissed, just long enough for him to think everything was okay between them. Then she ran to the front door, unlocked it, and waved goodbye.

The party.

Rob.

Goodbye.

18

HE DIDN'T NEED to hear the Mustang's powerful V8 whining in pursuit.

He could feel them.

Always behind him.

It was a mixture of raw anger and lust, smoldering like coals behind their dead, angry eyes.

The girl, Ronnie, still throbbed in the throes of unfulfilled lust, and the boy, the roughneck from the diner.

Why were they chasing him?

Michel revved the bike, the night breeze singing through his long hair. The Mustang was suddenly left behind; then its front wheels jerked in response, and the steel beast screamed in rage and came for him.

Come. Let them come.

The wolf was leading the sheep.

He leaned into the turn at Locust Avenue and sped through downtown Stonebridge. He took a left onto King, past the lights flashing around the front of Brittingham's Furniture, past the shadows between the aisles of Charlie's Drugs.

He throttled down and stopped at the lone traffic light at King and Queen. The sheriff's office was two blocks up on King, but he wasn't going to give Hicks a reason to—

Headlights angled toward him from three blocks back.

He felt them. The boy was just steam and rage, boiling, looking for the release that only mindless savagery could give.

But the girl—

Her heat, her need, pulsed through the veins just beneath her skin. He could smell her sweat, her anger, even her confusion. But she should not remember being back there with him.

Then he understood. It was the boy. She was into him, his anger, his hot rage. This was pure lust. Ronnie wanted blood.

Funny.

So did he.

He tore right onto Queen Street and throttled up, heading for the rural roads that spider-webbed the edge of town, and the deep cover of the trees. He roared past the Patriot. His room felt stuffy and dark.

The headlights loomed closer, two blocks back. He punched it. A squirrel leaped in fear onto the road and froze at the scream of the bike. He saw it in the glare of the headlight. He reached out to it.

—GO!

And it sprang across the road, disappearing into the tall, unkempt grasses.

Two miles out of town, the road narrowed to an empty black line, ditches on each side. In the headlight he saw a road on the left, and a street sign leaning at an angle. He sniffed the air, felt the warm lives huddled in their flat homes and double-wides arranged sparsely down the road.

He barely slowed and bore left, leaning so far into the turn that he could have touched the asphalt with his fingertips, then he straightened onto the winding ribbon that was Black Snake Road.

There were no curbs or ditches here; only weeds and clumps of grass lined the fringe. He passed a tiny firehouse, red brick and grey cement, dark, and the night lay thick across the landscape, lit only by moonlight.

His headlight picked out a small plank bridge a few hundred feet ahead, and he crossed Craddock Creek as the slow brown waters underneath rippled with faint starlight, and the planks rattled beneath the tires.

The road grew darker, and the distances between homes grew longer. The Mustang was a low, constant threat behind him. Nearby he heard something big, probably a hawk, swoop down over the treetops and pluck a mouse off the ground. He could smell the boy behind the wheel –his foul sweat, reeking of alcohol, and the smoke from his Marlboro. The boy's heartbeat was rapid, fueled by his lust for violence. The girl had grown calmer, but she was breathing in hot anticipation.

He spotted the cut of a dark road on the right. At the corner was a broken wooden bus stop leftover from the 1920s, choked with tangles of ivy. He slowed and leaned into the turn, slowing just enough to let the boy see the flash of his taillight, and he roared into a leafy tunnel leading into dense, untended woods.

The Mustang's tires screeched across the road. The boy had missed the dark road, realized his mistake, and was now backing up. Michel slowed and gave him a few seconds to play catch up. Then he saw the yellow glow of the headlights, and he sped forward.

The road suddenly came to an end, blocked by three immense elms at the point of a ragged wedge of thick woods that divided two long-abandoned farms. On the left, the road led between two old brick gateposts, blocked by a thick iron chain. A faded NO TRESPASSING sign dangled from it by one corner. To the right, a dirt road led into the trees, overgrown with weeds and grass and scattered with a layer of leaves.

Michel took the dirt road.

The boy would figure it out.

Leaves and twigs spiraled out from under the tires. He heard deer in the thick woods on each side, clopping away from the roar of the bike, from the heavy rumble of the Mustang's V8. Their world had been violated. Predators were on the loose.

He rode onto the level lawn of an abandoned farmhouse, charred long ago by a vicious fire, illuminated only by the cold light of the gibbous moon. The pale dirt road led past the ruins to a barn whose bent tin roof had caved in. Two walls had crumbled to rotted timbers and crimpled tin.

Michel spun the bike through the wild grasses, angling its headlight at the opening in the trees. He was an open target. The boy could decide to run him down, but Michel was confident he would do nothing to injure his precious Mustang. This country boy would demand to fight, to feel his opponent's bones crack underneath his fists.

He would want to make him bleed.

The Mustang roared through the opening, casting a wake of spinning leaves. It skidded to a halt only thirty feet from where Michel sat waiting on his bike. The driver's side door flew open, and Kenny Cousins stepped out, a lit cigarette dangling casually from his lips as though attitude alone would beat his opponent into submission.

Ronnie stepped out into the tall grass. She watched the rider and adjusted her halter. She had reapplied her lipstick during the chase. Her lips gleamed in the moonlight.

Kenny reached behind his seat and pulled a baseball bat from the floor of the back seat, dull black tape wrapped around its tapered grip. His father had always driven around with three nightsticks and bats, all different thicknesses, hung horizontally in the back window of his pickup, just in case he ever drove into trouble, or felt like starting some.

Kenny was damn proud of his old man; proud of the way everybody in town knew to steer clear of Wayne Cousins when he'd had a few too many Pabsts down at Pearlie's Roadhouse. He smoked the same cigarettes, and used the same skullbreakers. Kenny had only the one baseball bat, but he carried it around just like his old man—*just in case.* Just in case somebody's head needed busting. Just in case he had to teach some asshole a lesson. Just in case he felt like it. He slapped the head of the bat into his moist, beefy palm.

This was a damn fine "just in case."

"All right!" he yelled. "Time to knock a lesson inta your fuckin' head!"

He strode toward Michel, muscles tensed like steel, the bat upraised.

Michel slipped off the bike and waited. "Son, you're making a serious mistake."

Kenny grinned. "You fuck! You made a mistake when you shot a fuckin' rock into my windshield!"

Ah. That was it. How *primitive.*

Ronnie's eyes gleamed, hungry in the pale headlights.

"Little man. What are you going to do about it?"

Ronnie giggled. She didn't know why. The fury burst from Kenny like an explosion. "Mother *FUCKER!*" He went for Michel with great, loping strides, closing the distance between them in seconds. He swung the bat at Michel's head. Michel stepped back, the angry breeze from the weapon tickling his forehead.

Then Kenny screamed—a rage-filled scream that came from the deep pit of his Neanderthal soul. He rushed Michel, and the long club was a pale blur as it slammed into the biker's forearm. Kenny brought it up blindly and swung a glancing blow off the biker's hip; then up again, and the bat thudded hard into Michel's temple.

Michel dropped to his knees. His eyes glimmered, filled with darkness, like a storm scudding across his vision.

Ronnie sat on the edge of the Mustang's warm hood. Her eyes were wide, and she shuddered with each breath. She felt herself growing wet. "Get him, Kenny!" She squirmed against the hood, pressure throbbing between her legs. "Show him!"

Kenny yelled, "—bash your fuckin' brains in, mother—" He brought up the bat, aiming for a crushing blow against the top of that bastard's head, and Kenny screamed, *"FUCKER!"*

Then the biker shoved off from a crouch and leapt impossibly high, somersaulting over Kenny as the bat swooshed through empty space and thudded into the earth.

Michel laughed. He rose behind Kenny, an avenging shadow with eyes of fire. Black blood trickled in a line down his temple.

Michel heard Ronnie gasp air through her teeth. Her blood was pounding, hissing like rock and roll brushes on a cymbal.

Kenny twirled around. Dirt and grass plopped off the bat. "How the fuck—"

He felt the boy's hatred, his raw jealousy, pulsing in the air between them. He felt the boy's rapid, powerful heartbeat, tasting of youth and wild grass. And the darkness rattling the cage of Kenny's soul roared in rage.

Ronnie stared at Michel. Her lust crashed over him in hot waves, fueled by the spectacle of men battling in primal fury, of blood spilled, but even more by this biker, this man-thing, an animal and a man, not a damn redneck town boy with a pack of cigs rolled up in his sleeve and a chip on his shoulder. A man, a man who could take her when she wanted to be taken.

The blood rushed through her veins in a hot, pounding river. Michel's head throbbed with her raw need. He tasted her lust on his tongue.

The *need* roared inside him. He had to feed, and her body responded to the gnawing at his soul.

Ronnie squirmed her ass against the Mustang's hood. Her taut nipples in the moonlight cast crescent shadows on her halter, and one hand absently rubbed herself between her legs. A hard, steady song on the radio pounded out something about teeth, and a hydra.

Michel felt Kenny's heart as it suddenly lurched into overdrive, manic, pounding with an out of control beat. Kenny grunted, loud, and he rushed Michel, a bullet of muscle and arrogant rage.

The club came up. Kenny screamed something incoherent, saliva flecking his lips, and he brought the weapon down toward Michel's head in a swift, brutal arc.

The night rang with a loud smack as tempered wood met flesh.

Ronnie laughed.

Kenny stared at his precious bat, locked in the iron grip of the biker's hand.

Michel ripped the bat away and tossed it to Ronnie. —*Catch!*

She caught it with both hands and stared at it.

Michel lashed out, and his fingers circled Kenny's throat in a steel grip. He visualized the windshield, and pushed the thought toward Ronnie.

—*Finish it.*

The thought came completely out of nowhere, but she smiled at it immediately. *Yes. Good idea.* Then she went around to the driver's side of the Mustang, and slammed the bat straight down into the windshield, laughing.

Kenny gurgled, his eyes widening in shock as Ronnie turned his windshield into a curved plane of glass spidercracks and empty craters. She shattered a headlight and the driver's side window. Then Kenny's feet left the ground. His neck muscles strained with his beefy weight. The biker lifted him with one hand. Kenny clasped the biker's wrist with both hands and thrashed his legs, struggling to free himself.

Michel smiled, his white, long teeth, his deep, ebon eyes, shining with cold moonlight.

With a single, inhuman thrust of his arm, Michel slung the boy away. Kenny thudded onto the ground at Ronnie's feet, an offering. He blinked in the Mustang's headlights, his neck aching with fire.

Michel glided toward Ronnie, a shadowed silhouette between the vehicles' headlights. She licked her lips. She felt his eyes burning into hers. The bat fell to the ground. The biker's massive hands seemed unnaturally elongated, like claws, black and shiny.

Kenny struggled to his knees. He started to cry out, "Ronn—" but the biker's grotesque fist backhanded him in the side of his head. He flew back against the Mustang. Blood arced from a long, deep gash in his cheek, spraying Ronnie's legs.

She stared at the sprinkle of crimson stars spattered on her flesh. Michel brought up his hand, and Ronnie hungrily licked Kenny's blood off his fingers.

Her eyes rolled back, and her sudden, spontaneous orgasm jolted her, blinded her. She rocked back against the hood, shuddering, grinding her ass against the hot metal, gasping repeatedly as she smeared Kenny's sticky blood across her thigh, between her fingers, and her eyes locked with the biker's, swallowed by their bottomless depths.

Kenny whimpered on the ground. "Ron? Ronnie?"

A shadow moved over him. He spat blood onto the ground. He wriggled up to his knees. He smelled the grass, felt the earth between his fingers. He saw his own blood and spittle freckling his hands. From the Mustang, the radio sang, "Gettin' ready, 'cause here I come."

His voice was a ragged whisper. "Ronnie? Come on, Ron, I—"

Michel was a shadow shape flickering in the headlights. Ronnie smiled. His eyes burned with crimson fires, and his teeth, his long razor teeth, smiled at her. She moaned once, and her fingers tugged at the knot behind her neck. The black fabric fell down, and she ripped the halter away. Her white breasts bounced in the yellow headlights, and she parted her legs, popped the button on her shorts, and pulled down the zipper.

She laughed. Someone, somewhere, a million miles away, was singing, *Hey there, Little Red Riding Hood.*

His breath permeated her. She wanted to lick the sweat from his bare chest, his stomach, and then down, down, below his navel, she wanted to lather his manhood with her tongue, make it hard and deadly.

He clutched Kenny by the back of his head. His voice was a command, and Kenny instinctively acknowledged the authority, the limitless power, of this beast, this night god.

—*Watch.*

Kenny wavered unsteadily on his knees as Michel glided toward Ronnie, his head lowered in some kind of feral crouch, his eyes frozen on the girl as her heat, her blood, transfixed him, pulled him.

Ronnie spread her legs, cocking her hips. She flipped back her long auburn hair, clinging with sweat. The biker smiled, and she felt his love filling her, saw the fire and attraction in the gleam of his magnificent teeth.

"Ro— Ro— Ronn—" Kenny tried to call out. Then his head was snapped back. The biker's voice filled his mind.

—*SILENCE!*

Then Michel stood before her. One arm snaked around her waist. She tingled where their skin touched. He nuzzled his teeth against her sweat-slick neck, then licked her skin down to her breasts. He raked his teeth across her rock-hard nipples, then caressed them with his long tongue.

Ronnie moaned, grinding her crotch against him, and whispered, "Now."

He grinned, exposing the length of his sharp, ivory teeth. He nuzzled his hard lips against the side of her neck.

Ronnie's neck suddenly went cold, burning cold, as he sank his teeth into her tender flesh.

Her body shuddered against him as she came, again, and again, her breasts bouncing against his chest. Her hot blood spurted in jets from her jugular, welling into his mouth. It burned down his throat. He tore deeper into her. Electric life sizzled through him, waking him. She moaned, low, and an image came to him: Kenny, beefy and naked, thrusting into her. He tasted the sharp scent of a joint, and beer, and the smell of her perfume as she sprayed it under her neck, between her breasts, and the sweetness of the chocolate shake she'd had last night, and the taste of Kenny's sweat on her tongue.

Michel jerked his mouth away. Her hot blood cascaded down her round, bare breasts.

—*COME HERE!*

Kenny crawled toward him on his knees. Then Michel plucked him from the ground by the back of his neck. He pushed Kenny's face against Ronnie's gaping neck, smearing her blood across his mouth and face.

—*Drink.*

Kenny lapped her blood into his mouth. He gagged once, and snot and spit ran out of him as he wept silently, mouth clenched upon her torn flesh.

—FEED.

He bit her. Michel's powerful hand pressed his head against her, hard. This time Kenny bit deep, a crescent-shaped wound that filled with blood. He sucked it, like he was still in high school, giving his girl a hickey in the back seat, and then his tongue found a ragged tag of flesh stuck between his two front teeth.

His head jerked back in Michel's grip. Kenny saw the cold moon sailing high above them, suddenly blotted by a bestial shadow face of fiery eyes and long, feral teeth, a Halloween monster movie nightmare, oozing blood from its jaws, and then it all swirled into utter blackness, into sweet, black silence.

And the moon laughed.

19

SUMMER STEPPED INSIDE and shut the front door with her butt. The old house was dark, except for the fluorescent over the kitchen sink and the blue light from the living room television. Her mother sat hunched on the green velour sofa in the living room, focused on the TV. Her hair was a little too long, and it stuck out strangely at the sides. Summer opened her mouth to say something, then decided against it. Her mother would definitely not appreciate her resemblance to a screech owl hunkered on its perch.

"Charlie Chan was always stupid," Louise said, blinking behind her glasses.

Summer glanced at the black and white Zenith. Merv Griffin had gone off at 1 a.m., and *Nite Owl Theatre* was showing a Charlie Chan movie starring Warner Oland. The movie featured a stereotypical black comedian, wearing a fez, and she watched as Chan and company passed through the chambers of a buried tomb.

The dim sets reminded Summer of her own house. But the resemblance ended with the lighting. The movie's shadowy Egyptian sets, detailed with hieroglyphics and paints, were beautiful and exotic. There was more life and lushness in this old black and white movie than in Stonebridge, and Summer suddenly felt a hollow spot open in her heart.

"I hate that nutty Charlie Chan," Louise said. "And that stupid Stepin Fetchit."

"Then why are you watching it?"

Louise shuffled over to the TV. She turned up the volume. The soundtrack was suddenly scratchy, popping electrically in the silences between dialogue. "Nothin' else on. Just Number One Son." She laughed at that and went back to the sofa—Summer called it the Green Blob—and sat down, adjusting her rear. "Carolina Clem is pretty funny when he wants to be. I do enjoy all his comical going-ons."

Carolina Clem was the host of *Nite Owl Theatre.* He wore baggy overalls and a floppy straw hat, and he sang cornpone parodies of "whatever songs them kids is listenin' to these days." At least it wasn't that hairsprayed evangelist Ma watched sometimes.

"I'm going to bed, Ma."

"Watch out for them bedbugs," Louise called after her. "You know what they do," she cackled.

Her mother had said that since Summer had been a child. "I know, Ma. I know."

And you look like the Tootsie Pop owl.

She went to the kitchen and opened a bottle of Coke. She took a sip, thought for a second, then glanced into the living room. Ma was enrapt by the movie she hated, watching as Charlie Chan examined a body under a sheet.

Summer opened a small cabinet above the sink. She pulled out a bottle that had been hidden there since the day her dad had walked out. She unscrewed the cap and raised it to her lips. The Jim Beam seared down her throat, tingling and stinging at the same time. She took a swallow of Coke, then slugged the bourbon again.

She started upstairs, feeling the bourbon's mellow rush on top of the wine and beer. She wobbled a little at the top of the steps, and whispered, "Whatever," smiling at herself.

Moonlight frosted her bed. She locked the door and let her purse slide down her arm to plop onto the floor. In the darkness, she toggled her radio on. The linear dial winked with golden backlight, and she turned the knob to her favorite stations, but they had powered down for the night. Even WGH from Hampton Roads wasn't worth listening to—she could barely make out "Magic Carpet Ride" through the crackling static—so she dropped to her knees and flipped through her albums until she came to one by James Carr.

She put the record on the turntable. She peeled off her t-shirt and tossed it into a corner. A low, soulful organ twanged from the speakers. She dialed back the volume. Carr's gravelly voice rang out in pain, almost crying, about how they had to hide in the darkness to be together.

She unzipped her shorts and tugged them down, then remembered her sandals were still on, and she flipped them one at a time across the carpet. She took a swallow of Coke as the alcohol buzz hummed around in her head. She smiled and dropped onto the bed, shorts peeled around her knees. The singer's voice lulled her like the splash of soft waves. She closed her eyes, tasting the sugar and soda on her tongue, and then the music carried her from her bed and into the shadows, and then on to the dark end of the street.

20

SHE WOKE TO the sound of the needle skipping at the end of the album. The plastic numbers flipped inside her alarm clock. 3:36 a.m. She was still buzzed, and she smiled at that, but *God* did she have to pee.

She rolled off the bed, saw that her shorts were still halfway on, and pulled them off. She shuffled down the hall. The living room light was out. Her mother's bedroom door was ajar, and Summer heard her snoring into her pillow.

A minute later, she went back to her room. Moonlight, the clock, and the stereo were the only focal points of light, and she glanced from one to another, feeling strangely like there was something she was supposed to do.

She toggled the stereo from **ALBUM** to **AM/FM**, and the mournful tones of "Only the Black Rose" came in from Hampton Roads with barely a hint of static.

The moon was high, shining down from a clear sky. She moved to the window to close the drapes. Moonlight slanted across her body, shining white along her curves, the line of her belly.

And she stopped.

Someone was in her garden—*HER* garden—cupping a white rose to his nose.

She stepped back from the window. She was only in her bra and panties, and if he should—

He looked up, straight into her heart, with those huge, lonely night eyes.

Michel.

His lips parted—and then she was twisting the doorknob when she remembered she was in her underwear. She found her shirt and shorts in the pale moonlight while a heavenly commercial for Rolling Rock—brewed from mountain spring water—played on WGH, "in old Virginia—Gateway to Dixie!"

She stepped into the hall, barefoot and quiet, and listened to the purr of her mother's snoring. Then she tiptoed down the stairs. She crossed the cool kitchen tiles, glanced through the back door window—*Oh, shit, it really is him!*—and she gently opened the door.

The warm night air embraced her. The moon silvered her roses. They were growing a little wild—she hadn't pruned them since May—but the moonlight made them ethereal and brought out their secret, wine glass poetry. He was a dark mass in the center of the blooms, where the power and the weight of the night seemed to coalesce.

Summer stepped onto a pathway of concrete circles, painted with the sun and moon and Orion and the Dippers, that she had laid out six years before, and came up to him. He seemed pale in the moonlight, troubled, as he stared at the long, white flowers bowing toward him.

"So much life," he said. "So much beauty."

She crossed her arms as if to ward off a chill, but she had already broken a sweat between her shoulders. "Shh," she whispered. "What are you doing here?"

He had changed into jeans and a black t-shirt that molded to his wide shoulders and his brawny arms.

He stared into her wide, ice-blue eyes. What was he doing here? He really didn't know. After what he had done tonight—after he had reveled in the hunt, and the taste and the sweet cascade of crimson—what had he been thinking? What had he been seeking?

He focused on the way the moonlight rippled down her blonde hair. "Couldn't sleep?" he said softly. "Bored? Thinking of you? Take your pick."

She straightened. "How did you know where I live?"

He looked down at a waist-high bloom in front of him. "I followed the scent of roses. Somehow, I found you."

"How corny can you get?"

"And yet, here I am."

They looked each other over in the warm, still silence.

"Thanks for the dinosaur," Summer said.

"Spur of the moment. Hope you like it."

"I have him on my bed."

"I'm glad he's got a home. I would have brought you flowers, but you seem to have enough of those."

They smiled simultaneously. Then she said, "You know you're bleeding?"

"What?"

"You've been hurt. There's blood all over you."

He tried not to appear shocked. Had the presence of this woman so confused him that he hadn't even smelled the girl's blood speckling his cheeks?

She turned abruptly and sneaked back into the house. She came back a few seconds later, carrying a paper towel dripping with cool water. She balled up a towel and gently wiped down from his cheek to his jawline. "Jeez. Who was she?"

As if she didn't already know.

He shrugged. "I guess I shouldn't ride my bike without a helmet. Even a little twig can scratch the hell out of you."

He had washed up back at the motel, but he had missed a few drops without the benefit of a mirror. Then he had climbed onto his bike and rode, blindly, into the solace of the night, looking for—

What? Forgiveness?

Love?

Her?

She glanced into his eyes. He stared back, impassive.

What wasn't he telling her? She decided, *A lot.*

"Blood can tell you a lot," he said.

Can he read my mind too?

She moved away and sat at the far end of a concrete bench she and her mother had bought at Williamsburg Pottery. Summer had painted it night blue with white and silver stars, and in her fourteen-year-old hand she had painted a quote in floating, cloud-like lines across the seat.

We are such stuff as dreams are made on;
And our little life is rounded with a sleep.

"There are things only blood can tell you," Michel said. He sat at the opposite end. "Things that are hidden. Feelings concealed deep within your soul."

He looked out over the patches of roses, white and yellow and red. He whispered her name. She waited, and he finally said, "Summer, do you have any idea who you are?"

She looked into his eyes. What was he really asking?

Do I know who I am?

Or did he mean that I don't know who I am anymore?

She looked out over the roses, surrounded by pink albas and floribundas, tea roses and romanticas, and a single yellow and orange bush of talisman roses in the heart of the garden.

Dad leaving. And dying. Mom's bitterness. Herself, growing up, reaching out, rebelling. Christ, things were different now. They had been for a long time.

"When I was twelve," Summer said, her voice as soft as the touch of the night air on her skin, "everything changed."

He watched her, his dark eyes transfixed upon hers.

"Nothing dramatic happened. Nothing big. But something clicked. Inside me. One day I was one person, and the next I was someone else. Someone new."

He nodded gently.

"I looked around, at everything, and I just wasn't happy. And I realized that nothing was really the way that people wanted me to believe. Church—" She shook her head. "I used to be in junior choir. I used to write religious poems for the church bulletin. And then, it all seemed worthless. All the people, and the choir, and the reverend, were just as false and hypocritical as everyone else. They all—not just church people, but everyone—cheated on each other, and lied, and hurt each other. And school wasn't a real education. It was training. Training kids to grow up just as stupid as their know-nothing parents. I woke up, that's all. I've grown up. Grown away. But my mother and Rob and Stonebridge, they'll always stay the same."

"Who's Rob?" It came out suddenly. A sudden surge of jealousy burned in his heart.

"A boy," she said. "My—" She averted her eyes. "A boy. No one."

He nodded once, silent.

"No. I don't know who I am. I guess I just know who I'm not. I'm not the little girl my mother wants me to be. Something's inside me, like it's trying to break out. And I don't belong here. Does that make any sense?"

"Too much sense. I said almost the same things to someone a long time ago, to a woman very much like you."

Their eyes locked, and an image came to her with an electric kick.

Reddish-brown hair. Full lips, and an even smile whose warmth she could feel.

"Angeline," she whispered.

Michel's eyes widened. How can she remember? *Before she has even—*

"And you," Summer said. "Michel. Michel— D'Arnot?"

He stared at her silently, then reached out and took her hand. His voice was barely a whisper.

"I left Vietnam and came here—I thought—because of an old friend. But now—" His eyes softened. "I didn't know that you were calling to me. I didn't know I would find you again."

His hand on hers was both warm and cool at the same time. "Again?"

He could not answer her.

"Michel, how old are you?"

He shrugged. "Twenty-eight."

"Hm. You've lied to me again."

"Listen—"

"You may look twenty-eight, but—" Summer knew, then, that she was on the edge of something. She stood on the verge of something terrifying—a bottomless chasm—where, in its darkness, burned an infinity of wondrous possibility.

Did she dare?

He held out his hand. *He's not leaving, is he?*

He cocked his head, waiting. He could see there was something on her mind.

She took his hand.

She wanted to say, "*Take me for a ride on your bike.*"

What came out was, "Get me out of here."

He gazed into her cool blue eyes, recognizing the strength, the need, in her voice.

"Come," he said, leading her toward the street. "Let's ride the night."

21

THE WIND WHIPPED through her long hair as Michel sped west on Route 28, winding up toward Blue Top Mountain. Summer's arms were wrapped tight around his waist. He bent into a curve and she leaned with him, like he'd shown her. The breeze on her skin tingled like fire. And she smelled him. Musky. Animal. A dangerous, spicy scent that made her want to burrow her face into the curve of his neck.

Primal.

She felt as though this were a dream, more crystal clear and tangible than reality. With Michel, riding with her bare feet just inches from the rough road, feeling the pulse of the engine between her thighs, she was flying. Soaring.

Free.

The road began to rise, bordered on the outside by dented guardrails. The purr of the engine echoed off the rock face. They drove through the rising woods and passed a driveway blocked by two whitewashed steel gates, secured by a thick chain and padlock. A faded sign arched over the driveway, and Summer smiled at times gone by.

Then she placed her lips at his ear. “Hey!”

“Hey!” he shouted.

She grinned. “You want to do something wicked?”

He smiled over his shoulder. “As often as possible.”

“Go back.”

“Where?”

“Back there. I want to show you something.”

Michel slowed and made a U-turn, then gunned it. She pointed toward the driveway underneath a faded sign.

Welcome to
Storybook Hollow

He stopped in the road. A sign hung from the right gate.

OUT OF BUSINESS
NO TRESPASSING!

“I think it's closed.”

“That's why it's wicked.”

They drove over to a narrow gap on the far side of the gate. He cut the engine and walked the bike into the protective cover of the thick trees. Moonlight poked through the treetops as they followed the curve of the overgrown gravel drive, dappling the path with silver and shadows. Summer instinctively took the lead, hands in back pockets, as they stepped into a dirt and gravel parking lot, wild with weeds and tall grass.

"They closed a couple of years ago," Summer said softly, as though in a deserted church. "The family that owns it couldn't run it anymore, ever since the new highway was built. It killed off most of the business. Then the old man who started it all died, and they don't know what to do with it."

They stood at the top of a small, kidney-shaped valley that stretched between Blue Top and Dog Mountains. The opening to the hollow was blocked by a two-story facade of plaster and plywood that had been painted to resemble a line of old books. Above the spines of *Mother Goose* and *Cinderella* and *Black Beauty* were white, plywood clouds, framing a rainbow that read **STORYBOOK HOLLOW**.

Michel said, "An amusement park?"

"No, not really. There were bumper cars and a few kiddie rides, and some carnival games way in the back, but mostly it's just scenes out of the fairy tales."

"What's a place like this doing out in the middle of nowhere?"

She shrugged. "They always said old Mr. Waddell was crazy. He spent all this money to build his dream. And then it went away."

She pointed out a dark rectangle in the center of the giant bookshelf. The title above read *Through the Looking Glass.*

Two turnstiles blocked the entrance. Leaves and twigs littered the concrete floor. Michel hopped over, then reached out for Summer and plucked her off the ground. She felt the hidden strength in his arms, a touch that seemed somehow familiar.

An empty, buffet-style restaurant building occupied the left-hand side of the facade, and on the right stood a gift shop. Summer peeked through a window. The shelves were barren, but she remembered the rows of souvenir mugs and snow globes and fuzzy animals.

"I've still got a diary that I bought here," she said. "And a yo-yo too." She glimpsed her reflection in the grimy glass. She was nothing but a pale, moonlit face—and where Michel stood was an amorphous mass of darkness.

She spun to face him. He looked down at her, wondering. "What?"

She stared into his bottomless eyes. "Nothing." Then she pointed out a gravel path that led into the trees. "Come on."

He smiled. "I suppose sneaking in makes us characters in a story, right?"

She smiled back. "Okay. *The Invaders of Storybook Hollow.*"

"No. *The Princess—*"

"*—and the Midnight Rider*," she finished.

"Much better than *Invaders*."

"Believe me, I am no princess."

"Hm. Okay. A brat then."

"Brat? You can't call me a brat! You don't know me well enough." She slugged his arm. *Like punching a sand bag.*

He laughed. "I know a sneaky little brat when I see one." She tried to punch him again, but he laughed and danced out of her way.

"Just wait till I get you back." Her eyes sparkled, and she ran off, following the overgrown path.

The pines thickened, climbing up the incline of Blue Top. The winding gravel path was scattered with dead leaves and pine needles. Michel made out the roofs and outlines of tiny buildings limned with moonlight—castles, towers, thatched roofs, a giant shoe. He almost laughed aloud at the childishness of it all, but Summer was just ahead, glancing back at him. He had recognized the memories, the wonder, in her eyes. This place meant something to her.

She led him to a fifteen-foot-high playhouse built to resemble a medieval castle. A faded, red pennant hung listless from its highest tower. They stuck their heads through the child-sized doorway. The walls were painted with simple murals: a fairy godmother and a pretty cleaning girl. In the center stood a column painted to imitate marble. Shards of glass or clear plastic glittered on top: all that was left of the precious glass slipper.

She pulled him back onto the path. "Princess," Michel said.

"What?" She tucked a strand of blonde hair behind her ear.

"See? I was right the first time. You are a princess."

"Nope," she said. "You were right the second time." Then she punched his arm and laughed and ran away up the path. She was a milk-pale ghost flitting through moonlight and darkness, and her hair bobbed behind her, a halo of golden yellow.

They passed fairy tale characters made of plaster and chicken wire, frozen in grotesque simulations of life. Three plaster pigs in bowties watched on, horrified, as the Big Bad Wolf huffed and puffed at a house of bricks. The wolf's tail had broken off, leaving a jagged hole in the bottom of his plaster pants. Inside the house of the Three Bears, the walls were scrawled with graffiti: PEACE. FIGHT THE POWER! SMOKE WEED!

The stable for the pony ride still smelled of dung and old hay, and as Michel reached the Gingerbread Cottage, Summer jumped at him from behind a cart that had once sold cookies. He reached out to grab her, but she twisted away, laughing, and then ran beneath a shadowy overhang of trees forming a sinister wood.

She waited for him just inside the overgrown arch. "We're entering the Dark Forest. I used to love this. Wish I had a flashlight."

He reached down and took her hand, enveloping it in his gentle grasp. "There's enough moonlight. I can see for both of us."

With the mere touch of his fingers, her playfulness was gone, replaced with a blossom of warmth in the center of her soul that slowly spread its tendrils, reaching for the secret parts of her.

He pushed aside a long branch that dangled over the path and let her pass underneath. The trees were closer back here, darker, and he realized that most of them were artificial, painted with faint, phosphorescent faces stretched in horrific grimaces.

They walked past the castle of Beauty and the Beast, past the moonlight-speckled gingerbread house of Hansel and Gretel, and into an area with wooden picnic tables. Summer sat atop a table. Michel sat next to her, and in the stillness they listened to the night sounds and the crickets, and enjoyed the tentative touch of the warm breeze on their faces.

She gestured back toward the castle. "There used to be a stained-glass window in the wall. Beauty's rose. I would play in there for hours. That's where I got the idea for my garden."

He looked over his shoulder, saw the tip of the Beast's castle against the sky. "Your roses are beautiful."

"Not really. They need a lot of trimming. I've been working too many hours to get anything done."

"The diner can't be that busy."

"This town has maybe seven or eight restaurants, tops. People have got to eat somewhere."

He looked toward the empty structures in the back. "Stonebridge is pretty quiet, isn't it? Peaceful."

"Dull is more like it."

"All small towns move at a different pace."

"Stonebridge doesn't move," she said. "Evolution doesn't work here. It's so old-fashioned. Look around. This is where dreams come to die."

"No. That's Vietnam," he said. "Your town may be slow, but there's something here. I feel it."

She stared at him as though he were crazy. "Sure you do."

"I'm serious. I came to Stonebridge to see an old friend. I suppose he needs my help. But I found someone, another reason to—"

Her cheeks grew hot.

"It's just too quiet here," she said. "Too empty. That's all. I mean, hell, you've been to Vietnam. You've been all over the place, I bet. I've only been here. I want to see things, you know? See Hollywood. Go to New York and drink at a bar, like they do in the movies. A real bar."

"You don't have bars in Virginia?"

"This state only allows mixed drinks to be served in restaurants, right? And that's only for the last couple of years, I think. We can't even have a real bar to drink in. Can you believe it?"

"You've never been to a big city?"

"Not unless you count Richmond. Hell, they're still fighting the Civil War there." She looked at her toenails, frosty pink in the scattered moonlight filtering through the trees. "I want to see London. And New York. And Miami, and Rio De Janeiro, and Paris—"

"Rio?" He frowned and looked away, into the trees.

"Yeah. And I need to see a volcano, up close. Tahiti. Black sand beaches. Night clubs, and art galleries, and plays, and book stores, and Rome. The pyramids. And the ruins down in Mexico. How wonderful would that be?"

He nodded. *Rio. Did she remember?*

"There has got to be more out there for me. I know it. I feel it, inside. Ever since I was a kid. Out there is where things happen. Out there is—" She paused. "Out there, it's rock and roll. Here, Stonebridge, it's hymns and Hank Williams."

"There is much more out there," he said, so quietly that she could barely hear him. He looked up, above the tree tops, and into the sky. She saw the stars reflected in his eyes.

"Chichen Itza," he whispered.

"Yes! That's the one. The Mayans."

"I've never been there. It's a place that is both ancient and new."

She watched him silently, felt his gaze prickling her skin.

"The Mayans rose and fell only a few hundred years ago. But it seems like thousands, doesn't it? Millions. Even their most recent cities are buried in the jungle, ruins, home only to monkeys and parrots. Theirs was a magical civilization. A young people, and violent, yet somehow immortal. They understood the stars. Eternity. And blood."

Michel's gaze followed the leaf-strewn path toward the back of the park, into the shadows. Summer watched him, her thoughts swirling with images of temples poking through the green, tangled jungle; of statuary and murals and pigments and blood, choked with vines.

"*National Geographic*," she said. He looked up. "That's how I escape. Books. Novels. The library has the old *National Geographics*. That's where I read about Chichen Itza."

"You hear the call of the road. The need, the urge."

"To get out, to go anywhere."

"Anywhere but the place you're in." They smiled together. "That feeling and I are very old friends," he said.

"I'm feeling it more and more. Especially—"

She caught herself. *Now that you're here.*

"It's not always as good as you'd think. It gets tiresome when you're alone. Whenever it's empty, and it's a long road between where you were, and where you want to be." He spoke of the roads he had been on, traveling across deserts, up tiny, cobbled streets in Italian villages, winding through the firs across Canada; but his voice itself held her, and she was lost in the cadence of his words, the almost hypnotic way he recreated the streets of London, and Paris, lamps flickering, reflected in puddles, and the hot palm-lined lanes of Johannesburg.

Does he always talk like this? she wondered.

It's poetry. *He* is poetry.

"Don't get me wrong," he said. "The road is beautiful. Romantic, even. But you can always ride into trouble you never foresaw. Or—" He paused. "Or trouble can follow you, like a curse. And there's no road you can take to escape it."

He looked out through the gaps in the trees, but his vision was focused on other landscapes. "And there are some roads, some paths, you cannot avoid. They find you. Ley lines, some call them. Lines of power, of essence, stretching in a web across the earth. The aborigines of Australia call them songlines." He shook his head. "I prefer *dreamlines*."

"I've heard of them," Summer said. "In a paperback I've got, about ghost stories and strange events."

"Someone like me." He paused. "I can find them, usually. I kind of sense them. They connect between places, points of power. Energy." He looked at her. "Like here."

She said, "So what exactly brought you here?"

He stared, eyes wide. How could he explain in a way she would understand? How much truth could she accept?

"An old friend. Ben Castle."

"Mr. Castle? You know him?"

"We served together in the Army for a while."

But Ben is so much older than you. She stared into his eyes, and saw only truth. "Vietnam?"

"We were in Saigon." It wasn't exactly a lie.

She smiled. "I like him. He came in for a week during my junior year in high school. He taught us painting, some illustration. I didn't get much past stick figures though."

"I saw some of his paintings yesterday. He's good. Quite good."

"When you said you were brought here, I thought you were going to say one of your dreamlines led you here."

He was silent for a while. "Ben wrote me a letter. I thought he called me here. But now I know that I rode in on a dreamline, one that took me completely by surprise."

She listened to the song of his voice, and the way his smile held her eyes, as if he could smile only for her. She imagined the heat of his touch, the feel of his lips pressed against her own.

"I thought I was coming to find Ben Castle," Michel said. He looked into her eyes. "Instead, the dreamline led me straight to you."

22

SUMMER LEANED BACK, disbelieving. "You know that sounds a little bit crazy, don't you?"

He shrugged.

"I suppose you're one of those ancient astronauts too." She knew it sounded crazy. No, it was just plain insane. But she also knew how she felt. This feeling inside her—warm, new.

Overwhelming.

It was just as crazy as he. She had known him for only a day, and already he had become a part of her, a part that thrilled her beyond her understanding, and a part that scared her, pushing away all sense of reason.

He stepped closer, just inches from her. He sensed her heat, her heartbeat, and her fear. But he was speaking only the truth. He had not known it at first, but he had accepted it.

She had brought him here, just as Ben, living here in Stonebridge, was no mere coincidence.

He reached out for her hand. "Summer, please."

She placed both palms against his broad chest and held him away. "Just wait a sec."

He stepped back.

"Look," he said. "I couldn't help coming here. First it was Ben's letter. Then I found you. Both of you. Here."

She watched him silently, lost in her own tangled thoughts.

"You said you dreamed about me," he said. "You knew my name. You knew about Angeline. How? Is that a coincidence? As soon as I rolled into town, I found you. And, and you said—"

"Is it you?"

"I know what I said." Summer hopped off the picnic table and brushed pine needles and dirt off her shorts. She looked up the dark path. An owl *whoooooed* twice in the distance. She turned and faced him. She started to speak, then abruptly shut her mouth. She turned and strode up the path, into the shadows.

"Summer?" He watched her go. "Summer?"

Over her shoulder, she called, "Yes, I'm going somewhere. And you better hurry your ass up if you're coming with me."

He caught up to her at the ruins of a fortune teller's tent. It had once been painted in bright, gaudy colors and covered with arcane symbols that had been copied out of a book. Now the tent was splotched black with mildew and faded from the sun, sagging with the weight of stagnant rainwater and sodden leaves.

Dark trees, both real and plaster, closed in on them. Branches over the path reached for them with gnarled, misshapen fingers. And he heard her whisper, perhaps to herself, "I love this part."

The trees parted, revealing the battlements of a plaster and plywood castle. The center portion stood almost two stories tall, and the towers on either side cast deep shadows across the moonlit path.

Summer peered through the dark opening on the other side of a child-sized drawbridge. "This was always my favorite," she said. She glanced at him. "I wanted to live in here. I guess none of it works any more. But it was really cool when it did." She stepped on the drawbridge and tested it with one foot. "Come on."

The moat had been poured with cement and was now littered with paper cups and twigs in a long swirl of mud and brackish water. A cement crocodile watched them cross under the portcullis.

The room had been painted *trompe l'oeil* to resemble a medieval stone chamber. A suit of armor stood in one corner. The right wall held a collection of portraits: witches, some with green skin, some with warts and crooked noses. A black coffin took up the center of the room. A gold, spray-painted crest on top read, simply,

"It seems so small now."

"It *is* small."

"Oh, I know. But not when Daddy brought me here. This really was a haunted castle back then." She pointed at the armor. "That would come to life and shake every few minutes. I thought it was coming after me when it first happened." She looked at the portraits. "Then these would all start talking. Tape recordings. Speakers behind each one, I guess. My friends told me my third-grade teacher was one of the voices." She pointed at a portrait. The brass plate read MILDRED. "That was her."

"Was her name really Mildred?"

"Mrs. Halloway. Teachers never have first names. Don't you know that?"

"I sincerely beg your pardon." He gestured toward the coffin. "Did someone get buried here every day?"

"That really would have been creepy!" She grinned. "No, some high school guy in a cape and make-up would pop up every now and then and scream. Scared the hell out of my mother once." Summer's eyes sparkled with mischief. "She said she almost peed in her pants."

She went into the dark back room. A hole in the plywood ceiling let in a shaft of moonlight. A bank of fake electrical switches took up one wall, and thick wires led up to a tall ceiling where a metal platform hung. Michel saw a green rubber hand hanging over the side.

"Frankenstein's laboratory," Summer said, hugging herself. "I always got chilly in here. I used to spook myself and think it was ghosts. You know, like cold spots or something. I'm chilly right now."

It was cooler in here, he realized. He sniffed the air. Fresh and cold. Clean.

"There was always thunder and lightning," she said. "And electrical sounds. Screams." She gestured toward a two-headed skeleton hanging from chains in a corner. "Then he'd start dancing around, like he was being electrocuted."

Michel bent over a metal grate in the center of the room. "Moaning used to come from there," she said. "The Dungeon of Doom."

Summer pushed open a secret door in the back wall, painted to look like a bookcase filled with mysterious volumes of lore, and together they stepped outside. The children's maze was ragged and overgrown, and smelled of honeydew and wild blackberries. She pointed into the darkness at the far end of the park, between the two mountains. "There's a path back there that leads to the natural bridge." Michel stared into the darkness as though it were lit with sunlight. A thin, worn path wound along the mountain, leading down. "They've got it blocked off with a fence so no one falls off and kills themselves." Summer turned back and started up the path toward the entrance.

They walked side by side, silent. Crickets chirped in the shadows on every side.

She sneaked a glance at him. "Your turn."

"My turn?"

"Yep. Spill it. Tell me everything."

"About?"

"About you."

"Oh."

He stayed silent for a few minutes, and finally spoke up as they reached the Peter Pan Pirate Ship, where Summer had once spun the wheel to starboard and had hoisted the skull and crossbones. She had waved at her daddy, who had watched her from the ground below as she set sail through lagoons and azure seas and through the mists of make-believe.

"Well," he finally said. "My name is Michel D'Arnot. I left France when I was in my early twenties and roamed around for a while. Well, actually, my parents sent me away for a while."

"Sent you away? Deliberately?"

"It wasn't as heartless as it sounds. I was a little wild back then. Rebellious."

"You too? I guess I should have been kicked out of the house a long time ago."

He smiled. "I don't think you ever stole the village priest's biggest hog and locked it inside the church. The night before Easter."

Her eyes went wide. "You what?"

"Services started at dawn. They had to hold Mass outside in the rain. And it took them two weeks to finally get rid of the smell."

She burst out laughing.

"I was shipped off two days later. My family was quite well off, so I was sent money on a regular basis, to keep me fluid, and to keep me far away. I have always been different. And there are a lot of people who will never understand that. They think I'm dangerous. And they'll stop at nothing to find me. That's why I roam."

"Are you?" she said.

"Am I what?"

"Dangerous."

He looked at her and said, "Yes. Oh, yes. People like your sheriff hate people like me. I represent things they will never comprehend."

"Hicks never liked me either," she said. "I told him off once when I was in junior high school, during an assembly about integration. Guess which side he was on."

"I'm sure," he said.

"I couldn't take it anymore, about how the darkies—that's what he called them—about how they weren't the same as us. And I pretty much cussed him out. Called him a racist pig. Some of the teachers even applauded. I got suspended for a week. So, he's never forgiven me. Or Ben Castle."

"Ben? What did he ever do to Hicks?"

They were passing a wide facade painted to represent the Emerald City of Oz. Faded green glitter sparkled in the moonlight. "Mr. Castle and the sheriff went to high school together," she said. "But Ben has long hair and a ponytail—I think it's kind of cool—and he's an artist, and fairly famous too. He spends way too much time in the big city, you know, and Hicks probably thinks he's just a dirty old hippie. Plus he has medals and Army awards that Hicks could never have."

"Jealous," Michel said.

"Jealous," Summer said.

He looked at her, almost with pride. "Junior high school?"

She nodded. "Yep."

"Good," he said.

"So," she said. "Are you some kind of criminal?"

"What? No."

"You said people are after you."

Leaves crackled under their feet. From somewhere on Dog Mountain, he heard the tinkling sound of a brook, of water bubbling over stones.

"My nature is what they despise. In their eyes, I'm worse than a criminal. And I know that more than a few would like to see me gone."

"Gone? You mean, like, to jail?"

"I mean permanently. Dead. But, no, the law isn't after me, if that's what you mean."

"So that's why you go under a fake name."

He nodded. "And, to tell you the truth, I am tired of hiding. It seems like I've been hiding forever."

"Then, you weren't even in the Army? Or Vietnam?"

They passed Snow White's Cottage, and a blank, tamped down rectangle of dirt and straw where a petting zoo had been. "Oh, I was there. First Infantry. But I also did a lot of other things—some things no one will ever know about."

"Like what?"

"I volunteered for special night missions. I was a tunnel rat."

"What's that?"

"You probably haven't heard about them on the nightly news. The VC has dug tunnels across Vietnam. They built complexes underground that had miles and miles of tunnels, even booby traps. I would go into the tunnels and do as much damage as possible."

"All underground?"

He nodded. He remembered the tang of the earth as it swallowed the blood of his enemies.

The tunnels had been a feast.

She said, "I would feel so trapped."

"Everything I did over there, I did only to survive. There was no joy in it at all. But there are others still over there." He paused. "I've never seen so much contempt of life. There are things, atrocities, that the U.S. will probably never hear about. Soldiers collecting the ears of the villagers they've killed. Decapitations. The torture of innocent civilians. Wholesale slaughter." He looked into her eyes. "I'm tired of running. And I'm tired of senseless death. I need peace. I need life."

Summer felt the sadness swimming behind his eyes. With the moonlight falling across his face, she suddenly saw the poster in her bedroom: the night-clad gentleman of eloquence and death, stepping from the dark shadows of dreams to glow fierce in the cold night. Some part of her made a sudden, instinctual connection. She thought of the blood she had cleaned off his cheek. He said he'd been scratched. But she hadn't seen any scratches.

The death.

The blood.

No, she thought. *That's just crazy. Impossible.*

She brought her fingertips to his cheeks and felt the warmth against her skin.

But, she thought. *But.*

What if—

She shivered once, in the warm moonlight.

What if?

And she wasn't afraid.

"Dreamlines," she said.

He gazed into her eyes, silent.

And she whispered, "A pair of star cross'd lovers—"

He grinned. "Beautiful *and* literate," he said.

She blushed and hoped he couldn't notice in the dark. "That and *The Tempest* were my favorites in English class."

They crossed the wooden bridge over the Jiminy Creek-It that flowed gently toward the bottom of the tiny valley, and they walked in silence toward the front of the park.

He had a duty to Ben. He owed it to him. It was stronger than a blood oath. It was a bond of brothers, forged by death and fire and courage.

He didn't like it. He wanted better for Ben. But this is what Ben wanted. *Needed.* It was his one chance to have a future. How could he say no?

But Summer—

He scented her beside him. Her aroma, her essence, permeated his soul.

Part of him wanted to jump on his motorcycle and tear out of there right now; to say *sayonara* to Stonebridge, and Hicks, and leave Summer far behind, safe from his pursuers, safe from him—and very, very much alive.

But it had been no coincidence that had brought him to Virginia. He wondered if Fate or Destiny or whatever would let him leave if he tried.

Destiny and dreamlines.

Must I ride this road for the rest of time?

Summer walked ahead. The still shadows beckoned to her, and he watched as she stepped up on a round, abandoned platform beneath a roof of ornate scrollwork and pastel landscapes. She weaved between brass poles and wooden horses, between the black, galloping silhouettes.

Michel stepped onto the carousel and watched her slip between the ponies. Finally, he heard her gasp softly, and he came up alongside her as she climbed onto a pink horse that exploded with color. Carved red and white ribbons draped its chest and flanks. A golden saddle still shone with layers of shellac, and roses of vibrant reds and yellows and purples decorated its white mane and tail. Its head was raised, as though it were challenging the sky.

Summer ran her hand along the carved roses. "She's still beautiful," she said, quietly. "But look at the cracks."

Her eyes were shadowed, but he saw they were filled with sadness. "Flower," she said, "meet Michel. Michel, this is Flower. She's the best horse on the whole merry-go-round."

Her eyes welled with tears. "In second grade, Sally Bailey saw me trying to get on, and she jumped on first so I couldn't. I punched her in the face and pushed her off."

He smiled, then saw a tear roll down her cheek. "Summer?"

She said it suddenly, her eyes focused on Flower. "You're going to leave soon, aren't you?"

"I—" He paused. There was no sense in lying. "Summer, I can never stay anywhere for too long. There are people—"

She ran her finger along the rim of a yellow rose. She wouldn't look at him. "I want to go."

"Oh." He stepped away from her. "All right. I'll take you back."

"No," she said, shyly. "I want to go with you."

It all fell on him at once, and he shifted on his feet uneasily, suddenly claustrophobic, trapped in her teary gaze as she looked up into his eyes.

The perfume of her soul had pulled him to this old valley, like light trapped for eternity by a black sun.

But she was too good. Too alive. He could not condemn her to a life like his.

"You don't know what you're asking."

"I don't care. Take me with you. Wherever. I want to go. Tonight. Right now."

"There are people after me. Dangerous people. And then they'll be after you. Do you want to live the rest of your life on the road, being chased? To hide like an animal? Wandering the earth? Hiding from the light?"

Her blue eyes flashed, darkening in anger. "Do you have any idea what it's like to be stuck in one place for your entire life? Where nothing changes? With a mother who not only chased away your father, but is absolutely nuts?"

He tried to speak, but she pounded her chest with her fist. "I feel the damn world! In here! I *feel* it, like I've— I've ridden your dreamlines before. I'm supposed to be with you, aren't I? You came here because of me. You said so. And I've seen you in my dreams for as long as I remember. I've written about you in my diary. I saw your eyes. I felt your face in my palms." She hopped off the pink horse and came up to him. "I knew Angeline's name. She's— she's in me somehow. I can feel it. Horses. No, one horse. You and she, riding it together."

He pulled away.

Yes. It had happened. A field in spring. County Cork, Ireland.

He could not deny it now, no matter how much he wanted to. He could not deny her.

"But you will be damned, Summer," he said.

"If I stay here, I'm already damned. And that is why you came. To take me away. To take me. This is what you have to do."

He was the night; a shadow riding through her dreams and into her mundane reality.

She was the light.

Whether delivered by chance or by destiny, he had been pulled here for a reason. Demeter had called to him from the depths of her soul, and he had answered the call, to guide her from Hades up into a world of wonder, of glittering starscapes and sweet, moonlit dreams.

"No," he said, but there was no steel in his voice. "Not for you. You deserve better. Much better than I."

She pressed herself against him. Her nipples hardened against his chest, and she looked into his infinite eyes.

Her wide blue eyes became his world. He inhaled her, the scent of her hair, her sweat. Her lips came closer.

"No," she whispered. "I belong to the night. I belong to you."

He took her in his wide arms and crushed his lips to hers. She tangled her slender fingers in his long hair. Their lips parted. Their tongues touched, tentatively. Then their hunger commanded them, pulled them together, binary suns dancing an endless ballet in the darkness.

His sharp teeth raked her lip. The tiny scratch blazed with electric fire, and then his mouth moved across her cheek, down, down her long throat, to nuzzle against her hot flesh.

The fire built inside her, molten, pulsing deep in her belly. She pulled his mouth to her neck. Her pulse was a drumbeat against his lips. She moaned, softly. "I need you."

Her scent, her being, flooded him, and he felt as though he were drowning in her. His lips parted. His long teeth pressed against her flesh, seeking the hot blood coursing just underneath.

He pulled away. No, this was not what she deserved.

Without thinking, she yanked his head back down to her neck, hard.

A flick of his tongue—a low growl deep from the back of his throat.

She shivered, sensing the wildness barely concealed in the cage of his skin.

No! He fought to resist. *No! I cannot.*

Her fingernails dug into the back of his neck, sharp. And he could not hold back. He lashed out with his teeth: just a razor-sharp sting that drew only a few drops of her crimson soul; just a taste, silky and hot, a swirl of sunlight in the hollow of his tongue.

She arched against him, lighting jolting through her with the echo of a woman's scream.

She tastes her own blood on his tongue. She feels her body clutched tight in his arms, feels the swell of her breasts as he feels them, hot and soft; she feels the small of her own back against his rough hand.

A woman—brunette, streaked with red, twenty-three, smiling down upon him, freckles lightly dappling her nose as she straddles him in a field of waving yellow grass.

Angeline.

She jolts against him, her body wired like a marionette, her own body no longer.

Fireworks explode in the black sky over Rio de Janeiro. Angeline beckons to him in the chill night, surrounded by masked revelers, laughing and holding each other, kissing.

Angeline's eyes widen in shock. Her arms reach out. A splotch of red blossoms near the center of her chest.

Her dress pokes out unnaturally. She coughs blood, and it spatters to the street. "Michel."

Then the sharpened point of a long, wooden pike rips through the silk and cotton, dripping with her dark blood.

She stares at the sharp, wet point that has erupted through her chest, dimly registering the sharp agony where the obscene thing has been driven by an unknown hand.

She stumbles toward him. Black blood spurts hot from her heart, a crimson burst around the fire-hardened point. "This isn't— Oh. Oh, Michel, I wanted so much to show you."

She crumbles into his arms. The masked assailant merges with the drunken crowd as they dance and cheer. A burst of fire in the sky. Her hands wear gloves of dripping blood.

And Michel is screaming, "Angeline!" into the night, and he swears as the light passes from her eyes that he will never break his promise.

The stars burned brighter in Summer's eyes, sizzling pinpricks, like the tips of sparklers, opening like roses in the night; and the scent of roses.

Her roses.

It was overpowering, intensified, floating to her on the still air from miles and miles away.

She saw galaxies reflected in Michel's eyes: worlds unknown, spinning around their blazing suns like lovers.

She saw Michel, gazing into her eyes, a smear of her blood along his lower lip.

The name came to her in an eddy of distant memory, beneath the mask of Angeline's face.

And then, *Nichole.*

And another.

And another.

And she knew.

It came to her, calm, the acceptance of a lineage that had sung through her dreams.

Angeline.

Genevieve.

Nichole.

Elinor.

Lisabetta.

Celestria.

This was unreal. Impossible. No, it just couldn't be true, not a word of it.

But logic has no say in the poetry of the soul. The truth that sang in her heart knew the dreamline that had brought Michel to her was the road she had to ride, to the same indefinite point, to the same crimson future.

Wherever it took her, she needed to go.

Blood doesn't lie.

The call of dreamlines cannot be denied.

She blinked, and he was holding her away from him, watching her.

Weakly, regretfully, he said, "Enough."

She tried to speak.

"Enough, Summer," he said. "This is not what you deserve. Or need. This isn't—"

The sound of the slap across his face echoed under the tent of the carousel, across the hollow. Her eyes flared with rage.

"You've been in my dreams for as long as I can remember. I have your eyes, a drawing of your eyes, in my diary. You are not just going to leave me here alone like some helpless little girl. It's wrong. It feels completely wrong. I know you now. I know this dreamline." She stared into his eyes. "This was meant to be. And I need more. I need to be with you."

23

THEY RODE DOWN the mountain, her arms around his waist, her head nestled on his shoulder.

He wanted to drop her off a block away, so her neighbors wouldn't be awakened by the bike. But she felt something now, something fierce inside, and she insisted he drop her off at the edge of her driveway, because the bike was loud, and she no longer cared if it woke up the nosy neighbors, or even her mother.

She swung off the seat. He stuck his hand in his pocket and came out with the motel key dangling from his fingers. He placed it in her hand, and she looked at the blue plastic oval with 34 imprinted in white.

"Wait for me in my room tomorrow night."

She smiled. "It's already tomorrow."

"Yes." He took her hand and kissed it. "I have to meet Ben first. I'll come to you around 9:30 or 10:00, I hope."

She nodded, absorbed in his eyes.

His hand wrapped around the back of her head, and he pulled her to him. Their lips met, hungry, and he crushed her to him, awakening his blood.

You have it wrong, he thought. *So wrong.*

It is I who belong to you.

He let her go, and kissed her gently, one more time.

She had forgotten about the beer bash in the woods. She had forgotten Rob.

Michel was her night, and her day, and her heart.

He rode away, waking old Mrs. Carey in her creaky bed from a dream of a mystery lover touching her *there* with his warm, wet tongue.

Her mother slept, oblivious, as Summer returned to her room and slipped naked between the sheets.

And Michel, his skin already tingling in the scant minutes left before the sun would rise behind Dog Mountain, followed their dreamline straight back to Storybook Hollow.

nocturne in fantasia

I feel the earth move

saturday, july 3, 1971

1

THE DREAM SWAM slow, thick, eddying like a muddy river.

Angeline, reading a book in a large bay window; and men—

—men that, somehow, she knew—

Colin

and Vicente

—but had never seen before.

And Michel. He was there. She couldn't see him, but in each flash of vision, she felt him, a presence, hovering.

She woke up, and her mother yelled again from downstairs, "Summer! Phone! It's the diner!"

And *damn* the light filtering through the drapes was bright. Her clock read 8:36. She hadn't even gotten four hours of sleep.

"Be right there." Her head throbbed. She pushed herself out of bed and closed the blinds and curtains on the east wall. She started for the door, then twisted around and closed the other curtains. She wanted it dark.

She went downstairs in nothing but a t-shirt. Her mother sat at her coffee and crossword perch in the kitchen, smoking her third Winston of the day. "Hmp," her mother muttered. "Catting around again last night, I see."

Summer glared at her, but said nothing. *It's just not worth it.* She picked up the handset. "Whoever this is, I am not happy."

The man on the other end tried to laugh. "Hey, sorry about this. It's Ralph."

"Yeah, I'm sorry about that too."

He chuckled uncomfortably. "Hey, Summer, I hate to call you like this, but Sarah can't come in today, she called in sick. Think you can come in for me? At least for the lunch rush?"

She leaned her forehead against the wall phone. Her head was pounding, and the light in this old house was just too damn bright. She had a couple of friends who suffered with chronic migraines, and she figured this was the painful light behind their eyes they were always talking about. And *damn* she was tired.

"Yeah, I definitely need the bread. But I need to leave around four."

"Yeah, yeah," Ralph said, quickly. "Sure, sure. You're a lifesaver, Summer. Thanks a mill—"

She hung up and closed her eyes, wishing this day were already over. Her mother was watching her. "I've got to go in," Summer said.

"Supposed to be your day off, ain't it?"

"Supposed to be. One of the girls is sick."

"Girl like you needs to stay home sometimes. Ain't gonna do you no good working so hard the way you do. Staying out all night."

"Mom," she said, tired and furious and feeling it all boil up in her. "Mom, just shut *up*."

Her mother's mouth fell open. "Now, just who do you—"

Summer's voice was hard, like steel. "It's *whom*, Ma. *Whom*. And I'm talking to you. I don't want to hear it. Understand?"

She trudged back upstairs as Louise stared after her, puffing her Winston. She peeled off her clothes and stepped into the shower, relaxing in the hot tingle of water. The scratches on her neck were tiny pink lines, and she thought of Michel, his heat, his strong touch. *And, oh God, his lips*. And she thought of her mother, staring at her, bug-eyed.

And she laughed.

The night had been— She didn't know the word. Wonderful? Beautiful? Perfect? The way their mouths had merged, the way his arms held her. And the electricity his passion had sent through her.

She laughed. Water sprayed her belly, tickling between the V of her light-haired mound and down her long legs.

Joy sang through her, a voice of strength and life and magic. And she laughed away the stench of her mother's foul cigarettes, and sang to Creedence and hummed to Booker T. as she put on her makeup, and she left the house in her stiff, pastel uniform and her round, blue John Lennon sunglasses, still smiling, thinking of tonight, of him.

Michel.

Of him.

Only him.

2

THE FOYER DOOR slammed against the wall. A tower of paper cups rolled off a file cabinet and across the floor.

Iris Salmon looked at the sheriff over her glasses and said, "Get that, will ya?"

Sheriff Hicks crushed one of the cups under a thick-soled shoe. "Crystal Blue Persuasion" came from a transistor radio atop a deputy's desk. "Cut that shit off," he said.

He was late coming in, thanks to the goddamn waitress who never showed up at the Dixie Dinette. The place had been packed, as usual in the morning, but orders always backed up when Ralph tried to fill in and pull waitress duty.

Hicks made straight for the IN box on his desk. He rustled through reports on a late-night speeder out on Route 81 and a hitchhiker just inside county limits.

Nothing.

He shouted, "Iris, did you get any answers to my—"

Iris bent up from the floor, the roll of paper cups wobbling from side to side in her hand. "Does it look to you like I'm doing something?" She placed the tower of cups back on the file cabinet. "They're on my desk. I would have given them to you, but some asshole knocked all the paper cups onto the damn floor."

He picked up a small pile of papers off her impeccably neat blotter. Eighteen pages. A report from the FBI, the hippie's Army record from General Services, and crap from one of the credit bureaus.

He looked up at her and nodded once. It was the only thank you the old bat would get.

The glass rattled in the office door as he slammed it shut. He slung his campaign hat onto a chair and squeezed his bulk into his creaking chair.

The credit report was clean, too clean. Trager had no outstanding bills or debts, no rent, no car, no mortgage, no nothing. That said a lot.

Trager was a bum. Shiftless. Riding from town to town on that hippie cycle of his; no job, no bills. He probably robbed filling stations and grocery stores to buy drugs and live on potato chips and Twinkies.

Hicks reached over to press a button on the intercom, but stopped when the door burst open.

"Just put down those fingers," Iris said. She held his coffee mug in her hand, steam curling from the surface. "Do I ever forget?"

She put the mug on his desk, then waddled to the door. "I spit in it though." She slammed the door and walked away, her blue hair bouncing.

He read the records from General Services. Major Trager had been shipped out to Vietnam in '66. Served in the 1st Infantry. Volunteered for front line duty. Saw action in Srok Dong and Operation Attleboro in some place called Suoi Da.

Received a field promotion to Lieutenant Colonel at Ong Thanh in '67. Saved four men and was wounded in the Tet Offensive; received Purple Heart.

"Bullshit," muttered Hicks. He opened the bottom desk drawer, unscrewed the cap on the scotch, and poured a slug into his coffee. His back was aching again, a result of a high school football game, and the fight afterward. He had been suspended a week for breaking the opposing quarterback's nose. He took two pills from his pocket and swallowed them with his coffee.

Trager secured a village of friendlies in '69, got wounded again, received another Purple Heart. Promoted to full bird colonel in January of 1970. Retired May, 1971. Shipped back from Saigon to Los Angeles. Pension checks going to a bank in San Francisco.

Hicks slung the report onto his desk and took a long drink from his mug. There was nothing there he liked, and nothing he could use. The bastard had the whole goddamn Army fooled. *Purple Heart, my ass.*

He sipped his coffee and stared out the office window. He felt a familiar warm buzz starting in his head. The weatherman on the TV last night had said today was going to be a scorcher, and damn if he wasn't right. 81 degrees already, according to the sign over at the bank. The sky was clear and heat waves shimmered off Main Street, reflecting the sky in shallow, wavering pools.

The FBI had sent pretty much the same information the Army had. But he sat up straight when he came to a mention of a task force report, and an entry by a CIA operative in 'Nam. He read one portion repeatedly.

RUMORS REGARDING SUBJECT'S REPORTED ABSENCES FROM DUTY AND POSSIBLE ACTIVITIES ON VN BLACK MARKET ARE INCONCLUSIVE AS OF YET. DAILY ACTIVITIES INDICATE POSSIBILITY OF INVOLVEMENT IN VIETNAM-THAILAND DRUG TRADE. INVESTIGATION ONGOING.

Hot damn! A druggie!

He barely read the rest of the report, and all but ignored the conclusion at the end of the collaborative report.

COMMITTEE CONCLUDES INSUFFICIENT EVIDENCE IMPLICATING SUBJECT. INVESTIGATION CLOSED PER US/VRN TASK FORCE S-1712, 03 FEB 70.

He stacked the papers neatly on his desk.

CRIMINAL ACTIVITIES.

Hicks did like the sound of that.

He knew that this report was all he would get from the G-men, and to even bother asking the CIA for anything would be a waste of time. Hell, the spooks would not only deny having any intel on Trager, but they'd deny that the sky was blue, that the president was Nixon, and that the sun was going to come up tomorrow.

Insufficient fucking evidence.

He saw a squirrel hopping across the street, and he imagined crosshairs centered on it. A tug of his finger—*BLAM!*—and the squirrel exploded in a cloud of fur and blood.

God*DAMN* if he hadn't been right all along. He knew, he just knew, there was something messed up about that hippie. Something seriously wrong-a-rooni. And he'd be damned if he was going to let a low-life son of a bitch like that get away with pushing drugs in his county.

He smiled and drank his coffee. The scotch tingled down his throat. He took another pill.

No sir-ee, Jim Bob Dandy.

The hammer was coming down.

He'd get that hippie bastard.

Oh, he'd get him.

3

WHEN SUMMER WALKED into the Dixie Dinette, the first thing she did was go to the kitchen and pop three aspirins with a glass of ice-cold 7-Up. Then she started taking orders, and a customer called out to her, "Hey, Hollywood! Can I get some more coffee over here?"

That's when she remembered her sunglasses were still on.

Tina laughed behind the counter. Summer tucked the glasses into her purse, but Tina and Ruthette called her Hollywood for the rest of the day.

By noon, her headache had softened to a dull throb behind her eyes, and she decided the first thing she'd do when she got home would be to take a long nap, with the air conditioner on HI. She wanted to be ready for Michel tonight—ready for a good time, ready to dance with him, maybe to the radio in his motel room, with his hands roaming over her body.

God! What am I thinking?

And no headache—no *nothing*—was going to stop her.

And then the bells on the front door jangled, and Rob walked in.

A wave of guilt flushed over her, and she flashed a half-smile at him. She held up her pen as if to say, *Just a minute.* Then she turned back to Joanie Windsor, asked her to repeat her order, then read it all back.

Rob found an empty seat at the counter. Ruthette waved to him through the order window, and he smiled back and mouthed, *Hey.*

Summer went around the counter, poured four glasses of iced tea, and a Coke for Rob. She slid it across to him, dropped the tea off with the Windsors, then came back around.

"Hey, Crash."

He rolled his eyes. "I called the house. Your mother said Ralph pulled you in today."

"Yeah. Sarah called in sick. Probably her period again."

Rob noticed dark, puffy crescents under her eyes. "You okay? You look a little pale or something."

"Headache. And I was awake half the night, I guess. Couldn't sleep." She looked away, pretending to check on her customers. She could not look him in the eye. The scratch on her neck seemed as if it were red hot.

"You want aspirin?" Rob said. "I've got some in the car."

She shook her head. "If it doesn't go away in a while, I've got some in my purse."

Rob gulped most of the Coke and slid the glass toward her. "Okay. Just get better. The party's not going to get really going until nine or so, so we've got plenty of time. Why don't I pick you up around eight and grab dinner? I'll bring the cooler." He grinned. "And wine."

A bald man in a black shirt waved to her from his booth, Reverend Hayes from St. John's. "Gotta go."

Rob saw Ruthette watching him from the window, and he waved. "See ya, Ruthette."

She smiled back, and Tina's head appeared in the window. "See ya—Crash."

Rob blushed. "Oh, man."

Tina laughed. Ruthette watched Rob walk through the door, then she looked over at Summer, totaling the reverend's check. Summer placed it on the tabletop, said something with a smile, then looked up and saw Rob climbing into his car. She watched as he backed up, then drove off. Then she sighed, and her eyes lost a little of their spark.

And Ruthette knew.

Summer came in with the reverend's dirty plates and stacked them in the sink. She leaned against the ice machine, enjoying the feel of the cool metal against her cheek.

"Your head ain't any better?" Ruthette said.

Summer closed her eyes. "Yeah, but—" She trailed off. "It's still there, a little. And I am beat."

"You should've told Ralph to take a hike."

Summer shook her head. "Can't. I'm saving up. I've got to get my own place."

Ruthette slipped a spatula under a beef patty and slapped it onto a bun. She squirted on some ketchup and mustard, rang the bell on the counter, and yelled, "Tina! Order up!"

She turned to Summer and wiped her hands on a dish towel. "How are you and Robbie?"

"Same old."

"Nice kid," Ruthette said.

Summer looked away. She did not want to be having this conversation.

"The boy worships you."

Summer stared at anything but Ruthette. "Maybe that's the problem," she said softly, as though she were talking to herself. "He's still a boy."

Ruthette nodded, but said nothing. She turned to the counter and picked up a ticket Tina had just left, but the order may as well have been written in Sanskrit.

Poor Rob, she thought. *He has no idea.*

Summer went through the swinging doors to check on her tables. Ruthette tossed the ticket onto the counter.

Poor Rob. And poor Summer.

Because she knew this wasn't right.

It was the biker.

She felt it in her gut, the same way she felt that there was something about that stranger.

Something just plain wrong.

4

DEPUTY DUKE CRAWFORD was parked in the lot of Wayne Cousins' Texaco station, in his usual spot between a rusted-out Packard and a 1948 Good Humor truck that Wayne would probably never finish repairing. Hicks and Wayne had been tight in high school, bullying the kids they thought were the weakest, and then having a laugh about it over beers they shoplifted out of the market downtown. The sheriff and Cousins now had a deal: whenever a car was pulled over to the side of the road, a deputy was to determine immediately that said car was a traffic hazard, and Cousins Towing was to be called. The daily rate to hold a car on the Cousins lot was more than the price for a night at one of the local motels, and at the end of every month, a check from the Texaco would arrive at the station house—just an appreciation to good ol' Buddy Hicks for his lifelong friendship.

Speak of the devil. Duke watched the sheriff pull up to the light, flick on the bubble on the cruiser's roof, and make an illegal turn without a stop onto Route 81. The sheriff put the pedal to the metal and squealed toward the outskirts of town.

Duke reached for the mic to find out what Hicks was all hot for. There was nothing special happening; no emergencies, no radio chatter. Just Hicks tearing toward the mountains—

Then he knew.

Hicks was headed out to the Patriot.

He was going to roust the biker.

Duke burned rubber turning onto Route 81. The sheriff was already two blocks ahead. Duke brought the mic to his mouth, but paused with his thumb on the button. There wasn't a thing he could say to talk Hicks out of whatever he had planned—at least, not over the radio. Hell, Hicks would probably order him to head back to the office and mind his own business.

He placed the mic back in its holder.

Between town and the mountains, Route 81 dipped between low green hills, speckled with grazing cattle and long rows of cotton, puffed white amid tufts of green collards and lettuce and rows of grey earth. The corn in Jack Holly's fields stood tall, reaching for the sun. Then the farms gave way to wooded, ancient hills, thick and verdant in the heat of summer. Duke spied the Patriot Motor Inn up ahead and watched the sheriff kick up a cloud of dust as his brake lights flashed and he angled the cruiser into the driveway. Hicks parked parallel to the spaces in front of the office, and was hauling himself from behind the wheel when Duke crunched over the gravel and parked behind him.

Hicks scowled as Duke got out. "Boy, what the hell you doin' out here?" He screwed his hat onto his bullet-shaped head. "I put you in town on traffic, didn't I?"

Duke put on his own hat. "Had a speeder in sight. He tore out of town like a bat out of hell. I realized it was you." The engines ticked in the silence between them. "Thought I'd see if you required assistance." Yeah, that sounded better than the truth. "What're we doing out here, Sheriff?"

Hicks glared at him. "I don't require any assistance, Deputy."

"Sheriff, what are you wanting to do? We don't have anything on the guy yet."

Hicks took a step toward him, his left eye twitching. "He's a goddamn pusher," he said. "Report came in from the Army. Some kind of black-market big shot in Vietnam. Well, I ain't gonna let him pull any shit in this town." He pointed toward the last room. "His motorcycle is gone. And I want to know what that fucker is up to."

"Jesus. We need a warrant."

Hicks scowled and started for the front office. "I don't think the management here will have any problems giving local law enforcement a harmless little look-see, do you?"

Duke stared at him, wide-eyed. He got a whiff of scotch off the sheriff's breath. "We can't do that. You know we can't. If we find anything in there, it'll never hold up in court."

Hicks shoved open the office door. Millie Watson sat behind the desk, checking off room numbers on a clipboard while a bowling tournament played on the black and white. Millie was fifty-five, had dyed brown hair, and painted-on eyebrows that arched high like rainbows. She looked up at them, from Duke to the sheriff, noted the badges shining on their shirts, and tried to hide a frown.

"Well, Sheriff. Duke. What can I do you for today?"

"Miz Watson," Hicks said, smiling. "I was hoping you could get Carlton for me. He around today?"

She raised an eyebrow. Almost every room was booked for the weekend. The annual Fourth of July fireworks show was at nine tonight over at the natural bridge, and they didn't need a single guest to be scared off by the sheriff's shenanigans.

"I think he's out back, cutting the grass. Why don't I go and get him?"

"Thank you kindly," Hicks said.

"Whyn't you boys have a seat? I'll just be a second."

Hicks stood. Duke nodded and smiled.

Millie crossed through the empty dining room. A sign read, "*Cousin Abner sez it's the BEST country breakfast buffet in Stonebridge!*" She went through a back door toward the rectangular pool.

Hicks stared through the glass in the front door, lost in his own counsel. Duke watched Millie through the large dining room windows. She called out to a man who was pushing a gas mower in ever-decreasing rectangles across the lawn. Millie pointed toward the office. The man glanced over, mouthed, *Aw, the hell!*

then let go of the mower. He started their way, taking long, damn-it-all-to-hell strides.

He opened the dining room door and held it open for Millie. She walked with him into the lobby. Duke touched the rim of his hat. "Mr. Haynes."

"Duke." Carlton Haynes was tall and gangly, but late middle age had gifted him with a paunch as round as a basketball. He pulled a white handkerchief from his back pocket and tamped the back of his neck. His gold Ban-Lon shirt was soaked dark under his arms. "Sheriff. Please tell me we ain't gonna have any trouble up here now."

Hicks smiled way too broadly. "Won't be any if I can help it." He stepped up to Haynes and spoke low. "Carlton, one of your guests has come to our attention. Seems he may be wanted by the authorities."

"Let me guess." Haynes combed back his thick, snowy hair with a ten-cent black plastic comb. "The guy with the motorcycle."

Hicks' eyes narrowed. "Has he done something?"

Haynes shook his head. "Perfect guest. Gone in the morning, and he's usually back at night. No trouble at all. He's hardly here."

"Then, you're keeping watch on him?"

"Not at all. Tucker, my night manager, told me all about him. Checked him in, what, Thursday night? Said he's a bonafide war hero."

Hicks scowled. "Yeah, we heard all that." He put his hand on Carlton's shoulder and pulled him close, a confidant. "Now, Carlton, this is a matter that needs to stay quiet, am I right? Between you and me."

"Well, Sheriff, I don't know what I can do for you."

"Carlton." He looked Haynes in the eye. "We just need a few minutes. Just to take a little walk through this biker's room. It's as easy as pie."

Carlton's eyes grew wide. "Sheriff, now, you know I cain't—"

Hicks squeezed the man's shoulder. He spoke softly, so Millie, sitting back at her desk, couldn't hear. "All I need is just a quick lookie-loo. No harm, no foul. And, just so you know, I consider this a personal favor between you and me. Now, I'm not permitted to divulge all's what I know of this James Trager, but let me assure you: you will be doing Stonebridge a huge favor." Hicks leaned in closer, almost cheek to cheek, and whispered, "I don't want what he's selling—you know, out on the streets—to get in the hands of our kids. Do you?"

Carlton's face went ashen. "You mean he's one a' them druggies? Like on *Hawaii Five-O*?"

"Now, I didn't say that, did I?" Hicks patted Carlton's shoulder. "But I believe you have a firm grasp of the situation." One eye twitched, and Haynes noticed that his other seemed too large.

Haynes looked over at Millie, who was not paying attention to anyone at all, no sir.

Carlton blotted his upper lip with his handkerchief. Then he stepped behind the counter and removed a key from a metal cabinet on the wall. He came back around the counter and headed for the door.

Hicks stopped him. "Carlton, now, it'd be best if Duke and I did this on our own. He could be armed."

"You don't mean—"

"He's probably not even in there. But you can't take that chance, now, can you? That's our job." He held out his hand.

"Carryin' a gun on vacation? That—that just ain't right." He placed a key for room 34 in the sheriff's palm.

Hicks moved toward the door without a word. Duke said, "You and Millie need to hang tight. We should be right back."

Duke stepped out into the sweltering heat and followed the sheriff. Carlton closed the door, turned to Millie, and said, "I don't think I like our sheriff, Millie. Not one bit."

Millie peeked through the blinds and watched the sheriff stride down the sidewalk like a king. "A very bad man," was all she said.

Hicks took long strides, gunning for room 34. Duke ran to catch up. "Sheriff, we just can't do this, not without justifiable—"

"My town, my rules," Hicks said.

"Where'd you get all that stuff about drugs?"

"Report from the Army. Don't you listen?"

"Jeez, Sheriff." His voice went up an octave, almost pleading. "If that's true, he might have an arsenal in there."

Hicks unsnapped his holster and pulled out his .38. "He just might."

"But we need a warrant. Buddy, nothing we find in there would stick. They'd rule the search illegal."

"You let me worry about all that," Hicks said.

Duke started, "But, but, guns, and drugs—"

Hicks thrust his big index finger into Duke's chest. "I don't give one shit about evidence, or warrants, or this cocksucker's rights. I need to know what that piece of shit is doing in my county. My town. Got me?"

"Yeah, yeah. But, Sheriff, we gotta do it right."

The sheriff's cheeks grew splotchy. "You listen to me, you little fuckin' pansy. Ain't no way I'm gonna let this sumbitch get away. His ass is mine. I need a deputy who ain't some little queer bait. If you can't back me up like a man, don't bother clocking in tomorrow. You copy?"

The muscles in Duke's face grew taut. "When have you ever not been able to count on me, Buddy?" He stepped up to him, face to face. "When have I ever failed to back you up? Goddamn it, I'm trying to get you to see straight. We're the law—not law breakers. So fire me if you want to, goddamn it. Take my badge right here and right now. I'm just trying to make you see reason—and keep us both on the up and up."

Hicks glared at him. Then his shoulders sagged, and he let out the breath he'd been holding. "Duke." He nodded, more to himself than to the deputy. "Duke. Goddamn it. Something just ain't right about this guy."

"I get it, Sheriff. I get it. But—"

Hicks turned toward the door. Room 34. "I'll take point. You take the side."

Duke sighed. He had tried.

He pulled the revolver out of his holster and flipped the safety. He stepped past the door and hugged the wall, pistol pointing to the ground.

Hicks stood to the left and rapped the green door with his knuckles. "Mr. Trager! It's the manager! May I have a word with you?"

A crow cawed from atop the Patriot's road sign, and in the distance they heard the low rumble of a riding mower. Beyond the door, they heard nothing.

Hicks knocked again. "Mr. Trager? May I come in?"

He tightened his grip on the revolver and slid the key into the knob. He twisted, felt the knob turn. He counted down silently, mouthing to Duke, *3—2—1—*

"NOW!"

Hicks shoved open the door and rushed in, gun leveled. Duke charged behind him, crouched to fire.

The room was empty. Hicks moved toward the bathroom, peered inside, then lowered his gun.

"Close the door," he said. He slipped the revolver into his holster. "Keep watch at the window. Let me know if he comes back."

Duke shut the door. He found a small gap between the thick curtains where he could look out and not be seen.

The bed was messed up. A water glass and a toothbrush had been used. Clothes hung in the closet alcove. Hicks looked inside the duffel on the floor. Nothing. He looked under the bed and between the mattress and box springs. He pulled out the dresser drawers, the nightstand drawer, and flipped through the crinkled pages of a Gideon. He ran his fingers around and behind a framed print of the Founders signing the Declaration of Independence. He looked under the sink, then took off the top of the toilet tank.

"Nothin'," Hicks said. "Not one damn thing. The room is clean."

Duke glanced over at him, then looked back outside without a word.

"There's got to be—" Hicks snapped his mouth shut and thought for a few seconds, looking around.

Bed.

Sink.

Dresser.

Clothes.

Duffel.

He stared at the olive-green duffel bag on the floor, TRAGER stenciled in black.

Army.

That's it.

"Go on, Duke. I appreciate this," Hicks said. "Get back to the station. Ask Iris for everything that's come in on Trager. I want you up to speed. I knew I could count on you."

"Okay," Duke said. "What are you going to do now?"

"Nothing much to do," Hicks said. "All's well and good." He cleared his throat and adjusted his hat. "I'm going to get me a nice cold cherry Coke at the drive-in. Then I think I'm going to go for a little ride."

5

SUNBEAMS GLOWED THROUGH the tall trees that lined Three Stump Road, scattering shimmering clouds of golden light across the winding asphalt ribbon, over the undulating lawns of green grass. Hicks parked in front of Ben Castle's ranch home and let the car's air conditioning wash over him. Iris Salmon's voice crackled on the radio, talking to a deputy out in Mosby about a drunk walking down Powhatan Road.

There was no sign of the hippie's motorcycle. It could be in the shed out back, he supposed, but the wooden doors hung ajar, and the only things he could see in the shadows were a yellow lawn mower and a red metal gas can.

He got out of the cruiser, grunting, feeling in his legs the pull of gravity mixed with the weight of age. Getting too old for this shit. But by God, he wasn't going to let anything stop him. Not old age, not a do-gooder deputy, and not some old, pony-tailed bum.

No sir-ee, Jim Bob Dandy.

The brass door knocker was in the shape of a lion's head. He slammed the ring in its mouth four times, hard. The sound echoed like gunshots through the house.

Seconds later, he heard heavy footsteps crossing the floor. The door whooshed open. "Who the hell is—" Ben Castle paused, staring at Hicks. "Sheriff," he said. "What the hell did my door ever do to you?"

There was no room for sarcasm in Hicks' life. Sarcasm was another language; a math he couldn't understand. Everything was straight and linear to Hicks. Cause and effect; A to B to C. Clear and simple.

Sarcasm, however, was a language that turned corners.

"This ain't no social call," Hicks said. "I need to talk to you about that biker."

Castle held a long horsehair paintbrush in one hand. His smock, an old dress shirt rolled up at the elbows, was stained with burnt umber, magenta, and thirty other pigments. He blinked at the sheriff. "Give me a break, Buddy. I'm working."

"Work? You mean paintin'."

"Why, of course, I'm paintin', Sheriff Hicks. It is my job. They actually pay me for it too. Quite well. Say, why don't you come in and enjoy the glorious air conditioning that God in His infinite wisdom has provided us?"

Hicks nodded. "Obliged."

Ben closed the door. He turned around, and Hicks had stopped in the center of the living room and was facing him.

"You lied to me."

"What are you talking about, Buddy?"

"You know damn well what I'm talking about."

Ben stared at him for a moment, then sighed. "Oh. Jesus, Hicks. Why do you have such a hard-on for this guy?"

"What the hell do you know about him? He's got a jacket! And I'm betting you know all about it."

"Christ," Ben muttered. "*Wrong*. When you came by yesterday, I had never met the guy."

"Bullshit."

Ben felt the heat rise in his face. "Bull*SHIT*, you dumb bastard. You asked me about Trager. Somebody named Trager. Okay? So this guy knocks on my door last night. Last night, Mister Hicks, okay? *After* you paid me a visit. And he introduces himself. Okay? His mother, Mr. Hicks, is the daughter of my best friend in the Army. The man who saved my life in 1917. And I never, ever, heard her married name before you mentioned it to me yesterday."

Hicks' face went slack. "Huh?"

"Precisely, you dumb ass. You don't fucking get it. My friend's name was Reese. His daughter's name was Reese. But her married name is Trager. And Colonel James Trager, your long-haired hippie friend, is the grandson of my best friend, Don Reese. Do you get it yet? You fucked up, Buddy. I never met Colonel James Trager until last night, after you came here. And he came to tell me his grandfather had died. That's all. No conspiracy. No collusion. And, just so you know, his grandson is just like him. A war hero. A man with guts. A man who won't take any shit from small-minded morons like you."

Hicks' face turned beet red. His jowls quivered in rage. "Trager's a drug-dealing commie! He's a long-haired queer, just like you! Neither one of you deserve to be called a hero! My brother—"

Hicks stopped suddenly, his eyes wide. Castle had taken a step back and was laughing.

"Really? A long-haired queer?" Castle sat down in an armchair and laughed at the sheriff. "My God. You really are just a typical redneck dumb fuck, aren't you? A queer. Christ."

Hicks took a step toward him. "My brother!" he shouted. "Cecil was a God-fearing, genuine war hero! He fucking led his platoon into an ambush to save our country! And the goddamn Chinks blew him up in some village in Korea that nobody can even find on a map anymore! And here you are, paintin' your pretty pictures, and Trager, pushing his heroin on—"

"Heroin? Where did you get that from? Come on, you can't be serious."

"That's straight out of your boyfriend's jacket, my friend. Heroin, opium, mary-g-wanna, what have you. A goddamn criminal. My brother, Cecil, was a real American hero. Not pinko scum like you."

Castle grinned and said, softly, "Get out." His fingers were claws digging into the arms of the chair. "Get. Out."

Hicks shook his finger. His eyes seemed too large, bulging. "I swear to fucking God that I'll throw Trager in the clink—and anyone else who aids or abets him. You got that, homo? Now, where is he? I know you know."

"I have no idea." Castle walked to the front door and opened it wide. Sunlight streamed into the dark room. "I have no idea, and I don't care. Now, get out of my house. You are not welcome here. And don't come back here without a search warrant. Am I clear?"

Hicks quivered with restrained fury. His red face turned a pasty white.

"Do you understand me, Buddy?"

"That's 'Sheriff' to you."

"No. You're just a clown to me. A redneck rodeo clown who stinks of hayseed and horseshit." Castle smiled. "Get out."

Hicks' lips trembled. His fingers fumbled with the snap on his holster.

"Out," Ben said. "This is my property, and you are now trespassing. Out."

Hicks forced himself to step forward. He stopped in the doorway. "Faggot," he muttered.

The door closed behind him. He heard the deadbolt slide into place, and then he heard Castle, behind the door, laughing.

Ben watched the sheriff through the window. Hicks walked back to the car, squeezed himself in, and slammed the door.

Ben let the drapes fall together, then walked back to his studio and tossed the paintbrush onto a work cart. The flat top was mottled with a spectrum of oils and acrylics. He gripped the edges of the cart and shook his head, trying to comprehend the manic bullshit that had just gone down. *Shit.* There would be no more work done today. Hicks had drained the joy, the energy, from him.

He poured himself a shot of Maker's Mark, thought better of it, and doubled it. Then he slugged it down in a single gulp.

The story he and Michel had come up with would hold Hicks off for a little while. But that redneck was a hunting dog, and he wouldn't give up until his quarry was either treed or killed.

"Damn." He thought he had buried all the suspicions about Trager and the black market. But he had missed an entry somehow; probably just one single line item in the Army's bottomless well of carbon copies. It was a stupid rookie mistake.

"Damn it."

Now, the situation had changed. Hicks had documentation, suspected charges—serious ones—and he could potentially use them as probable cause.

Obviously, careful hadn't been careful enough.

Michel had to help him now. Together they could figure out what to do about Hicks, and how to get rid of every trace of the original Army investigation.

To help Michel, Michel had to help him.

To save him.

To help him live.

6

HICKS SAT BEHIND the wheel in front of Castle's house, his knuckles clenched white around the steering wheel.

He shook out a Pall Mall and lit it with the dashboard lighter. He sucked the smoke in deep, his mind seeing only the muddied, olive image of his brother, floating in a Korean rice paddy, choking on his own blood, a torn, red crater in his chest.

He screamed then, his rage echoing inside the cruiser. A flock of starlings scattered from the nearest tree. He pounded his palms against the steering wheel, and he screamed and screamed until his throat was raw, and his voice echoed in his ears.

He finally came out of it, spittle dripping down his chin, and he realized the ringing in his ears was the radio, a scratchy voice calling his name.

He picked up the mic and squeezed it, shaking. He spoke slowly, deliberately. "This is Hicks. I copy."

Duke's voice crackled through the speaker. "Sheriff, we need you to get out to Riverdale, pronto. Ronnie Sheffield's daddy just called. They're in a panic. Ronnie went to the drive-in show last night, and she never came home."

Hicks cleared his throat. "Okay. So?"

"Here's the thing," Duke said. "The boyfriend is missing too, Kenny Cousins. And so's his new Mustang."

7

SUMMER TURNED THE black Camaro onto Croatoan and parked in front of her house. Her mother's 1959 Cadillac was in the driveway. She sagged in her seat. She looked at the old green siding, the dead plants in planters on the whitewashed porch. Home. Again. *Jiggedy jig.*

She listened to the radio for a few seconds, and to the low hum of her Camaro. The interior was cherry red, the exterior glossy black—Rob told her it was called "tuxedo black"—with custom red detailing, and it rode on custom tires with red trim. She had bought it from her mom's sister, Bessie, who took only $300 for a car worth maybe a whole grand. Aunt Bessie and Uncle Frank had bought the '69 Camaro brand new for their son, Dale. Dale had named the car Carlotta, as in, "*Come ride with us to the malt shop! It's a whole lotta car!*" Yeah. That was goofy old Dale. Just out of high school in '68, Dale got called up by the draft in October, only a month after they gave him the car, and found himself six months later, fresh out of boot camp at Fort Benning or Fort Bragg, *somewhere*, in some unpronounceable and mosquito-ridden Vietnam hellhole that the military called Hamburger Hill.

Then he went and got his legs blown off in a Viet Cong RPG attack, less than thirty seconds before a second shell blew away the rest of him. They shipped back his duffel bag and his dog tags. There was still dried blood in the middle of the A in DALE.

Bessie hated that car. Frank drove it sometimes, but Bessie just wanted to be rid of it. She said it still smelled like Dale. When she suddenly decided that Uncle Frank was going to buy her a new Galaxie 500, she mentioned the Camaro to Louise; and when Summer overheard her mother on the phone, she took $750 out of the savings account that her mother didn't know about, and had Rob drive her to Bessie's place across town. She threw down $200 on the Formica table in Bessie's kitchen and said, "Why not keep the car in the family?" Bessie sucked on a Chesterfield and pursed her lips. She really had been hoping for about $900, but on sight of Summer's instant green—and it *was* her own niece—"Well. I was thinking more like $450," Bessie said. Summer pulled another hundred from her purse, said, "Three hundred, Aunt B. Cash." She snapped her purse shut and crossed her arms. Bessie looked at the bills on the kitchen table, and started to cry. A few minutes later, Summer signed the registration and snapped up the keys.

She looked at her house, and a little laugh bubbled up from somewhere unexpected. God, her mother had been so mad. Aunt Bessie must have called her as soon as she'd driven away—in *HER NEW CAR!*—and Mama had been pacing back and front across the front porch, in some yellow and black blouse that made her look like a bumblebee. She had parked the Camaro at the curb. It had gleamed in the bright sunlight. "Doesn't it look nice, Mama?"

"GodDAMN it, you ungrateful girl!" Louise had been shaking in rage. "Who gave you permission to up and get that car from Sissy?"

Summer slowly walked up the sidewalk, head cocked, looking at her mama as if she were crazy. "It's all my money, Mama. I made it. I can spend it any way I want to."

"How the hell a girl like you get three hundred dollars to spend on such foolishness?"

"I work, don't I?"

She had shaken a bony finger at the Camaro, as if blaming it for all her troubles. "That's trifling! It's a waste of good money! You don't need a hot rod like some hoodlum!"

"But it's not—It was Aunt Bessie's."

"Sissy never had a lick a' sense and she never shoulda sold you that piece of trash! Now, you take that damn thing right back to her now and get your money back! You hear me?"

"Mama, I am *not* taking it back."

"You hear me? Now, you TAKE that GODDAMN HOT ROD *BACK* TO BESSIE RIGHT NOW! No daughter of mine—" Louise's whole body was shaking now as she jabbed her finger toward the Camaro. "Ain't no good girl that— Can't have a decent— You can't just up and—"

And then Summer had laughed. Clara Barkley across the street had been watching from an open window. The Willert boy had ridden by on a bicycle, then stopped to watch when Louise had started shouting. And that's when Summer knew for the first time, truly knew, with people watching, seeing exactly what her mother was, that her mother no longer held any power over her.

Louise had fallen quiet, still shaking. Then she turned around and slammed the screen door behind her. Maybe she had realized something then too.

Summer sat back in the driver's seat and looked at the front door, closed tight. "Oh, Ma," she whispered, and she turned off the engine. The radio stayed on. Sly was singing a simple song, and she snapped the knob to the left. The radio went silent, and she heard a mockingbird screaming at something across the street.

Her hand hesitated on the door handle. Sometimes it was just too much to go inside and deal with her. She shoved open the car door and pushed herself into the sun. She felt the weariness in her shoulders, closed the door, and started up the sidewalk, just wanting to get inside, away, into the coolness of her own room—and then she stopped, craving something warm and bright and alive, and she crossed across the lawn toward her garden behind the porch.

The scents hit her as a slight breeze wafted through the roses. She sat on her bench without even thinking. Her purse slid to the end of her arm and plopped onto the white gravel. She bent over, elbows on her knees, and rubbed her forehead with her palms. She whispered, "What am I doing?" Because it was him, wasn't it? And it was Rob. And him, and Rob.

"Shit," she whispered. "Shit, shit, shit."

She curled up on the bench, fetal position, one hand over her eyes.

And then her eyes blinked open.

How long have I been asleep out here?

She didn't get up at first, because she felt she couldn't even move. She had never felt this way before—completely at ease, without a single care—and she wanted to enjoy it forever. Her whole body was so relaxed. She smiled and murmured, "I feel like a Slinky." Was it because she fell asleep outside? Maybe she'd needed a quick nap like people needed a cup of coffee. Was it sleeping in the warmth of the sun? *Whatever.* But she forced herself to sit up, and like water through a funnel, she felt as though all the crap she had been dealing with had simply drained away in the warm embrace of the sunlight.

She glanced at her watch. 5:45. She pushed herself onto her feet and went through the front door. Smoke from her mama's Winstons, and the tinny sound of some black and white movie on the TV.

Louise sat absorbed in the afternoon paper's crossword puzzle and an old '40s movie on TV, and didn't look up as Summer walked by. She climbed the stairs, staying close to the wall where she had learned the steps didn't creak. She dropped her purse onto her bed and flipped off her shoes, then twisted the A/C dial from LO to HI. She went into the hall and took the upstairs phone off the maple gossip bench, stretching the cord as far as she could into her room. She closed the door and sat on the floor, her back against the door. She stared at the phone cradled in her lap.

Get the damn thing over with.

She dialed Rob's number and heard it ringing on the other end. She squeezed her eyes shut, listened to the metallic, hollow *riiinnnnggg*—

She hung up.

Her stomach was twisted in a knot. She didn't want to hurt him. It was wrong, she knew it. But she also knew how she felt last night in the garden, and in the shadows of Storybook Hollow.

Shit shit shit.

She put the handset to her ear and dialed.

The ringing through the wires sounded distant, unreal. Then someone picked up the phone. She heard the sound of fabric rustling as the phone moved across someone's shirt.

But no one said anything. She listened, then said, "Hello?"

She heard Rob say, "No, Dusty! Oh, oh man—" The phone rustled again, and she thought Rob said, "Hold on."

Someone said, "Crap!" in the background, and then Rob was on the phone. "Hello?"

"What was all that?"

"Oh, hey. It was Dusty. He pooped in the kitchen again." She tried not to laugh. "Now I've got to throw my sneakers in the washer."

Then she laughed once, and Rob said, "The brown smear goes halfway across the kitchen." And then she lost it, and Rob finally laughed with her.

"You're gonna hate me," Summer said when there was lull in the laughter.

"Give me a break. How can I hate the woman I love?"

Her breath stopped. She was silent for a second, filled with guilt that was a heavy weight in her gut. Then: "I've got to cancel tonight. I'm not feeling right."

"What? You're not still mad about the other night, are you?"

She shook her head. "I don't know. I just—" She trailed off. "I'm still tired from yesterday, and with the rush today."

"Look, why don't you take a nap? It won't start getting really good till at least nine or ten, just like every year. So I can still come pick you up in, like, three hours. Okay?"

She closed her eyes. "No, I don't think so. I think I'm just going to relax and get into bed. Why don't you go and have a good time? I know you will."

She heard him snap his fingers. He said, "Hold on," then, in the background, he said, "Let's go out." He came back on. "Sorry. Had to put Dusty outside." He sighed. "Ah, what the hell. I don't want to go without you. I'll just stay here and watch the tube. I picked up some new paperbacks last week in downtown Richmond, Ace Doubles. Chandler and Goulart, remember?"

"Who?"

Rob sighed theatrically and said, "Woman! How am I going to edumacate you to the science fiction world if you doesn't pay attention?"

She faked a laugh. "You don't have to."

"No. No, look. Tell you what. Hell, it's early. Why not?" He was talking to himself. "Listen, I'll drive to Roanoke. Why not? *McCabe and Mrs. Miller* is playing. I hear it's supposed to be pretty good." He didn't mention he had just seen the nude pictorial in the new issue of *Playboy* down at People's Drugs, which was now on his desk in his bedroom at home. "So, don't worry about it. We'll go out Sunday or something. Go to bed."

"Rob, you sure? I hate doing this to you."

"Summer, jeez, I'm fine. Just feel better. And get to bed. Okay?"

She felt her whole body sag in relief. Her stomach still squirmed from the guilt, but she knew this was what she had to do. And something quieter inside her, yet no less urgent, whispered to her with words that were secret and sexy.

"Okay?" he said.

"Yes, Crash," she said.

"Seriously, go to bed. Don't worry about me."

"Okay. Thanks, Crash. Don't enjoy the movie too much."

He laughed. "Not without you. 'Night."

"'Night, Rob."

She hung up and stared at the phone, then let out a long sigh. *That was done.* She closed her eyes. She still felt the weight of her lies, down deep in her gut, where secrets stirred.

He was going to find out. It was inevitable; she knew it, just like everybody in this damn podunk town knows everybody else's business the next day, like there was some kind of secret gossip hotline through the telephone wires.

He'll find out. Somebody would see her car at the motel. Then one of his buddies will let him in on it. Or maybe it'll be that Donna Cross from high school. She always had a thing for Rob, and she'd probably love to swoop in with the latest *Have You Heard?* and lay it all out there, and try and get Rob all for herself.

She could cancel with Michel. Yes. She *should* cancel.

Hell no. She wasn't about to cancel. They could go to the movies. Not the drive-in though. Somebody would see them there. The Hillview Theatre. Something just started, or was held over.

But someone could still see them.

The motel room. She nibbled her lower lip. *His room. Alone.* Maybe pick up some beer beforehand, or hit the ABC store. Ray Ray would sell her a bottle. Turn on the radio, maybe the TV, and just wait and see what happens. *Yes.* Sure, someone might recognize the Batmobile parked outside his room, but that was something she could explain away. *No, my car was in front of my house, because I was asleep in bed.* Or, *There are a lot of '66 Camaros across the country, and the one at the Patriot wasn't mine. What kind of girl do you think I am?* And that rumor probably wouldn't get back to Rob.

No matter what happened tonight, Summer knew in her heart that she was going to have to break up with him, and soon. And it wasn't just Michel—although he had certainly woken something up inside her. It was more. She just didn't feel the same about Rob as she had only a year ago. Maybe even a month ago. There was an empty spot in her soul that almost made her want to cry, because Rob had been a part of her for so long.

But now—

She carried the phone back to the bench, then locked the bedroom door and pulled off her shoes. She unzipped and stepped out of her stiff, pastel uniform. She pulled the drapes tight. The room was dark and cool. She had just enough time to rest up an hour or so, and then get ready.

Her stomach squirmed, in a way that was slinky and smooth, and the guilt tasted delicious.

She peeled off her under clothes and let the cool, soft sheets caress her bare skin.

She let out a breath, and she fell asleep in moments.

8

THE LIGHTS AROUND the mirror snapped on, and Summer liked the way the tiny white bulbs shone like crescents across her breasts.

Maybe he'd like it too.

"There's a Kind of Hush" rolled out of the speakers, whispering with static from distant WGH, and she mouthed along with the words. It was just after seven, and the sky was turning grey. She sat at her vanity and blow dried her hair, simultaneously brushing her long blonde hair. She squeezed out a mist of Aqua Net in a quick halo that would keep her hair where she wanted it without getting stiff. She wanted to look perfect for Michel—natural, like she was born looking perfect.

She slipped into her skimpiest pair of panties, two pink triangles with red, satin trim and a little bow in front. She tugged on a sheer, silk bra, the thinnest bra she owned, and realized her nips were going to poke out like she was going braless.

She smiled.

She opened the closet. She had no idea what she wanted to wear—nothing too fancy, just something simple. And sexy.

She picked out a blue, checkered blouse that accentuated her curves, and she left the top two buttons undone. Then she pulled on a pair of tight blue jeans and slipped on a white belt that hung low on her hips.

Nothing fancy. Just natural.

She picked up her mascara, and then her mother yelled up the stairs, "Summer! Come on down for dinner!"

What the hell? Mom hadn't cooked dinner in months. Usually Summer brought supper home from the dinette, and they ate separately, Mom watching TV, Summer up in her room, five or six records stacked on the turntable.

She opened her bedroom door and smelled grease and pepper and a hint of vinegar floating from the kitchen. She had planned on picking up something from the Atomic again. "Um, okay. Be right down."

Louise was at the stove as Summer walked in, watching four thin pork chops sizzle in bacon grease in a cast iron skillet. Steam rose from a bubbling pot of canned collard greens, next to a small pot of mashed potatoes. "Wow," Summer said.

Louise flipped the pork chops with a salad fork. "Felt like something homemade for a change."

Summer glanced at the box of instant potatoes on the counter, said, "Okay," then carried plates and silverware out to the dining room. She grabbed a bottle of Tab and some paper napkins off the kitchen counter, and in a few minutes her mother slid the pork chops onto a plate and scooped the collards and potatoes into old serving bowls trimmed with blue, stenciled roosters.

Her mother smiled as she sat at the table. "Now, this is nice."

Summer slid a pork chop onto her plate. "What's the occasion?"

Louise helped herself to the collards. "Nothing. Just thought we'd have a nice dinner together for a change. And besides, I thought we could talk a bit, and then watch some TV together."

"I can't, Ma," she said. "I've got time to eat, but I can't stay. Going out."

Louise looked up from her plate. "Again? Tonight?" She was silent as she sliced into a pork chop. "Going to the movies with Rob?"

Summer looked down at her plate. "Yeah." She took a bite of pork. *Damn.* It tasted just as good as when her mama had cooked them growing up. "With Tina too; some friends." She wasn't about to tell her the truth. No way.

Her mother's face tightened, and she gazed at Summer with eyes clouded with stern disapproval. "Trifling."

"It's the weekend, Ma."

Louise looked down at her daughter's blouse. "We had this discussion last night. You're *my* daughter, and I thought I taught you to dress like a lady."

Summer laid her fork across her plate. "I think this looks nice. It's not the 1950s anymore. This is the way girls dress nowadays."

"That is not the way a young lady should dress. I don't care what year it is. And those damn dungarees! I always hated it when you insisted on wearing those things to school, like a farm boy. And that top is too tight. It'll give Rob ideas."

Summer laughed. "You let me handle Rob."

"Boys. They'll all think you're a common tramp."

"Ma, come on. You know me better than that."

"But you don't know men. Kids your age think you know everything. But you don't know anything."

Summer pushed her plate away. "Why are you starting in on me again, Ma? For once, I'd like to have a day when you don't come down on me for something that doesn't meet your approval."

"That's what I wanted to talk to you about. You are going out way too much, little girl. You are trifling around with boys who aren't good enough to kiss your feet."

"Ma, Rob is the single nicest guy I've ever—"

"And what about that filthy biker from the other night? I know you've been seeing him behind my back."

Summer's eyes flared. She couldn't know. "Rob. Rob's my boyfriend."

"He's a goddamned male. Men are dogs. Trust me. I knew his parents, and they hung around with a loose crowd, just like you."

"Ma, it isn't 1930 anymore. You have got to—"

"You should be married at your age. Having children. Living like a proper woman. *Not* going to the picture shows all the time, and listening to your damn music. You need to settle down, with a man who respects you—not some lowlife biker. Not like your damn father."

Summer stared into her mother's eyes and whispered, "That is never going to happen. I hate this place. I've tried to tell you this, to get you to understand. But you never listen. You just want me to be a little, silent doll baby. I'm not like that. I've never been like that. There's nothing here for me. Not one damn thing."

Louise sat back, surprised. Her head trembled on her pale neck. "What more could you want? We have everything a girl could want right here."

"Shit, Ma. Junior League every Wednesday? In a frilly, pink dress? Friday Pot Luck with the drunks over at the Lions Club? Church every Sunday? Should I join the choir and sing 'Holy Fucking Holy'?"

Louise's mouth fell open.

"The same four ugly walls, the same dumbass TV shows every night, just don't cut it." She slammed her hands down on the table. Silverware clanged against the plates. "I do not belong here. Not anymore. Nobody sane would want to stay in this hillbilly town. Someday, you're going to have to let me go—or, goddamn it, I'll walk out on my own, and you can kiss my ass on the way out."

Summer stood up. She wadded her napkin into a ball and threw it onto a pork chop. "I guess I'm not hungry. But thank you so much for the fucking conversation."

She turned her back on Louise and went upstairs. She locked the bedroom door, then let herself breathe. "Jesus fucking Christ."

She sat on the edge of her bed and stared at herself in the vanity mirror. She thought she looked pale. She was brown and had the bikini lines to prove it, but in the pale light from her vanity, she seemed whitewashed, and she suddenly hated herself, hated this room, this house, this whole damn town.

She stood and snapped on the radio. James Taylor was halfway through "Fire and Rain," and she took a cigarette out of her purse and lit up. She kept a glass ashtray on her desk, filled with spare change. Her father had brought it back from a Stonebridge Volunteer Fire Department convention in '61. The bottom of the ashtray was printed with *Greetings from the Atlantic City Boardwalk!* She poured the coins onto the top of her vanity, letting pennies and dimes roll into the thick shag carpet.

She sat at the vanity and stared into the mirror. She took a drag on the Salem and tapped the ashes into the ashtray. Her reflection stared back at her.

Tramp.

She looked down at her checkered shirt. Hell, she looked like Ellie May Clampett.

"Fuck this."

Summer started on her eyes—light blue eye shadow, black eye liner, and mascara down the length of her long lashes. She wiped away her lipstick with a Kleenex, then pulled out a dark shade of lip gloss from the top drawer and rolled it onto her lips.

Joe Cocker's voice came through the bathroom window, and she went to the closet, peeling off her blouse and jeans, and tossed them into a corner.

Tramp.

She shoved aside coat hangers and yanked out her tightest jeans, a pair of white, hip-hugging bell bottoms. She wriggled her ass into them, holding her breath as she buttoned the waist. Then she pulled out a soft white cotton top with bell sleeves and pulled it on around her neck and shoulders—then stopped. She unsnapped her bra and threw it onto her bed. She tugged down the top and tied it in a knot directly under her breasts. She left the buttons undone.

Summer looked in the mirror. Her nipples poked out like bullets, and the vanity lights gleamed off her tanned stomach.

She smiled.

She stood in front of the open closet, looking at the shoes lined up on the carpet, and picked the new high-heeled sandals she had bought a few weeks ago down at J. M. Fields. The heels and soles were cork, and the straps were off-white rope. She pulled them on, then looked at herself in the mirror. She tugged her white hip huggers down an inch, exposing more of her stomach, getting daringly close to the top of her pubic hair, the way the girls wore pants in *Playboy*.

She sprayed Cachet—the good stuff—on her throat. On impulse, she unzipped her jeans and sprayed once just above her panty line. That might get his attention.

She checked herself in the mirror and nodded. She threw her keys and cigarettes into her fringe purse, then stared at the pack of matches from the movie last night.

She turned down the volume on the stereo and stepped softly to the door. She opened it a crack and listened. Louise had cut on the TV in the living room, and she could smell the smoke from her Winston as it trailed up the stairs.

Summer pulled off her sandals and stepped into the hallway. Her mother's bedroom door was open, and she slipped inside and pulled open the bottom drawer of her mother's cedar dresser. Louise had hidden a woven straw basket underneath slips and garters that hadn't been worn in thirty years. Summer lifted out the lingerie and saw what she wanted—her father's lighter, on top of a pair of ivory dice, a poker chip, and little mementos he had left behind that her mother, for whatever reason, had kept to herself. She replaced the underwear atop the basket and sneaked back into her room. The lighter was a shiny silver Zippo, painted with the Marine Corps emblem on the side. She tested the lighter with her thumb, and it caught on the second try, casting a warm, yellow glow across her face.

One more glance in the mirror. She was a tall, blonde vision in white cotton and tanned flesh. Wide hoop earrings gleamed against the brown smoothness of her skin. Bangle bracelets jangled on both wrists, a mixture of silver and turquoise and gold plate. The light gleamed off her glossy lips, and the aroma of her perfume hung around her in a floral haze.

"Dressed to kill," she said.

She slung her purse over her shoulder and picked up her heels by the straps. She went barefoot down the stairs, a ghost in the house's twilight, and listened at the bottom. Some TV theme song played—a tune she had heard almost every weekday for years, in endless reruns. *Gomer fucking Pyle.* She knew what she would write in her diary for today. *I listened as the mindless, endless music played on in the background, and felt like I was going mad.*

She had planned on slipping through the front door while Ma was focused on Gomer's hilarious hijinks. Instead, she tiptoed through the kitchen, past the greasy iron skillet on the stove and the half-filled pots of mashed potatoes and greens. She slipped on her John Lennon sunglasses and her shoes, and she disappeared into the twilight maze of dusky roses, growing wild and tall.

9

HE FELT IT as the sun dropped toward the curve of the earth. It tingled through him like a fever in the dense, cool darkness, though sunlight had never once kissed the spot where he lay. The temperature was dropping imperceptibly to those walking in the sun, but to him, it ticked lower and lower toward the embrace of the night.

Michel rose from his bed roll on the floor of the cold, stone chamber and pulled on a clean shirt from his pack. Then he stood in the darkness, silent, staring into the still emptiness.

It was wrong. He wanted nothing to do with this. He only wanted to move out, to ride. He wanted to meet Summer at his motel room and take her away; to ride the world with her arms around his waist and the endless road winding beneath his tires.

But it was wrong, for both of them. He felt an obligation to help Ben, and would never shirk his duty as a friend. If this were the only way Ben could go on, to fulfill his life's dreams—

Damn. He would do it. He had to do it.

But Summer didn't deserve the long fate he had borne. They had found each other once again in the long, endless night, but something felt different this time.

He loved her. He couldn't help but love her.

But Summer, she deserved the light.

He looked at his black, Army-issue watch. 8:45.

Almost sunset.

Outside, he hopped onto his bike. The blue-grey sky was streaked with blood-tinged clouds. He revved the bike, spitting gravel and leaves, and drove the snaking mountain road to the quiet homes on the outskirts of Stonebridge. He parked in front of Ben's house, and as the bike's engine fell silent, he listened to the crickets, and the locusts high in the pines, and the low murmur of a television from across the street.

Ben had the door open for him before he reached the stoop. Michel smelled the aroma of butter and charred steak coming from the kitchen, and Ben's breath smelled of French Cabernet. "I wasn't sure you'd be coming back." Ben smiled, but there was something else, tremulous, behind his eyes.

Fear.

"Just finished supper. Thought I'd get some work done if you weren't going to show."

The lights were on in Ben's studio, and Michel moved moth-like toward the paintings angled against the walls. He flipped through the oils closest to the doorway, and behind him he heard Ben pop a cork from a bottle of wine. These were football players, suggested by splashes and dabs of color. He almost said, "Leroy Neiman?" Then he noticed darker lines underneath the bright swaths, overlapping thin, dark lines on top, creating shadows and depth, suggesting subtle facial features and details that went beyond magazine art and entered another realm. A blur of brown and gold arcing over the team. A running back in red and white, catching a pass. A blonde cheerleader hanging in mid-air in the background, her pom-poms an explosion of color. Neiman was good, but Ben—he was on another level.

Ben came in with glasses of deep, ruby red Bordeaux, the open bottle canted awkwardly under his arm. A smile came to Michel's lips. He could smell the wine over the scents of paint and seared meat. "Is that a '62?"

Ben shrugged and handed him a glass, then held up the bottle. He grinned. "You're good." He looked at the glass of red in the light. "Latour."

Michel let himself smile. "I know."

Ben took a sip of wine and gestured toward the painting. "Had a magazine in D.C. call me. They wanted an illo to go along with an article about Virginia football rivalries. The editor told me, 'We want it like those sports pieces Neiman Marcus does for the glossies, you know?'"

"Neiman Marcus?" Michel laughed. He was actually happy to be here with Ben, enjoying an old feeling that he didn't even know he'd been missing: togetherness.

"So, I said, yeah, I know Neiman," Ben said. "And this is what I came up with. Hung out at a coupla Stonebridge High games a few years back, made some sketches, found a coupla Leroys for reference, and I gave 'em a genuine Neiman Marcus."

"It's better than Leroy Neiman. The shadows. The details. Compared to him—"

Ben shrugged. "Yeah, well. So I get a call from the editor, and he says, it's not what they wanted at all. Not like the sports guy at all. Looks like some monkey threw paint and shit all over the canvas and called it art. That's what he said."

"But it's clearly—"

"Doesn't matter." Ben sipped his wine and stared at the canvas. "So I kept the kill fee. I've got the painting. And maybe it'll sell to some rich New Yorker next month for two or three times what they were going to pay me. You'd be amazed at what sells. Doesn't matter how good it is. Only if somebody likes it, and has enough money."

Michel pointed at the figure in the background. "She—"

"Hm," Ben said, swallowing wine. "Beautiful girl. Summer Moore. Cheerleader, three years ago, I guess."

Two swirls of cadmium red and a curve of white. Daubs of flesh-colored acrylics, and a question mark of yellow-white. Legs curled, breasts floating in mid-jump—and he's recreated Summer.

Ben said, "You've met her, I hear."

"Word gets around." Michel moved to another row of paintings. Ben had painted a series of portraits, all writers: Doyle, Darwin, Verne, Dostoyevsky, Twain, Dickens, Melville, Poe, Shakespeare, and even Edgar Rice Burroughs. Quotes from their stories were woven into their clothes, around vases and tables, merging in three dimensions with the backgrounds. Another series showed animals frozen in mid-motion, the backgrounds blurred, as if they were captured in freeze frames. Another row held exaggerated landscapes of mystical places—Stonehenge, Delphi, Machu Picchu, the moai of Easter Island—limned with unearthly light from stars and nebulae and a whorl of galaxies. "One of my latest series," Ben said. "I don't know if they'll ever sell or not, but I like doing them."

Michel ran his finger down the length of an archway of tilted stones. "Arches, openings—the ancient Mayans believed they were doorways to the beyond. The afterlife."

Ben sipped his wine. "That's the kind of feeling I'm trying to evoke. That we just have to open the door, and walk through."

Then Michel stopped. Ben cleared his throat behind him. Michel's hand was on the painting of the battlefield at St. Mihiel. He stared at it, silent.

From somewhere outside, they heard the muffled pops of fireworks exploding in the distance. Ben said, "July Fourth fireworks up at the hotel, the new one by the natural bridge and Carter Caverns. Tourists won't hang around for sundown tomorrow since it's a Sunday, so they're setting them off tonight."

Ben took a seat in an easy chair. Michel took the other chair. Ben placed his glass on the walnut lamp table between them.

"All right. So, what's the deal with 'Nam?"

Michel stared at the light playing through his wine.

"What the hell happened with you? Why did you go dirty?"

Michel sipped the Latour and stared into its depths. "It wasn't exactly like that. Not the way you think."

"Everything we had on you—"

"You had nothing except accusations and innuendoes. Most of which *I* planted myself."

"Why the hell would you plant allegations against yourself?"

"Look. I *was* dirty. But I wasn't as bad as you were led to believe—not the way you think." He took a drink and placed the glass between them. "You had testimony, I'm sure, that I was dealing black tar and opium and thai sticks. Right?" He didn't wait for Ben to answer. "I never dealt in any of that. I only dealt in grass."

"That's not what we—"

"I know, I know. Look. I just sold marijuana. I never stole American supplies and sold them to the VC. But I needed to make money, and I needed to change things. It was absolutely mandatory that I established a bad rep over there. I needed to deter the amateurs. I didn't need any redneck soldiers trying to carve a drug empire back home when they shipped out. I was after the pros already over there. The bad ones. Evil. I was after their cash."

Ben stared at him.

"I used most of my profits to create new lives for the GIs here in the states.

You were over there. Some guys got into it. They went animal. Wearing VC ears and scalps as mementos."

"None of that has been proven."

"I saw it, Ben. I was there. You were only a consultant. But I lived it. I breathed the blood on the wind."

Ben looked away. "Christ."

"I did a lot of things over there that I'm not proud of. Some were for sheer survival. And I realized, once I landed, that I could actually help some of the guys who had been drafted into it—the ones who were too poor or too ordinary that their parents couldn't buy them out of Vietnam. The ones who couldn't take it were easy to spot. They drank too much. They laughed too loud. So many were just boys." He held a fist against his chest. "I could feel them in here, Ben. Going berserker, or suicide, was the next step for them. So I decided to help them come back home, no matter what it took. And it takes money. So I stole arms and supplies and drugs, all from the NVC, and I resold it on the black market. I did it to help, Ben. My influence"—and he looked up, into Ben's eyes—"and you'll learn this—*your* influence—can't replace dollar bills."

Michel sipped the wine. "Not all men are wolves like you and I."

Ben found himself nodding. He understood all too well.

"I ended up helping some Vietnamese families too—homes, villages, that our guys destroyed, simply for fun."

Ben looked up at him. "There was no evidence that you—"

Michel smiled. "No, there isn't. The things that are most important, I do in the shadows. That's why I don't want you cursed with this semblance of a life—or anyone else, for that matter." He gestured toward the St. Mihiel painting. "I didn't save your life all those years ago just so I could curse you later."

"It's a goddamned gift. A second chance." He refilled their glasses, and he stared at the shimmer of light playing through the cabernet. "Okay. 'Nam. You saved lives. You lived a life. You lived. This is my only chance. Mikey—" He fell suddenly silent and took a long, deep breath. "Mikey, I don't want to die alone. Hell, I don't want to die. Not like this, to something black and invisible. Give me a sword in my hand and a woman in my arms." Ben grinned softly. "Give me another shot."

Michel turned away. "You're asking for a life without light."

"Yeah. I guess I am."

"You'll have to change. Everything will have to change. Including your identity. Many times."

"I've thought about that. Thinking about New England. Change my painting style, my subjects." Ben's eyes twinkled. "Maybe become a popular, yet reclusive, artist you'd read about in *Time* or the *New Yorker*."

"You will have enemies."

Ben laughed. "Worse than the Krauts? Worse than Hicks?"

"You have no idea. White knights. Families. Organizations. All on the same mission—to destroy those who they consider inhuman. And if they find you, they will try to kill you."

Ben shook his head. "Michel, my soul, here, is dead already. The only thing keeping me going is my art. It's more alive than I am."

"You will need to feed." Michel touched Ben's arm. "The people you walk among will soon become as cattle to you. There will be times when the need is upon you, and you may not be able to maintain control." He stood, wine glass in hand, and went to the window. He moved aside the drapes and peered out into the night, but all he saw was a Mustang convertible, and the blurred swing of a bat, and two pale breasts smeared with blood. "Can you ever be prepared for that?"

"There are days I hate myself. I won't lie to you. I dream about 'em sometimes. I've killed men in three wars. Kids, pointing their damn guns at me. What other choice did I have, Michel? And I'll kill again, if I have to."

"Yes, you will," Michel said. "And that is what makes us both monsters."

Ben stared at his wine. Michel went across the room, flipping back canvases, becoming absorbed in Ben's various visions of the world.

He finished his wine and stared at the empty glass. He turned around. Ben's wine was long gone, the bottle emptied.

Michel rolled up the sleeve of his right arm. He pulled the knife off his belt, and looked at Ben.

The old man pushed himself out of the chair. Michel grabbed Ben's wrist, and his grip was cool, strong like iron. He pulled Ben toward him and twisted his wrist, palm up. "This could take minutes," Michel said. "Or it could take days. Believe me, my friend. There will be pain. I know of a place, close by, where no one will walk at night—where you may turn. There, no one should hear you."

"Oh. Okay," Ben said.

"Ben. Seriously. There will be pain."

Ben stared emptily into Michel's eyes. "Pain? With a second shot at—" He stopped. Nodded. "Whatever it takes, Mikey. Okay? What else do I have?"

Michel's eyes were wide and dark. Unreadable. He sliced the blade down his forearm. Thick black blood oozed up from the gash like oil. Ben shivered. The rich, heavy aromas of earth and blood intermingled, swirling up into his nostrils like some intoxicating smoke.

And, impossibly, he smelled a hint of roses.

Michel held out his wrist to Ben. He smiled, humorlessly, his eyes nightblack, dead, his long canines gleaming.

"Drink, my friend," Michel said, "and be damned."

10

SHE PULLED INTO the motel parking lot with a spray of gravel and almost parked in front of Michel's room, but even at dusk the sky was still too light, and she definitely didn't need any rumors about her car being seen anywhere around the Patriot, proving that them two sinners must be shacking up at the no-tell motel. A gravel drive led around the back of the Patriot, so she followed the drive behind Michel's room and parked on the nearby grass, in the shadow of a dumpster. There was no way anyone could see her car unless they were looking for it.

She walked around the end of the motel and unlocked the door. She stepped in, looked around, found what she wanted, and then she walked to a breezeway near the main office and filled the square, plastic bucket with a loud tumble of ice from the ice machine.

She went back to the room, made sure the drapes were shut tight, and tore the crinkly, white paper off a drinking glass. She had stopped by the ABC store after leaving her mother sitting in her usual spot on the sofa, and bought a bottle of Jack Daniel's from Ray Ray Pollard behind the counter. She poured herself a cup of Jack on the rocks. The bourbon sloshed cold on her tongue, down her throat, and she poured another. She fluffed the pillows against the backboard of the bed closest to the window and turned on the black and white TV. Her only choices were reruns: *The Andy Williams Show*, filled with dancers in white, sequined bell bottoms dancing to ancient big band tunes; *Mission Impossible*, which she thought was boring and an outgrowth of the American War Machine; and a couple of daytime game shows taking up prime time. But all she saw were images of her mother, and the echo of her voice, and she still smelled those damn greasy pork chops.

She snapped off the TV and turned on the radio next to the bed. She found WGH and let the jangle of "Green Tambourine" wash over her. She stared at the blank TV, and a lone tear trickled down her cheek. A sip of bourbon, and another tear, and she couldn't hear the music for her sobbing.

This town, this fucking town.

It came out of nowhere, a raw burst of silent, incomprehensible rage; and she threw the glass blindly, heard it crash against the mirrors and tinkle into the sink. Then larger pieces clattered down like heavy rain, crashing like church chimes.

Oh.

Oh shit.

A jagged corner of the mirror dropped off the wall, into the sink.

She stood and saw only half-reflections of herself in the spider-webbed glass, one hand on her cheek, her mouth open in surprise.

"Shit on a stick."

Then she took a swig of Jack straight from the bottle, and laughed.

11

THAT SNEAKY LITTLE *bitch!* Louise slammed Summer's bedroom door. She had sneaked out, damn it, right out from under her nose.

I didn't teach her that. Her damn daddy did that. Taught her how to sneak around! "Damn that little girl!" She walked back downstairs and stood in the entry hall, *tap-tap-tapping* the newspaper against her thigh like a metronome. That little girl of hers was always looking for trouble, and *damn* if she hadn't found another way to make her angrier than ever.

She lit another Winston. The television was singing about ring around the collar. She muttered, "Bleh," and clicked the dial from CBS to NBC to ABC. Nothing. Not one goddamn thing to watch. She turned the dial to UHF.

"—course, sinners, you know, don't know they're sinning."

"Ah." *Finally.* A low organ hymn played in the background, and she sat down while her favorite TV evangelist, Brother Enos Purvis from Virginia Beach, Virginia, pontificated on his righteous, godly, weekly broadcast, *Pathway to the Light.*

She put the crossword on the arm of the sofa and wondered about Brother Purvis' hair. All that silver-white, combed straight back and fluffy on the sides, sure did make him a handsome fella.

"—and neither do the kids these days. They don't know what they're singing, or listening to, or even doing! I was preaching one Sunday on the evils of the kids' music today, what they call the rock and roll music. And afterwards, a mother came up to me and told me about her teenage son, and how he listens to rock and roll all the time, and how rebellious he has become. Rebellious, and argumentative—defying authority at home and in school, and even refusing to go to church on Sundays."

Louise said, "Oh, yes." That was Summer, all right.

"That junk is on the transistor radios and on their record players 28 hours a day. And you can't tell me they're listening to the beautiful lyrics, because you can't understand a word that the Beatles or Mick Dagger are saying. No, the kids are hearing only the beat of the jungle music! It twists inside them like a vile serpent, hypnotically making them dance like heathens in Africa, praying to their vile, un-Christian gods. Those jungle drums go straight into their bodies, causing them to move like hoochie-coochie gals in the big cities, to dance wantonly and without moral guidance—the guidance of the Bible!"

Oh. Lord, yes. Some of these things she had believed for years, about the music's heathen jungle rhythms, and what kind of filthy, dirty thoughts the beat could provoke in today's youth, and about the blatantly obscene lyrics. And to think this is the music her little girl listened to! No wonder.

"It is a lure of the Devil. Rock and roll is a demonic symphony, and Satan himself is its infernal composer! Sure, it all sounds so sweet and safe at first, even though most of us can't understand the words! And that is why this rock and roll music is so insidious. It's like a drug.

It is! Addictive gibberish! And it's no wonder that so many kids who listen to this garbage day in and day out are doing the drugs, now, is it? See, the music starts off innocently enough, but then the jungle beat comes in, pulse-pounding, and it starts kids wanting to move their bodies. Then the electric guitars start playing, making these weird, hellish sounds no instrument here on God's earth should make, sounding like nothing so much as the fevered whisperings of demons. And, trust me, friends, this gets the kids to start thinking sinful, lustful thoughts—and worse.

"Burn them. Burn their filthy records and their blasphemous tape tracks. It's the only answer. Burn them in a bonfire of righteous destruction, dedicated to the Glory of the Lord! And when the black smoke of evil rises to Heaven, the Lord our God will smell the fires of salvation and will smile down upon us, and our children will bathe in the light of Almighty God."

She stared at the television. Smoke curled from her cigarette, and an inch of ash fell off and landed on her right slipper.

"Well," she said to the television. "Well. I wonder what that tramp daughter of mine is up to tonight."

12

SOMETHING WILD HUNG in the night air, a perfume without a scent. Michel felt the summer heat rising off the black road beneath his tires. The taste in his throat burned like raw alcohol. The doctor's diagnosis had been correct. It was the poison that burned; the cancer that had tainted each drop of Ben's blood.

To Michel's eyes, the pale floodlights focused on the Patriot's sign were as bright as lightning bolts. He parked in front of his room. The purr of the bike wound down. He sniffed the air, smelled the bike's engine, and the smell of cut grass. And he detected Summer, her own soft scent underneath the aroma of her perfume. It was the sweet scent of her skin, the soft aroma of her long hair, drifting from under the door of his room. Then—

He leapt off the bike. He detected two other scents, faint, like ghosts—and then he tasted the sharp tang of blood on the air. His hand closed like iron around the doorknob. The metal bent beneath his grip.

Summer stood at the sink with her finger under the cool, running water. Suddenly the mirror was filled with a swirl of darkness, glaring at her with two crimson eyes, a glowering beast. She spun. "Michel? What the hell?"

He stopped in the center of the room. "Where are they?" He took in the broken mirror, a pile of broken glass on the sink.

"Who?"

He sniffed the air. They had been there, hours ago. "Were you here? Did they hurt you?"

"Who?"

"The sheriff and his lackey."

"Lackey?"

"Blood. I smell it. I swear, if they hurt you—"

"No, no one's been here. Just me." Summer held up her hand. He took in the blood dripping down her finger. "I broke a glass. And the mirror. A little. I cut myself cleaning up." She looked in the glass shards over the sink. No beast. No red eyes. Only Michel.

"I never would have forgiven myself if—" He gently took her injured hand. Just a scratch on the tip of her index finger. He kissed her palm.

"Are you making the boo-boo go away?"

He had been too worried when he crashed into the room. Yes, they had been there—hours before Summer ever arrived. Now he saw her really for the first time tonight. Her white top and pants contrasted against the dark tan of her skin, her golden hair.

"You're beautiful."

Her lips parted, as though to say something, and he crushed her to him. He tasted the bourbon lingering on her tongue, and he was filled with her. He held her tight, their mouths merged together, and felt the guilt wash over him—about Ben, about putting Summer in harm's way, and about the depth of his feelings for her. He did not want to turn her. She deserved a life in the sun.

He had to tell her what he was—what the darkness was truly all about.

Their lips parted, and he held her away from him. He looked at the cracked mirror, concentrating on his reflection.

"I've got to take care of this," he said.

"Where are you going? It's after ten."

"I've got to see a guy about fixing the mirror. And I kind of messed up the doorknob."

She walked with him to the door and saw the mangled metal that had been the doorknob. "Wow."

He stepped out onto the sidewalk and said, "Stay here."

Tucker Coe sat in the padded office chair behind the counter. In the gap between his thighs, foam rubber bulged out from flaky cracks in the worn vinyl seat. A rerun of *Mannix* played in a monotonal static on the black and white. Mike Connors sat behind the wheel of his Cuda convertible, speeding after a black sedan along the turns of the Pacific Coast Highway.

The bell jangled on the door as Michel came in. Coe had his feet up on the desk. The office smelled of stale cigarettes and boiled cabbage. Coe looked over his shoulder. "Oh! Mister—I mean, Colonel Trager! Nice to— How are—" He swung his feet off the desk to stand at attention. "What can I do for you tonight?"

"Tucker," Michel said slowly, "I need a favor."

Coe seemed to sway on his feet. "Oh, oh, anything, Colonel. Anything."

"Good, Tucker. Good." Michel lowered his voice to almost a whisper. —*Why don't you sit down, Tucker?*

The chair creaked as Tucker sat back. His watery eyes stared without blinking.

—Tucker. I need something fixed in my room.

"Oh," Tucker said, softly. "Oh, sure, sure, no problem."

—Tucker, I need a new mirror over the sink. And a new doorknob. You can do that for me, can't you?

"Sure, Colonel, sure. Easy peasy."

—Easy peasy, Michel said, smiling. *—The doorknob needs to be fixed tonight. Tonight, so I can lock the door.*

"Tonight. Okay, okay, I can do that tonight, sure. Got an extra out in the shed."

—Sheriff Hicks broke the mirror and the doorknob, Tucker. He wants me to take the blame. Did you know he sneaked into my room, Tucker? Sneaked into my room like a

common thief?

Tucker squirmed lower into the chair. Michel felt the man's heart start racing. "I heard he'd come by, and Mr. Haynes, he had to let him in, he HAD to, but, but he, the sheriff, he—"

—Tucker, Tucker. Not to worry, trust me. The shadows lengthened. The room grew colder, darker. *—See, you're going to bill the sheriff for everything. Everything.*

"The sheriff?" Tucker's heart raced erratically. His hands gripped the edge of the chair. "But I can't, Colonel. He'll lie about me to Mr. Haynes, and tell him *I* did it! He'll blame it all on me, I know—"

Michel tugged at the edges of Tucker's concentration, willing the room to grow darker, colder. Tendrils of night swirled along the floor, seeping from the shadows, the places where light could not reach. They snaked up the swivel chair, wrapping themselves around Tucker's arms, his legs, holding him in the chair.

Tucker's breath slowed. He sagged in the chair.

—Tucker.

His eyes blinked open.

—Tell me what happened here today with the sheriff. Everything.

Tucker focused on Michel's black, infinite eyes. "Sheriff and Duke came by 'fore I come on tonight. They made Mr. Haynes give 'em the key to your room. I don't know what they did. Mr. Haynes thinks they was after something—maybe looking for guns or somethin'."

—What else?

"Nothin'. That's alls I heard."

There was nothing in the room to find. All his cash was either on him or hidden in a compartment on his bike. But if Hicks had been in there for some other reason—

—Tucker. Repair the doorknob to my room. Tonight. Understood?

Tucker nodded.

—You will have the mirror repaired in the morning. Listen to me. Tonight I entered my room, only to discover that someone had broken in and trashed the room. They broke the mirror and a glass and the doorknob. I do not know who or why. Understand?

"Yeah," Tucker said. He licked his dry lips. "Yeah."

—Good. I then came straight here to see you, and you promised to fix the doorknob immediately. You told me nothing about the sheriff. Your secrets are safe.

"Yes, sir. Yes, sir."

—Good. Now, please go get me some band-aids.

"Band-aids?"

—Band-aids.

Tucker shoved out of the chair and went into the back room. He came out with a handful of band-aids in his palm. "I think I'll go get that doorknob now."

Michel said, "You do that," and he went to the front door.

As soon as he stepped outside, he smelled her. Summer's perfume hung in the still, warm air, and he knew she had been out here, at the door.

Watching.

He looked across the parking lot. She stood by his motorcycle, smoking, staring at him.

Does she know?

He led her back into the room. He kissed the cut on her finger, then covered it with a band-aid. Then he went through the room, looked in the drawers, behind them, under the bed, between the cheap mattress and box springs. "The sheriff and that deputy were in here earlier. The owner let them in. They probably searched the room, looking for anything illegal. And I needed to make sure Hicks didn't leave something behind that he could use against me."

"Like drugs," Summer said. "A setup."

He nodded.

"I wouldn't put it past him," she said. "He's always been a crooked bastard. He's been needing to be taken down a notch for years now."

She crushed her cigarette in the ashtray. "You want to get out of here for a while, or—"

"Yes," he said. "I've wasted too much time on your backwater lawman."

Summer picked up the bottle of Jack Daniel's off the nightstand, took a swig, and held it out for him. The bourbon slid smooth down his throat, weak, like tea. It wasn't like Ben's bourbon.

"If you want to go see a movie—"

He opened the door for her and peered out into the night.

She had to learn. She had to understand who he was, and why she could not be allowed to love him.

"Actually, there's something I need to show you."

He looked into her eyes. She met his gaze without blinking.

She knows.

"There's something you need to see. In the woods."

13

THE BIKE'S TIRES rumbled like thunder over the planks in the Craddock Creek bridge. Summer's hair whipped behind her, and the night seemed to sing, beating with a secret heart she had felt only in her dreams.

She had known his eyes for years; but she hadn't known that he was—

Hadn't she? When she watched him in the office, manipulating Tucker like a marionette, hadn't something inside her, some secret grey cells, already known what she would realize?

Last night, when she had offered her neck to him, he had scraped his teeth against her bare flesh, and memories had welled up, exploding like hot tears—

His eyes.

And they were the eyes of the beast she had seen downtown.

I know.

I know what he is.

She pressed her nose into his back; smelled the scent of the detergent on his shirt; smelled the deep, earthy aroma from his skin.

And I want him so bad.

Michel slowed the bike. Black Snake Road. And then Michel said, "Hold on," and they leaned into the turn, at the old ivy-covered bus stop at the intersection with Nicewander Road.

"Oh shit," she breathed, almost inaudibly; but he heard her over the snarl of the motorcycle.

"What is it?"

Her stomach twisted. Her friends, they'll all see her. With *him*. Oh God. And she was sure that, by tomorrow morning, someone would tell Rob all about her.

"I thought you wanted to show me something."

"Yes, I do. I—"

She peered ahead, over his shoulder. "You want to go to the party?"

What party? Then he got a whiff of smoke, of cigarettes mingled with grass. He smelled sweat, and perfume, and heard rock and roll and laughter on the breeze. He had been so caught up in Summer—in her closeness, and in his duty to her, to save her, even from himself.

"Shit," Summer murmured. "Shit."

He pulled up between the two gates and the overgrown private roads. To the right lay darkness, and the shame that hung over him in a cloud of clotted blood.

He looked down the path to the left. The iron chain had been broken, and its two rusted strands lay across the drive. There were already more than a hundred people back there, and he was sure more would come soon.

He wanted to bolt. This was too close.

Way too close.

"Summer."

She gestured toward the left gate. "It's this way. The Sugden place. These two farms have been abandoned since forever."

He looked into her eyes. Wide and wondering. And her soft red lips.

There are no coincidences.

The bike thumped over the thick chain on the drive leading toward the party.

The rutted gravel drive led in a gentle curve through the trees. Stars blazed between the branches. Twigs and a covering of years-old leaves blanketed the drive, but Michel could tell that cars had come through here tonight, casting leaves to the roadside.

He saw the glimmer of lights, low through the trees. He scented a mixture of perfumes and colognes, and gasoline and carbon monoxide from cars, and old hay, and fox spoor intermingling with the high grasses, and the fresh aroma of the pines. Cigarette smoke, and the tang of salt and sweat, merged with the scratch of car radios, most tuned to the same station, sounding tinny and distant through the trees.

He slowed the bike as he came to the first few cars parked back in the shadows between the trees. Summer's breath felt hot on the back of his neck, and Grace Slick's powerful voice echoed with a plea to go ask Alice. Michel flicked his head toward the silhouettes of a couple making out against the bole of a tree. The boy's hand was up the girl's blouse, and the girl was moaning softly into his hot mouth.

"Oh my God," Summer whispered. "That's Christy Conner." A wicked gleam appeared in her eyes. "But that isn't Hoss."

"Hoss? The big man on *Bonanza*?"

She squeezed his waist. "Hoss Calvert. Her boyfriend." She smiled, looking at him sideways. "God, no one watches that stupid show anymore." Then Michel aimed the bike off the drive and into the trees, toward a clearing lit by a ring of headlights.

He pulled up just outside the innermost ring of cars. Some had big transistor radios playing on their hoods, angled antennae gleaming in the headlights. Most were Fords and Chevys, but he saw a hardtop AMC Ambassador and a VW bus, and most were running with their headlights on and their radios cranked. He cut off the engine, and the first thing she heard out of WGH was, "It's too late, baby, it's too late."

She brushed her hair. Two other rings of cars formed semi-circles of light across the overgrown farmland. Away from the headlights, a small farmhouse stood long-abandoned. Its tin roof was gutted, and the side walls were covered in tangles of ivy.

Past the farthest ring of cars, an old, dilapidated barn squatted at the end of the overgrown gravel drive. Its doors had fallen off and lay splayed outward like broken wings, and the roof had bowed in, bent like tin foil where a broad tree spread up through the roof.

She already felt their eyes on her. On *them.* They walked into the circle of light, and Summer felt all the girls staring. She knew what they were thinking; she'd be thinking the same things.

I've never seen him *before.*

Who is that? Someone new?

But she's not with—

And then their mouths would fall open, gaping at the newcomer.

Her new guy.

Two guys laughed and hung around two shining tin trash cans filled with ice and some mystery mixture. "Hey, Moon," Summer said.

Joey Mullins looked up. "Summer! Hey!" His eyes glanced at her tight blouse. He reached out and backhanded Tank Purcell across his arm. Both were barefoot, wearing faded t-shirts and jeans. "Here we go!" Moon Mullins said. Tank looked up, then stood straight. They flanked the trash cans and said, in unison, "Welcome to the hall of the Mountain King!"

They had poured Kool-Aid, 7-Up, and five gallons of grain alcohol into each trash can. As others arrived with bottles, they poured in vodka, gin, bourbon—everything—as they passed through the first ring of cars. "Hairy Buffalo Party," Tank said, slurring his words. He scratched his chest through his Led Zeppelin t-shirt. "Pour somethin' in. Don't matter what."

Summer glanced over her shoulder at Michel. She poured some Jack Daniel's into the closest trash can. Moon Mullins stirred the mixture with a boat paddle, humming to the song from the car radios. Then he dipped a paper cup into the swill and offered it to her as though it were a goblet of molten love.

"Hell. That may be the best one yet," Tank said. Summer smiled and took a sip. She winced, then swallowed. "Damn! Could it be stronger?" Then she laughed softly, and took another swig.

Tank and Moon laughed together. "Told ya!" Tank said. "Best one yet!"

"Get bent!" Moon said. They both tasted the concoction, then rocked back on their heels. Moon looked up into the sky and howled like a wolf. "Yes!" Tank yelled. "Yes! Yes!"

Then the ground popped in tiny explosions. Grass spewed in tiny tufts as a wad of firecrackers exploded near them, hopping like jumping beans. Summer gestured for Michel, and together they moved into the headlights.

Girls stared from across the clearing, flicking back their long hair to get a good look at the stranger. She thought she heard someone say, "Dreamy." Summer nodded at Gloria Jewett, home from her sophomore year at William and Mary. Gloria wriggled her fingers in a wave, openly eyeballing Michel. Then she looked at Summer and raised an eyebrow, as if to say, *What do we have here?*

Summer shrugged and gave her a slight grin.

She offered the cup to Michel.

"That smells like turpentine," he said.

"Tastes like it too." She poured it into the grass. "I'm sticking with the good stuff." She opened the Jack Daniel's and took a swig, then gave it to Michel.

They crossed the circle of headlights and observed the crowd leaning against their cars, drinking or smoking. Most of the guys were dressed identically in t-shirts and faded jeans, the uniform of choice for the too cool, too tough, American teen. The women, though, were dressed to take advantage of the evening. Some wore tight blouses, unbuttoned to casually expose a little cleavage, tucked into snug, belted shorts. Others wore hot pants in white or yellow, and a few wore psychedelic t-shirts and peace sign necklaces with wide, bell-bottomed jeans. Windy Tarver from high school wobbled by in a peasant blouse and cut-off denim shorts, and smiled at Michel. He smelled the marijuana smoke in her lungs. Long strands of multicolored love beads swung from her neck as she made her way toward a group of girls standing near a pickup truck. The tailgate was down, and the guy sitting cross-legged atop it wore a brown, paisley dashiki and strummed an acoustic guitar. Girls hovered near him, talking softly and singing along as he played "Eleanor Rigby." He had to be someone's college boyfriend; no guy from Stonebridge would be hip like that.

A girl squealed behind them, and suddenly Summer was enveloped in a warm hug. Tina laughed in her ear, then pulled away, holding her at arm's length. "Hollywood!" she squealed. She wore flared hip-hugger jeans and a bright, flower print halter, exposing her midriff. Her hair sprang out in a frizzy wedge from the hot night's humidity, and she embraced Summer again as if they hadn't seen each other in years. Summer smelled alcohol on Tina's breath and smoke in her hair, and realized Tina had been partying for a while.

"Look!" Tina reached into her purse and handed Summer a Mason jar filled with some clear liquid, slightly pink and swimming with strawberry slices.

"What is it?"

"Girl, it's that strawberry wine you like. Well, a little, I guess. Mostly it's mountain moonshine. With that strawberry wine you like."

Summer unscrewed the cap. "Cousin Irvin?"

Tina laughed and looked Michel up and down. "Mm hmm." Then her eyes went wide. *The biker?* "Oh!" She spun toward Summer, her mouth hanging open. Summer took a sip from the Mason jar.

"Hot *damn*!" Summer coughed into her hand, smiling. "God, that's good!"

Tina's eyes glittered in the headlights, and she looked at Michel. "Well?"

Summer said, "Tina, this is—James. You saw him the other night."

"Yeah, I sure did." Tina grabbed her arm and started to pull her away. "Oh, man, we have got to talk."

She pulled Summer between two empty cars, their radios blaring something about the mind of the universe. Tina opened her mouth and stared at her, but nothing came out.

"What?" Summer said. "What?"

"Oh my God!" Tina said, and she broke into a wide smile. "The biker!"

And then they started laughing.

Across the clearing, Michel found an old picnic table near some trees and sat on top. He thought perhaps he had stepped into a situation here, but he wasn't exactly sure.

Oh. It was that boy who had driven Summer home Thursday night.

Summer took another drink of the strawberry shine. Tina lit a cigarette. Summer plucked it from her hand, took a drag, and slipped it back between Tina's fingers.

"So," Tina said. "Have you done it with him?"

"Tina! Jeez!"

Tina glanced his way. "So what's he like?"

Summer flicked her eyes toward him. "He's nice. He's, just, so confident. He just got out of Vietnam. He's riding across the country."

Tina pulled Summer's hand toward her and took a swallow out of the jar. "How'd you two get together?"

What could she tell her? That he magically appeared in her garden? That they went for a ride to Fantasyland? "Drive-in, last night. He recognized me. I was kind of hoping we'd go to a movie. Some place alone. But we wound up here."

"Is he gonna stick around?"

"No idea what his plans are."

"But, what about Rob?"

Summer looked down into the jar, where the strawberry pieces were swirling in a slow, drunken dance. "Yeah. Well. He went to some movie of his."

"Roanoke?"

Summer nodded.

"Okay. So. What are you going to do?"

"Hell if I know. He—James—he's probably going to leave soon. Maybe a few days. And I—I'll have to handle Rob tomorrow. I guess I have to. Don't I?"

"Yeah. Because he'll hear it from somebody else if you don't do it first."

Summer looked toward the ground. "Jesus, what am I doing here? With him?"

"Looking for trouble."

Summer suddenly laughed. "So what else is new?"

Tina motioned for the jar and took a long drink. "How do you drink this stuff? The wine makes it too sweet." She reached in her purse and pulled out a Mason jar three-quarters full with clear moonshine. "I'm sticking with Uncle Irvin's Special."

Summer sipped her own shine. Girls in another clearing far in the back were cheering about something. "Starting to get a little wild."

"Yeah," Tina said. "Sonny Barrett and Eddie Pugh wanted me to drop acid with them."

"You didn't."

"Aw, hell no. Who knows where that shit came from?"

Summer looked back at Michel. He watched the crowd, seemingly bemused by it all. She couldn't help but notice that most of the girls were sneaking glances at him, then whispering to each other.

"Magpies," Summer said.

"They've got to talk about something. And he ain't ugly, you know."

"Did you see Ronnie watching him the other night? It looked like she was gonna eat him up alive."

"Shit. That girl is just plain horny for any dick with legs."

Michel turned toward Summer then, and they smiled at each other across the circle of lights. "I better get back."

"Yeah, you gotta stake your claim on that one," Tina said. "I should find Denny. He didn't like it that the guys asked me to trip with them."

"Two guys plus Denny? Maybe all that stuff about you on the men's room wall really is true."

"It better be," Tina said. "I wrote it."

Summer started toward Michel, sipping her moonshine and swinging her hips. She was mellow with a warm, strawberry-sweet buzz. She felt men's eyes on her, appraising her curves, the way she moved. And she just didn't give a damn. This little wiggle and shake was for an audience of one.

She put one foot up on the long wooden seat and held the jar of moonshine toward him. "We're going to be the only thing people will be talking about tomorrow."

"We can go, if you wish." He took a sip and smiled. "I do like it strong."

"No point in leaving now. We've been seen by too many people who know..."

She turned away from him, filled with a cold, empty feeling in her stomach. The guilt had been waiting there all day, crouching like a wildcat. Now everyone knew, and if they didn't, they would soon.

"Okay." She took the jar from him and sipped the moonshine. "I've been dating a guy—Rob—since high school, okay? Everybody around here—hell, as far as they're concerned, we're almost married." She saw two girls staring at them. She recognized them from some class in eleventh grade. "Now, here you are. And I'm suddenly not here with Rob. And you ride a motorcycle. You're something new. And dangerous. This is network news to these hillbillies."

"Maybe so. But I don't care about them." He took her hand. "What they think is inconsequential. You're the only thing that matters to me."

The WGH jingle played from a dozen radios around them, and then "Mississippi Queen" echoed into the night, the beat pounding fast and strong. She smelled beer and cigarette smoke, and a whiff of pot on the slight breeze. A couple started dancing in the headlights, and a girl in jeans shorts and a Coca-Cola t-shirt waved for her boyfriend to join her in the lights. Summer wanted to laugh. Rose Wilkins was never going to get Dunk Miller to dance in front of a crowd.

But the music's hard beat was getting to her. She felt a wildness growing inside her. "We shouldn't be here," she said, almost a whisper. "I shouldn't. But I don't want to leave."

A bottle rocket shot into the air from the ring of cars next to theirs. It exploded in an umbrella of sparks, and people around them whistled.

"That's ironic," Michel said. "I felt the same way earlier. But now, I can't tell you how glad I am to be here. Away from the war. With you. I just don't want you to regret—"

"I don't. I won't."

"—or come to, perhaps, despise me—"

She whispered, "I could never do that."

"Summer, there are so many things you need to know about me. I fear that..."

"I know more than you think."

He stared into her eyes. "I've known you for only two short days, but you have changed already. You're not the same woman you were the night we met."

"I'm not different," she said.

"Perhaps you don't see it."

"No. You just don't understand. I'm the same. The same person. But it's you. You've made the difference. I don't know how to explain it. But meeting you. Knowing you. I feel like, like I've been asleep for a long time, and I'm just now waking up." She took a sip of moonshine. "I'm tired of pretending that everything is so wonderful. Tired of living in a place where time stands still." She looked away, toward the far edges of the party. "The stone bridge. That's really what this place is all about. The past."

Another bottle rocket *whoofed* into the sky, an arc of yellow fire, then exploded into sunfire rain. Kids laughed, and the song ringing from the circle of radios was "Temptation Eyes," and she wrapped her arms around his neck and pulled him down to her mouth. Their lips parted, and their tongues touched, tasted each other, and she closed her eyes and felt only his hands on her waist, his mouth hard against hers. The music was a symphony singing through her, blinding her to the rest of the world; and when she opened her eyes they were inside the circle of cars, and her hips were swaying, and she gave him a wicked grin and pulled him with both hands into the headlights.

He shook his head, but she placed his hands back on her waist and pulled him into the rhythm of the Grass Roots. She wrapped her arms around his neck and kissed him again. She felt the hot burn of eyes upon her; but her lips were merging with his, and he was all there was, all that mattered, and the music was the sound of their intertwined hearts.

"Come and Get It" rang out between the cars, and she sang along with Badfinger, and they danced in the circle of flattened grass. He smiled, enrapt in her strong, clear voice. She felt his cool skin under her fingers, his iron hands hot near her belly. Something hot, like an ember, flared inside her.

The song faded. She looked into Michel's eyes. The car radios sang out, "WGH—famous 1310—" then "Dancing in the Moonlight" spilled out of the speakers. Someone shouted, "Oh yeah!" behind her. Michel looked over her shoulder, smiling.

"What?" she said.

"I think we started something."

Dunk Miller was dancing with Rose Wilkins in front of a '70 Gremlin, and another couple came into the light from between cars, and another. At least twenty couples danced to the radio, caught up in the joy of the rhythmic night. She felt it on the warm night air: a coming together. It was a sparkle of wonder, and they were at its epicenter. And she laughed and swung out from him, then spun back into his arms; and they danced, and she whirled in an ethereal, velvet haze that tasted of roses and bourbon, and Michel's wine-sweet breath hot against her cheeks.

Song merged into song, and they lost time, lost in each other's eyes, lost in themselves. Sweat trickled down her back, and the heat in the circle seemed to swell, and the crowd grew from twenty couples to almost forty, all singing and dancing along with Eric Burdon and War, and Cream, and Friends of Distinction, and the Stones, and Deep Purple, and the Bar-Kays, Mayfield, and Shocking Blue: a bacchanalia of youth and freedom under the sweet kiss of the summer moon.

"Venus" faded into a serenade by Rhinoceros, and couples came together to hold hands and dance, and take their first fumbling kisses. She led Michel back to the picnic table. She had lost some of her buzz, and she wanted the taste of bourbon on her tongue. She took a long swallow and set the bottle beside him. He took a swig as she lit a Salem and inhaled. "God, how long were we dancing out there?"

"Forever," he said, smiling. He checked his watch. "Almost an hour. Twenty to midnight."

She took the bottle and lifted it to her mouth, taking a long drink. She sighed and looked around. "Fireworks'll go off—"

A barrage of firecrackers *pop-popped* like gunfire near them in the trees, and she lurched out of the way, into his arms. He laughed, and she shouted into the trees, "Jesus Christ! Go back to kindergarten!" Drunken laughter rang out from the shadows. She turned to him, saw him laughing, and hit him in the chest. "Not funny," she said. And that made him laugh even more.

She smiled and took another drink. She felt her buzz coming back. "Want to see what's going on back there?"

Michel shrugged. "Whatever you want, princess."

She slung her purse over her shoulder and carried the bottle in her hand. "And don't you forget it." She felt tight and all right, and she led him around the edge of the headlights and walked into the twilit space between the rings of cars, where it was darker and quieter. His arm felt strong, solid, like a tree trunk, and she watched where her sandaled feet stepped across the crunchy grass.

A Frisbee sailed past them, and Joe Burwell waved and said, "Sorry!" Horsey Cole caught it and waited for them to walk out of their path. Summer pulled Michel towards an arrangement of metal kegs angled in huge buckets of ice. An overgrown path led toward the old, abandoned barn.

Dave Raynor was pumping a keg of Bud. He'd grown a moustache since the last time she'd seen him. "Summer Moore. You look really great. Haven't seen you since high school. Where you been?"

"Stuck here. You still in school, Davey?"

He grinned and handed them both paper cups sloshing with foam and beer.

"Junior at Tech. Me and a coupla other guys from Kappa Sigma paid for the kegs. I mean, what the hell, it's a party, right?"

"What the hell."

"We got Rolling Rock too."

She sipped the beer. "Naw, this is cool. Thanks, Davey."

They moved toward the closest semi-circle of cars, their amber headlights angled on the crumbling barn. A portable 8-track on the hood of a new, green Pinto played "Wild World." Two girls sat on the tailgate of a beat-up 1950s pickup, drinking beer, as a college guy with a scraggly beard theorized that maybe we all lived in a world that wasn't real; that maybe this was all a dream—no, a nightmare—of some unknown deity. "I mean, look at Vietnam!" he said. "Ain't that the Pit of Nothingness? The something-something Circle of Hell?"

They crossed the path into the semi-circle of cars, then laughed together. "With all these educated jerks around, maybe I'm glad I didn't go to college," Summer said.

Michel shrugged. "You would have done quite well. You're a lot smarter than you think."

She sipped her beer. Her buzz was back, and she felt fine and mellow. "No, I mean, I don't want to be somebody like that. A pretentious know-it-all."

Michel smiled. "University isn't all like that. The right courses, and the right teachers, can open minds; show you things you couldn't imagine if you stay in only one place all your life."

She stared at him.

"What?"

"Just thinking," she said. "If my counselor or teachers had said anything like that to me in high school, I would have jumped at the chance to go. But my grades weren't always As and Bs. And my mother never wanted me to leave."

She thought she heard someone call her name. Michel stopped, and Summer noticed Tina taking long, fast steps towards them. She was biting her lower lip, and she grabbed Summer's arm.

"Hey," Summer said, "don't spill my—"

"Summer, you've got to get out of here."

"Huh? No way."

"You have to. Now. Rob is here."

"What? No, he said he was going to the movies."

"I just saw him! He's back there talking books and shit with Jesse Moyer. Summer—"

"He told me he was going to Roanoke." She pulled Tina away and left Michel a few feet behind them. "I blew him off, T. I wanted to hang out with—Oh, shit. I didn't plan on coming here. It just happened. You think he knows?"

Tina glanced back toward the farthest area of cars. "No, he was laughing with the guys. He doesn't know anything. But you know he will. You have to get out of here."

Summer crushed her cigarette with the toe of her sandal. "Shit." She went over to Michel and took his hand. "Sorry about this. We've got to go."

"I heard."

She glanced back once at Tina, who mouthed, *Go!* Then they started down the path toward the motorcycle. She heard the low wail of a train rolling away in the distance. Nearby, in the shadows of the trees, she spied Lindsay Hayes, the reverend's seventeen-year-old daughter, taking turns making out with two guys.

She led the way between cars and into the headlit crowd, still dancing as the radios blasted out "Sugar, Sugar," and she aimed for the dark trees where the bike waited.

Then she heard Rob call out her name.

This can not *be happening.*

"Summer," Michel said. "Should we—"

"No. Keep walking. Faster."

They were at the far edge of cars. Moon Mullins was passed out on the hood of a '65 Skylark. Michel pulled her past the Buick. She saw the gleam of headlights shining off his bike not thirty feet away.

Then, from behind her:

"Summer?"

She whispered, "Shit," then stopped.

Rob trotted up to her, breathless, smelling of beer. "Hey. Didn't you hear me yelling? I wasn't sure at first it was you."

"Rob. Listen."

"What are you doing here? I thought you didn't feel good."

He glanced past her and saw Michel, halfway to the tree line, watching. Around them, the dancers and bystanders were growing silent, turning to watch as the Archies sang from the cars.

Rob smiled. "I wish you would have let me know."

Summer looked down at her feet. She couldn't look him in his eyes.

"Hell, I would have picked you up and bought dinner."

She said nothing, and he glanced at Michel again, watching from the edge of the shadows. He looked back at Summer.

She said, "Rob."

And it all clicked.

His eyes went wide, and he took a step away from her. He tried to speak, but he didn't have the words.

"Rob, this is not— I mean, I didn't want to—"

"No. Summer, no. No. I mean, what the hell?" He gestured toward Michel. "Who's that?" He looked at him, and finally recognized him. "Oh. Oh, fuck."

"Crash, you said you were going to the movies."

Rob's lip quivered. "You said you were sick." He stared, trying to think. The radios played behind him while the silent crowd watched. He looked at her as though he had never seen her before. "What is this? Why are you doing this?"

"Crash—Rob. I am really, really—"

"I must have done something. Did I do something?" Then it crashed down on him. It was all her, and she was doing it right in front of him. "Summer, what the hell are you doing this for?"

"Look, I didn't mean to—"

"Three years. Three damn years, Summer." A tear formed in one eye, and his face turned red. "And now I find you with a goddamned biker after, what, only two days?" He shook in rage, barely holding it in. "You told me you loved me. We were going to— I thought we—" He glared at Michel. "Are you fucking him?"

She took a step toward him, but he backed away.

"No. Don't even try to get close to me. I don't want you touching me with those hands." He stared at Michel, his right hand clenching and unclenching. "You son of a bitch."

"Rob, please," Summer said.

His face went pale, and his eyes seemed black with hatred. He stepped toward Michel, and Summer felt Michel's heat rise. It was like electricity on the air. He stood completely still, but she felt the air, tense, tight like a steel wire.

Rob roared, "You goddamned son of a bitch!" and he leapt to run past her, hell-bent to show that biker trash that Summer was *his* girl. But all her fear and guilt exploded then, in a wave of red-hot righteousness. Her arm flashed out, and she yanked Rob back with a rush of raw power flaring up from somewhere secret, deep inside her.

"YOU WILL *STOP*!" Her voice echoed through the trees, across the clearing.

Summer and Rob locked eyes.

"I didn't mean for this to happen," she said.

Then a boy across the clearing raised his voice. Eddie Pugh hopped from foot to foot, staring at his '62 Catalina. He pointed and yelled at the front grille. His eyes were wild, frenzied with one tab of acid too many. He screamed at the car, "You ain't gonna eat me!" He spun around and shouted to the crowd, "Hey! Who's got a baseball bat? This is one big damn snake!"

A couple of guys laughed. Eddie stepped away from the car, then threw a cup of beer across the hood. He slowly lifted his head and stared up into the trees. "The monkeys are laughing at us," he said. And he collapsed.

Sonny Barrett called his name, shaking his shoulder. Eddie's eyes blinked open. "Sonny, man. You see that thing? It's as big as a car."

Sonny looked up at the Catalina. "Yeah, man. I don't like it much either." He led Eddie away toward the trees.

Rob jerked out of Summer's grasp. She stared him down, arms crossed. She felt a cold hollow in her stomach. She couldn't go back to the way it had been. She had strung him along all this time, and she hadn't even realized it. She had been different then. Now she didn't even know who that lost, naïve girl was who had been with Rob for three years. All she knew was that she had to do the right thing.

"Rob, I didn't want this. I didn't plan any of this. It just happened. I'm so sorry."

He tried to look away, his eyes filling with tears. "What? Did I do something?"

How could she explain? All the stupid clichés that people used flashed through her mind. *I need my space. You deserve someone better than me. We're going in two different directions.* And the worst: *It's not you. It's me.*

"Rob, you didn't do a thing. I—" She shook her head. *No lame ass stories. He deserves the truth.* "You didn't do anything. You're the best boyfriend ever. I did it. It was all me. I caused this. And I didn't want it to happen like this."

"How then? How did you want it to happen?" Hot tears streamed down his cheeks.

"Rob, Rob, no, I didn't want this to happen, but—" She took a deep breath. "God, Rob, I'm so, truly, sorry." She looked him in the eyes and steeled herself. "But, it's over," she said, almost in a whisper. "I didn't really know it before. I didn't want to face it. But you deserve the truth. I'm sorry, Rob. I'm so sorry."

"Shit." He turned away and dismissed her with a wave. "Screw this. Screw you." He turned and started toward the back.

"Rob," she said.

"No," he said, without turning. "Just leave me the hell alone. Forever."

Summer watched him walk away, then noticed the silence of the crowd, and the ones still staring at her as if waiting for more of the show. The Monkees sang from car speakers about taking a giant step.

She wheeled around toward Michel, glancing back once at Rob as he merged into the crowds. Michel touched her arm. A bottle rocket went off from the middle clearing, then three others scratched the night with fire.

She headed for the bike. "Let's ride the fuck out of here."

14

THEY WERE IN the middle of a long, wet kiss, and Ricky's hands were way up Cindy's shirt, sliding across her breasts, slick with sweat, when the bottle rockets went off. Cindy Shuford grinned and pushed Ricky Hawley away and looked out the broken door of the dilapidated Nicewander barn, toward the Sugden property. "Rockets're going off early."

They had left the party a few minutes ago, and had stumbled through the thick wedge of dark trees between the party on the Sugden farm to smoke some grass and make out—among other things, Ricky hoped—in the ruins of the collapsed Nicewander barn.

"Can you see the mountains from the other side?" Cindy said. She brushed a sweaty strand of brown hair behind her ear.

"Fuck if I know," Ricky said. She walked past him, kissed him hard and deep, and then went over to a splintered wound in the far wall. She looked toward the mountains. "They're supposed to go off over at the caverns at midnight."

"We missed the big fireworks. They set 'em off early this year." Ricky checked his watch. "It ain't midnight for another five minutes, and I got us some grass I bought especially for tonight. C'mon."

Cindy didn't say anything. She stood at the gaping tear in the wall, looking to the right.

"Cindy?"

"Come look," she said.

Ricky came up beside her. A dark green Mustang was angled half in the grass, half on the overgrown drive leading back to the road.

"Shit," Ricky said. "That's Kenny's new Mustang."

"Kenny Cousins?"

"Yeah."

They stared at it, silent. Firecrackers popped at the now-distant party.

"Then where's Kenny?" she said.

"Hell if I know." He pulled a plastic bag out of his pocket. "Come on. I rolled these—"

Cindy stepped out of the barn and went in the direction of the Mustang.

"Goddamn it," Ricky said. He jammed the joints in his pocket. "Cindy! Come back here!"

He went out to stop her. She crept up behind the Mustang, and he caught up to her and whispered, "Come on! Him and Ronnie are probably out here screwing!"

"Then how come I don't see 'em in there?" she said. She tiptoed a little closer, craning her neck to see through the windows.

Above them, they heard a soft *whuuuuzzz* as a bottle rocket sailed into the sky from the party. Then the sky erupted into shimmering cascades that lit the landscape with flashes of red, white, and blue.

"Oh, shit," Ricky said. "That's blood."

Cindy took one step closer.

And that's when she started to scream.

15

"WHAT ARE WE doing up here?" Summer said.

Michel had driven into the mountains. He idled the bike at the thick iron chain across the gateway to Storybook Hollow.

"I told you earlier there was something you needed to see."

"I thought you meant the party."

"No, not at all. I thought you wanted to go to the party."

"No," she said. "Christ, no."

"This is my fault. I wanted to show you something else back there. I hesitated." He was silent for a moment. "Or perhaps I misunderstood you deliberately. I was going to show you the kind of man I am."

"I already know."

"Perhaps. Perhaps not," he said. "But this is something else."

He drove through the gap in the foliage, past the wall of the restaurant, and up the leaf-strewn path.

Summer had been quiet on the drive to the mountains, her arms clutched around his taut waist, feeling his muscular flesh against hers. She ached with the guilt of hurting Rob, and once came to tears, her cheek snuggled against Michel's back. But she had finally admitted to herself that this day had been inevitable. Things would never be the same.

She had found the man whom she had dreamed of for years.

And she could no longer ignore her dreams.

Michel rolled to a stop beside the Haunted Castle, and the bike roared down. Crickets slowly filled the silence. Summer climbed off and ran her fingers through her hair, then turned to him. "Okay, so why are we here?"

His dark eyes twinkled, and he gave her a secret smile. "Something beautiful."

He pulled a flashlight out of his pack behind the seat, then took her hand and led her into the castle's dungeon room. He knelt at the grate in the floor and lifted it out. "Your cold spot," Michel said. "I came back up here last night after I dropped you off." He leapt into the hole. Only his head and shoulders remained exposed above floor level. "There's a crawlspace down here. Come on."

He helped Summer into the hole, and they crouched in the four-foot tall space beneath the castle. Michel flicked on the flashlight. "That's where the moaning you heard came from." A plastic speaker lay nearby, covered with dust and leaves. He shined the flashlight on the underside of the floor. "And a trapdoor, so the guy in the coffin could get in and out without anyone seeing him."

He led her to a far corner, against the angled rock wall of the mountain. "Sometime, not long after this park was built, I'm guessing, part of the ground underneath this castle collapsed. Right here. And this," he said, "is where all that cold air you always felt is coming from."

The flashlight illuminated the ragged edges of a six-foot wide hole in the crawlspace floor, angling into the mountain wall. A new, shiny aluminum ladder poked up through the black hole.

"It's opened up even more, I'm sure, since you were a kid."

"What is it?" she said.

"Something no human has ever seen before."

A cold chill ran up her back. "How do you know that?"

He smiled. "I know." He held out his hand. "You're the first."

He led the way down the ladder, and he shined the light on the rungs so she could see where to step. "Don't worry," he said. "It's only about twenty feet down." She went down the ladder and stepped onto an uneven rock floor. It was colder down here, not even sixty degrees, she guessed, and he suddenly snapped off the flashlight. It was darker down here than she had expected, darker than anything she had ever experienced.

"Michel?"

Her voice echoed around her. She reached out for the ladder she knew was there and gripped the cold metal. "Come on, Michel. Don't try to scare me."

She heard a match strike, saw the glow of the tiny flame on Michel's face. "I wouldn't do that to you," he said, and he lit a kerosene lamp. With a twist of a brass knob, light filled the chamber around her, exposing smooth rock walls and the sloping curve of an underground tunnel only feet away. Stalactites hung just inches from the top of her head.

He took her hand. "I call this the antechamber. Come on." He led her into the tunnel's curve as it descended gradually, then let her step a few feet ahead of him as the opening widened, and she paused at the grand vista that he had discovered under the earth, flickering with firelight.

Her eyes widened, filling with wonder. "Welcome," he said, "to the Hall of the Mountain King."

The rock floor was smooth and irregular, shaped by underground waters that had receded in the far-distant past. This was a royal palace sculpted by the secrets of the earth. Stalagmites had formed from millennia of water and limestone slowly dripping from long stalactites high in the ceiling. The immense chamber was lit by kerosene lanterns atop smooth outcroppings and wide stalagmites.

"It's wonderful," she whispered.

"I've never quite seen anything like it," he said, looking at her.

"Where'd you get the lanterns?"

"Same place I got the ladder. The hardware store downtown, after I dropped you off this morning."

"They were open that early?"

"Not exactly."

"You didn't. You broke in?"

He grinned.

"I'm not sure I like my boyfriend being a thief."

"Hm. A thief. I've sometimes had to do worse. Besides, I left two hundred on the counter. More than enough to cover it."

"Two hundred *dollars*?" Her eyes went wide. "Are you rich or something?"

He smiled. "Something."

She looked at him askance and walked by him, stepping carefully along the smooth, eroded rock. She pointed at dark openings in the rock wall far in the back. "Where do they go?"

"Farther down into the mountain. I haven't gone through them all. But I found an underground lake that's simply amazing. Some of the caverns are so deep they lead underneath the town."

"And these are all part of Carter Caverns?"

He shook his head. "As far as I can tell, they're not connected at all. These caverns are ours. They put Carter Caverns to shame."

"Ours," she said. Lit by the flickering lanterns, it was as though they were standing inside an immense and timeless cathedral. The light danced on her tan skin, her bright hair, and she was a queen in a forgotten temple devoted to her.

"I stayed here last night," he said. "Explored as much as I could. I'm keeping the motel room just for appearance's sake. Keep the sheriff guessing. Make it look as normal as possible. Being here is much safer, for me at least. The first day I was here, I slept in a mausoleum."

Her lips parted, as though she would say something, then she closed her mouth and nodded once to herself. In the background somewhere, she heard the trickle of a small stream, the last trace of the powerful underground river that had once flooded these chambers.

"There's something else over here." He took her hand and led her to a wide alcove in the rock wall. Beneath an overhang of stalactites was a smooth flowstone almost three feet high, brilliant in ivory and beige drippings that had solidified from eons of calcite flowing down the sloping wall of the cavern. His bedroll had been left rolled on top.

"I call it the Devil's Altar."

She smiled. Their eyes met, and suddenly he seemed brighter, happier than he had before. "What?" she said.

"I love it when you smile."

She watched him for a moment, and then she kissed him, hard, their mouths merging, filling with the heat of their mutual need.

"Summer, it's time you learned the truth. About me."

Summer said, "I know it already."

"I'm not so sure about that."

"Michel, I've seen you. I've dreamed you, your face, the way you hold me, since forever." She ran her finger along the length of his strong forearm. "The beast. The other night, on top of Rob's car. The way you made me feel things, with just a scratch from your teeth. I *know*. I've known you forever. You're waking me up, taking me from a bad dream, into the dream I always wanted to come true."

She had intuited so much. He was sure, now, this is what was meant to be. But could he put her through the terror, through the constant fear he lived with every moment? The fear of being found—and destroyed?

"There are no coincidences," he whispered.

He opened his bedroll and stretched it across the flowstone, then picked her up under her arms and sat her on the cushion. She laughed. "Think you're gonna get lucky?"

He smiled, but there was no mirth behind his dark eyes.

She pulled the bottle of Jack out of her purse and took a long swig. She held it out, but he shook his head. She took another drink, and waited.

He opened his mouth. Closed it. Looked into her eyes. "Summer," he said.

"Michel," she said.

He watched her silently for half a minute.

"Very well. You were right. I'm not twenty-eight. I'm older. I was born in March of 1846, in a village a few kilometers outside of Paris."

She said, "That's one hundred twenty-five."

"Quite so," he said.

He let it sink in. She took another drink.

"I was named after a good friend of my parents, an explorer, like Stanley and Livingstone, or Burton. He once came for a stay with us after one of his South American excursions, and he brought back boxes of uncut gems, mostly emeralds, and gold. I would play with the stones and imagine I were the explorer, discovering ancient ruins, digging for treasures deep in the earth.

"I was something of a black sheep in my teens. By the time I was twenty-three, my parents had had enough of my behavior, and they shipped me off. They gave me money to book passage and to live—in a manner befitting a gentleman—and would wire it to me wherever I roamed. I met many others in likewise positions. Remittance men, they called us; going from one port of call to another, but never returning home.

"So I became the explorer I once pretended I was. And something of a rogue. I went all over the world, by steamer, by train. And I learned a little about a lot of things, about life and growing up.

"And then— There was Angeline.

"I booked passage to cross the Atlantic for my first voyage to America. Liverpool to New York. October, 1872. It was the *Adriatic*, one of the new steamships, on its sixth voyage, I believe. I always booked a first-class cabin, but I spent a lot of time those first few days down in steerage. That's where the real fun could be found.

"October seventh, I came out on deck in the early morning. I had won a few hundred in a game of Faro below decks—a card game no one plays any longer—and stood at the rail, enjoying a fine Havana. I gazed westward, and noticed her standing at the bow, staring off into the distance. She had dark hair, with a reddish hue that seemed to shine with strands of gold.

"She stood with her back to me, yet, the curve of her figure, the magnificence of her tresses. I was intrigued, to say the least.

"I took a step toward her. It was only later—much later—that I realized something was pulling me toward her as if we were tied together. And as I approached, I opened my mouth to introduce myself, and she spun around.

"She stared at me. I apologized for scaring her. And as soon as she heard my voice, her eyes softened, and she asked me, 'Is it you?'

"Something— I had never felt anything like what I felt in that moment. It was as though something bright opened up inside me. Like a flower opening to the sun. And I knew her voice, somewhere deep inside me. I had heard her voice, seen her face, somewhere. Some when.

"And I said, 'Yes.'"

She and Angeline.

Michel, coming here, to a tiny little hole-in-the-wall Southern town he had never heard of.

And then she knew why. This is why she had always felt like an outsider. Something inside her had always known there was a better life for her. Her past and future were now mingling, and she and Michel had been living and reliving their lives over and over—for centuries perhaps—dancing a ballet that could span eternity.

Michel was right. There are no coincidences.

Summer said, "I had a dream when I was twelve, I think. It was night, and I was in a field somewhere. And there was a woman riding a horse. I've always called her the Shadow Woman. She was all dark, but her eyes were burning, like fire, and she had long, very dark hair. There was a man standing in the field, like he was waiting. The moon suddenly gets bright, and the woman jumps off the horse and runs into his arms." She looked Michel in the eyes. "They fell into the tall grass, and then they got naked, and then—then, all I remember is a lot of moaning. And kissing. And the blood."

He answered in a whisper. "October sixteenth. Three days after the *Adriatic* docked in New York. The night Angeline and I became one. The night I was turned."

They watched each other silently. Summer felt in her heart the truth of his words, and wondered if, tonight, it would be she who—

No, Michel thought, not tonight. Her soul was too beautiful, too full of light, to let him corrupt it. Already, the earth of this town was red with blood he had spilled. Summer deserved better. Why should she be fated to a life in the shadows, always on the run from the monsters who wanted him?

No. If he refused to turn her—if he rejected the future that destiny had written for them—then perhaps this damned waltz through eternity would finally come to a proper end.

"I must leave soon. Tomorrow would be best. Summer, I want you to be with me forever. But for your sake—to keep you safe—I must go. Alone."

"The hell you will," she said. "You're not going anywhere without me."

"Summer, listen to me. I'm a killer."

"You were a soldier."

"I was. But I kill because I have no choice. It is my curse. I cannot change who I am, and I do not want you to become like me. You deserve a far better life than the one I can bequeath you."

"Bequeath?" She took a drink of bourbon. "Big, stupid word."

"Summer, there are people after me. Powerful people, who travel the world looking for me. They've been trying to kill me since the day Angeline and I—" He turned away from her. "No. They'll find out about you soon enough, and they'll come after both of us. If we are together, it will be easy to destroy us simultaneously. Helena Hawkbourne and her family of maniacs."

But Summer no longer heard him. *Hawkbourne*? She knew that name.

Angeline.

Angeline Hawkbourne.

"Who are they? The Hawkbournes."

"Self-appointed white knights, determined to wipe me off the face of the earth. They've followed me across the world, relentlessly, continent to continent—and they'll come after you too. There are almost two centuries of history behind their vendetta, and they will never stop." He walked away from her. He would not allow it to happen this time. Not to her. "No. I can't let anything happen to you. Not ever again."

He had to leave, as soon as he could. He would cheat this damn entwined fate of theirs. She'll grow, and live a full life, in the sun, and he will deny her a destiny of blood and darkness.

To give her up.

To let her live.

After only a few days.

After lifetimes.

This was how much he loved her.

Then Summer spoke from close behind his shoulder. "So, teach me."

He shook his head, afraid to turn. If he saw her face, her eyes, he would melt, or be tempted to give in, to—

Something soft hit him on the side of his head, then plopped to his feet.

Pink fabric, wadded with elastic. A tiny, red satin bow.

He turned.

She had stepped out of her pants, somehow magically keeping on her high-heeled sandals, and had left the white jeans in a pile on the cold stone floor. She stepped toward him, naked from the waist down, save for a slim, gold belly chain sloping around her hips. Her fingers untied the knot under her breasts, and she let the white cotton blouse slide down her back to the floor. Lantern light danced along her light brown skin, highlighting the sensuality of her bikini tan—the pale triangles that made her full breasts seem even rounder, and the wide, pale V between her legs that pointed toward a trimmed tangle of soft, sandy hair.

He felt himself stirring. She stepped closer, and he scented her: beneath her perfume and the aromas of woods and bourbon and tobacco, he smelled her muskiness, her sweat, the heat pulsing between her thighs.

"Teach me," Summer said. Her lips grazed his, then slid across his cheek, tingling with warmth. She whispered low into his ear, "Teach me."

Her hand found the front of his jeans, and she felt him in there, hardening at her touch.

If he had thought he had a choice before, his body told him he had never had a say in it. With her naked skin on his flesh, the swell of her breasts against his chest, the smell of *her* intoxicating his every sense, he knew he had been naive. And when she rubbed her hand lightly up and down the front of his jeans, he knew that he was now hers.

"Teach me," she said, breathing into his mouth. She unbuttoned his shirt and yanked it off. "Everything." She pulled down his zipper, exposing a web of soft black hair that thickened below his abdomen. "You're the only man I've ever truly wanted. The only one I've ever wanted inside me. Teach me."

He took off his boots and socks, and she pulled down his jeans. Her bracelets jangled as she ran her fingernails down his hardness, then gripped him, feeling the strength inside his long, thick shaft. Its tip glistened pink under its uncircumcised sheath, and as her hands closed around his length, his cock throbbed against her palms. She pulled back the foreskin and exposed the head, and with her red fingertips she rubbed the tip in circles, lubricating the head with his own juices. Michel breathed deep, the low purr of a lion, as he grew harder in her soft hands. Then she led him by the cock over to the Devil's Altar.

Their tongues merged; living things, becoming one. His hands cupped the curve of her ass, fingers slipping between her, squeezing. She pumped his cock, feeling it swell in her grip. Then his mouth was on her breasts, his tongue tracing a wet line down the curve of one, coming up from underneath to find a stiff, brown nipple. He sucked gently, teasing with his tongue, one nipple, then the other. She moaned and ground against him, and his cock dug hard into her belly as she bit his neck and teased with her own tongue, down the line of his neck to his muscular chest.

Then she let go of his manhood and pressed her hands against his chest. She shoved him back against the flowstone and sucked his nipples, then crouched down slowly, licking down his chest and abdomen, to the top of his black pubic hair. She grabbed his thick cock and pulled back the pale foreskin to expose the head, and she looked up at him. "I want you," she said.

Her lips enveloped him. He arched back, moaning low, as her tongue swirled around him, and she dove her mouth farther down along his shaft, until she felt him on the back of her throat.

They moaned together, and she teased him under the head with her tongue, flicking against his cock's puckered lips. His fingers wrapped themselves in her hair, and she felt his head throb, grow larger against her tongue. She swallowed his whole length, moving her tongue along the base of his shaft. His moans echoed through the cavern as she cupped his balls and massaged them, moving her mouth up and down the slick curve of his cock.

He pulled her by her long hair and kissed her deeply. Then he tongued his way to her round breasts and raked her nipples with his teeth, then flicked them with his tongue, sucking each hard nipple in turn. Then he lifted her, his mouth melding with hers, and laid her across the bedroll.

She spread her legs for him, and he crawled between them, kising her abdomen, nuzzling his nose and tongue through her blonde mound. He inhaled and smelled the hot muskiness inside her. Then he tasted her juices with long, slow laps of his tongue along her moist lips. His hands found her breasts and cupped them, his fingertips caressing her rock-hard nipples in slow circles. Then his tongue found her rosebud at the point of her sandy hair. He teased her, gentle, and her moans rolled through the cavern as he flicked her with the tip of his hot tongue. She squirmed, her fingers tangled in his thick black hair, and ground herself against his mouth. His tongue darted gently between her labia, into the hot center of her lust. Her fingernails dug into his scalp. Then he came up to make love to her red, swollen clitoris, and she thrust shamelessly against his face, her legs wrapped around his back.

He hungered for her. Her heat and smell drugged him, intoxicated him. He felt her heart racing, her blood thumping through her veins, pulling at his need, his lust for her.

She pulled his head away and looked into his eyes. Her own juices gleamed on his lips. He came up above her. The head of his stiff cock pressed against her clit. She leaned up and kissed him, bit his lip, tasted herself on it. And she whispered, "Take me."

The head of his cock bulged from its pink cowl, and he thrust his shaft into her, sliding in easily. She gasped, and her eyes rolled up at the feel of him inside her, filling her as nothing had ever filled her before. She cried out as he thrust deep, pulled back, almost out of her, then he plunged his thick shaft deep inside her. She dug her fingers into the cheeks of his ass, moaning with each deep, powerful thrust as his cock ground against her clitoris, sending a jolt of untamed lust through her.

Their gaze met. Michel saw it in Summer's ice-blue eyes. The Want. The Need. The heat tingled in his teeth. He pounded into her, her scents of perfume and sex intermingling. He suckled one breast, teasing the nipple with his tongue. The blue vein throbbed just beneath the skin. His mouth was on it, tonguing it. His mouth clamped onto her pale flesh and his teeth pierced her smooth skin. His mouth filled with hot crimson.

She moaned at the sudden razor pain, realized dimly, *This is what I want!* and she yanked his face to hers. Their mouths met, smearing her own hot blood over her lips, mingling with their saliva, swirling on their tongues, and she shivered as the taste and the blood and his moans and the thrusts of his cock intermingled.

She bent forward and bit his neck, her teeth clamping hard. A single drop of dark blood welled from his skin, and she sucked at it, wanting more, needing more of him.

Then the knife from his belt gleamed in his hand, and he drew a short, deep line across his neck. His blood dripped onto her mouth and chin, and she panted at the heat, at the aromas of blood and sex, and she closed her mouth over the throbbing wound and sucked as he bent back to her soft, round breast and drank deeply of her. Crimson spurted across her tongue, filling her; and his cock plunged into her, deeper, as they drank each other, and she rocked against him, her fingernails digging into his ass, and she exploded against him, thrusting her pelvis against him, surging with him in rhythmic waves.

The cavern spun in a whorl of musk and ecstasy, and her moans of pleasure echoed against the cool rock. Her eyesight went dark, then a deep red. And she drank of him, each thrust of her against him sending ripples of electricity through her.

His thrusts deepened. A moan began low in his throat as he sucked her breast. She felt it then: their pulses, beating as one, thrusting, pounding in tandem, locked in blood and lust. And then it was as though she could see through his eyes, and they were one, for he could see through hers. They were linked, now and forever, and as each other's sweet blood cascaded over their tongues, they touched the burning hearts beating in the core of their eternal souls.

And he moaned, thrusting, his orgasm rocking her, and he pummeled her with his animal need. Their moans mixed together as she came and came, her sweet lips burning with fire, jets of his hot seed shooting deep into her.

Their cries echoed forever in their cavern beneath the earth, and flesh and soul and heart became one.

aubade

here comes the sun

sunday, july 4, 1971

1

SUMMER NESTLED IN the crook of his arm, her golden hair spilled out over his broad chest. Her finger toyed gently with his nipple, and she heard their voices distant in her head. Angeline, Nichole—so many, so long ago—whispered softly together as one, a constant murmur far away in her soul. She couldn't hear them all, or remember every name or voice. Her songlines with Michel had been intertwined for centuries, for so long and so far back that she couldn't see where it all began.

She sat up on her elbow. Her long hair was stringed with crimson. She reached across his chest and grabbed her bourbon, opened the bottle and took a long swig. Her buzz was wearing off, and she wanted this high, this night, to last forever.

She tasted things in the bourbon she hadn't tasted before. Wood, and smoke. The lantern light flickered brighter, and the shadows throughout the cool cavern seemed to have slunk away. She felt a calmness in her now. She felt as though she could accomplish anything.

She felt unleashed.

She gave Michel the bottle and he took a drink, then placed it on the cave floor. The blood on his flesh was cologne. She smelled *him*, the darkness and the earth that were part of him.

He stared at the ceiling, hung with stalactites pointing at them like sharpened stakes. He almost laughed at the irony.

"What?" Summer said. "What are you thinking?"

"So much." He stared at the shadowed ceiling. "Something I read once in a museum."

She kissed his nipple, ran her tongue around it in a circle.

He whispered, "*I will breathe the sweet breath which comes forth from your lips, I will behold your beauty every day. My prayer is to hear your voice, sweet like the north breeze. Your limbs will be young in life, through my love of you, and you will give me your arms which bear your spirit. I will receive it, and live through it. You will call out my name for eternity, and it will never fail on your lips.*"

She kissed his chest. "That's beautiful." She nuzzled her lips down his belly, then kissed his cock with her moistened lips, licking it softly, flicking her tongue along its crest. It stirred at her touch, and she climbed up on him, slowly smearing her juices up his belly. She straddled his chest. Blood oozed thick from punctures in her breast, dripping down to a nipple, then along the curve of her breast. Love and blood. That's what it was all about, wasn't it?

She ran her fingers through his long black hair, then pulled his face against her hot, crimson mound. His tongue found her, and she smelled their juices, their heat, swimming together. She pulled his mouth tighter against her wetness.

"More," she said. "More."

2

THE CHERRY-RED flashers atop four squad cars threw silent lightning across the empty field, casting long, staccato shadows through the branches of the trees. Squad cars were arranged in a rough semi-circle, headlights focused on Kenny's Mustang. Each deputy had already walked up to the car to peer through the blood-splashed windows.

Headlights bounced in the distance as a squad car turned through the old gate. Three deputies—Curly Jackson, Collie Nettles, and Billy Tate—stood together as the car stopped halfway between them and the gate. Another squad car followed through the gate, then parked behind the other.

Sheriff Hicks stepped out of his Fury, still in uniform. He looked at his watch. Almost 12:30 a.m. He lit a Pall Mall and said, "Well, shit."

He and Duke had driven out to the Sheffield house late Saturday afternoon. Ronnie's parents had gotten back from Carolina in the morning, and there was no sign of their little girl. Lulie Sheffield couldn't stop crying. "She just ain't like this. She's never not come home before. Never." Ford Sheffield was furious, sure as shit that Kenny had talked his precious little girl into running off with him. Duke checked Ronnie's bedroom while Hicks had talked with them; none of Ronnie's clothes or personal items were missing, so that told him they hadn't run off to elope. A night of screwing around in a Richmond motel? Maybe. And then Lulie cried even harder when he suggested such a thing.

"Shit," Hicks said, again.

Duke came out of the cruiser in back and walked up to him. Duke was in jeans and a white t-shirt. He wore his badge and gun on his belt.

"I was minutes from getting into bed, goddamn it," Hicks said.

Duke stared at the scene in the headlights. He smacked his palm against his forearm. "Mosquitoes are bad tonight."

"Don't you worry about them bloodsuckers," Hicks said. "They ain't gonna kill you none."

Something tight felt knotted in the pit of Duke's stomach. "I've got Enfield on the gate to the Nicewander farm."

"I saw him. You think I'm stupid?"

Duke smelled alcohol on the sheriff's breath. Strong. Hicks must have had a nip or two driving here from town—probably that cheap ass scotch, like he had hidden in his desk.

Hicks said, "Radio him. Tell him to park across the damn entrance. No one gets in or out." Duke started toward his car. Hicks turned. "You too. Go block this gate, then walk back up here."

Duke drove backwards the way he'd come. Hicks bent into the front seat of his car and grabbed a flashlight. He angled the white beam on the rutted dirt drive leading to the barn. He scowled and looked up. The deputies watched him. "Goddamn, I should fire you all!" he shouted. "The only tire tracks here are from your own goddamn tires! Any of you fuckin' college boys think about the evidence you ran over to park this close to the scene?"

They all looked away. Hicks aimed the flashlight onto the dirt road. He heard footfalls running up behind him, and Duke fell into place at his side, his own flashlight picking things up in the still darkness. "It's a mess out here," Duke said. "Looks like Kenny spun out a couple times through the grass."

"Hm," Hicks said. They were only feet away from the deputies when they heard someone throwing up in the dark trees to their right. They both focused their flashlights into the shadows, and picked out the olive uniform of a deputy.

Jackson spoke up. "It's, um, Cobb, sir. He got here right before you. He just looked in the window, and—"

"Pussy," Hicks said. He and Duke came up beside the deputies. A few feet away, a young couple stood huddled, his arm around her shoulders.

"Cindy Shuford and Ricky Hawley," Jackson said. "They called it in from the pay phone up at the fire station."

Hicks turned toward the Mustang. He played his flashlight over the broken headlights, the blood-smeared windows, the windshield woven with jagged veins. The interior was a mass of shadows. "Christ on a crutch."

"Yeah," Duke said.

Hicks stared toward the Mustang, aiming the flashlight in front of his feet. He yelled over his shoulder, "Jackson, get the girl's statement. Nettles, take the boy." He stopped and turned around. "Who's in unit six?"

"Tate, sir," Jackson said.

"Tate!" Hicks yelled. "Take Cobb, if the sorry son of a bitch can clean himself up. Go through the woods and canvas that party. See if any of those kids saw anything. And no one goes home until I say so!"

Tate ran to pull Wilmer Cobb out of the trees. Hicks spat on the ground. "I knew there'd be trouble up here sooner or later," he said to Duke. "I should've cracked down on this little shindig years ago."

"Hell, Sheriff. It's just kids letting off steam. I came here too, back in the day."

Hicks spun around to face the deputies. "And goddamn it, Tate, take notes! No mistakes, got me?"

Tate waved at Hicks. Cobb, beside him, wiped his mouth with the back of his hand.

Hicks pointed his flashlight at the Mustang. He winced and rubbed the side of his head. "Headache?" Duke said.

"Shit," Hicks said. "It's amateur hour around here." He took a pill out of his pocket and dry-crunched it.

They stepped off the drive and into the tall grass. The mix of headlights cast multiple shadows as they walked toward the Mustang, stopping to point their lights into the grass and to make sure they weren't stepping on evidence. Duke focused his flashlight on a swath of grass that was darker than the others.

"Shit, that's a lot of blood," he said. "That's a lot of blood."

Hicks stared at the Mustang, ten feet away. Blood smeared the inside of the windows and windshield, and stained the hood and front grille as though it had been driven through a crimson waterfall. The canvas top was shredded across the center, as though mighty claws had ripped through tissue. The headlights glowed dim, ghostly yellow, and Duke thought he heard music, scratchy, coming from the radio. "Battery's almost dead," he said.

"Um hm," Hicks said.

They aimed their flashlights through the windows. With the smears blocking the light, the interior was mostly shadow. But they made out small patches of pale flesh through the glass, and what appeared to be a male's silhouette in the back seat.

"Oh, lordy," Duke said. "They've been in there since last night. Jeez, in this heat."

Hicks cleared his throat. "All right. Let's round up everybody we can. We need 'em here now. Secure the area, question the hippies at the party. Get Iris on this. She can do all the calling. She'll need to call Elmore at the paper, and tell him to bring lots of film. You can expect that lady reporter to be right behind him. Right now we secure the scene, get Elmore to take pictures as it is right now, and the rest we do at sun up. We need more light. That's all there is to it."

Duke nodded. "Yeah. Okay."

"And get Iris to call Doc Bragg. Get him up here pronto."

"Jesus, Buddy. The coroner?"

Hicks nodded.

Duke started back toward the nearest squad car, then began to run.

Hicks aimed his light at the ground between him and the Mustang, casting the beam from side to side. A few feet from the grille, he spied the hilt of Kenny's club, bloody fingerprints on the black-taped handle. Fragments of glass sparkled in the flashlight's beam.

He aimed through the passenger side windows. Two shapes were in the back seat. Blood had been smeared over the seats, the dash, Christ, everything. Nothing inside moved, save for the black flies that had made it through the ragtop and the cracked windshield and were scuttling across the windows.

Hicks heard Duke run up behind him. "I got Iris out of bed. She's on it. Heading straight for the office."

"She'll be a sight in the morning," Hicks said. "In her damn housecoat and those blue slippers."

Duke stared at the Mustang. "Yeah."

Hicks took a deep breath. "Let's get this over with."

They were five feet from the car when the smell hit them. The coppery tang of blood, mixed with the inescapable odors of urine and shit, smacked them like a slap.

"Oh, God. It was ninety-five degrees today," Duke said. That feeling in the center of his stomach suddenly clenched like a fist.

Their flashlights picked them out in the back seat. Kenny's head lolled back against the seat. Ronnie, naked, lay sprawled across him, as though he were holding her in his lap. Her eyes stared at nothing. Her stomach bulged unnaturally. She was covered in blood, evidently from the gaping wound where her neck had been torn open. Flies danced across her nakedness, and Duke looked away as one landed on her lower lip and crawled inside her dark mouth.

Hicks focused his beam on Kenny. His head was canted back, looking up at the headliner. Blood was caked around his mouth, on his hands and arms, soaking through his torn t-shirt.

Hicks grabbed the door handle. "Make a note that I'm opening the passenger door to examine the bodies."

Duke nodded silently.

Hicks opened the door. It was as though a fountain of blood had gushed over the interior, and the sickly smell made his head swim. He backed out and covered his mouth with a handkerchief from his back pocket. "I'm going to check her for a pulse." He reached in over the bucket seat and found her wrist. The radio flickered, and he could barely make out some rock and roll song. He looked back at Duke. "Ain't no pulse." He aimed the light at Kenny. A fly turned on the tip of Kenny's nose, then flew away as Hicks reached toward his neck.

Then Kenny screamed. Hicks jerked back his hand and fell out of the car. Duke shouted, "Jesus!" and backed off a few paces, then realized that Kenny was still alive in there.

Duke ran up and helped Hicks to his feet. "Ambulance!" Duke yelled to the deputies. "We need an ambulance!"

Hicks leaned into the open door, and Duke ran around and opened the driver's door. "Kenny? Kenny? You hear me?"

Kenny rocked in the back seat, holding Ronnie. His eyes were glassy, empty. One hand stroked her blood-streaked hair as he whispered something to her deaf ears.

Hicks cocked his head and listened. "What's he saying? Is he saying something?"

Duke leaned in. The smell was getting to him, and he struggled to keep his stomach under control.

"He's just—something, repeating—London?"

Duke strained to understand. Then he shook his head and stood up, breathing deep the clean, warm air.

"Sheriff—" Duke just stared at Kenny. "Sheriff, he's singing."

"Singing?"

Duke leaned into the car again, then stepped away and took a deep breath of the still night air.

"It's a rock song, Sheriff. 'She's Come Undone.'"

3

CASTLE LOOKED AT his watch in the moonlight. After 2 a.m. The fireworks over Dog Mountain had stopped popping in the night five hours ago. Michel had left, what, about ten or so, he guessed, and nothing had happened so far.

He had tried to paint, but his only idea had been a variation on an abstract he had finished a year ago. It had been a bad idea then, and it was awful now. He had put his brushes away, then picked up a bestseller someone had given him for Christmas. He started it several times, but he just couldn't get past the opening court scene with an Italian named Bonasera.

Michel had said it could take up to three days. It was different for everyone, he'd said. *It could be tomorrow; it could be Tuesday.*

But the change will come.

All the lights were off. Only the streetlights, and a floodlight from a telephone pole way off in the back yard, shone through his gauzy drapes. He wondered if he should change out of his day clothes and try to sleep, but he conceded it was pointless. He walked into the kitchen and made a cup of tea and warm milk and stared at his long, white-haired reflection in the window over the sink.

Tea and warm milk.

I am an old man.

He sipped his tea and sat in an easy chair in the living room. The drapes hung open, and he could see out across the dark street, the still trees dappled with moonlight, and the clear, endless sky glittering with stars.

He thought, for the first time, that maybe this was all just too unreal. Maybe Michel was not what he thought. Maybe—

No. He had shared blood with Michel tonight. He had seen for himself how Michel's eyes had gone black, and his teeth—

No.

It was all *too* real.

And he still tasted Michel's blood on the back of his tongue.

What have I done?

In the black shadows between the homes across the street, he spotted a small brown rabbit chewing grass. Its head perked up as it listened for danger, then it hopped once and started munching grass again.

Ben smiled. He had had rabbits when he was a child, in a hutch in the back yard his Daddy had built for him with leftover wood from—

Hold on.

He looked from house to house across the street. Far to the right, he clearly saw the soft beige drapes in Jasmine Winters' front windows. To the left, moonlight exposed the brilliant red brick of Sam Rodd's chimney. In the darkness in between, he followed the rabbit hop towards Sam's back yard, and he spied a small black beetle scurry over the concrete curb and into the grass.

He went over to the window.

The sky was ablaze: a nebulous river of suns, whirling across the blue-black horizon.

He snapped on a table light, then flinched away. The light *burned.* He snapped it off.

His stomach rumbled. He burped, tasting the tea and milk on the back of his throat. *The light in his eyes.* It had started something—some kind of cascade—

He stepped away from the lamp, and his stomach clenched. His muscles wrenched, dropping him to his knees. Then his stomach heaved, and a gush of tea and milk and black bile erupted from his stomach and splattered onto the carpet. He tried to crawl away, then his stomach heaved again. The fire in his belly seared up his throat, and tonight's steak and bourbon spewed out in a thick black torrent.

He staggered toward the front door. Michel had told him what to do, to protect himself, to protect his neighbors.

He stumbled down the front steps and started the pickup. He tore through the streets, barely pausing at stop signs, until he made it downtown.

He parked the truck behind Howard's hot dog shop, and stumbled through the alley until he reached the end of the block. He hugged the shadows, then suddenly fell to his knees, vomiting black bile into the grass. He looked across the street. Just a few more yards.

He ran for the brick wall that surrounded the property. The black iron gates were locked tight with a chain, so he climbed over the wall and into the cemetery.

There. The dark, angular shapes in the back. He weaved through the tombstones to the line of mausoleums, and he read the names chiseled in marble.

His stomach sent blinding spasms through his body. He stifled a scream, even as he remembered Michel's advice. *I found a place you can go. No one will go downtown at night, tonight or tomorrow. Hide in the cemetery. It will be safer there for you and everyone else. But nowhere is safe until the change is over.*

The iron gates below the name GARDNER were unlocked, just as Michel had said. They creaked open, and in moments he was in the cool darkness of the grave, huddled in a corner blanketed with dirt and crackling leaves as his insides squeezed as though in a vise. He screamed into the black night, and his pain was muffled from the world by the thick marble walls of the dead.

4

HICKS STOOD IN the center of the overgrown drive, smoke curling up from the Pall Mall in the corner of his mouth. The bright flashes from Elmore Eubank's camera lit the scene with silent white bursts. An ambulance waited, engine running and rear doors open. Ronnie Sheffield's body lay on a gurney, and Gordon Bragg, the county's informal coroner, stood over her with a flashlight. He shook his head quietly. He snapped off the flashlight, then pulled up a white sheet and covered her. Blotches of red soaked through the white linen. He turned to the attendants. "You can take her. The M.E. in Richmond has already been called."

Bragg walked over to the sheriff and ran his fingers through his white hair. "Near as I can tell, she's been dead near about twenty-four hours."

"That's what I figured," Hicks said.

Bragg looked around the scene, at the barn and the Mustang. "How do you see it?"

Hicks rubbed the bridge of his nose, then threw his cigarette to the ground. His headache was throbbing, and he wanted to be home, sipping an ice-cold whisky. And his damn eye wouldn't stop jerking. "They came out here to fool around in his new car, smoke some marijuana—found a baggie in his pants pocket. Something set him off. She probably said something that made him angry. It wouldn't take much, not for Kenny."

Bragg nodded.

"So. She pissed him off; he pissed her off. Who knows? She takes the baseball bat and bashes in his windshield, and it just drives him crazy."

"There's skin under her fingernails."

"Figures. So, they got in a big fight. She scratched him up some. Took it out on his shiny new car. And he killed her."

The attendants closed the ambulance doors, and they moved off down the drive. Ronnie's body lay next to Kenny, who was held tight with leather straps on a gurney, guarded by a deputy. Bragg had declared him stable, but the docs up at Stonebridge Hospital wouldn't be able to do anything for him, so he was bound for Richmond.

"Jesus, Buddy. Chewing into her neck like that. You sure Kenny could have done this?"

"Oh, he done it all right. All that blood, all over him. And you saw his teeth."

Bragg nodded. In the light from his flashlight, Bragg had found a piece of flesh wedged between Kenny's incisors. "Yeah."

"He was hopped up on something. LSD. Speed maybe." Hicks spit into the earth. "Fucking kids."

They heard footsteps behind them, and Duke came up with his notebook. "Hey, Gordy. Sorry you had to get called out here tonight."

"You know how it is."

Duke flipped open the notebook. "We've got statements from the kids who found the car. We've got six kids over at the party who heard Cindy screaming when she saw the body, and we've got their statements as well. Plus we're talking to all them that are left over there. A lot tore out after they figured the cops were coming."

"And?" Hicks said.

"Nobody saw a damn thing. Not a single witness."

They walked toward the crowd of onlookers that had stayed behind to watch. Two girls wept, holding hands. Carla Akins, the Record-Progress' editor, was asking questions and taking notes.

"I've sent the ambulance on to MCV," Bragg said. "Kenny needs to be looked at by somebody proper. Neurology, eventually. And Psych. We've probably got a Ward Eight, here."

"I need Kenny gone over like a crime scene," Hicks said. "Call the docs at MCV and tell them this is a murder case."

Bragg nodded.

Hicks looked up at the sky. "Sunrise in about an hour. We'll start searching as soon as there's light. And I guess I got to tell the parents." In the crowd, Hicks spied a teenager talking to Deputy Nettles, gesturing toward the Mustang. "Who's that boy?"

Duke looked up. "The Everett boy. Danny."

"Danny Everett. Another punk like Kenny."

"I'm going home," Bragg said. "You don't need me here, right?"

"Go," Hicks said. "Get me a report later today."

Bragg nodded, and turned toward his car. Hicks cupped his hand to his mouth and shouted, "Nettles!"

Deputy Nettles perked up, then trotted over. "Sir?"

"What's the Everett boy want?"

Nettles looked back over his shoulder. "He just heard about Kenny. Says he's Kenny's best friend."

"Bring him here." Nettles walked back to the boy, then led him over. Nettles said, "This is Danny Everett, Sheriff. Says Kenny got into a fight yesterday. That's how he got the money to pay for his car."

Danny's eyes were wide as he alternately stared at Hicks and at the blood-spattered Mustang.

"All right, Mr. Everett," Hicks said. "You come out all this way. Tell me what you know."

Danny swallowed. "All I know is what Kenny told me. He and Ray Ray got into a fight a few nights back."

"That's Ray Ray Pollard," Hicks said. He glanced at Duke. He had heard that Ray Ray was dealing marijuana out back of the ABC store, but he couldn't prove anything just yet.

Danny nodded. "Yeah. Kenny said that Ray Ray owed him a bunch of money, and he didn't want to pay up."

"Did he say what for?"

Danny shook his head, trying not to look nervous.

"You know," Hicks said, "there's rumors that Ray Ray deals drugs on the side. You heard anything about that, son?"

Danny shook his head again, a little too quickly. "No, sir. All I know is that Kenny said, 'If I want my money, I'm gonna have to beat it out of him.' He said it was like two hunnert bucks." He looked across the field at the wrecked car. "Jeez."

Hicks said, "You know anything about Kenny dealing drugs in town?"

"No, sir! Never!"

"So you don't know a thing about why Kenny loaned Ray Ray $200?"

"Loan? Oh, hell no, Sheriff. I'm just saying— Look, that's just what Kenny told me, Sheriff."

"When did you see Kenny last?"

"I saw him and Ronnie at the drive-in. Last night. Monster show."

"Anything seem unusual about either one of them?"

Danny thought about it. "Nope. Same old Kenny. We were supposed to meet up tonight. Over at the party."

Hicks lit a cigarette. "What time did you see them last?"

"Eleven? Eleven thirty? The Frankenstein movie was still on. Kenny tore out of there like a rocket."

"What for?"

"I don't know. It was, like, right after some motorcycle rode out of the drive-in. I remember, 'cause that chopper was loud."

Hicks narrowed his eyes.

Motorcycle.

Duke looked at Hicks. The sheriff's face was flushed, and his twitching eye seemed to wobble in its socket. Duke said, "Danny, can you describe the biker?"

"I didn't really see him that good. Long hair. Cool-looking bike, though."

Hicks watched the boy. "Don't go anywhere for the next few days. I might need to ask you some more questions. Jog your memory some. You hear me?"

Danny nodded. "Yes, sir. Hey, Sheriff. You think Ray Ray coulda done all this to get back at Kenny?"

"Forget all that shit. You just let me know if anything else comes to you."

"All right, Sheriff."

Hicks watched him walk away, then said to Duke, "Why would Kenny go after that biker?"

Duke sighed. The biker again. "We're not sure he did. All we know is that Kenny left in a hurry. *After* the biker left. Hell, maybe Ronnie pissed Kenny off at the drive-in. Maybe he drove out here so they could have it out."

Hicks turned toward him. "Call in the bears."

Duke stared at him. "You want the stateys in on this?"

"I need searchers. I need the scene here canvassed right, damn it, and I don't have enough men. Get Iris to make the call. It's almost dawn."

Duke said, "We've got to pick up Ray Ray. Sounds like drug money could be behind it all."

"Shit," Hicks said. "You and I both know it wasn't fuckin' Ray Ray."

Duke watched him. Ray Ray was weird all right, but he had never been considered a threat. "Still, we—"

"No. We've got to find that goddamn biker."

"Buddy, Ray Ray is a possibility. You and I both know Kenny did it, but we've got to eliminate Ray—"

Hicks looked Duke straight in the eyes. "Trager. Now. Sumbitch needs to be hunted down." He shot a pistol with his index finger and thumb. "Pronto, Tonto."

5

MICHEL DROVE DOWN the mountain. Summer held on to the seat, leaning with the bike, still buzzed, and smiling at the tingle of the warm wind as it whipped her long hair. She wore one of his shirts and a tight-belted pair of his jeans so that her white outfit would be free of the blood that had dried on their skin.

The motel room's doorknob had been replaced, and Tucker gave Michel a new key. Michel lulled him into forgetting about tonight, and Tucker promptly fell asleep in his chair.

Summer stripped, and they showered together and washed off the blood, and they made love with Summer pressed against the tiles, her legs tightening around his waist as he drove deep into her. She felt her body shuddering, rising to climax, and she buried her face into his neck, muffling her cries as she bucked against him, her body clenching with each powerful thrust.

She towel-dried her hair as best she could, and when they were dressed Michel peered through the curtains at the purple sky. Dawn was not far off.

He held her close and kissed her, the physical bond between them now as strong as the steel knot tying together their souls.

"We must make plans to leave," he said. In the caverns, their love had convinced him. Fighting against their destiny was useless. "At sunset, we need to disappear from Stonebridge. We'll stay in the caverns at first, so you can turn in safety, with no fear of being discovered."

"I feel it already. I feel *you.* You're a part of me."

"That's only part of it. We drank of each other. It could get violent for you. The change unleashes the beast inside of us all. Over the next few days, inside the earth, with me beside you, you'll be safe. In the dark."

He looked into her eyes. "You need to understand something—something you'll find out for yourself soon enough. Survival must be our number one imperative. Sometimes we will be forced to do horrendous things; even to coerce others to commit horrendous acts for us. Even upon the innocent.

"I am a killer. It is part of my nature. But you are so different. The things I've done— Summer, your heart is so much purer than mine. I didn't want you to become one like me. You're so—"

He cupped her chin and gazed into her eyes. Her skin seemed to glow, and her bright eyes were wide with wonder.

"Magic," he said, softly. "Your soul is so bright. You glow like the sun I can never see again."

She opened her mouth to speak, but he put a finger to her lips. "You deserve a life in the sunlight. You deserve far more, far better, than to never again feel the warmth of daylight."

She smiled up at him, and there was hard steel in her gaze. "This is magical to me too. But you need to understand. No matter what, I'll always be who I am, and it won't matter what I'm forced to do. You don't know who you're dealing with, mister." She smiled. "I'm tougher than you think. And I'll never hide. I thrive in the sunlight. Nothing is ever going to take it away from me."

"Summer, you no longer have a choice. It will kill you now. Sunlight—even mirrors—exposes us for who we truly are. The sun burns through our veneers, down to our souls. This is what we are. You chose the darkness, Summer. You chose it over the light."

"No." She kissed him. "It was you. I chose the prince of darkness. And I'll choose daylight, and moonlight, and you, and whatever else I want. Because of you, I feel the real me growing here, inside. And I am done doing the things I'm supposed to do, or pretending I'm someone I'm not. I'm done following the rules. I will never give up the daylight." She ran her hands down his cheeks. "But I'll live for the night."

"You cannot," he said. "You will die."

"Then I'll die. Do you understand? From now on, I live my way. Or not at all."

He held her hands in his and stared into her eyes. If sheer will could change the course of reality, then Summer would be able to change the path of the sun through the galaxy. But he also knew that there was a border between the realms of light and darkness, a sharp line their kind could never cross.

She couldn't accept that yet. In time, he knew, she'd find out for herself.

"Stubborn."

"Get used to it."

He pushed a strand of damp hair away from her face. "Very well. Come to me in the cavern after sundown," he said. "We'll hide your car from view, and we'll wait it out. Together. Then we'll leave town when you're ready."

"And go where?"

"I have a house outside of Boston."

"Boston?" Summer had never been farther north than a Washington, D.C., field trip.

"It's safe. I'll make a call. My servants will ready things for us."

"Servants?" she said, eyes wide.

He opened the door for her. Out on the sidewalk, he pulled her to him, and they kissed long and hard. Then she backed off toward her hidden car, running her hand along his motorcycle. "I think I need a bike of my own."

He laughed and waited until she drove off. Then he turned toward the mountains. It was dark, but he could feel the heat of the coming sun tingling on his skin. He had to hurry.

He turned north on Route 81. Seconds later, he heard an engine gunning behind him, and saw a flashing red light as it washed over him.

He looked over his shoulder.

Damn.

Dawn waited ahead of him.

And Hicks was right behind.

6

THE HORIZON GLOWED violet with the rising sun. Summer pulled up to the curb, stepped out, then crushed her cigarette on the road. She looked up at the house and thought of facing her mother when she walked through the door. *Aw, shit.* She took one last swig of bourbon—*Why the hell not?*—then steeled herself for her mother's onslaught.

She went in and closed the door behind her. The television was off, and the only light on was over the window in the kitchen. Her mother had gone to bed—but she had stayed up for a while, waiting for her. The ashtray by the sofa was overflowing.

"Dodged that bullet," she said.

Her mother's door was closed. Summer went into her bedroom, turned the air conditioner on high, threw her clothes onto the floor, and snuggled into bed, basking in the glow of Michel's body against hers, inside her.

She fell asleep within seconds.

Louise, however, was not sleeping.

She lay in bed, silent and still, staring at the ceiling, her heart thumping in an irregular, furious beat. Her mother's Bible lay at her side in the darkness. But she had tried to memorize the chapter—at least, the important parts—and she lay there in the dark, whispering.

"—the tokens of virginity be not found for the damsel, and the men shall stone her with stones that she die at her father's house, because she hath wrought folly to play the whore."

She repeated it, a mantra, as dawn rose over Stonebridge.

Virginity not found.

Play the whore.

The whore.

The whore.

7

HICKS COULDN'T TAKE it any longer. His headache had turned into a bass drum beating inside his skull, and his never-ending football injury had flared up again with jolts of fire. He had to get out of there. He put Duke in charge so he could go to the station to coordinate things with Iris and the state police.

But he didn't. He drove north, toward Route 81, where that motherfucking biker was staying in that no-tell motel.

Their initial search through the fields revealed nothing. A deputy found a switchblade, but it was old and rusted, and Hicks was sure it had nothing to do with the scene.

Kenny did it, high and pissed off and drunk.

At least, it looked that way.

But Hicks was sure that biker had something to do with it.

Hicks stopped at a gas station and yanked a bottle of Coke from a machine. He downed some pills, two reds and a white, then went back to the scene and dealt with reporters from Richmond and Roanoke who had been paying attention to the police scanners. Finally, after a brief conversation with Chaz Barley, the Commonwealth's Attorney, he'd decided he and his throbbing head had suffered enough.

He was going to hunt down that biker.

Let somebody else suffer.

Hicks turned onto Route 81 and sped past the long cornfields. He radioed Iris to call the stateys again and make sure they got more searchers up here ay-sap. A black Camaro passed him, heading back toward town.

And then, at the end of his vision, he saw the biker, dead ahead at the edge of his headlights.

The fire needling his back was forgotten. He flipped on the flashing red bubble and hit the accelerator.

That sumbitch wasn't going anywhere.

Michel checked the sky. The sun crouched behind the mountains, but the horizon was turning blue. Damn. He was closer to town than he was to the shelter of the caverns. And Hicks.

Hicks hit the siren.

It was dicey. Michel had only minutes before the dawn would be bright enough to affect him, and he refused to lead Hicks on a chase straight to his only sanctuary.

He leaned into a sharp turn. Hasty attack? No. That tactic worked in Vietnam, but here? Hicks would put up a fight, guaranteed. It could take too long.

Michel squealed the brakes, burning rubber, and spun to a stop, facing the way he'd come. He leapt off the bike and stood his ground.

Hit and run was the only viable tactic.

The squad car barreled around the turn. Hicks suddenly saw Michel only yards in front of him, standing in the road.

"Shit!" He slammed the brakes, and only feet before he hit Michel, he spun the wheel to the right and dug a swath into a cornfield. Then he was out of the car, crashing through broken stalks toward the road. He stepped onto the asphalt, and found Michel leaning against the parked bike, smiling.

"I guess I'm in a heap o' trouble," Michel said.

"GodDAMN it, you son of a bitch!" Hicks fumbled to open the strap of his pistol. "You had your chance to get outta my town. Now you're under arrest for murder."

Michel laughed.

Hicks leveled his gun at Michel. "You ain't no fuckin' war hero. You're a pusher. You and your goddamn drugs from Viet-fucking-Nam."

"A murdering, drug pushing biker? Good story." Michel stepped toward Hicks.

Hicks pulled back the hammer with his thumb. "You just stay right there, boy, or you won't be going anywhere but the morgue."

Michel took another step. "Been there."

Hicks looked into Michel's eyes. They had turned solid black. He took a step backwards. "You stay right there. I'm telling you."

Michel took another step. Hicks fired.

Michel staggered back, a splotch of dark blood welling in his chest.

He smiled.

"What—?" Hicks said.

Then Michel leaped. He cleared the space between them in a second and slammed Hicks to the road. The sheriff's back erupted with electric fire. Michel's fingers clenched around the pistol and ripped it from the sheriff's grasp. Something snapped. Hicks grunted, fire spreading through his middle finger. Michel threw the gun into the corn.

He pulled Hicks up by his collar. Hicks ploughed a beefy fist into his face. Michel grabbed the sheriff's left arm and bent it back, back, until Hicks' face was white with pain, and it felt like the whole arm was going to come off, and he was crying out, "Stop! Stop!"

Then Michel let go. Hicks' arm hung useless, his hand limp on the warm road. Michel pressed his right hand against the sheriff's forehead and forced his head back, laying bare his fat throat, exposing the irregular line of the external jugular.

Michel bent down, exposing his sharp teeth, smelling the sweat and the fear coming off Hicks with the stench of garbage. His teeth grazed the man's flesh.

Then Michel screamed, and a shaft of sunlight seared the back of his hand.

He threw Hicks to the road and crouched, out of the sunlight that peeked between the mountains. His eyes bulged, as black as night, and his voice was filled with feral rage.

"You're a tiny little man, Hicks. Men like you—officers, Napoleons in camo—they'd disappear during the night. They'd get killed in battle by friendly fire that no one could trace. They'd go off to piss in the jungle and get a barrage of bullets in their backs. I served my time. Crawling through flooded tunnels. Feeding off the blood of Vinks and tunnel rats that tasted of snakehead and curry. I was killing men halfway across the world when you were shitting in rags. You're nothing but a worm."

Then a thin beam of sunlight angled across Michel's forearm, and he screamed.

He dropped to his hands and feet, smoke hissing from his blackened forearm, and he crawled toward the bike, fast, natural, like an animal.

He grinned at Hicks, then leaped onto the bike, kickstarted it, and tore off, back toward town, riding low in the shadows until the roar of his bike faded down the road.

Hit and run.

Hicks forced himself to his feet and stared down the road. What he saw—the teeth, those eyes.

No! He's a biker, just a biker. A goddamned, no-good, fucking biker.

Then he screamed. His arm dangled at his side as he screamed to the dawn, and his cries echoed through the long rows of tall corn. And he screamed, and he screamed, and he stood there until he could scream no more, his muscles aching with rage, his face mottled with red, one eye bulging; needing to strike out, needing to hit, needing to hurt.

Needing to kill.

8

"SUMMER!"

Summer's eyes fluttered open. Early morning sunlight filtered through her drapes. She managed to murmur, "'M sleepin'" and closed her eyes, then her mother shouted again.

"Summer! Get your butt out of bed right now. We're going to church."

Summer blinked and turned over. Her clock read 7:28. She closed her eyes at the brightness. Her head throbbed.

"I am not going to church. This is my day off, and I am sleeping in."

Louise came in and stood over the bed. "You traipse around all night like a common whore and don't come in until almost daylight. You are going to church, little missy."

"Ma, I haven't been to church in years, and neither have you."

"Young lady, you will do as I say right now. As long as you're living under my roof—"

"Ma, knock it off. How much longer do I have to listen to this?"

Louise shouted, "Get your ass out of bed and get ready, you little tramp! I will NOT let my daughter become the town whore! Only the grace of God will save your ungrateful ass now. You better be ready in an hour for the 9:00 service, or there will be hell to pay."

Louise spun around and marched out. Summer blinked after her, her stomach doing somersaults as drums beat in her head.

She threw off the covers. "Shit on this," she said.

The voices of the congregation rose, and throughout St. John's Church, "Holy, Holy, Holy," echoed hollowly—almost as hollow as church made Summer feel.

Her mother had told her to drive, and as soon as Louise climbed in and closed the door, she wrinkled her nose and said, "Has someone been smoking in here?" Summer didn't answer. She slipped on her sunglasses and drove away, hoping to get this over as quickly as possible.

She fidgeted in the hard, wooden pew. A headache knotted behind her eyes, and she felt the hangover, combined with only two hours of sleep, rushing to make her pay for last night. Then she stood with the congregation as the choir filed in, holy, holy, holying, and her stomach sloshed, and she knew she was in for it. She tried not to look at the flowery sundress she'd thrown on. The reds and greens were too bright, but not as bright at Louise's dress. Her mother wore a painfully yellow sundress that came down just above her knees.

She looked like Tweety Bird.

Summer hadn't been to church since seventh grade, when she told her mother she was never going back to be bored again. Yet she recognized almost everyone that had been here back then, all sporting their Sunday finest, spruced up for the Jumpin' Jesus show. The same people came for absolution every week. The same people still cheated on their wives, or shoplifted, or lied on their taxes. And her mother wondered why she hated church.

The sunlight streaming through the centuries-old stained-glass windows stung her eyes. She wanted to wear her sunglasses inside, but she knew she'd get a slap on the arm from her mother. She giggled, covering her mouth so Louise wouldn't notice.

She only caught bits and pieces from the psalms and rituals. Her stomach was swirling, and she felt dizzy. *He came flying upon the wings of the wind. He made darkness his secret place.* And all she could think of were Michel's hands on her, caressing her, the feel of his body against her flesh. *They are dead, they will not live; they are shades, they will not arise.* Well, we'll see about that, she thought, 'cause Michel sure did a lot of rising last night. *The truth will make you free.* She rolled her eyes. I'm not free; I'm trapped in here. *He descended into Hell.* And she stifled a laugh. Hell? I'm there right now, with Tweety Bird.

Reverend Hayes peered through his wire rims and read the Collect and Epistle for Independence Day, then stepped to the pulpit and read his sermon, equating true independence with the acceptance of Jesus into your life.

She tuned him out, instead thinking of how free she had felt in the cavern last night, as though her soul had been unshackled to soar. Slowly she became aware of whispering behind her, around her, throughout the congregation. She looked up and saw Reverend Hayes standing at the top of the marble steps leading to the altar. He held his prayer book clasped tight in both hands. Ordinarily, at this point he would make church announcements, thank people for flowers, ask for prayers for those in the hospital. But his expression was one of disbelief.

"My friends, I fear I am at a profound loss. The Fourth of July is usually a day of great celebration. Of family get togethers, and picnics, and bands playing in the park." He waved a hand, fingers opening wide. "And fireworks. Beautiful fireworks. A celebration of life." He looked down at the prayer book in his hand and pressed his palm on it. "I do so love fireworks," he said, softly.

He looked out at the expectant faces. He took a deep breath.

"It is my unfortunate duty to inform you— Please, I am so sorry—" He cleared his throat, struggling to stay poised. "A tragedy has befallen a young couple in town, one of whom is—was—a part of our St. John's family."

Gasps went up from several people in the congregation.

"Early this morning, Ronnie Sheffield was found— I mean—" He paused. "I regret to say that she is—no longer with us." More gasps went up.

Someone in the back cried, "Oh no!"

"I have been told by Ronnie's father that police believe her boyfriend was involved in her death. He is now in custody. The exact details, we don't—I haven't been—" He floundered for words.

A woman began to cry in the choir.

"Please, forgive me. It's only because the Sheffield family asked me to pray for them."

The storm roiling in Summer's stomach suddenly felt hard and tight, as though she had been punched.

Ronnie.

Dead?

She said out loud, "How?"

Her mother snapped her head around and shushed her.

Reverend Hayes went on about praying for the family, and the blood of the innocent. *Ronnie.* She was no innocent babe.

And Kenny. Minor criminal, major bastard.

She giggled, and covered her mouth with her hand.

Oh my God. Innocent? She looked around at the people she had grown up with, these Sunday morning pretenders, and wondered who in this church was truly innocent?

Sunlight streamed bright through the stained glass, too bright, reflecting with needles of light off the massive gold cross over the altar.

The Devil's Altar.

She laughed aloud, and her stomach was spinning, telling her to move. Church, the liars in their Sunday finest. It was all too much. Her mother stared at her, and Summer made a sound, something between a laugh and a cry.

Summer sobbed aloud and leapt to her feet. She crawled over people's knees, trying to get out of the pew, trying not to laugh or cry while neighbors watched, whispering, "Oh, the poor thing," and, "She and Ronnie were best friends," and, "Bless her heart."

She ran out into the sun, onto the red brick path through the graveyard. Her eyes stung with tears, and she was laughing and crying simultaneously, taking in great gulps of air. She staggered to a cement bench in the shade beneath a weeping willow. Her body ached in shock, as the faint strains of the closing hymn came from the old pipe organ, and she saw the spatters of blood on Michel's face, Friday night, in her garden.

No. No, he couldn't have.

Horrendous things.

And then she heard the doors burst open, and suddenly women were around her, friends from high school on each side, their arms around her. She didn't hear them say, "She's in a better place," or "There's a reason for everything," or "The Lord works in mysterious ways."

She told them she would be all right, that it was just so sudden, a complete shock. Then her mother was there, standing in front of her, her lips pursed. "I hope you're proud of yourself. Making a scene in my church."

She wheeled away toward the car, and Summer's friends stared after her. She heard one girl say, "What a bitch." And Summer laughed and wept, trying to breathe through the tears clogging her nose, and said, between sobs, "You don't know. You just don't know."

They held her while she cried, "Ronnie, Ronnie," and the girls cried with her, running their hands down her hair, and someone behind her said, "That goddamn, no good Kenny."

And Summer wept and laughed, because she knew; and her mascara ran black down her cheeks as Louise stared disapprovingly from the car, as the world spun around them, as Ronnie lay cold and lifeless somewhere on a metal tray, and the sunlight beneath the willow slowly turned to shadow.

And she knew.

9

THE DOOR BANGED against the bathroom wall, and Hicks slammed open the medicine cabinet and didn't give a good goddamn if the mirror broke.

He could move his arm a little now, but it still hurt like a son of a bitch, and he was pretty sure his finger was either sprained or broken. He fumbled with a bottle of aspirin, finally screwed the black cap off the Bayer bottle, and he plopped four white tablets straight onto his tongue. He swallowed them with handfuls of water from the faucet, then dried his hands, wincing at the pain that shot through his middle finger.

It had taken him almost half an hour, trudging through Louis Crowder's cornfield, to find his revolver. The gun was intact, but the barrel was clogged with dirt. Then he backed his cruiser out of the field, spitting corn and soil from the tires, U-turned across the road, then tore off to his house. No way he was going back to the station looking like this.

He found an old bottle of Doan's Pills tucked behind an even older bottle of Bactine, and he carried the last three pills into the kitchen and washed them down with a slug of Gilbey's. He put the bottle on the counter, lit a Pall Mall and took a deep drag, then drank another shot, and another. For the pain.

He opened the cylinder of his revolver and blew the dirt out of the barrel. Then he twisted a paper towel tight, scowling, because he hated wasting his own good money on paper towels, and twisted it into the barrel, pulling it out the muzzle, along with any extra dirt. "Good enough for God's work," he murmured, unaware that he was talking to himself. He reloaded the gun and holstered it.

He drank another long swig of scotch, staring out the back window; but all he could see was Trager's goddamn long hair, his hippie face, and he swallowed three more pain pills from his shirt pocket. He was going to find that biker.

I shot him! And it didn't even slow him down!

That's just crazy. And no way he was going to tell the office what happened up the road. He and Trager got into a fight; they both got themselves a little beat up; but ol' Buddy Hicks got the drop on the hippie bum, and Hicks saw him off at the county line.

That's what happened. Yes sir-ee, Jim Bob Dandy.

But the sumbitch drove off somewheres. Into town.

Where?

A hidey hole? Maybe. And he sure as shit didn't go back to that motel.

He grinned.

The only place he could go.

Ben Castle's.

He filled his flask with scotch, shaking, and spilled it over the sides and onto his fingers. Damn, his eye would just not stop jumping. He licked his fingers clean, then gulped one last shot from the bottle.

He drove through town and pulled into the parking lot of Stonebridge High, then cruised back behind the practice football field to the edge of the woods. A winding path through the trees led to a neighborhood just a few hundred yards away, and only three houses down from Ben Castle's backyard.

He stepped off the path and weaved through the trees. The scotch felt warm in his belly. He felt pretty good now, with the pills and the booze dulling the sharp edges. Leaves and twigs snapped under his feet, and he stopped ten feet inside the tree line behind Castle's house and took a swig from the flask and watched the house for ten minutes.

No movement.

No lights.

He stepped out of the trees and went over to Ben's storage shed. Lawn mower, yard equipment, some old furniture. Trager's motorcycle wasn't there.

He walked to the back of Ben's house, moving from one window to another, glancing inside. No movement; only shadows and furniture and paintings. Ben's bed was unmade and empty.

Hicks checked his watch. 7:15. This early and nobody's home? He figured the old hippie would still be asleep.

Good. This way he could look around all he wanted.

He stepped up to the screen door and rapped on the aluminum frame. He waited a minute, then knocked harder.

He tried the doorknob. It turned easily, unlocked, like most doors out in the country, and Hicks whispered, "Thank you, you faggot cocksucker."

He stood in the kitchen. The clock ticked over the dinette table. The house was shadowy and still in the morning twilight. And there was a smell, a weird, earthy smell, almost like dirt and oil and vomit.

The drapes were drawn in the dining room. The smell was stronger out here, and he found a spot in the living room: an irregular pool of black bile that had soaked the thick carpet.

He checked the bedrooms. No Ben and no biker. His middle finger throbbed dully. He found Ben's bottle of Maker's Mark and threw back a slug, then another, and he said, "Fuck this," and decided to search for something harder.

He slung open Ben's medicine cabinet, and a clear plastic bottle stood out on the bottom shelf. A Charlie's Drugs prescription label read

MEPERIDINE

Take 1 for pain every 12 hours.

"Mee— meeper-eye—"

Aw, hell. If he couldn't pronounce it, it *had* to be good.

He popped three pills and swallowed them with a slug of Maker's Mark. He glanced at himself in the mirror, and for a moment he saw the biker's face.

His soulless black eyes, the smoke hissing out of his skin.

He slammed the cabinet door, slammed it again—*It didn't happen!*—until the mirror shattered in a glittering, silver rain.

He went down the hall. He found the kitchen knives and picked the longest, sharpest he could find. He strode into Ben's studio. The steel knife gleamed in the gold morning light as Hicks slashed painting after painting; and when he had had enough, he threw paintings across the room and shoved over Ben's painting table with his foot, spilling vermillion and oils and linseed onto the carpet.

He went into the living room and broke a row of photos on the mantel. He lashed out with his good hand and smashed a lamp, and he was laughing and gasping for breath when he noticed he had cut himself across the back of his hand. He yelled, "Shit!" and pushed over an easy chair, and then threw a crystal ashtray into the wall, punching a hole into the dry wall.

He ran cold water over his hand, then wrapped a white, flowered dish towel around it. Dishes stood in a drying rack next to the kitchen sink. He scattered the dishes with a wide sweep of his arm, and smiled as the china shattered against the wall. He turned at the back door and took in the carnage he had wrought.

It'll be a nice present for that fuckin' faggot when he gets back.

He left the back door wide open, and disappeared into the woods, his head buzzing with a mindless, seething, bottomless rage.

10

SUMMER WEPT AS she drove home, and Louise smoked and stared out the window. She parked in the driveway behind her mother's Cadillac. Louise was out of the car before Summer could cut it off. She flicked her Winston into the grass and stormed for the front door.

Summer closed the car door gently, so the sound wouldn't reverberate through her skull. She stepped into the cool house. Her mother stood in the hall with her back to her.

Summer closed the door. "Ma? Are you okay?"

Louise suddenly spun around, her face stretched in a grotesque rictus of rage, and she slapped Summer across the cheek so hard her head snapped to the side.

"*You ungrateful little BITCH!* You're high on something, on some kinda *DOPE*, aren't you? You are *NOT* the daughter I brought up to obey the Good Book! You're just a goddamn bitch *JUNKIE*, aren't you?"

Summer's cheek stung bright red. "Are you crazy? I don't do drugs!"

Louise's hands balled into arthritic fists. "That, that *boy*. You've been doing it with him, haven't you?"

"Ma!"

"You've been *FUCKING* him, haven't you? That bastard has gone and knocked you up, hasn't he?"

"Knocked—Jesus, no!"

Louise took a step closer, snarling her words. "You're nothing but a common little whore. No good like your goddamn father! And now you're going to have a little bastard baby, aren't you? A little, fucking, bastard baby."

"Mama, I haven't— Rob and I have never—"

"Not *him*, you tramp! That boy's too stupid to know where to put his pecker. You know who I'm talking about. That hoodlum. That biker the whole town is talking about."

Summer's eyes widened.

"You spread your legs for him, didn't you? You let him fuck you, didn't you, you SLUT? You did it with him, you fucked him!"

Louise slapped her again. Then she swung her hand again. Summer snapped her arm up and blocked her mother's blow, then shoved her away. She hurried up the stairs. "You're crazy!" Summer yelled. "You're crazy!"

Louise stood at the bottom of the steps, her hand clenched tight around the bannister, and yelled up, "It's that goddamn music of yours! That devil-fornicating music you listen to! No daughter of mine—"

Summer slammed the bedroom door. She cranked up the stereo and changed into jean shorts and a short-sleeve blouse. She needed out. No way she was going to stay here with that crazy lady. No fucking way. She needed answers, about Ronnie and Kenny, and what happened after they left the drive-in.

She slipped on her blue shades and slung her purse over her shoulder. Maybe it didn't really matter. Ronnie was dead, and nothing would change that.

Horrendous things.

Whatever she found out, she'd be ready for it.

She was going away with Michel.

No matter what.

She turned off the radio and strode downstairs, past her mother smoking in the living room.

"Just where do you think you're—"

Summer slammed the door.

Louise stared at the blank TV, at nothing. Her Hummels stood quiet in their places, beautiful, quiet, perfect little babies. The grandfather clock in the dining room corner ticked, second by second, the way it always should. She sat surrounded by order; her very own, precise, order.

And her ungrateful bitch daughter.

She smoked the Winston down to the butt, and stubbed it out in the ashtray at her side.

"Well."

That hellion had left her no choice, hadn't she?

"Well."

She walked into the kitchen and reached for the phone.

She dialed only one number, and waited for the operator to pick up.

11

ELVIS WAS SINGING "Guitar Man" from the jukebox when Summer came through the front door and saw Tina taking an order, her eyes red and puffy. She looked up at Summer with an empty expression of disbelief, and nodded toward the kitchen. Summer went through the swinging doors, and didn't even have time to say "Hi" to Ruthette before Tina came in behind her. They hugged, and tears welled in Summer's eyes.

"I can't believe this," Tina said. "I know Kenny's a son of a bitch, but this?"

"It doesn't feel real," Summer said. "I mean, we both were there with her Friday night."

Tina grabbed her purse from under a steel counter and lit a cigarette. She closed her eyes and forced a laugh. "Are you as hungover as I am?"

Summer nodded. Even with her sunglasses on, the light stung, too bright, and she felt the knot squirming in her stomach, writhing like eels.

Tina blew smoke. "It's all over town. I don't know what's true and what isn't. Somebody found them in Kenny's car at the old farm, right next to the party."

"All that time, we were drinking, and they were right there?"

"I feel so guilty, like somebody should have known."

"You can't do that to yourself. How were we supposed to know?" But she felt the guilt too.

"Everybody's heard something different. Kenny found out she'd been sneaking around behind his back. Or she said the wrong thing, and he just blew up."

"He's done stuff like that before."

"Yeah. But—God, this is gross. Bailey Evans knows one of the deputies. She said that Kenny was trying to eat Ronnie's skin. And he— he chewed through her neck."

Summer stared at her.

No.

"And the last time anyone saw them was when they left the movies."

No, please.

"She said that Danny Everett was there last night, with the cops. He saw Ronnie's body. He heard her throat had been torn out."

"This just can't be happening."

"And Danny told her that Kenny tore out of the drive-in like he was crazy or something. Right after some hippie guy left on a motorcycle."

And there it was.

She had feared it all morning, since Reverend Hayes told everyone that Ronnie was dead.

She had fought against it. She hadn't wanted to accept it.

Kenny.

It came to her suddenly, a flash of insight she couldn't deny.

Kenny had done something. Somehow, he had provoked Michel. He'd started a fight. He'd picked the wrong guy, big time. And he'd paid for it. He and Ronnie both.

Horrendous things.

Ruthette cleared her throat. "Tina, baby, you better get on out front and help Sarah." Tina looked over at her, then jabbed her cigarette in a red plastic ashtray. "This is terrible," she said, and she went out to her tables.

Summer went over to the grill, and she and Ruthette hugged. Then Ruthette held her out at arm's length and looked at her. "Girl, are you okay?" Summer's skin was ashen, and dark circles surrounded her eyes. "I know y'all were close."

Summer seemed to deflate, as though her strength seeped out of her. "I'm just shocked. Sick to my stomach."

Ruthette looked into her eyes. She was telling the truth; Ruthette could see it. But there was something different now. She was pale, and sad, and teary-eyed.

But she wasn't frightened at all.

Ruthette sighed and pulled her to her bosom.

She had grown up, just like that. And even though she couldn't know that this was the last time she would ever see her, Ruthette knew for a certainty that Summer had outgrown Stonebridge, just like that.

Summer didn't belong here anymore.

Just like that.

Then the kitchen doors banged open.

Sheriff Hicks and Duke Crawford barged in as customers stared at them. The sheriff's left eye fluttered. He winced in pain as he lifted his arm and pointed straight at Summer.

"You," he said. "Summer Moore."

Duke came up beside her and placed his hand on her arm. He wouldn't look her in the eyes. "I'm really sorry about this, Summer," he said.

The blackness behind the sheriff's eyes seemed alien. He grinned, but instead of mirth, she saw only blind hatred.

"Let's go for a little ride, girly girl," Hicks said. "We gotta talk about last night."

12

IT USED TO be a storage room, but Hicks got the idea for an official interrogation room from a low budget Fred MacMurray cop movie during his second year as sheriff, and convinced the board of supervisors to allocate the funds in 1951. It came complete with one too-bright, hanging lamp, a steel table bolted into the floor, and a top of the line two-way mirror in the wall.

Summer had been left alone in there for almost two hours. The deputies on duty had stared at her as Hicks had pushed her into the dark room, telling her to, "Get comfy, Goldilocks."

She was smoking her third Salem, tapping the ashes into a blue aluminum ashtray on the table, when Duke came in. He tried to avoid her eyes as he sat across from her. She didn't deserve this. They had the guy responsible for Ronnie's death. Duke couldn't figure out why Hicks wouldn't let go of this biker thing.

"How are you?"

She stared at him, one arm across her sloshing stomach. "Why am I here?"

"You don't look all right." She seemed pale, but it could have been the light from the hot bulb over the table.

"My stomach."

"You want a drink? Coffee?"

"A Coke would be nice. My stomach is killing me."

"The party last night?"

"I thought I was going to throw up in church when—" She teared up. "Ronnie," she whispered.

Duke saw the tears. He was sure she didn't know anything about Ronnie's death, but other women had cried in that chair before.

"What am I doing here, Duke?"

"The sheriff's got some questions for you about last night. Anything you can remember about Friday night. About Ronnie and Kenny."

"But I don't know anything. The first thing I heard about her was in church. And I saw them at the movies Friday night. Jeez, how could you think I'd know something about—"

He stood up and touched her hand. "I'll go get your Coke."

He left and closed the door. In the hall, he opened the door on the right and entered a dark space that used to be a closet. Hicks had been watching them through the mirror.

"Sweating her down," he said. "Sweatin' the bitch down."

"You heard her," Duke said. "I believe her, Buddy. She might be hiding something about her hangover—maybe drugs or something—but she doesn't know anything about Ronnie's death."

Hicks said, "Yeah. But she knows the biker."

Knowing someone isn't a crime, Duke wanted to say. "Be right back," he said.

"You ain't gonna give her that Coke."

It was an order.

Duke stared Hicks down. "She's had enough, goddamn it."

He went to the refrigerator and popped open a bottle of Coke. He took it to Summer, who drained it, and she handed him the bottle. "Thanks. Hot in here."

"Supposed to be," he said.

The door behind him opened, and Hicks walked in. Duke stood. Hicks scraped the chair across the floor and eased his bulk into it. Duke hung near the door.

"So," Hicks said. "Miss Summer Moore. 56 Croatoan Avenue. Age 20. Obviously hungover. Miss Moore, I could charge you with underage drinking, you know that?"

"I'm over eighteen, Sheriff. I can drink beer legally."

The sheriff's eye twitched. The Moore bitch was being a smart ass, all right.

He lit a Pall Mall and blew smoke toward her. He offered her one. She shook her head. "No, thank you. Got my own." She lit another Salem. The smoke curled toward the hanging light bulb.

"Okay, Miss Summer Moore. When was the last time you saw Kenny Cousins and Ronnie Sheffield?"

"Friday night. At the drive-in movies."

"Friday. Okay. What were you doing?"

She narrowed her eyes at him. "At the movies? I was watching the movies. With my boyfriend."

"Boyfriend."

"Yeah. My boyfriend, Rob. Rob West."

Hicks grunted. "What were the movies?"

"*Dracula* and *Frankenstein*. They weren't the greatest."

"Where'd you see Ronnie and Kenny?"

"They were there. They were a few rows up from us, in Kenny's new car."

"What were they doing?"

She shook her head. "I didn't keep tabs on them. I saw Kenny's head from behind. And I didn't see Ronnie till she went to the bathroom."

"When was that?"

"Hell, I don't know for sure."

"You don't know a lot."

"I definitely don't know what I'm doing here. I didn't even talk to Ronnie Friday night."

"And where were you yesterday?"

"What? All day? You really want to know where I was all day?"

"You bet your ass, Goldilocks."

"I was at work. I got called in. Sarah called in sick, and it was supposed to be my day off. Then I went home and took a nap."

"And what about last night?"

She took a drag on her cigarette, deciding what to tell him. *Aw, what the hell. He already knows.*

"The Fourth of July party, over at the old Nicewander farm."

"Yeah. The illegal party you kids think we don't know anything about. With all the underage drinking, and the druggies." He cocked his head, and in the light, one eye seemed bigger than the other. Wilder. "And I guess you were there with your boyfriend. Rob."

She took a last drag on the cigarette and crushed it out. She crossed her arms. "Not exactly."

Hicks laughed, a little too loud. "Not exactly! That's goddamn funny! Ain't it, Duke? Huh? Ain't that funny?"

She stared at him. Hicks had always been a tough son of a bitch, but this behavior wasn't like him. She looked past him at Duke, but he wouldn't meet her eyes.

"So. How'd you get hooked up with him?"

"Rob?"

He smacked his hand flat on the table. "You know goddamn well who, Miss Moore. The goddamn biker you met Thursday night. Trager. James Goddamn Trager."

She sat back, as far away from him as she could. His head bobbed nervously, hungrily, and his eyes held a crazed, empty look.

"We met. At the drive-in."

"Doing what exactly?"

"I went to the snack bar. He was there. He saw me. And he asked me out. We went to the party last night."

"Where is he?"

"How would I—"

"You were seen with him last night by half the kids at that goddamn illegal hullaballoo! Now where the goddamn hell is he?"

Duke took a step toward Hicks. "Sheriff, I think we need to—"

"You fuckin' stay right there, Dudley Do-Right." He leaned across the table. "I remember you, Miss Summer Moore. Raisin' hell in high school. Makin' fun. Disrespectin' me. Authority!" he shouted. "Me! You don't respect your betters! You think I forgot?" Hicks laughed and leaned back into the hard chair. "Now. That new boyfriend of yours ain't up at that motel. I been checking on him. Now, where the hell is he holing up?"

"I don't know. I haven't seen him today." Her stomach felt like it was doing flip flops. The Coke tasted like acid on the back of her throat.

Hicks watched her, silent, then sat down and forced himself to stay calm. "Are you aware that Kenny Cousins was seen chasing after him Friday night at the drive-in?"

Kenny chased him? "No. Why would Kenny—?"

"Now. Just how well do you know this Trager?"

"I don't see how that's any of your business."

"And I don't think you can see past the tip of your nose, girly girl." He stood up, bandaged hand on the table, looking down at her. "Now, I asked you a goddamn question. Just exactly what is the nature of your relationship with the suspect?"

"Suspect? But, I thought Kenny—"

"Kenny. Shit." He grinned, shaking his head. "Do you even know anything about your new boyfriend at all? Who the hell do you think he is?"

"We only went on one date. Last night. I don't know what you want me to tell you."

She was trembling, and Hicks saw how pale she was, and how she was favoring her stomach. Sweat had broken out across her forehead.

Guilty as shit.

"Can the crap, missy. You're high on something, aren't you? What did he give you? Pills? Bennies? Reds?"

Summer laughed in his face. Pills? Oh, he'd given her something better and redder than he could ever imagine.

"Drugs." She leaned back in her chair. "You and my mother should swap stories sometime. Nobody is ever up to any good except for you two."

"Well. At least she ain't blind. She knows bad news when she sees it."

Summer sat up straight. "Excuse me?"

Hicks grinned. "I thank God for loyal Americans like your mother. Who do you think called me and told me all about you and the biker?"

13

HICKS GRILLED SUMMER on and off for another three hours, but he didn't get anything out of her that he didn't already know. He let her stew alone in the interrogation room for another hour while he sat in his office, shuffling papers and nipping off the bottle of scotch in his drawer. Around supper time, he looked out the window and saw how low the sun was, and he finally told Duke to get Summer the hell back to the diner.

She was silent in the back seat of the squad car, hugging her stomach. No one had offered her anything for lunch, and now the acid in her stomach felt like whitecaps crashing to shore. Her eyes stung from the sunlight.

"Summer? Are you all right?"

Duke watched her in the rearview mirror. She managed a grin. "I feel like shit on a stick, okay?"

"How much did you have last night?"

"Beer, bourbon, and moonshine. My stomach feels like it's a lava lamp. Christ, Hicks kept me in there for four hours, Duke. I'm hungover, and I have just been completely embarrassed in public, and none of it's called for. I didn't do a thing."

Duke turned in to the dinette's parking lot. "I know you didn't. I told him that, but he wouldn't listen." He turned toward her. "Look, Hicks wants to pin Ronnie on Trager."

"What? But he—"

"The evidence points straight at Kenny. But the sheriff wants Trager for this. I mean, he wants to nail him bad. So if you know anything—anything at all—you've got to come clean."

She stared him down. "Duke, how long have you known me? You're becoming just like him." She tried to open the cruiser's back door, but it wouldn't budge. "Open this damn door and let me get home."

Duke came around and opened the door for her. "Summer, look, I'm sorry about—"

She stepped out into the diner's parking lot. Her stomach squeezed like a fist: clenching tight, then relaxing, then squeezing again. "Just forget it, Duke. I thought that if any of you cops believed me, it would be you."

"Summer, I didn't—"

She slid into her Camaro and slammed the door. She watched him climb into his cruiser, and a jolt of pain deep in her belly doubled her over the steering wheel. She sat back, took deep breaths, and watched Duke drive off in the rearview mirror. Then she backed out of the lot and headed home.

She turned onto Croatoan. Her mother's car was parked in the driveway. She had been hoping Louise would be out somewhere, riding her broom or luring children into gingerbread houses. She didn't want to deal with her right now. She just wanted to *hate.*

She got out and walked up the sidewalk. She paused in the shade of the porch, wondering what to say to her. Nothing came to mind that wasn't full of curse words, so she went inside and closed the door.

Her mother sat in the living room, watching television. *Screw it*, she thought, and she strode past Louise and her smoke and a Tarzan movie on the black and white, not even acknowledging her existence.

She started upstairs, then grabbed the bannister as her stomach lurched with an intensity she hadn't felt before. She willed herself to hold it all down. All she wanted to do was pack her bags as fast as she could and go to Michel.

She turned up the air conditioner in her bedroom, then glimpsed herself in the mirror. She looked ashen in the light, and her eyes seemed sunken in. Cold sweat beaded on her skin.

"I look like hell."

She went to the closet and reached for the suitcases in the back. Then her stomach *lurched*, stopping her in mid-reach. Gases gurgled in her belly.

She yanked open the bedroom door and rushed for the bathroom. She forced herself to keep it down.

Not yet not yet not—

And locked the door. She reached for the toilet seat, started to kneel, then her stomach erupted in a torrent of blackness that splattered across the toilet. The smell overwhelmed her. Her stomach heaved again, choking her with the foulness of shit and earth; and she heaved again, and her black bile dripped over the rim and down the outside of the toilet. She fumbled for the handle and flushed, and her stomach clenched again, and she vomited blackness and blood, and she struggled for air, and she heaved blood into the toilet, onto the fuzzy green toilet rug.

Oh God, what IS it, the smell, I'm BLEEDING, my blood, am I—

Her sinuses filled with the dank, coppery tang of her rich blood. She flushed again. She waited for the next spasm to rip open her insides and spew them against the white porcelain. Nothing came. She staggered to her feet, then thought better of it, and sat on the edge of the tub.

Then it came again. Her stomach knotted, and she vomited blood and darkness onto the floor.

She slid down the outside of the tub, breathing slowly, and she pressed her hand on her chest.

Then she froze.

Her heart.

Beneath her fingertips—

She couldn't feel her heartbeat.

The light was growing dim, fading.

No. NO! This can't be—

Her left hand plopped to the floor, limp. Her face thudded onto the rug.

Michel? Please, help—

She dimly felt the fibers of the carpet against her cheek, and as her eyes lost the light, she saw only the green bathroom rug, the carpet sticking up near her eye, speckled with black bile and crimson.

And then her eyes glazed over, and she saw nothing.

14

A GLORIOUS SUNSET, in the summer, in Stonebridge:

The Independence Day Festival at Washington-Jefferson Heritage Park was long over. Corky Seward, owner of Corky's Maytag and Appliances, once again read aloud the Declaration of Independence from the park gazebo, dressed in his very own tri-cornered hat and his royal blue Revolutionary regimental uniform.

The high school band played Sousa and patriotic marches and a slew of American standards, and Roberta Ledbetter, the children's librarian at the Hendrick J. Cordell Memorial Library, finished the concert with her best imitation of Kate Smith, in both size and voice, and belted out "God Bless America." The Lions Club Jug Band came onstage and got the crowd laughing while performing in underwear and women's wigs, using instruments made out of saws, hula hoops, and pogo sticks.

Children ate cotton candy and candy apples in the shade, while others caught June Bugs and tied thread to their legs and laughed as the giant insects spun in tethered circles above their heads. Adults drank beer out of coolers and played cornhole after their picnics of hot dogs and fried chicken and potato salad.

It was July Fourth, and the sun was high and hot, and as Stonebridge's good citizens went through all the annual celebratory motions of firecrackers and parades and charcoal flare ups, the gossip and conversation invariably turned to Ronnie Sheffield and her gruesome death; to examinations of her character, based on the currency of common knowledge, which was that she had been a mild to moderate tramp who may or may not have deserved a fate commensurate with her low morals, but perhaps not a fate so horrible and brutal as the death God granted her. And, as to Kenny Cousins, hmph, good riddance. Over beers and bourbons, the adults admitted to themselves that Kenny's end was long- and well-deserved, for everyone knew exactly what type of boy he had grown up to become, and how could he escape it, with a father who had done time in the state pen, and was a worse man when he got out than when he went in? And, try as they might to shield the children from Ronnie's murder, the story made the news in both Richmond and Roanoke, and Stonebridge's kids made the obligatory hickey jokes, and called Kenny Cousins, "My cousin, the cannibal."

Now, with the sun sinking below the Crescent Valley ridge, a soft haze settled over the green mountains, and families began to settle in. While birds chirped and bats swooped and squeaked between the trees, the sky turned purple, and the air was still and hot. Every now and then, an errant firecracker went off and echoed down the quiet streets. A lonely train whistle blew in the distance, from a southbound Norfolk and Western. Kids playing with sparklers and trying to catch lightning bugs were called inside for the night, because it was time for dinner and Walt Disney, or *Hogan's Heroes,* or Red Skelton, or *Bonanza*, and the Batman movie would be on the TV soon. Old people sat out on their porches in rocking metal lawn chairs and smoked, and drank Schaefers out of ice-filled buckets, and talked low about how they couldn't understand what had got into Kenny, and how that boy coulda done that to that girl. And oh, ain't that a cryin' shame.

Then the mountains were black silhouettes against the sinking sun. It was 8:44 p.m., and the bathroom at 56 Croatoan Avenue was lit only by the last hazy light of the waning sun filtering through the curtains.

Summer's eyes snapped open.

And the world was born anew.

She felt each individual fiber in the strands of the shag rug touching her skin. She heard the soft fibers spring up, crackling, as she rose in the darkness. Her nausea was a dim memory; all she felt inside was a warm, pleasant serenity, and a sense of inner strength she had never felt before.

Her mother had turned up the television—*No.* She heard the hum from the back of the black and white in the living room, and the dialogue from the TV show, as though she were standing in front of the set; and under that, her mother's slow snoring. She had fallen asleep on the sofa again.

Her hearing was better. Stronger.

She heard a radio playing, "It's Just a Matter of Time," some country song with a tinny organ playing in the background—from the Whitehead house, three doors away. She heard the footfalls of a boy rushing home down the street, and heard a couple kiss, smacking lips, down the block.

The bathroom light was off, but she saw the cracks in the paint along the bathroom trim as clear as if it were daylight. She saw old stains on the toilet and sink, and in the last grey light coming from the drapes, dust danced like snowflakes. She parted the drapes. Lightning bugs dipped on the soft air currents, blinking as bright as streetlights.

She was reborn, and the world was new. The night was alive, and her soul sang with myriad voices, a harmony of sopranos and echoes, singing an endless song.

Their voices, Angeline, Nichole, Genevieve, the others, lost down the centuries, lived in her now. She felt the long, eternal story—a story beating in her heart—that was entwined with her very being as tightly as DNA.

She and Michel had been predestined to come together, to set her soul free.

He was always on the run, and now she knew why.

It was time for her to run with him, side by side, through the long night.

She balled up the bathroom rug stained with her black fluids and stuffed it into the paper grocery bag that doubled as the bathroom trash can. She did the same with her top, stained with vomit and blood, and she cleaned the toilet.

She showered and put on jeans and a striped, low neck, sleeveless top, then went to her vanity to put on her makeup.

And she froze.

Her reflection stared back at her with black, dead eyes, wide with horror. Her flesh was white and bloated, and the hollows under her eyes and cheekbones were deep blue shadows. Her mouth was a gaping wound, and her tongue was a black-red snake hiding behind long, sharp white teeth. Wisps of blackness curled around her, seeping from her pores like tentacles of oily smoke.

She took a step away from the mirror, blinking at the thing she had become.

Control.

A whisper from deep inside.

Mastery. At all times.

Until the beast can be loosed.

And she said, "No."

It seemed like the air popped. She looked in the mirror, and she was herself. Tanned, sandy-haired, ice-blue eyes.

She started piling her clothes on the bed. Then she stopped. Under the sounds of the television, she heard footfalls. And she smelled something, a familiar scent, outside, in her garden.

Yes.

This was destined to happen as well.

She took the stairs, soundless as a breeze. She opened the back door, instinctively willing the night to muffle the creak of the hinges. Then she was in her garden, and she felt his heartbeat throbbing through the air, and smelled his scent—a scent that, until now, she never knew he had.

"Rob," she said.

He had been pacing in the garden, afraid to knock, wondering what to say. He snapped his head up at the sound of her voice, and there she was, right next to him.

He stared. Her eyes, her lips, shone brighter, rosier, as though she had blossomed overnight into something ethereal.

"How'd you know I was out here?"

I smelled you from my bedroom just wouldn't do. "I saw you through the window. How long have you been out here?"

She went toward him, almost gliding across the pebbled garden.

"A few minutes, I guess. I didn't know what to do. Or say. Since last night, I feel so, so empty, I guess. Without you. And now, with what's happened to Ronnie. And Kenny, jeez. Kenny, going to the hospital, or jail. I mean, what the hell is happening? It's like a storm of shit, all at once. It's all coming apart. And, and *you*—" His eyes welled with tears. "I didn't know where else to go. I mean, who else do I have? Who else have I ever talked to about everything?" He wiped away a tear. "Look, I'm sorry. I didn't mean to. Aw, hell. I can't believe this is happening. I mean, what did I do? I must have done something."

"Rob, don't do this to yourself. You're the best boyfriend a girl could ask for."

"Then why?"

She couldn't tell him everything that had happened—hell, he wouldn't believe it—but he deserved as much of the truth as possible.

"This is all on me. It's my fault. I can't tell you how sorry I am. You don't deserve—"

"But why him? You don't even know him. You just met him."

Her voice softened. "I didn't know any of this was going to happen. I didn't know that he would come here. But it happened. I can't tell you if it was an accident, or fate, but—"

Rob was leaning toward her, listening, and she realized he was captivated by her, by her voice, by her—by *her*. She was doing, instinctively, what Michel had done yesterday with Tucker at the motel.

He said, softly, "But I thought we were in love. I thought, you and I, after I graduate in a couple of years..."

She ached with guilt, but she knew there was nothing else she could do. "We were. And I was." She focused on him, and to Rob, her voice became a song that echoed down to his soul. "Let's sit down, Rob. You're tired."

His eyes clouded over. They sat on the bench, and she placed her hand on his. The blood beneath his skin rushed like a river.

"You thought we were always meant to be together," she sang, "and maybe we were. Just not forever."

She smelled the sweet scent of roses, stirred with the hidden undercurrent of his blood. "I had dreams I never, ever told you about. Dreams—about him."

Rob's eyes closed. He leaned toward her, *just a kiss*, knowing down deep that this may be the last chance he'd have to prove his love.

"You don't want to do that, Rob," she sang. She *shoved* him, a gentle nudge of her will, and he moved back from her. Her voice was strong now. She would make him listen.

—*I am not the one for you*, she said. —*You know that now. You've accepted it, Rob. I am not the woman you will dream about. You're letting me go. You have to move on. You and I will always be a part of each other. We had wonderful times, and we'll always love each other. But we were not meant to be together forever.*

He whispered, "Summer."

—*Rest.*

He lay down on the bench, and Summer felt his heartbeat with her senses; touched the blood flowing under his skin, just beneath her fingertips.

Her eyes *shifted*, cold and black. Her teeth ached. No, they *throbbed.*

An emptiness, a hunger, burned in her soul.

A hiss of air passed between her lips, and she needed his blood, Rob's blood, on her tongue, down her throat, feeding the thirst.

—*No*, she whimpered. All she wanted was Michel, to find him and get the hell out of Stonebridge.

"Summer," he whispered, and his need for her clawed like a slavering beast inside her.

—*Relax.* And she opened her mouth, revealing her long, white teeth, and a tongue as black as midnight.

Her lips tingled across his neck. And then his blood welled between her lips, and she tasted him, knew him as if for the first time. His blood was a crimson magic, flashing Polaroids of his life. She tasted the scent of old books bound in leather; saw Rob in a small room—his dorm room—at Tech. She tasted Smithfield ham at Christmas, and the scent of his Old Spice at his sister's wedding. And she saw herself, golden, glowing, beautiful to him, tasting of cinnamon and wine. And she drank of him, a sweet, dark communion.

Then her eyes flew open, and she jerked away, realizing what she had done—what she had been ready to do. Her hunger was too raw; she would have drunk of him until he was no more.

Instinct. She bent down, licked the blood off his neck. The twin wounds sealed as though they had never been, leaving only pink puckers in his skin.

—*You don't love me, Rob.* She kissed his temple, and as her corn silk hair brushed his skin, she knew she would forever remember the sweet taste of his love. —*Find your one true love. She's out there.*

—*And—please forgive me.*

She twisted around and sensed the air. She felt a pressure, a *knowing*, building through her, a whirlwind of angry wasps.

Then she heard, from street after street in the distance, the sounds of gunfire, shot after shot. Her shoulder jerked back with an invisible impact, and an image of Michel blossomed in her mind, her vision splattered with blood and hot red pain.

Her shoulder erupted with fire, and she staggered across the gravel path.

Michel.

He had been shot.

15

SHERIFF HICKS STAYED holed up in his office since he let Summer go around six p.m. He asked Iris to stay late, and told her and Duke he was beat from the all-nighter out at the farm, and that he had fallen and sprained a finger and his arm. He was going to write reports and take some aspirin for the aches.

Behind the closed door, Hicks pulled the bottle of scotch from his desk. Those pills of Castle's had been damn fine, but they had worn off an hour ago, and god*damn* his arm felt like a three-alarm. The scotch went down his throat warm, an old, comfortable friend. He drew the blinds and sat in the twilight, trying to dull the pain; trying to take the edge off the red, sharp hate that burned in his chest when he thought of Trager. Fucking Trager. And that— What was that black stuff? Smoke? Coming out of his skin?

No. Forget it. Didn't happen. Hicks took another long swallow. No way did he see that. Never happened. They'd put you away for imagining weird-ass shit like that. Fucking loony bin stuff. Hell, maybe he'd get to share a padded room with Kenny Cousins.

He threw back four different pills from his pocket with a long slug of scotch, and for the next two hours, he fielded calls from the *Record-Progress*, the Richmond, Roanoke, and Newport News newspapers, and from reporters with TV affiliates across Virginia. The State Police called to let him know they were evacuating the Nicewander farm. The crime scene was clean; all the evidence, what little there had been, had already been discovered and tagged, not including all the empty beer cans, cigarette butts, and withered condoms they had found inside the old barn.

When the phone rang around 8:15 p.m., Hicks was courting a thick scotch buzz and he let Iris take the call. Then his intercom buzzed, and Iris said through the speaker, "Sheriff, it's Willie Weeks, over at St. John's."

"Who the hell is Willie Weeks?"

"Willie, the old caretaker over at St. John's. He says he was closing up the graveyard, and he says there's a motorcycle hidden behind one of the mausoleums."

"A motorcycle?" *Hot damn.* "A black one?"

"Hell, Buddy," Iris said, "I didn't ask about the color. But Willie says it looks like the door to the mausoleum has been broken into, and he ain't about to go in there. He says he thinks he heard—"

"Iris, you tell Willie Weeks to stay clear of there. And you get Duke and all the boys still on duty, and get them out there right now. Have 'em meet me out front of the church—and tell 'em stay clear of the cemetery. No sirens, Iris. Got that? Code two. Code two, Iris."

"Code two, Sheriff, I got it"

But Hicks was already out of his chair.

I got you now, you son of a bitch.

Four minutes later, he pulled up in front of the old brick wall around St. John's. He waited in the Fury and smoked, drumming his fingers on the wheel, his eyelid jumping. He saw Willie Weeks at the front gate, alternately looking at him, and then back towards the mausoleums.

Duke followed two minutes later, cherry flashing, but silent, and Hicks got out and explained the situation. Within twenty minutes, Hicks had eight more deputies standing around, waiting for orders. Cobb was the last to arrive, and Hicks just shook his head. "Idjit."

He gestured for Willie to come over. He shook Willie's dark hand, rough from years of handiwork around St. John's, as though he were a visiting VIP. "Mr. Weeks, here, called in a break in. Looks like one of the mausoleums out back has been broken into. Mr. Weeks, tell us what you saw."

Willie wrangled a faded, blue baseball cap in his hands. His voice was gravelly and deep. "Sheriff, I was just closing up, making sure all the gates was locked, just like every day 'bout this time. And I was coming up on the back gate, and I saw something in the weeds behind the Gardner crypt. They's a motorcycle parked between the mausoleum and the fence."

"What color?"

"A nice black and white one, Sheriff. Shiny."

"What did you do then?"

"It's real dark in there, Sheriff. I think I heard someone move around in there. I watch the grounds, sir; but I ain't going to try and kick no bums out of there, no, sir, not if I don't know if they's gonna pull a knife on me, no, sir."

Hicks placed his hand on Willie's shoulder and said, "You did good, Willie. Now, going in from here, which one is the Gardner mausoleum?"

"Last one on the right, Sheriff. Name's above the gate. Carved in marble."

"All right, Willie. You get back behind the cars here and keep clear. We're going in and have us a look see. You make sure no one gets through this gate."

"Yes, sir, Sheriff."

Hicks stared towards the row of mausoleums. The sun was behind the mountains, and the cemetery was a silent landscape of stone and grey. One faint star hung in the violet eastern sky.

"Okay, boys," Hicks said. "We're going in armed. Duke, I want you to get that tear gas out of my trunk." He threw Duke the keys.

"Tear gas?" Duke caught the keys one-handed. "Sheriff, if it really is Trager that's holed up in there, don't you think all this is a little overkill?"

"He's a biker and a hippie and he's probably armed, damn it, and ready to shoot!" Spit flew from Hicks' mouth. "Now, get that tear gas! I'm gonna smoke his ass out! You got a problem with that, boy?"

Duke stared at him, shook his head, then opened the trunk. He pulled out a black object that looked like a short, squat billy club. A shiny thumb stud stuck up from the handle. Duke slammed the trunk. "Holy shit," he said. "What are you still doing with this? We all stopped using these years ago. These things can kill."

"Never you mind about that," Hicks said. "You just get ready to use it when I say so. You fucking understand me?"

Duke stared him down. "Yes, sir."

"Good fuckin' thing."

"What about gas masks?"

The deputies looked to Hicks.

Hicks said, "Don't be a pussy, Crawford."

Duke whispered, "Holy shit."

Hicks split them up. In the quickening darkness, three deputies followed close around the outside of the cemetery wall, positioning themselves behind the mausoleum. One of them, Nettles, carried a shotgun.

Hicks and Duke wove between weathered gravestones, while two pairs of deputies flanked them, twenty feet away on each side. Hicks halted beside a large monument topped with a marble angel, its arms open, its blank eyes facing the heavens. The others formed a loose semi-circle around the entrance.

The deputies hid behind two stone monuments and behind tombstones. All eyes watched the black gate of the Gardner mausoleum. The gate was still ajar. Each deputy aimed his service revolver. Duke held the tear gas billy with both hands. Cobb's eyes were wide and blank, and the pistol wobbled in his hand.

Hicks counted his men, in position, and nodded once at Duke. His eye quivered, and his heart raced in a wild gallop. He cupped his hand to the side of his mouth.

"Attention! You in the mausoleum! This is Sheriff Hicks! We know you're in there, Trager! We've got your precious motorcycle! You ain't goin' anywheres! Now, throw out your weapons and come out of there with your hands up high, or I swear to God I'll come in there and drag you out!"

A trio of silver haired bats chittered overhead in the still night air.

Hicks turned to Duke. "You ready?"

Duke said, "Sheriff, are you sure about this?"

"Goddamn it!" Hicks shouted toward the mausoleum, ignoring Duke. "Trager, it ain't any use hiding in there! Now come out! Before it gets ugly!"

No answer came from black opening.

Hicks nodded once. "You go," he told Duke. "Aim it right through the gate, and then get the hell out of there."

Duke stepped forward. Hicks called out, "Deputies! Take aim!" Duke looked over his shoulder at Tate and said, "You boys just don't shoot till I'm clear, all right?"

Tate nodded. "Run fast."

"Damn straight."

The mausoleum's marble steps were only thirty feet away, but getting there seemed to take forever. Duke's thumb twitched over the firing stud.

He stepped onto the first step. All he saw through the gate was solid darkness.

Second step. He heard the sole of his shoe scuff over the rough stone.

Third step. He lowered the billy and pointed it at the iron gate. The pad of his thumb found the metal firing stud.

He stepped onto the marble stoop. The black iron gate hung open a few inches, just as Willie had said. Cold sweat trickled down his spine.

He tensed his thumb, ready to press the metal button, and moved the tip of the club an inch, two inches, between the iron bars. Christ, it was dark in there. Even in the gloom of dusk, he would have thought he'd be able to make out shapes inside the mausoleum, but the darkness was like a cloud. It even seemed that it was curling around his hands in a chill, black mist.

Then the night exploded with a deafening roar. It was a howl, a scream, an animal cry of unearthly rage. The gate burst open. Black iron thudded into Duke's chest. He spilled backwards off the stoop. His back slammed hard onto the ground. The tear gas club spun away, and a huge, dark shape erupted from the doorway.

The beast was immense, as tall as a man, swirling with thick, black fur, its mane a streaked crown of silver and grey. It leaped from the steps, snarling, its shaggy snout only inches from the sheriff's pale and terrified face.

Deputies started shooting. Duke shouted, "Fuck!" and ducked behind a tombstone engraved with a cracked, mildewed skull. He fumbled his pistol out of its holster and aimed.

A deep, rumbling roar echoed from the mausoleum, and a monstrous beast of solid black sprang from the gate. It leaped atop Deputy Lang and crushed him to the earth. It screamed in fury, its eyes a fiery red in the swirling black mists. Hot drool spat from its mouth onto Lang's face, and the deputy screamed under the thing's incredible weight.

An onslaught of hot lead slammed into the beasts' broad, dark chests. Deputies screamed "Bears!" and "Wolves" simultaneously, but not one had ever before seen such hellish beasts. The black creature tore through the deputies, scattering them with its gargantuan arms. Deputy Tate ran up and blasted three bullets into its hairy chest. The beast backhanded him across the chest, casting him fifteen feet away.

It looked to the grey beast and roared. The grey beast responded, its deep growl echoing between the monuments. The deputies outside the cemetery jumped over the wall. Nettles ran up only feet from the grey monster, and fired both barrels of his shotgun into its side. Black blood burst out in a hot rush. The grey beast screamed. It rose on its back legs and spun around in a blur. With a howl of blood-red rage, it snapped its powerful jaws around Nettles' arm and wrenched it away with a single shake of its massive head.

Nettles screamed. Jets of blood spurted with each heartbeat from the red stump where his right arm had been. The deputies froze, staring at the carnage, at the beast with their friend's arm still between its jaws. Someone said, "Oh, sweet Jesus," and Collie Nettles collapsed to the grass.

Hicks gaped at Collie. How the hell could something like this be happening? And he screamed, "Shoot to kill! SHOOT TO KILL! SHOOT TO

K—"

Then Hicks locked eyes with the grey beast. The hair on the back of his arms stood up straight. The thing's eyes seemed to melt, and a frigid chill crept up Hicks' spine.

"Oh Christ," Hicks said. "Oh Jesus Lord."

The beast's bloodied jaws stretched back, almost in a grotesque smile, and the thing's eyes were filled with dark mirth. Hicks took a step back, another, muttering, "No, no, no, no—"

No, it couldn't, couldn't have been—no, couldn't be—

The creature roared, slinging the dead, bloody arm spinning hard into Hicks' chest.

It hit him like a bag of sand. Hicks flew backward. The back of his head glanced off a gravestone. Something inside him *snapped*, and a flush of sharp pain blossomed between his neck and arm. He tried to yell, "Kill him!" but his vision swam, and his words came out in an unintelligible moan. He heard popping, like popcorn; then dimly recognized it as gunfire. He opened his eyes, and saw the wolves or bears or—*things*—run across the cemetery, into the shadows, the deputies firing blind after them.

"Cease fire!" Duke shouted. "Cease your fire!"

Silence hung in the air like smoke. "Christ, this ain't Vietnam!" Duke limped toward Nettles, glaring at the deputies. "Those bears are gone! Just pray that you assholes haven't shot up anybody in town."

He kneeled on the red-drenched grass beside Collie Nettles, who stared up at him, breathing rapidly. Blood shot in an arc from the ragged stump at his shoulder. "You, Jackson! Get on the horn! We need an ambulance out here!" He stared at Collie's spurting flesh and whispered, "He's gonna bleed out."

He unlaced one of his shoes and glanced around. Finally he said, to no one in particular, "Somebody get me a stick, something strong! I need to twist this, hard!"

Lang ran up and gave him a plastic Bic pen. "Good enough," Duke said. Lang stood over them. "Jesus. Oh Jesus." So much blood.

Duke said, "Get some blankets. Collie's in shock." He wrapped the black shoelace around Nettles' stump and tied a knot around the Bic. He twisted the pen tight, and the blood spurting from the stump dwindled to a trickle. "Collie?" Duke said. "Deputy Nettles! You hear me?"

Nettles' head lolled sideways. He barely had a pulse. Duke knew he needed a doctor, fast.

Then someone screamed. "Get it off me! Get it offa me!" Duke looked up. Sheriff Hicks had come around and found a bloody arm in his lap, his shirt soaked through with Nettles' blood. He kept screaming, staring at it as though it were a poisonous snake. "Get it offa me!"

Duke saw Cobb standing at the periphery of the on-looking deputies. "Cobb," Duke said, "help the sheriff. See if he's hurt."

Cobb stared at the severed limb, swallowed, and stood over the sheriff. He closed his eyes, grabbed the arm with both hands, screamed, "Oh, God!" then flung it away into the tombstones as though it were diseased.

He started crying then, weeping, "Oh God, oh God," and finally walked away, back toward the cruisers.

Duke called after him. "Cobb! We need you over here! Cobb!"

Between his sobbing, Cobb shouted, "Shit, shit, I can't take this," and he bolted toward the cemetery gates.

Duke held the tourniquet tight. "Cobb! You get your ass back here!"

But a weak voice said, "Let him go. Chickenshit." Hicks struggled to his feet, his left arm dangling. He grimaced with each step.

Duke was glad. Starting with the tear gas, this whole enterprise had been one mistake after another, and it all started with Buddy Hicks.

He looked down at the blood soaking his shirt and pants, then looked in the direction the beasts had run. "Jesus."

Hicks wavered on his feet. Duke wanted to tell him to straighten up and act like a man, but he stayed quiet.

"You saw him, right?" Hicks said. "You saw him."

"What the hell are you talking about?"

"You saw him. Tell me you saw him."

"Saw who?"

Hicks looked back toward Cobb, fading into the dark, then back at Nettles, at the blood pooling between the blades of grass. One eye jumped like an electrical spark.

Duke said, "Who do you think you saw?"

Hicks stared at the pooling blood.

For an instant there, for just a second, as the wolf or the bear—the *thing*—looked down at him, its shaggy head had *shifted*, and the thing was suddenly wearing Ben Castle's smiling face.

Duke watched the sheriff as he stared at the blood, at nothing, and he wondered, not for the first time, if all was right with Sheriff Buddy Hicks, or if something was terribly, awfully, completely wrong. Because it sure seemed like the sheriff was walking along some thin border of normalcy and obsession, and was slowly losing his balance.

Before sunrise, Duke would know.

And he would bleed for it.

16

SUMMER'S FEET SCATTERED gravel over the tidy path as she stumbled, feeling bullets slam into Michel. She rocked with dull impacts as bullets ripped him in bursts across his chest. She felt his rage boil at this—this affront, by such officious little worms.

And he laughed.

He sang aloud his joy as he let his bestial nature to be set free, to loose his savage soul. To hurt.

Bullets ripped into him. His chest and side blossomed crimson.

She stumbled toward the back door. He was close, she knew it. She had to get to him. He needed her. Flashes popped into her mind: standing stones, grass, deputies firing, and trees.

The cemetery.

She went up the stairs for her keys. She felt where he was heading. Sanctuary.

Storybook Hollow.

She slung her purse over her shoulder and plucked out the keys. They jangled as she went down the stairs, two steps at a time.

Then her mother appeared at the foot of the stairs, waiting, her mouth a tight, thin line.

"Just where the hell do you think you're going?"

Summer tried to pass her. "Out."

"You can go straight back up to your room, little missy. I am not about to let you go see that hoodlum again."

Summer stopped on the bottom step and looked down on her mother. "Get out of my way, Ma. I'm going."

"The hell you are, Summer Moore. You are grounded!"

Summer burst out laughing. "Grounded? You think I'm still thirteen or something?"

She rushed past Louise. She reached for the doorknob.

Her mother slapped her hand away. Summer turned, red fire building in her eyes.

Louise stepped between her and the door. Her skin was pale, and her whole body trembled. "You will do what I say if you want to live in this house!"

Summer said, "After what you did to me today, I will never do a goddamn thing you say. Hicks had me in his interrogation cell for hours. All because of you."

"I did it for your own good! Hanging around with the wrong crowd. You're just a stupid little girl."

She turned away. *Michel. He was running; she felt the grass beneath his feet, the blood dribbling from a tiny wound.*

Safe.

She stared Louise down. "No. No, Ma, I'm not. I haven't been a little girl for a long time, but especially not right now. Face it. I've never been the quiet, orderly little girl you always wanted."

"That's your damn father in you."

"No, Ma. It's me. I'm not one of your little Hummel dolls. I've never been cute and cuddly. I'm different, Ma. I've always been different, and you just won't stop trying to change me into the perfect little doll you've always wanted."

She glanced over at the Hummels in the china cabinet. "God, those things are ugly."

Louise shook her finger at her. "They are not! They're beautiful!"

"No. They're all the same. Fake. Painted smiles. They never change. They never grow up. Just the way you want me to be."

"You were!" Louise said. "You used to be like that. You were always a happy child, always laughing."

"No, Ma. No kid was ever like these things. They're just unreal. Unnatural. They're hideous."

Louise shivered, anger building up inside her like an old boiler.

"I could never be like those things. And you just won't learn."

"You—" Louise's fists trembled at her sides. "You are evil."

"I'm evil? Hell, Ma. You bitched and moaned your way out of a good marriage. You chased Daddy away because you wouldn't stop fighting with him. About everything. Always sniping, saying nasty things about him and his side of the family. Always trying to get your own way. Fighting with him about everything—just like you do with me.

"You called the cops on me just because you're scared of a guy I know—someone you've never met. Someone you know absolutely nothing about. That, Ma—*that* is evil."

"You always try to turn it around on me! You—*you*—have *got* to change your *evil* ways."

Summer almost bowed over, laughing. "Ma. Oh, Ma. You really—"

"You hear me? You are going out too much! This is the Lord's day! You are not going out to see your smelly biker boyfriend, and do who knows what in the backseat like a common whore. You will march right back up those stairs—"

Summer slung back her hair. "Oh, the hell I will, you crazy old bitch. I refuse to spend another night under this roof. As soon as I get back, I'm moving the hell out. I'm leaving. No. Face it, Ma. I'm already gone."

Her mother stared at her, shaking. Her eyes looked empty, crazed, and Summer could feel her mother's heart, beating faster, thumping like a hard rock drum solo. The beat crescendoed, and her heart jackhammered as though there were something banging loose in her chest.

Her mother whispered, "Ah." Her face twisted in a silent grimace. "Oh."

And then she crumpled in a heap at Summer's feet.

17

TWO CALLS CAME in within minutes of each other. At 8:54 p.m., dispatch at Stonebridge General got an emergency radio call from a babbling, incoherent man who finally managed to say that he was Deputy Jackson, that they needed an ambulance at St. John's Cemetery, "Right now, for God's sake!"

At 8:58 p.m., an operator called the emergency room, requesting an ambulance to respond to an apparent heart attack at 56 Croatoan Avenue, the patient being one Mrs. Louise Moore, age sixty-two.

Ern Deese had just parked his ambulance in front of the emergency room after picking up take-out from the Atomic Drive-In, so he raced to the cemetery in Unit 1, wolfing down his Atom burger with extra mayo, and Porky Saunders drove Unit 2 downtown to the Moore house.

Porky had it a lot better than Ern. He and Pete Iverson rolled Mrs. Moore on a gurney to the ambulance, while the daughter climbed in back. Mrs. Moore was out of it, and while Pete took her vitals, Porky sneaked glances at her daughter in the rearview mirror. She sure was a looker, that daughter of hers.

Ern, though, didn't know what he was in for. He and Fred Horne parked out front, then ran to the scene. He took one look at Nettles, crimson oozing like mud from his raw stump, and he spewed his delicious Atom burger and fries all over a gravestone that read HOPE.

By 9:45, Collie Nettles was on the operating table, receiving pint after pint of O Negative as surgeons worked on him. Sheriff Hicks sat in a private exam room in the ER, waiting for the results of his x-rays and wishing Duke would leave so he could take a nip from his hip flask. Louise Moore lay in a hospital bed in Exam 7, wired to monitors and a saline drip, sleeping inside an oxygen tent while doctors bent over her.

"What the hell is happening tonight?" Duke said to no one in particular. He stood in the private exam room with Sheriff Hicks, looking through a glass window in the door into the ER. "Nettles. You. Three of our guys clawed and bleeding, and they're going to need rabies shots. Unbelievable."

Hicks grunted, sitting on a crumpled strip of thick white paper that covered the exam table. One wall was dominated by a glass medicine cabinet, filled with pill bottles and vials. "Ain't just tonight. It's been ever since that goddamn biker rode into town."

"I don't think you can blame a bear attack on Trager."

Hicks didn't hear him. He was focused on that *thing*, and its face, for just that instant, just that one second—

Nope. I didn't see that.

"Get down to the OR. I want you to stay with Nettles."

"They're not going to let me in the operating room, Buddy."

Someone knocked on the door, and Dr. Wilson Stoney came in, carrying x-rays. He was in his early forties, and his hair was already white. "Sorry to interrupt, gentlemen."

Hicks said, "Just go stand watch, Duke. I want to know what they're doing to him as soon as they do it."

Duke nodded. "Sure. It'll give me something to do."

The doctor closed the door. "I got the lab to speed up your films. It's pretty busy out there tonight, between you boys and Mrs. Moore."

"Mrs. Moore? Louise Moore?"

The doctor nodded. "Now—"

"What happened?"

"Mrs. Moore? Looks like a heart attack. They got her here just in time."

"Is the daughter here?" Hicks said.

Stoney jammed the x-rays in the light box on the wall and flicked the switch. "Came in with the ambulance." He pointed to an x-ray of the sheriff's skull. "Good news. No injuries here. With what you say you experienced—dizziness, blurred vision—I'd say you had a mild concussion."

I didn't see that. It was the concussion.

"Sheriff, are you okay?"

Hicks looked up. The doctor was talking. "Yeah, Doc. I've been up for 'bout thirty-six hours. I'm starting to feel it."

I hit my head after *I saw Castle's face.*

"Now," Stoney said, touching the middle x-ray. "Behind door number two, we have a fractured collarbone." He shrugged. "Not much we can do about it. The bone hasn't separated, which is good, but you can't be as active as I suspect you usually are. Finally, your arm. You've got a fractured ulna. You've also probably sprained your upper arm somehow, and pinched your radial nerve. We've got to set the bone and get you in a cast."

"I ain't got time for all that, Doc."

"It's not going to heal if we don't do something about it."

"My arm can wait. Just give me something for the pain. Every time my arm moves, it feels like it's on fire."

"Sheriff, that's because it's fractured. If we set it properly and pour a cast—"

"No can do, Doc. You take care of Nettles and my men first. I've got a murder to work on. Pain pills. That's what I need right now."

Stoney crossed his arms. "Buddy—" Then he sighed. "All right. A compromise. You get your pills, and I give you a splint—and a sling. And you get your ass back here tomorrow so I can fix you up right."

"You got a deal, Wilson. Let's do 'er fast. I got stuff to do."

Stoney unlocked the prescription cabinet and ran his finger along the white bottles. "What did you find out there?"

"Beside the bears, you mean?"

Never seen any bear like that before, no, sir.

Stoney said, "Well, I hear they come out in the summer, looking for food." He found a bottle, opened it, and shook out one pill. Hicks watched him place the bottle back on the shelf.

"Here." He dropped a white pill into the sheriff's palm, then went to the sink and filled a paper cup with cold water. "Take this one for now. I'm going to write you a prescription. Fill it down at Charlie's in the morning. They open at six. One pill every twelve hours. Strong stuff, believe me."

Hicks swallowed the pain pill. Stoney went to the door. "Try to stay as still as possible for the next few weeks. That collarbone has to heal. Now, I'm going to find my prescription pad and write you that scrip. And I'm going to send in a nurse to splint you up and fit your sling. Tonight, I want you to stay awake as long as possible. You've had a concussion. The longer you can stay awake, the better. Got it?"

Hicks winked. "Got it."

Hicks listened as Stoney's footfalls faded away, then he bent into the prescription cabinet and found the bottle of pain pills. He shook half the bottle into his palm, popped another into his mouth, and dropped the handful into his shirt pocket.

He turned back to the cabinet, looking from bottle to bottle, and finally smiled. He took a bottle of Dexedrine, popped one, and dropped the bottle into his pocket. He spied another bottle on the bottom shelf. He had seen the alerts from the Feds, and knew that the kids were using these to feel good. "And my back feels like shit," he said. He took the bottle labeled QUAALUDE and downed a pill with a couple of swallows from his hip flask. He swished the rest of the cold water around his mouth to cut the smell of scotch on his breath. He pocketed the bottle, then opened the drawers of the medicine cabinet and found thermometers, hypos, vials stoppered with rubber seals, rubber gloves, cotton swabs, everything an ER doc would need, right there at his fingertips, "Yes, sir, everything."

He stepped out into the emergency room and lit a Pall Mall. *There.* Through a slim gap in the pale blue curtains in the ER, Hicks got a glimpse of old lady Moore, mouth agape inside an oxygen tent. And there was Summer Moore, sitting beside the old lady, one hand on her frail arm. "Okey dokey."

The tip of his nose felt numb. Strange thoughts came to him as he stared at Summer, popping like firecrackers in a smoky haze.

"Okey dokey," he finally said, never once realizing he had been talking to himself.

He went back into the exam room, opened the drawers, and found exactly what he needed.

18

WEIRD.

Ma's skin felt thin and papery, as though she might crumble to dust if she peeled it away. It felt weird, holding her hand. All the two of them had had together for so long were the arguments. She couldn't remember the last time they had laughed together.

She thought of Tina, her close friends; she thought of their families, even Ronnie—wild, angry, yet passionate. They all hugged. Summer hugged her friends. Her friends hugged their siblings, their parents. Louise had never hugged her.

Not even once.

She felt the void between them as though it were tangible; an invisible wall of anger and resentment that forever kept them apart.

Her mother shifted her head on the white pillow. There was nothing else but the beeps from the heart monitor, the soft, steady rush of oxygen hissing into the tent, and the slow drip of saline into her arm.

The curtain parted. A nurse smiled at her. "I'm Nurse Baker, and this is Doctor Hoyt. We have to take some more tests."

"Can you tell me anything yet?"

The doctor, dark hair slicked back with a little dab of Brylcreem, shook her hand. "Rolly Hoyt."

He took the clipboard from the end of the bed, flipped through the notes, and glanced at Louise's heart rate. "She's stable for now. Your mother's had a mild to moderate heart attack. She's underweight, and dehydrated. And very weak. If she were a stronger person, younger, I'd say she's a candidate for a bypass operation."

"She isn't?"

"Well, not right now. We need more tests. We probably won't get the results back until tomorrow, at the earliest. But, because she's a heavy smoker—what, three packs a day?"

"Yeah," Summer said.

"No. A bypass right now might actually put her in more danger than she already is."

"She'll want to go home when she wakes up."

"I'm afraid she's going to be here a little while—three weeks, maybe more, depending on her progress."

"You're kidding."

"We'll know more in the next few days, I promise. But I suspect she's going to have to change her diet—less fat, more lean meats. She'll definitely have to stop smoking if she wants to live."

"Yeah, well, that ain't gonna happen."

"Hm. So, we're probably going to prescribe Coumadin, a blood thinner. We'll probably get her on a digitalis regimen too, for heart disease. And we'll give her a prescription for nitroglycerin pills, to take under the tongue whenever she feels a great deal of stress, or thinks another attack is coming on."

"So, she's going to live."

Hoyt took in a long breath. "I wish I could tell you that for sure. The next couple of days are critical. We'll know a lot more by Tuesday, Wednesday." He hung the clipboard onto the end of the bed. "If you don't mind sitting awhile in the waiting room, we'll get those tests started."

She took her purse and stepped out into the bright fluorescents of the ER. She followed the signs to a darkened waiting room past the nurse's station. Dark was all right with her. She wanted it dark. Soothing. All she could think of was her mother, limp in her arms as she carried her to the sofa and called the operator; and Michel, feeling the bullets as they ripped into him, howling with rage.

She wanted it dark and quiet.

She dropped her purse on a side table stacked with copies of *Look*, *Guideposts*, and *Time*. Elevator music played from a speaker in the ceiling tiles, and she wondered how "The Girl from Ipanema" could have ever been popular. She shook out a Salem and flicked open her lighter.

The flare lit her face, and she glanced at her reflection in the room's long glass windows.

The lighter clattered to the tile floor.

Her reflection had changed.

She stood in the center of a swirling cloud of pure, black mist. Her eyes stared back at her, black and empty, and her skin seemed to have shrunken to leather, black and desiccated. Sparks of crimson shone deep within the orbs that were her eyes.

Voices whispered to her, circling in her mind, whispers at the edge of understanding.

Then the mists parted, and she saw the shape of a great, savage beast, black-furred, streaked with yellow-gold hair—*blonde*.

Her reflection opened its sharp, feral jaws. The voices cried out to her, louder—

beast

—soul

And in the thing's black eyes, she finally recognized herself: a creature both beautiful and ugly, wild and passionate.

Untamed.

Black mist curled around the dark beast. This is me. This is the animal in my soul. Hungry. Savage. Made of shadows. *Magnificent.*

—control—

She steeled herself, for no one could be allowed to see this reflection, this monstrous thing that must remain hidden from the light. No one could ever see the terrible beauty she had become.

All the voices inside her came together as one.

"No."

And then her reflection was there again, blonde, blue-eyed, framed by the light from the doorway behind her.

"Good," she whispered.

She bent down to pick up her lighter, and when she stood up, there was another reflection in the glass, blocking the doorway. She smelled the tang of blood.

She lit a cigarette and stared at the reflection. "What the hell do you want, Hicks?"

His eyes jerked, glancing around the room. "That's Sheriff Hicks to you, girly girl."

She laughed. His face tightened. She felt an inner strength she had never felt before. And she knew, in her soul, this man could do nothing to harm her.

"I hear you tried to kill your mama," he said.

She wheeled around. "The hell, you bastard. She had a heart attack, not that you give a damn." Then she saw the blood soaked through his uniform. "Who the hell did you kill?"

He wrapped his beefy hand around her wrist and jerked her toward him. Her cigarette spun to the floor. With the pills working through him, his lame arm felt just fine.

She heard his heartbeat then. She felt the blood rushing beneath his skin. And she smelled scotch, and sweat. Something was in him, coursing through his blood.

He was high.

"Don't bullshit me, girl. I'm gonna nail your boyfriend once and for all."

He yanked her into the hall. The lights in the ceiling revealed how pale Hicks was, his temples dripping with cold sweat. There was nothing she could do now, not out here in public. But once they were away from the hospital, in the shadows.

Then there was a voice behind them, from down the hall. "Sheriff?"

Duke Crawford walked slowly toward them, his hat in his hands, staring at the floor. "Sheriff," he said quietly. "Sheriff. Collie. He—he didn't make it. They tried, but he, he'd lost so much bl—"

He saw Summer then, saw Hicks' hand around her slender wrist.

"Sheriff?"

Hicks didn't answer. He pulled Summer into the ER, and with his free hand he shoved aside the curtains concealing Louise Moore. Dr. Hoyt looked up from inside the oxygen tent, where he was listening to Louise's heart with a stethoscope. From the other side of the bed, the nurse said, "You can't be in here."

"Now, I do most certainly apologize," Hicks said, his spastic eye gleaming, "but I'm afraid I gotta ask you all to give us just a few moments here alone for some important police business."

The doctor stood up. "Sheriff, we're in the middle of Mrs. Moore's examination."

"I understand that," Hicks said. "I really do. But this will only take a few minutes, and y'all can get right back to what you were doing. This here's a private matter we gotta go over in here. You understand."

Dr. Hoyt took a step toward the sheriff. "I do not understand at all. This is unheard of. Mrs. Moore's health is at a delicate—"

Hicks unsnapped the safety strap securing his gun, and made sure the doctor noticed. His voice went low, and his eye twitched madly. "This is regarding a serious crime. And I do sincerely expect you to comply with my order."

Duke suddenly said, "We've got everything under control in here." He held open the curtain. "Please just give us a few minutes, and you can come right back and finish the exam."

Dr. Hoyt looked from Duke, to Hicks, then back to Duke. He shook his head. "A few minutes. That's all. Then get out of here and let us do our job."

He led the nurse out into the ER. Duke closed the curtain and said, "What the hell do you think you're doing?"

Hicks smiled crookedly. He turned to Summer. "You. You're gonna tell me where he is."

"The biker? Isn't he at the motel?" She reached out with her mind, just as she had done with Rob. She wanted to calm Hicks, control him. She *pushed* toward him. But all she sensed from him was anger; a kind of crazed emptiness where his thoughts should be.

It wasn't just the drugs.

Hicks had lost it.

"The goddamn motel?" Hicks said. "Nice try, little missy, but your Vietnam hippie friend has gone AWOL. Now I suggest you tell me exactly where he's holed up, or this is gonna get uglier than shit. And it's all gonna be on you."

"Sheriff," Duke started, "she doesn't know anything. We can get this guy, Buddy, but just let's get out—"

"Aw, fuck you, Duke," Hicks said. "When did you become such a little pussy?"

Hicks reached into his pants pocket, and slowly pulled out a glass and steel hypodermic. He pulled off a long, metal cap and let it *ping* to the floor, revealing a long needle, gleaming under the sharp fluorescent lights. The syringe was filled with a reddish-brown liquid.

He pressed the needle's tip against Louise's skin.

Summer made a move toward him, and suddenly his gun was in his other hand, aimed at Summer.

"Now, now," Hicks said.

Duke stepped forward, slowly. Hicks moved the gun to point at him. Duke froze.

"Morphine," Hicks said. "Got it from the doctor's treasure chest." He put his thumb flat on the metal plunger. "Enough to put a fuckin' elephant to sleep.

Probably enough to kill the old lady, don't you think, Summer Bitch Moore?"

Summer *pushed.* "You don't want to do this. You really don't."

—Put it down.

Duke took another step. "Sheriff, calm down now, Buddy. Calm down."

Hicks pointed the pistol at Duke's chest. "You shut the hell up, cocksucker." Then he aimed it again at Summer. "I'd hate to get blood all over those beautiful titties of yours. And if you think I won't, you're nuttier than squirrel shit." He laughed at that, and the fingers holding the syringe twitched. "Now, you sure as fuck are going to tell me where your biker boyfriend is. Or your mama's gonna get a big shot of Kickapoo Joy Juice that'll get her a' knockin' at the pearly gates."

She stared at him. Hicks waited, wondering what the fuck was taking her so long.

But there were voices, swimming through her consciousness, and she was listening, judging.

"Summer," Duke said. "Oh shit, he's serious."

She gave Duke a slight smile, then turned to Hicks.

"I'll do better than that," she said. "I'll take you to him."

19

HICKS ORDERED SUMMER behind the wheel of the cruiser. He locked Duke in the back seat, while he rode shotgun, his pistol leveled at Summer's waist. Hicks locked Duke's gun in the glove compartment. The ride up Blue Top Mountain was silent, the tension between them stretched taut, ready to snap. Summer ached to do something, to stop this, but couldn't think of anything that didn't end up with wrecking the car and getting Duke hurt.

She refused to take that chance. Duke was an innocent in this.

But Hicks—

She'd see it through to the end.

She braked suddenly, tires squealing. Hicks jerked forward. The headlights focused on a deer frozen in the road. "GodDAMN!" Hicks said, glaring at her. The deer leapt into the foliage down the mountain, and Hicks jabbed Summer in the ribs with the gun barrel. "Where the hell you takin' us?"

She put her foot on the gas. "Storybook Hollow."

He smiled at her, one eye larger than the other, twitching, and he laughed. "He thinks he's the fucking Gingerbread Man!" He kept on laughing. "I'll be damned. Fairy tales. Your boyfriend'll be behind bars pretty soon. Hope he likes the fairies in jail!"

Then Hicks started humming, watching the road as it wound beneath them, smiling, humming. He took a couple of pills out of his pocket and swallowed them with a shot from his flask. He kept humming, louder. Summer finally realized the tune. A hymn. "Onward Christian Soldiers."

She glanced in the rearview mirror. Duke shook his head, staring at the sheriff with growing disbelief.

They came to the chain across the entrance, and she parked. Hicks said, "Duke, now, I'm gonna let you out. You go move that there chain." He looked at both of them, grinning. "Either one of you do anything funny, somebody's gonna get a bullet in their fuckin' head. Understand?"

Summer nodded.

Duke said, "We're not going to do a thing, Buddy. We're just going to do whatever you say."

Hicks smiled. "That's a good goddamn thing, now ain't it?" He stepped out of the car and opened Duke's door.

Duke got out.

Hicks said, "Don't do anything stupid, Dukey-Duke."

Duke nodded. Hicks got back into the car and closed the door. Duke unclasped the chain and threw it to the side.

Hicks rolled down the window. "Go to the entrance. We'll be right behind you."

Duke started walking, his shadow bobbing between the headlights as Summer slowly drove behind him. Duke stopped at the turnstiles and turned around to wait. Hicks told Summer, "Shut it off. Hand me the keys."

She dropped them into his palm. He motioned for her to get out, then said, "Where?"

Out in the heat of the night, Summer lit a cigarette, took a long pull, and exhaled. "Inside there."

Hicks laughed. "Jee-sus! Ain't you a cool little cucumber?" He laughed again. "Go on, little missy. I'm right behind ya. Remember I got this here gun, so don't you do anything unless I tell you to do it. My finger's a little itchy today. Maybe I'll teach you the lesson I shoulda taught you in school, little missy. Hear me?"

"I hear you." She walked toward Duke and the dark entrance. She stretched out with her senses, and touched him, felt Michel in the shadows, waiting.

Summer and Duke leaped over the locked turnstiles. Hicks had to jump up on one of the waist-high metal bases and slide across to the other side, like a fat guy sliding on ice. Summer tried not to smile.

She led them up the path. No crickets, no locusts, no wind. The silence that had fallen seemed thick and unnatural. Duke thought back to the dark mist curling around his hand back at the cemetery. They just might be in some deep shit out here.

"Fucking place," Hicks said behind them. His fingers around the pistol were slick with sweat. Hicks had always despised Storybook Hollow, and had been secretly glad when it had closed. What kind of idiots read stories like this shit anyway?

Duke looked over his shoulder. "Buddy, seriously, we've got to think about what we're doing here."

"I know what I'm doing," Hicks said. "I'm getting me a murderer." He waved the gun at Duke. "Don't keep acting like such a goddamned pussy."

Ahead of them, Summer stopped and turned. She stood deep in the shadows, the tree branches bending toward her with gnarled claws. "The Dark Forest."

"So where is he?" Hicks said.

She shrugged. "Somewhere."

"Somewhere?" Hicks stepped toward her. "I suggest you tell me exactly where."

"Around, I guess," Summer said. "Everybody's got to be somewhere, right?"

His hand flew out and slapped her, hard, snapping her head back.

Duke cried out, "Sheriff!" and lunged for the gun.

The flare from the pistol lit the scene like a flash bulb: Hicks, teeth gnashing; Duke, hunched over, blood spurting from the left side of his chest, frothing between his lips.

Duke stumbled to his knees and looked up at Hicks, his hand over his chest wound. "Buddy. Jesus. Are you—"

Hicks pulled the trigger. Duke's shoulder exploded backward in a spray of crimson.

Hicks grinned. His bulging eye worked from side to side.

Summer helped Duke lay back against a tree. "You're going to be okay, Duke, I promise. I'll take care of you."

"Summer," Duke stammered, coughing blood. "He's crazy. He'll kill you. He'll—" He blinked. "Summer?" His hand clasped Summer's wrist. He shuddered in a paroxysm that spasmed the back of his head against the tree, and fell over.

Hicks screamed, "I told you, Duke! I told you! Don't be a pussy, Duke! I told you! I told—"

Then his eyes widened, and he remembered why he was there. He pointed the gun at her. "Where is he? Where the fuck is he? Get Trager out here now, or I swear to God you'll be next."

Then the shadows *shifted*, and a great beast lumbered from the darkness beneath the trees, surrounded with swirls of shadows. The thing snarled at Hicks, and suddenly Michel stood there, his black, gleaming eyes focused on him.

A twig cracked behind Hicks, and he turned to see Ben Castle step out of the darkness. Ben's wide, black eyes twinkled with starlight.

"Castle and Trager," Hicks said. "I knew it. You fuckers couldn't fool me."

Michel sniffed the air. He scented the drugs poisoning the sheriff's blood. "You shouldn't have come here, Hicks."

Hicks laughed. "You shouldn't have come to my town, boy."

Summer looked up at Michel. "We have to get Duke to the hospital. He's coughing up blood."

"You ain't going nowhere, girly girl, 'cept into a jail cell."

Summer ignored him. "We have to do something. I can't stop the bleeding."

Suddenly, Hicks screamed, "SHUT UP SHUT UP SHUT UP!" and he pulled the trigger. Summer spun backward, dark blood fountaining below her collarbone.

Michel pounced like a panther. He dropped onto Hicks and tossed him to the ground. He bent over him, his long teeth ready to snap through his throat. The gun went off again, and Michel roared in pain, blood oozing from between his ribs.

Hicks sat up on one elbow, laughing. "GOTCHA! I GOTCHA! I GOTCHA, YOU SUMBITCH, I—"

"NO!" Summer cried. She sprang off the ground, her black, bottomless eyes narrowed in rage, her long, white, sharp teeth bared in a feral smile. She landed on her feet, towering over Hicks. She reached down, her long fingers claw-like and sharpened, and picked Hicks up by his shirt. She brought his face just an inch away from her teeth. Hicks blubbered incoherently. Her breath was hot and rank and smelled of dead things.

"You were told not to do this." Her voice was a low, guttural snarl, the speech of an untamed beast. "Duke warned you. I warned you. He warned you."

She looked across at Michel and smiled, exposing her sharpened canines.

Michel stepped to the sheriff's side. Castle stepped out of the shadows and looked down on Hicks. Their deep black eyes glimmered with reflected starlight, and their cruel, inhuman smiles sent cold chills through him.

And he realized what they were.

He couldn't breathe. His body shivered in silent, jittering terror.

He felt them. *Inside.*

He felt them.

Hungry.

Summer lifted him by the neck, holding him at arm's length as his feet dangled above the ground. With a monstrous scream she slung him twenty feet through the air.

He thudded against the bole of a tree and plopped to the ground. The world spun around him.

She went toward him, her neck and head bent at a strange, inquisitive angle, as though she were sniffing out an alien thing, a creature beneath her. A worm.

She stalked Hicks as he scrabbled mewling through the weeds and gravel like a spider-thing. The sheriff's mouth moved uncontrollably, jabbering, and he tried to scramble backward, away.

Then she was on him, her black eyes smiling down at him as though he were a feast at a fairytale banquet. He jammed the barrel in her waist and shot her. The gunshot exploded out of her back.

And she laughed, a hiss of black mirth.

Her mouth stretched open, revealing by moonlight the length, the razor points, the death threat of her white smile. With a sudden lunge, she sank her teeth into his neck. Blood spurted across her gums, over her tongue. She tasted the dizzying emptiness of the chemicals swimming through him. She tasted his sweet, liquid fear, and felt joy, pleasure, as her hands tightened around him. A rib snapped beneath her grip. Hicks screamed, and Summer slung him to the ground.

She stood above him, her golden hair shining in the moonlight. She was a thing of darkness, born of a nightsong of crimson dreams. Blood dripped from her lips, and the voices whispered to her, a chorus that sang in her own voice.

Michel stared at her. She glowed in the silver moonlight like a goddess. She had become much more than he had ever imagined.

She was the beauty of the night incarnate.

She was whole.

Hicks crawled away through the weeds, whimpering. Summer ran to Duke. Blood bubbled from a red hole in his chest.

"His lung," she said to Michel. "We have to hurry."

She placed her hand over Duke's heart, and *pushed.*

—Calm.

—Be calm.

—Slow your heartbeat.

—Relax.

She felt his pulse slow as Duke fell still. In seconds, he breathed painlessly at her knees.

Michel came to her side. "He's dying, Summer. And we have to get out of town. Now."

Her head snapped up. Her black eyes bored into his. "The hell we will. Leaving now is not an option. He goes to the hospital."

She turned to Hicks, then leapt into the air, a roaring lioness, and landed astride him. "You thought you owned this town. These people. Me." He scrambled to crawl away, and she wedged her foot down on his crotch.

He screamed.

"You're a whiny little baby. A puddle of piss and shit."

Summer lifted Hicks by his fat neck. His legs thrashed in the air. Spittle dribbled down his chin. She gestured toward Michel and Ben. "Look at them. A child like you? You think you could ever defeat one like us? You're everything that's wrong, that's evil, about this tiny shithole town. You don't think. You don't dream. You dwell in the redneck slime like slugs. With your guns and your bullets—do you really think you can ever defeat the night?"

She ripped away his pants pocket and snatched his keys. The night shivered, trembled around her in the trees. She summoned the shadows, the black things fluttering at the edge of her senses. She leaned in to his face, her black eyes, her long white teeth, engulfing his field of vision.

She reached out, felt his confusion, his cold fear, felt the things rustling in the shadows, in the tall, secret pines.

She *pushed.*

And she whispered to Hicks: "Run."

The trees exploded with a deafening screech, erupting with hundreds of flapping, fluttering wings. Clouds of bats swooped down out of the trees, swirling around him in a black storm. Hicks staggered backward and fell on his ass, screaming, swatting at the black cloud. They rose and dove in a congregation of black wings, slapping his face and arms. He staggered to his feet, and the cloud shoved him toward the front gate.

Summer turned to Ben Castle, and gestured with her head.

—Run him. Herd the bastard back to town. His house.

She looked long into Ben's eyes, showing him what she envisioned, what was needed.

—This cannot lead back to us. No one else can be implicated.

Ben nodded, then looked at Michel. "I never would have known," he said, nodding toward Summer. Then he strode toward the gates, and faded into the shadows.

"Never would have known what?" Summer said.

Michel smiled softly at her. Ben had never been easily impressed. "You. The woman you've become. Your power."

Duke lay twisted on the ground. She sensed him, his heartbeat, his slow, irregular breaths. "I think he's okay for now." She glanced over at Michel. "Are you? I felt you getting shot."

"At the cemetery," he said.

"What were you doing there?"

"Desperation. Hicks cornered me on the road at dawn. It was quicker to hide there than risk the sunlight. I had told Ben to hide there if the change came upon him suddenly, to get away from his neighborhood, where people could hear him."

He touched the bloody hole in her blouse. "This has gotten out of control."

"I know. And I know about Ronnie."

"The boy. He gave me no choice."

"Hicks interrogated me today—for hours. About you. He's gone nuts."

"Yes. We have to leave Stonebridge—as soon as possible. But no one can know we left together."

"I can't go anywhere. My mother. She had a heart attack. She's in the hospital right now. I can't leave her."

"Summer, it's too dangerous for you to stay. The police have already linked you to me. If word about my whereabouts reaches my enemies abroad, they will come after both of us. If you're still here, they'll try to kill you—and probably your mother as well."

"I can't leave."

"You have to! Your mother will get better with or without you." His eyes pleaded with her. "And I need you. I was meant to find you. We were meant to be together."

"Forever," she whispered.

"Forever," he said.

She threw him the sheriff's keys. "We have to get Duke to the hospital. Then I'll go finish packing up, and then say goodbye to my mother."

"You can't tell her you're leaving with me."

"I'll take care of her. Don't worry."

"My bike is at the cemetery."

"Shit. That was hours ago. The cops will have it at the station by now."

"I can handle that." He looked at his watch. "It's almost eleven. We'll meet up at 3 a.m. And then we go away."

"To Boston?"

"Anywhere, as long as it's somewhere big. Crowded. We have to get lost in a crowd."

She smiled. "I want to go to the top of the Empire State Building and be part of the sky."

20

DR. ROLLY HOYT lit a cigarette outside on the sidewalk. Above him, the EMERGENCY ROOM sign buzzed softly, bright with large red letters. The electronic doors slid open. Nurse Gaynelle Baker stepped outside and took a deep breath. "God, it hasn't been this busy around here in a long time," she said, and she took a cigarette from him. "Muggy out here."

Hoyt lit it for her. "Yeah, but at least it's quiet. What a night."

"I've got Erica keeping tabs on Mrs. Moore. You can take a break if you want. Grab an hour in the lounge."

He shook his head. "Hell, if I did that, you'd never get me up."

A light glimmered in the corner of his eye, and a sheriff's car came slowly around the corner, its cherry red bubble spinning silently. Something was wrong with the driver; his head kept nodding forward, as though he were fighting sleep. He drove too slowly, and the car weaved over the yellow lines.

"What now?" Hoyt said.

Then the headlights focused on the Emergency Room doors, and the car kept coming, and coming.

"Christ," Hoyt said. "He's going to—"

Baker screamed, and the cruiser bounced up onto the curb. The car dove straight into the sliding, double glass doors of the ER. Shards of glass exploded across the empty lobby. The cruiser's horn went off, a bleating monotone that echoed down the green, tiled hallways.

Hoyt yanked open the door. "Deputy? Deputy! You hear me?"

Duke Crawford sat covered in blood, holding his hand across his chest. Blood trickled in rivulets from between his fingers.

Baker shouted into the ER, "We need a gurney!" She looked over and saw the blood soaking through Duke's uniform. "Holy shit." She turned back to the ER. "Come on, people, now! And prep the OR!"

Hoyt peeked between Duke's fingers. "Deputy, can you hear me? What happened? Were you stabbed?"

Duke's eyes blinked open. He shook his head. Air whistled out of his wound. Hoyt knew Duke's lung had collapsed—but how the hell had he been strong enough to drive?

"He shot me," Duke said between gritted teeth. "Hicks. Sheriff Hicks. Crazy son of a bitch—he tried to kill me."

21

THE BATS SWARMED him, thudding into his back like rubber balls. Hicks waved his arm to keep the squealing things from his eyes and face. His fractured arm flapped like a chicken wing.

His camp hat went flying. A bat smacked him across the bridge of his nose. He yelled, "Fuck!" and tasted a drop of blood on his lip, and he sprinted for the turnstiles, far away in the gloom.

His goddamn father! When Hicks was just a boy, playing at dusk in the summer, the bats would come out with the sinking sun. His father would taunt, "They'll get caught in your hair! Don't let 'em get near your head, boy! They'll claw your eyes out!"

His feet felt like dead weights.

Too slow! RUN! I'll never get away, Daddy! I'll never—

The exit came into sight, and the dark emptiness beyond looked like nothing more than a sweet slice of freedom.

He dove beneath the entranceway. The bats parted, some angling over the roof, the others colliding in a jet stream with his back as he tried to hurdle a turnstile. His feet tangled with the metal arms. Two bats slapped into his face and neck. He felt the sting of a claw rake across his forearm. Then his foot was loose, and he fell face first to the pavement.

—and from the shadows inside the park, he heard a snort of air, the chuff of a massive beast.

"It's—it's one a' them *things*," he whispered, and he clambered to his feet. His Fury loomed like a beacon in the middle of the gravel parking lot.

Bats cycloned around him in a black, screeching spiral. He ran, fumbling through his pockets for the keys. He muttered, "No, no," as his hands felt only shreds of fabric where his pocket had been. Then he was at the cruiser, his sweaty fingers fumbling on the door handle, and he screamed, "Fuck!" as it hit him that the doors were locked. He beat his fists on the window, leaving smears of sweat and blood across the glass.

Something raked the back of his neck. He spun for the road. His hand closed around a soft, furred body snagged in his collar, and he slung it to the gravel, grunting in sick pleasure as he stomped his heel into it, panting, until ichor dripped from his sole.

A roar erupted from the darkness. Red eyes glared at him from behind the turnstiles. Then a bat slammed into his forehead, snagging its claws in his hair, and he tore off for the road.

He stumbled over the chain and headed down the mountain road. Then the bats slammed him across his left side. He swung at them with his good arm. But they pummeled him to the guardrail along the edge of the road, where the mountainside was steep and wooded—and then their dense mass shoved him over the rail.

It was a sheer drop for fifteen feet. Then the mountainside angled out to a rough incline, and he slammed the ground hard on his shoulder, rolling sideways down into the trees. The ragged rocks scraped his flesh, leaving spotted trails of blood. The mountain suddenly sloped to the right, and Hicks went spinning. His shoulder collided with the bole of a pine tree, and as he heard his collarbone snap apart this time, he slid hard into a deadfall of two tall pines spilled from some long-ago storm.

Gasping, he leaned back against a cracked, dead tree. His collarbone throbbed. He jerked his head around. The bats had flown off, leaving him to die.

Then he heard it, above, somewhere on the side of the mountain: a low rumble from a savage throat. Two crimson eyes watched him from the shadows.

Hicks forced himself to his feet, his eyes on the mass of shadows watching from above, and grunted as he went over the fallen trees, one leg at a time.

He ran through the dark woods without thought. His sides ached, and jolts of sharp pain twanged up his back. Then the mountain leveled into a gradual slope, and the going got easier. He let himself slow down a bit, panting for air. Then he heard the thing crashing through the brush behind him, and Hicks ran as hard as his thick, tired legs could run.

His sides burned as he angled down the mountain. There—a patch of dim light between the trees. He lurched out, under the clear sky, on a dirt and gravel road that wound down the side of the mountain. He knew where he was—just three miles from town.

He corkscrewed down the mountain road, limping, following the rocky curves in the moonlight, away from the shadow thing, until the ground leveled and—*Finally!*—the trees parted as the gravel path widened into a pale driveway. Route 81 stretched toward Stonebridge under the open sky, and he ran to the right, heading south, toward the lights of town.

Cornfields lined each side of the road, crackling in a secret language in the warm, humid night. The stitches in his sides felt like they were going to burst, but he ran. A thousand feet up the road he spied a black skeletal structure silhouetted by a lone streetlight—the charred remains of the Stonebridge Motor Lodge.

Hicks ran toward a pale yellow light flickering above the edge of the road. The phone booth was the only survivor of the fire that destroyed the motor lodge in '67, and he grinned at the familiar shape of the backlit bell in the C&P Telephone signs atop the booth. The phone still worked—he'd used it some months back when his radio had gone out—and he could call the station and get somebody to come pick him up.

He looked over his shoulder. He was alone on the road. He slowed down, gasping, feeling safer as the phone booth grew closer.

He stopped at the booth and leaned on the metal edge, gasping for breath. His undershirt stuck to his skin. He stepped into the booth and slammed the folding door. He pressed his back against it to keep anyone from coming in, and he fumbled through his pocket, muttering, "A dime, come on, come on, just one goddamn dime."

He pulled out a handful of change, and he dropped a dime into the slot and heard the familiar metallic *ka-ting ting* as the phone activated. He put his fingertip into the hole for **OPERATOR**.

Then the door whammed into him from behind. His head connected with the dial on the phone. The change clattered onto the dirty steel floor.

His vision went dark. Then his sight cleared, and he watched as a pale hand wrenched the folding door off its steel hinges, and tossed it backwards in a high arc to crash into the motel's blackened ruins.

Ben Castle smiled at him, his eyes wide and black. In the pale overhead light, he looked stronger, younger. His long teeth seemed to shine like the moon.

Hicks' lips quivered. "Castle? Castle, you fucker!"

He reached for his gun.

Ben held up the sheriff's revolver. "You must be looking for this."

Hicks screamed, "That's mine! Give it!"

Then Ben yanked Hicks out of the phone booth with one hand and sent him spinning hard onto the road. "You goddamn crazy son of a bitch!" Hicks yelled. "I'll—"

Then Ben suddenly *shifted.* Standing over the sheriff stood a beast-thing of darkness, limned with swirling mists of black night. Its long white teeth grinned in a savage smile. Its narrowed eyes flickered red like burning coals in the darkness.

Hicks kicked out his legs. "Stay away! Stay away!" He pulled himself a few feet across the road. Pebbles dug into his palms. Then he was up, running across Route 81, and he jumped across a shallow ditch and plunged into the depths of Linwood Holbert's cornfield.

He crashed through the chest-high corn, away from Castle, away from the thing. Errant, crinkly leaves batted his face as he carved a crooked path through the rows of corn. He looked over his shoulder, and the darkness swirled, following him with eyes of red. He sped up, hoping the goddamn cornfield would just stop and he'd be out on a road he knew; then there was a roar at his right, and the thing snapped its teeth only inches away, and Hicks angled in a diagonal across the field, running up and over the rows of corn like a roller coaster, thrashing blindly through the whispering stalks.

The rows of corn ended suddenly and he stopped short, blocked by a rusted wire fence strung on four-foot-tall wooden posts. On the other side was a long line of trees, tall and still in the windless night.

Hicks squeezed between two stretches of wire, then ran into the cover of the trees. The darkness was thick here, and he had to feel his way between the pines and brush at one point. Then he was out, on the other side of the tree line, at the border of the Larkin brothers' collards field.

Sweat stung his eyes. Across the field stood a charcoal line of trees far in the back. He headed for them, crushing collards under his heavy tread. Then a low snarl rolled from behind, and he turned around to see that *thing* only ten yards away, trotting after him with shadows curling from its nostrils.

He fell backward over a collard plant. His back erupted with a jolt of fire. He climbed to his feet. His ankle ached with every step, and sweat ran in streams through his hair, down his neck.

He tripped over the bushy collards as though he were wearing clown shoes. Then he was halfway to the tree line, and he heard his own rough breathing, panting, gasping, his throat dry and scratchy, and God, he needed a drink, anything cold, ice, scotch on ice, scotch, oh God, a *drink*—

The collard field ended with a dirt border, and he ran into the shelter of the trees. He leaned against a slender pine and felt the rough bark against his cheek, thought maybe it would be okay to just rest here, just a while, only a minute or two, as sweat ran down his sides and he gulped air. Then the thing roared behind him, and his eyes snapped open and he spun between the trees and into the woods.

The trees were sparse, and the ground was covered with layers of brittle pine needles and leaves. He ran between trees blindly, trapped in a black maze. Deeper in, the trees became even sparser, and grass poked up from the leaf-strewn ground. Moonlight helped him pick his way between the tall pines, and his eyes finally made out a clear path that had been formed by countless feet over the years.

The path made a sharp right turn at a dense copse of ragged bushes, and he entered a small clearing. Empty beer cans and a moldy copy of *Playboy* lay near a fallen tree. Paper bags from the Atomic were crumpled nearby, and moonlight sparkled off empty bottles of Rolling Rock and Budweiser.

He fumbled to his knees. "Oh, God. Oh, God." He knew where he was. He'd had to chase hoodlums and dope smokers out of this clearing for years—and the path eventually wound out to the far edge of his own rural neighborhood.

"Shit," he said, gasping, hoping. "Oh shit, almost home. Almost home."

Then something large crashed down the path toward him. He got to his feet, groaning with his weight, and ran up the path toward safety.

Toward his house.

His booze.

His guns.

Grey trees blurred past him in the faint moonlight. He heard only the sounds of his own ragged breath. His world was only an unfocused cone of sight directly in front of him.

Minutes later, he spied a tree stump, and the path forked through grass on either side. He was on Northumberland, at the far end of his street. His house waited only a quarter-mile away.

His feet slapped the cracked grey asphalt as he ran past Meriam Teague's house, lit only by a fake gas lamppost in the front yard. The homes here were far apart, separated by long lawns or hedges, or the occasional vegetable garden. In a few minutes he huffed past Henry Williford's place. The old man's hound dog, Dawg, barked once from the backyard.

Then there was only the sound of his gasping, and his feet flopping on the street, and he passed house after dark house, shuttered for the night, for only criminals and ne'er do wells were out and about after nine in this fine, upstanding neighborhood, looking to raise hell or prowling for mischief.

And then:

He rounded a bend in the road. The first thing he saw was Barton Owens' place, silent in the still night.

And 100 yards farther, there was his house.

He reached for his keys, then yelled, "Shit!" when he remembered they were missing.

His heart skipped a beat. His front door was locked. He *had* to get inside.

He limped onto his driveway and went around the back. Dotty, long ago, had placed a decorative statue of a kneeling angel outside on the kitchen windowsill. Underneath she had kept the spare key, and he smacked the statue away with the back of his hand. His fingers touched the warm, steel key just as the statue dropped to the ground, one wing snapping off with a sharp crack.

He ran into the cool, quiet kitchen and locked the door. He took a dinette chair and jammed it under the knob. Then he went to the refrigerator and popped open a bottle of Pabst. Cold beer ran in wonderful streams down his chin, down his torn, bloodied shirt. Then he opened another, and another, and polished them off with a belch that brought beer back up into his mouth. He drank and drank, and no beers had ever tasted as sweet as those.

His back screamed, and his collarbone throbbed every time he moved. He fumbled in his shirt pocket and took out a handful of pills, and he downed them with a long slug of scotch that dribbled from the corners of his mouth. He took another long swig from the bottle and wiped his mouth with the back of his hand. "Now we're talkin'," he said.

The gun cabinet in the bedroom was locked with a combination lock. It took him a full minute to get his shaking fingers to work. Then he took out a 20-gauge shotgun and loaded the chambers. He placed the shotgun across his legs and took out a Colt .45 revolver. It had been his father's in World War I, and he oiled it once a year, saving it for a special occasion.

He guessed this was it.

Hicks placed the guns across the white linen on the dining room table. He moved a chair from the table and spun it so he could sit and watch most of the house from one vantage point and reach the guns in a split second. Then he went into the kitchen, swallowed a shot of scotch, and splashed cold water on his face.

He dried his face with an old dish towel and took another pull of scotch. It went warm down his throat, and he started to feel it, calming him.

He threw the deadbolt on the front door. He jammed one of the dining room chairs under the doorknob and wedged it tight. He opened the drapes.

He sat at the table, scotch at his elbow, and peered around. There was no movement outside in the moonlight. There were no sounds in his house, save for his own breathing, and the thump of his heart, and the *whisper-tick* of the kitchen clock.

Damn. Past midnight.

He had been running away like a fuckin' coward for more than an hour.

He leaned back in the chair and closed his eyes. He really felt it now, the booze and the pills finally kicking in, making him feel like he could do anything, that he could take on anyone and come out on top.

He went to the front window. Nothing but shadows across the street. Nothing moving at all from where he could see. Nothing to be scared about. Nothing at all.

He double checked that the Colt was loaded. He slipped it under his belt. Then he went into the bathroom and started laughing as he unzipped. "Racehorse," he said aloud, laughing. "Man, I gotta piss like a fuckin' racehorse." He laughed and laughed. After the night he'd had, pissing like normal was the funniest thing in the fuckin' world.

He zipped up and forgot to flush. He went straight for the scotch in the dining room and let it flow down his throat. He placed the bottle back on the table.

And stared.

His .38 service revolver lay next to the shotgun, gleaming in the silver moonlight.

"The hell?"

He reached for the Colt at his belt. Still there.

He leaned over the table and stared at the .38, almost afraid to touch it.

He lifted the scotch to his lips.

Castle. He—he took it.

A voice behind him said, "That rotgut's gonna turn your liver into a sponge."

He spun around so quick his hip bone hit the table, and he yelped aloud.

In the moonlight from outside, he could barely make out the shape sitting in his recliner.

"I brought you a present," Ben Castle said from the shadows.

Hicks reached behind him. His hand closed on the handle of his .38. Hicks grinned. "Castle, you old fucker." He brought up the gun and pulled back the hammer with his thumb. "You old FUCK!" He aimed straight at Castle's face—

Ben's eyes turned the color of dark red wine, then sparked, deep inside, glowing with rich, red fires.

—Buddy.

Hicks hesitated. Ben's eyes, his goddamn eyes. They bored into him like red hot screws.

—Buddy. Put down the gun, Buddy.

Hicks let his arm drop, and he slid the gun onto the white tablecloth. Ben's eyes. They were everything. They were all he could focus on. It was as though he were underwater, or moving in slow motion.

—Buddy. It's time, don't you think?

The sheriff's mouth hung open.

—Buddy. You're the sheriff. You're the king of the county. It's time for you to act like one. To act like a man.

A line of spittle and scotch oozed from the corner of his mouth.

—Sit down, Buddy.

Hicks sat at the table.

—There's something you need to do, Buddy. It's time to own up. Isn't it, Buddy?

Hicks nodded again. "I— I—"

—Look at the table, Buddy.

Hicks looked down. A ballpoint pen and a pad of writing paper had been placed beside the shotgun.

—It's time to own up, Buddy. It's time to make amends, and let everyone know what you've done—what you've been doing for a long, long time.

Hicks stared at the pen.

—It's time to confess, isn't it?

Hicks started to tremble. "Na— naa— No."

Ben's eyes burned like raging coals in the darkness. *—Oh, Buddy, it's too late for that. Don't even try to fight. Have a drink, Buddy. Have a nice, long sip of that scotch. Go ahead. You'll feel better. A lot better.*

Hicks glanced at the bottle, and thought it would be a good idea to have a drink right now. He chugged about three shots, and placed the bottle on the table.

There was silence for several minutes. Buddy Hicks contemplated the taste of scotch on his tongue. The world around him went numb.

—Pick up the pen, Buddy.

Hicks picked up the pen and pressed the top. The ballpoint clicked into place.

—Now, start writing it all down, Buddy. Everyone needs to know the kind of man you are. And that you're sorry for all the things you've done. All the innocent people you've hurt.

Hicks struggled. The pen shook in his hand. "But I—"

—Buddy, you're calm, now. You're doing the right thing. More scotch, Buddy. Relax. You can do this for me, can't you?

Hicks swallowed another shot of scotch.

Then Castle stood above him, his eyes burning down into his.

—Let's start with this. I'll help you out. You write in your own words, okay, Buddy? Understand?

The pen felt good in his hand. *Right.* He pulled the writing pad to him.

—You feel bad, don't you, about all the bad things you've done?

Man, that scotch felt good. He felt absolutely great. All the pain was gone in his arm, his back, his fingers.

He felt just perfect.

—Start like this. Tell everyone that it's time you came clean. You have to tell everyone about the bad things you've done. Go ahead. Start writing, and I'll help.

Hicks put the pen to the top sheet of writing paper.

To the Citizens of Stonebridge County,

It is time to connfess my sins.

—*That's a great start, Buddy. Keep going.*

I have changed over the years while I have been your sheriff, and have done many bad things while in office, for which I ask your forgivness.

Recent events, like Ronnie Sheffield's murder, have forced me to face the facts. That I am not a good man. For instance, I was going to try to put her murder on an innocent man, instead of Kenny who did it, I am sure. But what I did to Duke tonight is unforgivible to me

—*And you're going to make up for it, aren't you?*

is unforgivible to me. and now I have to pay the price.

—*Let it out, Buddy. Let it all out.*

A tear rolled down the sheriff's cheek.

I have stole guns and drugs out of peoples homes who were completely innocent. And guilty ones too.

I've lost paperwork deliberately to keep people in jail.

I have been stealing drugs and drug money from the evidence locker at work. And tonight from the hospital. My back has been hurting a lot.

I stop people driving lawfully and make searches that are illegal.

Many times, I put people in jail just because I have had personal vindetas on them, like on Ray Ray Pollard, and Ib Larkin, and the old colored that owns the Mosby junk yard. Maynard.

I faked evidence and lied in court just so I'd win many times. I shot and framed Clarence Duboy for the murder of Jenky Poole in 1962.

I bought guilty verdicts from Judge Flecher Macy for thousands of dollars over the years.

I am today the exalted cyclops of our local KKK Klavern, which also holds as members Wayne Cousins, County Superviser Mike Dunnell, and two of my deputies.

Ben's eyes widened. —*Buddy. Really. I'd heard rumors.*

Hicks' hand shook, and the ballpoint dropped to the tabletop. "No," he murmured. His eyes focused on the guns in front of him. His hand inched forward.

Ben's shadow elongated across the table. His eyes blazed scarlet in the shadows.

—*Oh, Buddy. Buddy. It's going to be all right.*

Hicks stopped trembling. His fingers closed around the pen.

—*You feel bad, don't you?'*

Hicks nodded slowly, and he wondered if it was the pills or the booze that made everything feel so slow, like he was floating in a cool blue pool.

But it felt good. Sweet and cool. Like he didn't have a care in the world.

—*Make it official, Buddy. Tell everybody. You have to atone for your crimes. Don't you?*

The time has come, and I've got to pay for the crimes I've committed. I have done wrong, and I cant see anyway out of this. Stonebridge deserves a better lawman than me.

Sorry, Duke. I hope I didn't kill you.

Tell my boy Lonnie I still love him.

—Good, Buddy. Good. Now, I'll be your witness. Give it the ol' John Hancock. Make it legal. Legal and binding.

Hicks signed the note ***Sheriff Amberson "Buddy" Hicks***, put the pen beside the writing pad, and let out a shuddering breath. He was crying, but he didn't realize it. He took up the scotch and took another swig.

"This—this is it, ain't it?" he said.

Ben was a spectre of darkness, looming over him with eyes of fire. *—Well, Buddy. You've got to do the right thing, don't you?*

Hicks nodded, his vision swimming with tears.

—You should probably stand up, Buddy. You think?

Hicks pushed himself up from the table.

—It all comes down to you, now. Your choice, Sheriff. What's it going to be?

The glow in Ben's eyes flickered along the shining steel of the guns.

Hicks glanced at the shotgun. Then he reached down, placed his hand on his father's Colt .45. "No," he whispered. He took his .38 service revolver into his hand. It was the gun he had carried longest. It was the gun that represented him, his position.

And his shame.

He cocked the revolver with a snap that echoed through the dark house.

He put the barrel between his lips. He tasted the cool steel, and the residue of gunpowder and smoke.

He heard the spatter of liquid dripping onto his shoes, into the carpet. Warmth spread down the front of his pants.

Ben looked down.

—Oh, Buddy—

The gunshot rang like a thunderclap across the neighborhood. A light went on in the house across the street. The front curtains parted, and Alicia Ryan peered out of her red brick ranch home, sure she'd heard a car backfire, but there wasn't a single thing moving out there.

In the next house up, Barton Owens was already on the phone, dialing the sheriff's department. He damn well knew gunfire when he heard it. He looked through his front window and craned his head to the left. It had to have come from near the sheriff's house. But damn if he could see anyone out in the dark.

They couldn't see the shadows at the back of the house. They didn't see the back door open. They never saw a tall black shadow, a sliver of endless darkness, cross the back yard, and merge with the long, warm night.

22

AS DUKE CRAWFORD plowed the sheriff's cruiser into the sliding glass doors of the ER, no one noticed two shadows, indistinct in the ill-lit parking lot, slip between cars and disappear into a night-black Camaro.

Summer drove silent through the parking lot, Michel beside her, watching through the back window as orderlies rushed to carry Duke inside. The band on the radio sang about a love that was out of line.

They made it to Queen Street, and Summer spun the wheel toward town. Michel glanced at her. Dark blood from her wounds had stained her blouse. She looked down at the holes in her shirt. "I don't even feel it."

He nodded silently. "Back there. The bats. How'd you do it?"

"The bats?"

"You commanded the bats."

"No," she said. "I didn't even think about it, really. It just came natural. I felt them, in the trees. It was like a buzzing in my head. And it just, kind of, happened. Natural. Like the reflection thing."

"Reflection?"

"My reflection. I saw it back at the hospital, in the window. It was me, but it wasn't me."

"Oh. Don't worry. In time, you'll—"

"So I sent it away. I made it change."

"You made it—"

"I made it look the way I look. I made it reflect me again."

"You controlled it? Your reflection?"

She nodded. The song ended on the radio, and the singer cried about Bill and their wedding day. Summer turned down the volume a notch. "Boo fuckin' hoo," she murmured.

He glanced at her in the rearview mirror—the beautiful blonde he had met last Thursday.

She was so different now. Her being, her essence, almost glowed, as though her heart had blossomed into a blazing star. He felt her inner strength emanating from her in invisible waves, a wild aurora of energy.

She was a natural force.

She was beautiful.

"What you did—the bats, your reflection—it took me a year to master."

"Well," she said, "I guess I'm not you."

"No, I suppose you're not."

She stopped at the stop sign at Matoaka, and then wheeled onto Croatoan. She pulled into her driveway and cut off the engine. She stared at him, then looked away.

They got out quietly. He walked in the deep shadows, so no one could see him. But Summer could, moonlight playing like silver in his eyes.

They stepped onto the porch. Summer turned to look across her neighborhood. "Weird."

"What?"

"Everyone's asleep. I can feel them, breathing in their beds. Soft, like the flutter of butterflies." She paused. "It feels like a dream. A couple of hours ago, they were all watching from the curb, or from behind their screen doors. The ambulance's light was flashing across the houses, and the drivers carried Ma out and put her in the back." She looked into his dark eyes. "Nothing's ever going to be the same, is it?"

He said, "Would you really want it to be?"

She unlocked the front door.

"You need to pack," he said. "Essentials only. The sheriff's station is close. And you need to get ready. We'll meet in the cavern. 3 a.m. or so. That will give us a couple of hours to get away, and find a place for the day. And then—"

She smiled, staring into his eyes. And then they were locked forever in each other's arms, and their kiss was a bond, as deep and as long as the eternity of night.

This one moment, this one kiss, would forever linger in their memories as the moment each knew they wanted to be as one together—one until the end of time.

And it was the last time they would see each other for many years.

Michel slipped out the front door and disappeared into the shadows. She closed the door and locked it, then went upstairs.

First she washed the blood off her chest. The bullet wounds had already sealed themselves, and all that remained were dark blood stains on her skin, and red welts where the bullets had passed through, the size of mosquito bites.

She changed into a bra and a black Jack Daniel's t-shirt. She put *Aretha Arrives* on the turntable and spun it into "Night Life." She pulled her red vinyl American Tourister bags out of the closet and opened them on her bed. Her mother had bought them for her in her sophomore year for a cheerleading trip to D.C. She had used them only that once.

She took her time, choosing her clothes carefully, leaving behind the clothes that were outdated, and pieces she could live without. She loaded her train case with makeup and toiletries, then filled the round tiara case with things she couldn't bear to leave behind: a scarf her father had bought her at Miller and Rhoads in Richmond; some pictures off her vanity; her dad's ashtray.

She threw in the diary where she had so long ago drawn Michel's eyes, then loaded everything into the trunk of the Camaro. Finally she brought down her stereo and the crate full of records. There was no way she could ever leave those behind.

Then she stood in the middle of her bedroom and looked around to see if she had forgotten anything. Her eyes watered, but she didn't cry. She knew this was right, but it was damn hard to let go of everything she had ever known for a new life.

The clock on her nightstand read 2:48. "Shit." She would be late meeting Michel. But she knew she finally had to do what she had been secretly putting off.

Ma.

She cut off the air conditioner, plucked the stuffed dinosaur off her bed, and held him. She balled up her bloody clothes and jammed them in her purse.

One last thing.

She went down the stairs and stood in the dining room. Those damn Hummels. The stench of Mom's Winstons. All the dead people staring at her from behind dusty glass. Dinners in the kitchen when Dad was alive, when life was all about playing outside and long summer days and the aroma of plastic Halloween masks.

She took a book off the sofa. She locked the front door behind her, and refused to look back. She refused to take one last walk through her roses.

They weren't her roses anymore.

They didn't exist.

They were ghostflowers.

She set the dinosaur in the passenger seat. Then she backed out of the driveway, threw the car into gear, and whispered, "Go to Hell, Stonebridge."

Two cruisers sat nose to nose in front of the shattered doors of the Emergency Room, their red lights spinning, stabbing her eyes with almost blinding intensity.

She put on her blue sunglasses.

A tow truck was lifting the back of the sheriff's cruiser. Both headlights were shattered, and the front bumper dangled at one end.

Three deputies stood at the doors, guarding the wreckage and sipping coffee. Ashton Ivor and J. B. Keever had been seniors in her sophomore year, and Red Waverly was in the senior choir at St. John's. Red had always been squirrelly, but now she watched him fidget in the warm night, scratching his head and shuffling his feet as though he wanted to be anywhere but here.

She got out of the car and walked toward them. Ashton saw her first and raised his coffee toward her. "Hey, Summer."

She stepped up onto the sidewalk. "Long time, Ashton. My God. What happened here?"

Red looked at Ashton for advice. Ashton shrugged. J. B. said, "We ain't supposed to say anything, Summer."

She raised an eyebrow. "Are you serious?"

Ashton stepped toward her and said, low, "Just keep this to yourself, okay?"

She nodded.

"Duke Crawford. He drove one of our units straight into the doors here."

"Duke? What happened?"

Ashton glanced at the others.

J. B. spoke up. "We don't know everything yet. He's in surgery now. We'll get it all straight when he comes to."

Summer looked from one to the other. "My mom's in the Emergency Room."

Red pointed a shaky finger down the sidewalk. "Can't go through here. Too dangerous. Gotta go around through the main doors."

"Okay. Tell Duke I said 'Hey.'"

Summer started down the sidewalk. Around the corner she came to a trash can, and she stuffed her bloodied clothes down into it, burying them underneath paper cups and greasy hamburger wrappers from the Atomic.

The lobby was dark, lit only by two table lamps with yellowed shades on tables near the windows. She heard the large clock on the wall ticking, making the empty room feel lonely and strange, and she followed arrows pointing down the stark, olive green hall toward the Emergency Room.

She turned the corner, and the scene became jarringly chaotic. Most of the county's deputies milled around, speaking low, sipping coffee in paper cups, casting nervous glances toward the Emergency Room. A woman was crying in the waiting room. Summer walked by and saw Evie Garland, Duke's longtime girlfriend, weeping into a tissue, her mother's arm wrapped around her shoulders.

She went toward the nurses' desk. A deputy turned and saw her. His eyes widened. She recognized Deputy Jackson. "Curly, what is going on around here?"

Jackson motioned for her. "Just the gal we needed to see."

"My ma is here," Summer said. "I need to check on her."

"This won't take long," Jackson said. He pulled her into the exam room where Sheriff Hicks had been treated. As they entered, Dr. Stoney looked up from the drug cabinet.

"Doc, you know Summer?"

Stoney nodded. "Heard your mother is stable."

Summer said, "Good. Thank God."

"One of the nurses here told us you were seen here earlier with Sheriff Hicks," Jackson said.

"Yeah," she said. "Keep that son of a bitch away from me."

"What happened?"

"That S.O.B has gone nuts. He threatened to kill my mother."

"Excuse me?"

"Her mother is in the ER," Stoney said. "Heart attack this evening."

"All right," he said. "What happened exactly?"

"What didn't? He followed me into the waiting room when Ma was being looked at. Then he forced the doctor, Dr. Hoyt, to leave, and he said he was going to inject her with morphine. He thought I knew something about some biker—"

For an instant, she glanced into Jackson's eyes.

—There was no biker. There was never a biker in town.

"—but I told him earlier at the station, I don't know anybody like that. He's gone nuts, Curly."

"So you're saying he accosted you here in the hospital?"

"Accosted? Hell, he dragged me out of the waiting room. He came out of here."

"This room?"

"Yeah, I saw him in here. The door was open. Then I went into the waiting room."

Dr. Stoney said, "Did you see him take anything?"

Jackson watched her. She shook her head. "No. I just saw him with a hypo."

Stoney sighed. "Yeah, he took something, all right."

"How did he threaten you?" Jackson said.

"How? He followed me into the waiting room, all angry. Duke came in and tried to calm him down. Instead, he got angrier. He pulled us into the Emergency Room and said he'd kill Ma if I didn't give up some biker that I don't know."

—There was never any biker.

"Those were his words? He'd kill your mother?"

"Yeah."

"And Duke was here too?"

"Yeah. Hicks tried to take me outside, but Duke pulled him aside in the hall and talked to him. Then Duke told me to get out and just leave. He said he'd handle the sheriff. So I got the hell out of here. I went home, but I couldn't sleep for worrying about Ma."

Jackson stared away, thinking.

Summer said, "So what happened here, anyway?"

"That's what we're trying to figure out. Sometime after you left, the sheriff must have driven Duke somewhere and shot him."

"Is he all right?"

Stoney looked at his watch. "He's still in surgery. Three and a half hours. Hicks—hell, he must have been drunk or something. It looks like he stole a bunch of pills from the cabinet." He opened a drawer and glanced at Jackson. "And a hypodermic and morphine are missing."

"Son of a bitch went off the deep end," Summer said. "He had a weird—a crazy look in his eyes. Twitching."

—Hicks did it all. He's crazy.

The deputy and the doctor looked at each other. Jackson said, "We've got to find him."

"Can I go see my mother now?"

Jackson nodded. "Thanks for helping. I might come 'round and talk to you some more."

"Okay—"

—Summer doesn't know a thing. Keep her out of it.

"—any time. You know where I am."

"Thank you, Miss Moore," Dr. Stoney said.

Summer touched Jackson's arm. "Get that bastard for me. And for Duke."

"Yeah," Jackson said. "Goddamn, what a mess."

Summer stepped into the hall and headed for the ER. Then she stopped short and turned around. She stood in the waiting room door. "Evie?"

Duke's girlfriend looked up and saw her. Then they embraced in a hug, and Evie started crying in Summer's arms.

She led Evie over to the chairs along the wall and took her hand. "I heard about Duke. I'm so sorry, Evie. The sheriff is a crazy bastard. They'll get him, I promise."

Evie nodded. "I'm just so worried about Duke."

"I know, sweetie. Don't be. If I know Duke, he'll be out of here in no time."

Evie sniffled and wiped her nose with a tissue. "What are you doing here so late?"

"My mama. She had a heart attack tonight. I better go see her. I'll bring y'all something for dinner when Ma is out of the woods."

They hugged again, and Summer went into the Emergency Room. She walked slower the closer she got to her mother. Then she stood in front of her mother's blue curtain and thought about what she had to do.

Michel. New York. The world.

This is the way it had to be.

She stepped through the curtain.

Her mother slept, mouth open, beneath the oxygen tent. Summer took the book out of her purse and placed it on the steel nightstand next to a pitcher of ice water. "I brought you something, Ma. Your *TV Guide* crosswords book. *Number Two.* For when you get better."

Louise didn't stir. The blood pressure monitor behind the bed beeped steadily.

Summer spoke low. This was only for Ma. She had to force the words out. It was a lot harder to say this than she had thought.

"I've got to leave here, Ma. I don't know if you can hear me or not. But you and me—we just ain't good for each other anymore. I love you, Mama, and I think you love me too. But I'm all grown up now. And you keep trying to turn me into something I'm not. I'm not the little kid you keep wanting me to be. And, you and me, we just can't stop arguing. So, I'm going to have to stop it myself."

She held back the tears and reached out with her soul. Her mother's heartbeat was weak, but strong—strong enough.

Strong enough to do one last thing for her daughter.

—Stay strong, Mama. Keep calm. Steady. Just let yourself relax. No stress.

—You've got to do this for me, Mama. In a minute, I need you to wake up for me. And I need you to say something for me. You need to say it loud. Real loud. And say it like you're mad. Real mad. But—

She felt their beings, their souls, touch each other. Poor Ma; she was so tired.

—You need to stay calm inside. Okay, Ma? Calm. After this, we're never gonna be angry again. Now, this is what you've got to do—

"Oh shit." Nurse Baker's head whipped around at Louise's first shout. She sprinted from behind the nurses' station.

Louise Moore's voice rose from behind her curtain. "I didn't raise no common tramp! If your daddy was alive—"

Deputies turned to watch as Nurse Baker whipped open the curtain. Louise struggled in bed, shaking a fist at Summer. Her daughter sat there, open-mouthed in shock. "Mama, please. You've got to stay calm."

Louise shouted, "I wouldn't treat a dog the way you treat me! No daughter of mine would act like a whore the way you do!"

Baker gasped.

"Mama! Please!"

Louise looked pale behind the clear plastic tent. "The way you traipse around! You and your slutty ways are going to give me another heart attack! This is all your fault!"

Baker pulled the tent away and pressed Louise back down. "Mrs. Moore, you have to remain calm." She looked up at the monitors. Louise's heart rate was slightly elevated. Baker shouted over her shoulder, "I need Dr. Hoyt *now*!"

Through tears, Summer pleaded, "But, Mama, you—"

"GET OUT!" Louise bellowed. "You are NOT my daughter! You ain't welcome in my house no more! Get out! GET OUT!"

Summer jumped up suddenly and screamed, "When will all this shit stop?" She ran out, tears and mascara trailing down her cheeks. A nurse came in and tried to calm Louise.

Nurse Baker ran after Summer. "Miss Moore, she's been through a lot tonight," she said. "It's the stress. She doesn't really mean what she's saying."

Summer wiped tears and makeup across her cheek. "That's just it. She *does* mean it. She means every damn word." She shifted her purse on her shoulder. "Tell her. You tell her for me. She doesn't have to worry. You tell her I won't be back. You tell her—she can count on it. I'm not ever coming back."

Summer ran down the hall, into the shadows. She sat crying in her car for ten minutes while Creedence looked for shelter from the rain.

She had set the stage. Everyone in the Emergency Room had heard. The whole town would believe it now. She had been kicked out. Disowned.

And the tears that ran down her cheeks, and the cold emptiness she felt inside, she would deal with.

She had always known she was different. Her own kind of loner.

Now, she was an outcast.

This was the way she knew it should be.
She looked at her slim gold watch. 3:23.
She started the car and threw it into **DRIVE**.

23

MICHEL STOOD IN the shadows of a broad, ancient elm across the street from the sheriff's station. A few aimless night birds fluttered over the treetops, but all else was silent around him.

His motorcycle was padlocked in the small impound lot behind a chain link fence around back. He focused on the station, and touched two heartbeats inside. A man. A woman. He strained to hear, and he could just make out through the walls snippets of speech, enough to learn that some deputies were still out at the cemetery, securing the scene, but most were at the hospital, waiting on word about Duke and mourning the loss of Collie Nettles.

He slipped between two county cruisers. He hugged the shadows in the foyer and passed unseen through the double doors. Through the interior glass doors he saw a short woman at her desk, her blue-grey hair piled in a towering beehive. A tall, lanky deputy in his uniform sat at a desk in the far corner.

He waited. In the main office, the lights grew dimmer, and the shadows in the corners stretched out, thickening with darkness. He slid through the crack between the doors and flitted from shadow to shadow until he stood in the blackness behind a filing cabinet.

The woman cried behind thick glasses. She picked up the phone and dialed it, then sat there blotting her tears with a tissue. Then she crumpled the tissue and slammed the phone down. "He's still not answering."

The deputy looked up. His name badge read JOYNES. "You know how he gets. If he wanted to be found, he would be."

Iris frowned. "Well, nobody's seen him since he went to the hospital. I can't believe he's just letting Collie's family wait. He should be out there. Collie's wife deserves better treatment than this."

Joynes went over to Iris. "You need to relax. You should have some of the sheriff's scotch."

"You ain't supposed to know about that, nosy."

"Damn, Iris. Everybody knows about it. He hasn't kept it a secret."

Joynes sat on the edge of her desk. "I know you don't want to hear about this. Hell, you probably already know. Word is the sheriff's an alky."

She glared at him. "You shut up now."

"Come on, Iris. It's bad enough the office thinks he's got a regular bar in there. And you know what Eddie said from over the hospital."

"He didn't steal no pills."

Joynes crossed his arms and kept his voice down. "Duke told me weeks ago that there's contraband missing from the evidence room. Drugs, Iris. And you know he and the sheriff are the only ones with the key."

"You just shut your mouth, Clinton Joynes." She straightened a pile of papers on her desk. "You just go on and keep your goddamn ideas to your own self."

Joynes yawned suddenly. He shook his head, trying to clear it, but what he wanted to do right now was go to sleep. "All right, Iris. Didn't mean to upset you."

Iris ignored him.

Joynes slid off the desk and started toward the corridor in the back. "I'll be back in the locker room. Put my feet up for a few."

Iris yawned as he walked away. It had been a long couple of days—and poor, poor Collie. "Come on, Buddy," she whispered to the phone. "Call me."

She took her purse out of her bottom desk drawer and looked at herself in her compact, then powdered one cheek. She yawned again, and her eyelids fluttered. She couldn't believe how sleepy she had suddenly become.

The compact clattered to the desk. The powder puff tumbled into her lap, and her head nodded forward.

Michel stepped into the wan light. Iris snored softly.

He looked on her desk first, searching for anything with his name on it. He knew for sure that Hicks had put his name into the system. This was his only chance to find out what damage this goose-stepping martinet had done.

He found nothing on her desktop or in the folders in the drawers. There were no loose sheets waiting in the Telex machine. There were no files in the filing cabinets with TRAGER written on them. There was only one other place.

He went into the sheriff's office. By moonlight shining through the window, he found it: a file angled across the sheriff's blotter. He flipped through the pages: Trager's service record, negative responses from the state police. Nothing important.

He took the file. He'd tear it up, then throw it away somewhere outside of town. He walked around the desk, then froze.

A single sheet of paper from the telex had been placed in the sheriff's inbox.

He picked it up.

The sheet bore a photostat of his military ID. The banner at the top read **INTERPOL.**

This had come through late Sunday. The sheriff's initial request had been telexed to Interpol on Friday morning.

Almost three days.

If his enemies had uncovered intel on his activities in Vietnam, they would have intercepted this immediately. He was sure they had operatives inside Interpol, probably stationed in the Paris office.

Three days.

The Hawkbournes could already be here.

They could already know about Summer.

The world seemed to spin around him.

Summer.

He had to protect Summer.

He took one step toward the door, then stopped.

He knew then what he had to do.

He snarled with rage, and his fist lashed out. The phone smashed into the wall.

He closed the office door behind him and stood over Iris.

—Trager. You've never heard the name Trager.

Iris whispered something in her sleep.

—You know nothing about any biker in town. Iris. Sheriff Hicks never requested any reports on anyone named Trager.

Her body trembled. She was struggling. He felt her loyalty to the sheriff, strong, deep in her heart.

He bent down to her throat. Her blood tasted of lavender and talcum.

—There was no biker. There was no Trager. Forget it all.

She moaned, almost purring, as though in an erotic dream. "Oh, Buddy—"

—Summer Moore is not involved in this.

"Mmmmmm," she murmured.

—Summer Moore is innocent.

Iris nodded.

—Innocent.

"Innocent," she whispered.

The phone rang.

—Answer it. Just like usual. I am not here. No one is here but you and the deputy.

She picked up the handset. "Sheriff's."

She listened. "Where'd you hear the shots, sir?"

She wrote down an address. "Oh my word," she said. "That's—" She nodded, nervous.

Michel felt her heart rate increase.

"You just stay put, sir. I'll send a deputy out there right now." She slammed down the phone. "Clint! Clinton! You get out here right now!"

Michel backed into the shadows.

Joynes came running down the hall. "What happened, Iris?"

"Get out to the sheriff's place right now! Somebody's heard shots!"

"Aw, the hell!" He snagged his hat off his desk, then ran out the front door. In seconds a siren started and a red light flashed, and Joynes tore a cruiser away from the curb.

Michel went outside. He wrapped his hand around the padlock to the impound lot, and he wrenched it off with a single tug. He threw the mangled lock deep into the trees behind the station. He kicked open the chain link gates, crimping the metal with his foot.

He ran his hand over his bike's gas tank. The secret compartment was intact.

He kick-jumped the engine, then he spun the bike between the bent gates and aimed for the mountains.

He felt numb inside. Empty.

There was one last thing to do.

One final duty.
To keep her safe.

24

JOYNES MADE IT to the sheriff's house in two minutes. He pounded on the front door. "Sheriff! Sheriff Hicks!" His voice echoed through the neighborhood. A light was on in the front room, so he knocked and rang the doorbell over and over.

Nothing.

He radioed Iris from the car, and she gave him Barton Owens' address. He ran across the street, and Barton already had the door open when he hopped up onto the stoop.

Barton told him what he had heard: not shots, but a single shot. Yes, it was definitely a gun he'd heard. Yes, he knew the difference between a firecracker and a gunshot, damn it. And yes, it came from the direction of the sheriff's house. Then Barton spat into the bushes beside the stoop and slammed the door.

Joynes walked back to his cruiser, stood around for a few seconds, then went back up to the sheriff's door. His knuckles ached from knocking, but there was still no response.

He sat behind the wheel, door open, and radioed the station.

"Iris, I'm going to stay here for a while. Ain't nobody home, but I'll be damned if I ain't here when he gets back."

He set the mic in its metal cradle and looked through the windshield at the houses on the street, silent and dark.

"Ain't this just a crock of shit," he said.

Something hard rapped the window, and Joynes jerked awake and shouted, "I ain't sleepin'!"

Deputy Jackson peered at him through the glass, shaking his head as he slid his baton back into his belt.

Joynes got out of the cruiser. "The hell, Curly."

"It's a good damn thing the old man didn't find you sleepin' behind the wheel."

"I was waitin' for him, is all."

"You've been out here for three hours." Jackson looked up at the house. "No word yet?"

"Naw. He hasn't called in?"

Jackson shook his head. "Iris has been trying to reach you."

"I wasn't asleep for that long. And I had the volume down on the radio."

"All hell's broke loose. We need to find Hicks right now. Looks like he shot

Duke just 'bout midnight."

"Duke? The sheriff shot Duke? For what?"

Jackson looked up at the house. "'Cause he's a goddamn lunatic. We think he's high on pills he stole outta the emergency room."

"Me and Iris was just talkin—"

"His house is all locked up?"

"Yeah, yeah. Tight as a drum."

"You try the door around back?"

Joynes stared at him.

"The back door? You go around to the back door?"

"Aw, shit," said Joynes.

"Jesus Christ, you dumbass."

Jackson started up the driveway. Joynes ran up beside him.

"Go get your flashlight," Jackson said.

"Oh yeah."

Joynes went back to the cruiser, then ran up the driveway with his flashlight. They snapped them on, and the yellow beams cut through the shadows around the side of the house.

They focused the lights on the storm door around back. Jackson tried the latch, and the door opened. He shone the beam through the glass in the back door. "Nothing unusual," he said. He turned the knob, and the door opened easily.

He looked at Joynes. "You fucking idiot."

They stepped inside. The kitchen was silent save for the ticking of a clock above the sink.

"What's that smell?" Joynes said.

"Sheriff?" Jackson's voice rang through the empty house.

They went through the doorway, and their flashlights froze on the blood pooling into the carpet. The sheriff's body lay sprawled in a viscous, crimson puddle, the back of his head only a ragged, empty hole.

"Oh," Joynes said. "Oh holy, holy shit."

One light was on, enough to sear into their minds forever the blood spattered across the ceiling and walls, speckled with pink nuggets of flesh and grey matter.

Joynes ran back into the kitchen. Jackson listened to him as if from a distance, crying like a baby, then he focused his flashlight on the blood-spattered note Hicks had left on the dining room table.

He read it slowly, carefully, then just stared at it as though it were an evil thing, something he didn't ever want to touch.

He said, "Holy shit is right."

25

ON THE WAY to Storybook Hollow, she pulled the Camaro into the parking lot of the Dixie Dinette and used her key to enter the empty restaurant. She didn't have long. Ruthette would be in at 4:00 a.m. or so to open for breakfast at 5:30, but Summer wasn't about to let Michel see her like this, her eyes red and puffy, her mascara tracked down her cheeks. She would settle on nothing but looking perfect for the first day of their new life together.

She freshened up in the women's room, then fixed her makeup, controlling her reflection in the mirror with hardly a thought.

She stepped into the dark kitchen, lit only by a pale, white work light over the sinks, and went into Ralph's office. In the shadows, she wound the dinette's key off her key ring and placed it on his desk.

She closed the office door and looked around the kitchen. In the front, she watched Tina serving a family, laughing at a joke, flirting with construction workers. In the kitchen, she saw Ruthette hunkered over the flattop, flipping pancakes and scrambling eggs. Hell, she even tasted the scent of Ruthette's Sweet Georgia Brown's pomade, sugaring her hair like—

Then the kitchen door swung open, and Ruthette's silhouette blocked the doorway.

"Summer? What you doing here, girl?"

"Ruthette," Summer whispered. "Why are you here so early?"

Ruthette stepped through and let the door swing shut. "Couldn't sleep. Thought I'd—" She watched Summer silently in the darkness. "Oh," she said. "Oh Lord, you've gone and done something foolish, ain't you?"

"My key. I brought back my key."

Summer looked different somehow. The girl stood a little straighter, shoulders thrown back. Stronger. Maybe even prettier, if that were possible. And she saw something new in her eyes. Something dark—a hardness that hadn't been there before.

"It's that motorcycle man, ain't it?" Ruthette shook her head. "I heard about you and Robbie yesterday. Been all the talk around abouts. Girl, you sure you know what you done?"

Summer shivered, holding back the tears. What could she say that could explain it? What could she say that would show Ruthette the truths in her heart? "I— I didn't—"

The cook put her purse on the counter and held Summer at arm's length. She looked into her eyes, and knew that there would be no getting back with Rob for her; she had woken up. She had seen too much, and maybe even touched her dreams.

The motorcycle man.

He was going to take her away.

"Girl, don't you go off and do anything you shouldn't, Summer girl. I know you. You get something in that head of yours, and you're like a damn bulldog with a bone. You can't just up and leave like this. What's that gonna do for your life? How are you gonna live? And your poor mama—"

"Shit. Why do you think I'm leaving? She doesn't want me here. She kicked me out."

Ruthette let go of her arms and took a step back. "Naw. Naw, she didn't. She's a crazy old coot, all right, but she ain't gonna kick out her only child."

Summer shifted her feet and stared into the kitchen. How much could she tell her? Could Ruthette live with the knowledge of what she had done? What she had become?

"Mama had a heart attack," she started, and she told her about her mother waking up and blaming her. Ruthette listened quietly at first, then teared up as Summer described the tirade at the hospital, and how she ran out and decided she wasn't going to come back.

In the pale kitchen light, Summer saw a tear slip down Ruthette's cheek. "I'm okay," Summer said. "But I can't deal with her any mo—"

"Your mama loves you, girl. No matter what. No matter how goddamn crazy she is. She loves you. She wouldn't just send you away. She'd never send you away. You and I both know that."

Ruthette watched her, really looked at her. Finally she said, "There's a shadow. It's in you now. Not sure if I understand or not." Then she said, "So soon. So soon." She rapped her hand once on the steel counter. "But this is yours. Whatever this thing is you gotta do; whatever this road is you gotta follow. It's yours. I ain't gonna try and stop you. You wouldn't listen to me anyway." She half smiled.

Summer stared at her, then suddenly found herself in Ruthette's embrace, holding her tight as she wept into her shoulder. Slowly, she pulled away. She held Ruthette's hands. "Let everyone think whatever they want. Don't tell them a thing. Ever. Please?"

Ruthette nodded. "Nothin' to worry about, baby girl. Just—stay out of trouble."

Summer laughed suddenly, and they both smiled at each other. "Like that'll ever happen," Ruthette said.

Then Summer placed her palm against Ruthette's cheek. "I'll write, I promise," and she spun around and almost ran out the back door. The door locked behind her automatically.

There was no way back.

She drove with the windows open, breathing the sweet night air as she sped up the mountain with Classics IV on WGH, singing about bits and pieces. New York City, she knew, wouldn't smell fresh like this. Clean. She had seen pictures in *Life* showing the thick pall of smog hanging over Manhattan, dimming the daylight.

She could accept the smog. It was all part of the magic that was New York City. There would be night clubs, and dancing. And the bands they would hear—Zeppelin, and the Allmans. Derek and the Dominos. Hell, maybe even Hendrix. She had read about them in *Cream* and *Rolling Stone.* They all played at the Fillmore East—she supposed it was like a grand palace theater from the early 1900s—and she decided that the Fillmore would be the first place she'd take Michel, on their first night alone together in the big city.

She pulled up in front of the turnstiles at Storybook Hollow and stepped onto the overgrown gravel. The warm night was quiet, and she looked up at the cloudless sky. The stars blazed with colors she had never seen before; with intensities so bright to her newborn eyes that she could see stars and worlds so faint and so distant that their number in the blackness had tripled.

New York.

The universe.

Michel.

This is what was meant to be.

She reached out for him, seeking their souls to touch.

And there he was, his heart beating, touching hers with their ethereal, unbreakable bond.

But it felt so tenuous. Distant.

"Michel?" she said.

She focused, and felt the wind singing through his hair, his tires humming over the road.

She vaulted over the turnstiles. The ground was a blur as she raced to the castle and plunged down the black mouth to land feet first onto the cavern floor.

"Michel?"

Only a single kerosene lantern flickered in the chamber, atop the altar, leaving the far reaches of the cavern cloaked in shadow.

"Michel!"

Her voice sounded through far, empty subterranean chambers.

She spun around. "*Michel!*"

Beside the lantern he had left a note and a thick envelope.

She felt a sudden, empty expanse, like a void between worlds, grow in the pit of her soul, and she screamed, "*MICHEL!*"

The long echoes of her soul's anguish rang hollow beneath the earth.

And she knew, in her heart, that he had left her behind.

Trembling, eyes watering, she picked up the note. She leaned against the smooth flowstone, then sank to the cavern floor.

The flap on the envelope hung open. Inside, she found three wrapped bundles of cash.

My Darling Summer,

His handwriting was bold and elegant, evocative not only of his cultured background, but of the gentleman and the romantic she knew he was in his secret, ageless soul.

I cannot tell you how much it breaks my heart to leave you.

A sob escaped her lips, and she read the note through a warm flow of tears.

It was not supposed to be this way. I wanted to show you New York. I wanted to show you Paris. All the places you spoke of just a few short nights ago, I swore to myself that I would take you there, and give you the world.

Now these things must wait.

Your sheriff requested intelligence about me from Interpol, and has unwittingly exposed me to my enemies. They have operatives in a host of international agencies whose sole goal is to ferret me out.

They will come here, I am sure. They may already be here. And if they find us together, they will do to you what they will do to me. They have no goal but to destroy me.

I cannot let this happen to you. I will not let this happen to you. You are mine to love, and mine to protect. And so, for now, I have to leave. I have to draw them away from you, as far from you as possible; no matter how much it hurts me, and no matter how much this feels so wrong. You and I must leave and go far away. But we cannot take the chance that they will find us. We must leave here now, and alone. And, above all else, keep hidden. Use aliases. Mail drops. Keep on the move. Hide in crowds and big cities. Stay in the shadows.

I've left you a portion of the funds I brought back from Vietnam. This should be enough for you to start elsewhere. I have no doubt your new talents will afford you to live however you wish, and in the manner which you deserve.

Very soon, I want you to go to Washington, D.C. There is an attorney there, Solomon Bronze, who handles certain sensitive matters for me. Look him up, and tell him you were sent by John Raven. He will ask you for proof that you know me. You will tell him:

"If then true lovers have been ever crossed, it stands as an edict in destiny."

He will give you a package that has been meant for you, and only for you, for decades. Take what he gives you, and learn from them. My journals will show you how I survived, and many things you need to know.

I adore you, Summer.

She could not stop the tears then. They came unbidden, no matter how she fought them, and her great, wracking sobs sounded more like the primal wails of someone driven mad.

I adore you, Summer. But you must know this. Though I write this beneath the earth and you are miles away, I feel our hearts beating as one, forever linked by one of your wondrous dreamlines. I had long ago lost hope in finding you, my one true love, but you have shown me that destiny cannot be denied, and that our love will last for all eternity.

In time, when I believe my enemies no longer have my scent, I will come for you. I pray that time will come soon, and that I am wrong that the Interpol report was intercepted. But if you do not hear from me, worry

not. I will always be looking for you, and when I believe we are safe, I will find you. Then, no power on Earth will be able to stop us from being together, and we shall show the world the force and the majesty of our fierce and undying love.

Forever, my love, my endless Summer,

Michel

The note fluttered to the cavern floor, and Summer cried and screamed until her throat burned raw. She pounded her fists against the side of the flowstone. This was not the way it was supposed to be, goddamn it, and part of her was furious with him for leaving without her, for abandoning her. But her heart accepted what he had done; the sacrifice he had made to protect her. She opened her soul and touched him on the dreamline. Farther away, dimmer; yet their souls kissed, light, just once, and then she drew away.

"Stay with me," she whispered to the empty cavern. "Stay."

She cried until she could cry no more, and people across the county woke before dawn, wondering why they had wept while they were asleep.

Summer forced herself to her feet. She folded the note and slid it into her back pocket. In the envelope she found cash. Twenty thousand dollars—more money than she had ever seen.

She left the lantern flickering on the flowstone. Her mother had told her, long ago, that when someone dies, to leave a light burning for them so they can find their way home.

She felt so barren, so alone, so dead inside, that she didn't know if the light were for Michel or for herself.

She stepped out of the haunted castle and looked up at the pale stars above the Hollow. Although the night was still full dark, her new eyes picked up the first ripples of sunlight in the east. Birds woke in the trees, chirping softly in expectation of the dawn.

She started for the exit, then paused. She thought for a moment. "What the hell," she said, and she turned towards the back section of Storybook Hollow.

Back here, a tall green hedge marked the border of the park. She pushed through a gap made by countless teenagers in years past, then followed a thin, overgrown path, strewn with cigarette butts and beer cans, that wound between Blue Top and Dog Mountains.

She came to a rusted chain link fence, ten feet tall and fringed on top with long strands of barbed wire. On the other side was the county landmark, the natural stone bridge that linked the two mountains, forged millions of years ago by the collapse of a cavern and the flow of an ancient river, now merely a trickle far below, down the pebbled stream bed that snaked through the archway. The stone arch had been discovered by George Washington, and had been later surveyed by Thomas Jefferson and James Madison—all their initials were still there: Colonial graffito they had scratched high up into the stone while on horseback.

She poked her fingers through the links and rattled the fence.

It didn't have to be this way.

Then it came from the pit of her soul. She rattled the fence again, harder, harder, watching the chain link undulate like waves as she screamed and screamed, and her fingers tightened, bending the galvanized steel; and she screamed her anguish, ragged and primal, the loss of Michel, the emptiness in her heart, erupting in a volcanic burst, echoing against the barren rocks below.

She unclenched her fingers from the mangled fence, then slipped through a gap where kids for ages had bent back the chain links to scramble to the other side. It brought back memories of sneaking out when she was twelve or thirteen, hanging out with older kids her mother would certainly disapprove of.

A one-lane road had been here once, running the length of the stone bridge's top until finally too many cars had driven off the edge to the rocks below, and the top had been fenced off. Now the road was cracked, overgrown with scraggly brush and unkempt shrubs, and the seams burst with tall brown grass. Only outcasts and kids came here now, looking for a cheap thrill or a cheap high.

She made her way through the grass and bushes and stood in the center of the empty road atop the stone bridge.

Old. Millions of years old, like her mother. A symbol of this dead, stillborn town, where nothing changes, no one grows, and no one ever leaves.

She had always been too afraid before to step too far, to step too close, to the edge.

But now she knew who she was.

She knew who she was supposed to be.

Stay in the shadows.

Hide.

She looked at the lightening sky beyond the mountains.

"Fuck the rules," she whispered.

She sat on the edge of the stone bridge and dangled her long legs over the side. She decided she'd send a few thousand each to Ruthette and Tina. They could split duties, going by to help out Ma after she got out of the hospital. That much money would help them both out, and no one she knew needed it more than Ruthette.

Summer slipped on her round, blue shades. She lit a cigarette and leaned back on her elbows and stared at the sky.

And she sang into the dawn, soft; a song about the morning, and an angel—a soul song by Bettye Swann—and she smiled.

"Bring it on," she said.

And she waited for the coming of the sun.

acknowledgments

I OWE ANNE Tibbets an extraordinary debt for accepting me as a client. I wrote ***Ghostflowers*** at a time when neither agents nor editors wanted anything to do with vampire novels, and the genre next door, the *paranormal romance*, was considered all but dead. Anne saw something in ***Ghostflowers*** that a few hundred other agents didn't, and she took a chance on me. I will never forget her kindness and her always encouraging notes; and I hope, someday, that her faith in me will prove even a little bit profitable.

Tin Wornom, my lovely cousin, and Mike Speller, one of my best and most honest friends, were beta readers for ***Ghostflowers***, and provided me with insights to which I was blind. My thanks to both for their critical wisdom, and for just being two of the nicest people I know. Tin is a wanderer who writes online about her worldwide travels; and if you'd like to hear tales of mystery, intrigue, and spooky ghost stories from a master storyteller, you can book Mike through *storytelling.org/speller/*. I'd also like to thank the super-talented writers and artists—and a dear friend who is also an incredible film and television actor—who were kind enough to write promotional quotes for ***Ghostflowers***. My most heartfelt thanks for helping get the word out.

My deepest gratitude goes to Scarlett R. Algee and Christopher Payne for bringing me and ***Ghostflowers*** into the JournalStone family. Thank you both for believing in my small-town vampire story, and for letting me get away without ever mentioning the V-word. And thanks to Sean Johnson for keeping me in line (by line).

Discerning readers may recognize that certain landmarks in my fictional town of Stonebridge, Virginia bear many resemblances to places in my hometown of Hampton, Virginia. My memories of downtown Hampton, Mercury Boulevard and Pembroke Avenue in the late '60s and early '70s are reflected in the business districts of Stonebridge, and are combined with just a splash of rural Caroline County, where I worked at the *Caroline Progress* from 2009 to 2012. Just so you'll know, the Atomic Drive-In is based on both Shoney's, formerly on Pembroke Ave. in Hampton, and Smitty's on King Street. While the Shoney's, where we were served outside by waitresses in roller skates, is long gone, Smitty's is still in operation, and if you order a Better Burger or a BBQ with extra hot sauce, please think of me. The Shenandoah Drive-In Theatre is an amalgam of the Hampton Drive-In and the Green Acres Drive-In, both of which closed down in 1981 and '82, respectively, but were great fun while I was a teen—including the night a bunch of us sneaked in by hiding in the trunk. St. John's Episcopal Church, where I was baptized, attended Sunday School, and got married, is almost identical to the fictional St. John's in Stonebridge; I added mausoleums to the old cemetery—just a little touch of

Dark Shadows. I think every Southern town has a St. John's church, but the St. John's in Hampton has a mysterious gravestone engraved with the deceased's date of death as "November 31." Downtown Stonebridge is mostly a mirror image of downtown Hampton, with a little bit of Phoebus' beer joints thrown in. Stonebridge's rural, residential areas are based on the country roads of Caroline County out near Cool Water Drive, and on the road going up to Fredericksburg. And there was a Feedlot night spot in Caroline County that I'm sure lived up to its name and reputation back in the day.

The stone bridge of Stonebridge is a fictionalized version of Virginia's Natural Bridge, and the caverns Michel discovers were inspired by Luray Caverns. I moved both destinations a bit to the south. Dog Mountain and Blue Top Mountain are completely fictional locales, but Storybook Hollow was based on my childhood memories of visiting Story Book Land in Woodbridge, Virginia. If you're so inclined, you can find a fine article all about Story Book Land at *insidenova.com*.

WGH, the radio station I mention frequently in these pages, was *the* powerhouse, Top 40 AM station—the radio leader in Hampton Roads (the World's Greatest Harbor) in the '60s and '70s, and the radio station I grew up with. WGH and the music of the classic rock era was an integral part of every teenager's life throughout Hampton Roads in 1971, and during the writing of ***Ghostflowers***, I instinctively knew that the novel needed WGH, especially since the town of Stonebridge would have been too small to have its own Top 40 radio station. Perhaps it's a stretch that a mountain town far to the west in Virginia could receive WGH from its radio tower in Hampton, but I do know that, to the south, WGH could sometimes be received as far as Florida. I hope purists and sticklers to facts about signal wattage will forgive me my liberties. By the way, you can find some of the WGH DJs and a lot of lifelong fans on the **WGH Radio 1310** Facebook page. And thanks to the late George Crawford and the Real Neal Steele for all the laughs way back when.

Ghostflowers was inspired deep in its secret soul by the 1960s' television series *Dark Shadows*. The show's melodramatic combination of love, mystery and blood was a subconscious influence at first, but when I recognized some of my novel's thematic parallels to *Dark Shadows*, I embraced the inspiration. Even my original title for this novel was a direct reference: ***Shadows of the Night***. *Dark Shadows* creator Dan Curtis' 1972 ***The Night Stalker*** was also an important, yet subconscious inspiration.

An equally significant influence was the *oeuvre* of Hammer Films and, specifically, its magnificently crimson vampire output. My intent from the beginning was to write ***Ghostflowers*** as *Hammer horror* for the 21st century. Coincidentally, *Dark Shadows* saw its final episode during the year 1971, when ***Ghostflowers*** takes place; and I viewed the very best Hammer horror film, ***Horror of Dracula*** (***Dracula*** in the UK) for the first time when it popped up on *The CBS Late Movie* in 1971. (It was the second movie of an unannounced Hammer Dracula double feature. Hardcore Hammer aficionados may not believe this, but on that night CBS somehow broadcast a print of ***Horror of Dracula*** that was complete with the intact decomposition scene.). Also, the Hammer double feature playing at the Shenandoah Drive-In in Stonebridge, ***Scars of Dracula*** and ***Horror of Frankenstein***, was indeed playing in drive-in theaters across the country during the summer of 1971, including at the aforementioned Hampton Drive-In on Pembroke Avenue in Hampton, Virginia. I wish I had been there that week, but I was probably at home, reading an Edgar Rice Burroughs novel.

My other intent with this novel was to emulate the technique used in the opening chapters of what I believe is the 20th Century's finest novel of the undead, ***'Salem's Lot***. In that influential portion, Stephen King developed and built a certain dramatic tension by showing the evil that would soon devour Jerusalem's Lot, without ever naming it. This heightened the internal reality of the novel—the big writery word here is *verisimilitude*—and truly made the reader suspend their disbelief. I challenged myself to write an entire novel using that same technique, and I hope I have succeeded. Thank you to Mr. King for his most vital influence, not only with the early, yet defining achievement that is ***'Salem's Lot***, but for his entire and all-encompassing body of literature. As Harlan once said, King is *sui generis*. (By the way, Steve: Whatever happened to Ben and Mark? Sure would like to read more of their story…)

The opening chapters of ***Ghostflowers*** were written in 1996, at a time when it was still possible for writers to sell a new novel from fifty pages and a detailed outline. Boy, has *that* changed. The remainder of the novel was written between 2013-2014, and everything was polished—and some parts were rearranged—in the intervening years, until I submitted the thirteenth and final draft to JournalStone in October 2021.

This novel would not exist if my wife hadn't prodded me with an awful and terrible and beautiful and unforgettable idea in 1996, which, within the span of a few minutes while I was shaving for work, somehow exploded into the novel you just read. I sincerely hope that you have someone in your life to hold and to love and to center your existence the way my wife is the soul of mine. From the very beginning, Maria has always believed in my goals as a writer, providing me with constant love and encouragement. She is the single finest person it has ever been my privilege and honor to know, and I'm a far better man because of her love and influence. And, yes, someday, I SWEAR to you, sweetheart, that we'll finally meet Steven Spielberg. Thank, you, my love, for everything you are, and for always staying that little girl on the swing with the biggest, brightest smile I've ever seen.

Rus Wornom
May, 2022

a *ghostflowers* soundtrack

SUMMER IN THE South in the 1970s was probably a hazy blur of similar experiences to Southern teenagers, no matter where you lived: behind the wheel on a date with your high school crush, heading for pizza and cartoons at Shakey's, or out to the Friday night game; or maybe just getting away from the parents at home; or hanging out at the beach in hopes of scoring second base behind the dunes as the tang of salt water blew in with the waves.

But there was always rock and roll. In the early seventies, rock and roll—with healthy doses of soul and pop on AM Top 40—ruled the airwaves, and was a part of every teenager's life, even if they didn't realize it.

I say that last part from experience. I was a nerd in the seventies, and still am in 2022. Hell, I didn't know that the Beatles had broken up until two years after the fact. I bought soundtracks to the movies I liked—***Silent Running***, ***The Exorcist***, all the James Bond films, and even ***Blazing Saddles*** and ***The Day of the Dolphin***—but I rarely bought a rock and roll album. Except for a few special songs, rock and pop were just like elevator music to me.

Nevertheless, I absorbed rock and roll via the radio, almost osmotically, without paying a lot of attention to it.

Classic rock, crafted from a commonality of cultures and a mélange of blues, soul, country and pop, was the background music we grew up on—the soundtrack of the seventies; and since classic rock is so integral to ***Ghostflowers***, I have created a video playlist on YouTube to accompany your reading, titled **GHOSTFLOWERS SOUNDTRACK**, available at

https://www.youtube.com/playlist?list=PLdPkP5ontMSQG9lVjvSYsTm K2fUvOLwqI.

Most of the songs—and there are a lot of them—are presented in the order in which the reader will experience them as they read the novel; however, a few are thematically influential, and perhaps were not even recorded at that time, such as "Brandy" and "Strawberry Wine." This playlist is entirely subjective, and mostly reflects the songs I heard repeatedly on WGH. But Summer, herself, is much more knowledgeable about rock than I ever was, and the list I originally envisioned quickly expanded because of her musical preferences; for instance, I never really cared for Janis Joplin, but Summer told me she loved her voice—so Janis had to be included.

Because my playlist is on YouTube, I also include the movie trailers that Summer watched at the drive-in theater on Friday night, and even a radio commercial or two. As to the tunes Summer plays on her stereo and the songs on the radios at the party in the woods, I did a ton of research on the music and

I've attempted to insure that every song that is mentioned in the narrative of ***Ghostflowers*** could have been heard on the radio during the weekend of July 4th, 1971. However, I'm sure mistakes have been made, and any anachronisms are solely mine. You can blame me and only me; I'll gladly take the heat.

This playlist is a cross section of June, 1971 mainstream radio—the buzz of the '70s teenage hive mind. It's what I heard coming from the dashboard speakers while driving in the summer with the windows down, scenting the aroma of wild onions and cut grass on the warm breeze, as the flicker of heat lightning flashed orange veins across the horizon.

Damn, life was sweet back then.

about the author

RUS WORNOM HAS written novellas for *The Magazine of Fantasy and Science Fiction* and three novels for Dungeons and Dragons. "Puppy Love Land" was published in the April, 1996 *F&SF,* and the story was later nominated as Best Novella on the Preliminary Ballot for the Horror Writers of America awards. His nonfiction has been published in such magazines as *Omni,*

Premiere, Gauntlet, and *StoryboarD,* and in newspapers and regional magazines. He participated in writing workshops with Harlan Ellison, Gene Wolfe, Brian Aldiss, and Kate Wilhelm. He studied in writing workshops at Old Dominion University with novelist Tony Ardizzone, and in the Graduate School of the University of Miami with Lester Goran. He lives in Virginia, but wants a stool to call his own at Capt. Tony's Saloon in Key West.

Find out more about the author at *ruswornom.com*, or contact him at *RusWornomAuthor@gmail.com.*